Sign up for our newsletter t
about new and upcoming releases.

www.ylva-publishing.com

Other Books by Jae

Happily Ever After

Standalone Romances:
Chemistry Lessons
Wrong Number, Right Woman
The Roommate Arrangement
Just for Show
Falling Hard
Heart Trouble
Under a Falling Star
Something in the Wine
Shaken to the Core

Fair Oaks Series:
Perfect Rhythm
Not the Marrying Kind

The Hollywood Series:
Departure from the Script
Damage Control
Just Physical
The Hollywood Collection (box set)

Portland Police Bureau Series:
Conflict of Interest
Next of Kin

The Vampire Diet Series:
Good Enough to Eat

The Oregon Series:
Backwards to Oregon
Beyond the Trail
Hidden Truths
The Complete Oregon series (box set)

The Shape-Shifter Series:
Second Nature
Natural Family Disasters
Manhattan Moon
True Nature

Paper Love

Jae

Acknowledgments

My sincere thanks go to my awesome team of beta readers for their feedback and support: Anne-France, Christiane, Claire, Danielle, Erin, Louisa, Melanie, and Trish.

A big thank-you to my editor, Miranda Miller from Editing Realm, for making this book better and for her attention to detail.

I'd also like to thank my womb mate, just for being herself.

Author's Note

Paper Love is truly a love story in so many ways: not only is it a romance novel, but it also combines many of my favorite things. Inspired by my love for notebooks and fountain pens, the book is set in a stationery store, and one of the characters is just as much of a stationery geek as I am.

The book is also set in Freiburg, the city where I live. So far, all of my novels have taken place in the US, so I decided to pick a city in Germany as the setting for my eighteenth novel. I'm excited to introduce you to some of the things that make Freiburg so special to me.

I hope you'll enjoy reading this book as much as I did writing it.

Happy reading!
Jae

Chapter 1

Don't ask, don't ask, don't ask, Susanne mentally chanted.

But, of course, her mother asked before the last of the fireworks had even faded away from the night sky over Berlin-Charlottenburg, as Susanne had known she would. It had been a yearly tradition since Susanne and her sister had been kids. "So what are your resolutions for the new year?" Their mother leaned against the railing of her balcony overlooking the courtyard and glanced from Susanne to her sister and back.

Susanne nudged Franziska. *Come on, Sis. Help me out here.*

But all Franzi did was nudge her back.

"Why do I always have to go first?" Susanne grumbled.

"Because you're the oldest," Franzi said.

A snort escaped Susanne. "Yeah, by a full seven minutes."

"Oh, now suddenly those seven minutes don't matter? You usually hold them over me any chance you get."

"Girls," their mother drawled. "No arguing on New Year's Eve."

"We're not arguing," Susanne said. "We're just—"

"You still haven't answered my question."

Damn. She had hoped her mother would let herself be distracted. No such luck. Lying to her was out; she would find out sooner or later, and Susanne didn't want to face her mother's disappointment when she realized she had been lied to on top of everything else.

The smoke that hung over the courtyard was so thick that Susanne could barely make out the familiar contours of the one-hundred-and-fifty-year-old buildings on the other side. But for her, there was no hiding behind the gray haze.

Oh, come on. Since when are you such a chickenshit? Normally, she didn't lack in confidence. Just a couple of days ago, she had marched into her boss's office and had tossed her resignation letter on his desk without hesitation. But telling her mother was different.

Franzi stepped next to her until their arms brushed, as if sensing that she needed the support.

"I only have one resolution this year," Susanne said.

Her mother waved her fingers in a let's-hear-it gesture.

Susanne took a steadying breath. "I, um, I'm going to start looking for a new job tomorrow."

Her mother put down her glass of champagne, while Susanne white-knuckled her own. "Don't tell me you got fired."

"No. I… I quit."

That might actually be worse in their mother's eyes. Job-hopping was what their father had done, moving from business to business, from failure to failure.

The firecrackers that had still been going off in the neighborhood stopped, and the silence was deafening.

"Yeah, well, your boss was a chauvinistic pig." Franzi tried a casual shrug but couldn't quite pull it off. "I would have quit a long time ago. Plus maybe now you can find a job where you don't have to travel so much and can stick closer to home most of the time."

Susanne gave her a grateful look but doubted their mother would see it that way. Would she think Susanne was like her father?

"Well, that's…" Her mother blindly reached for her glass and drained it in one big gulp. "…really good, actually."

Susanne shook her head as if something had stuck in her ears, affecting her hearing. *Oookay. Who are you, and what have you done with my mother?* "It is?" she asked with a tentative smile.

"Yes. And you don't even have to look for a new job. I already have one for you."

Uh-oh. Susanne traded glances with her sister. Why did she have the feeling she wouldn't like whatever her mother was about to say?

"Your uncle needs a little help with his business."

The tension in Susanne's shoulders receded. "Oh, sure. I can sit down with Uncle Bernhard and give him a few pointers."

"Not Bernhard. It's Uncle Norbert who needs your help."

"No problem. I can help him too. I admit I don't know much about office supplies, but I guess general business principles still apply. I'll call him tomorrow and—"

"No. A call won't cut it. He needs more substantial help, or he'll be bankrupt before spring."

This was the first Susanne had heard of Uncle Norbert's problems. Admittedly, she didn't have much contact with him or any of the relatives on her father's side. *Much? Try almost none.* "It's that bad?"

Her mother nodded. "Yes. And that's why I need you to temporarily move to Freiburg."

Now Susanne was the one gulping down the rest of her champagne. "M-move to Freiburg?"

"Yes. Don't sound so appalled. It's a charming little city."

"Yeah. With an emphasis on *little*. Mama, I'm used to Berlin, London, and Chicago. Freiburg is too small…too provincial. Whoever nicknamed it the metropolis of the Black Forest had a few too many."

Her sister grinned. "Who can blame them? The wine in the region is really good."

Susanne glared at her. "I'm not moving all the way across the country for the wine. If you like Freiburg that much, why don't you go?"

"I'm a dentist. Unless all Uncle Nobby's store needs is a root canal, I'm not going to be much help. As a business consultant, you're the perfect person for the job."

Thanks a lot, traitor.

"That's what I thought." Their mother smiled brightly. "Plus you're long overdue for a visit with your uncle anyway. I never understood why you never came with us."

"I told you I'm too—"

"Too busy with your job, I know." Her mother waved the objection away. "But now you don't have a job. Everything will work out perfectly. You can look for another job and spend some time with Uncle Norbert while you help him out for a few months."

"A few months?" She'd been thinking a week or two at the most.

"Just until Easter."

"Until Easter?" Susanne was starting to feel like a parrot constantly echoing the last thing her mother said, but her brain had problems processing this whole scheme. If she didn't know any better, she'd think her mother had planned it all out before even knowing she had quit her job. "But that's almost three months!"

"Yes." Her mother was still grinning as if she'd already solved Uncle Norbert's problems single-handedly. "By then, it'll be spring, and you'll get to enjoy a bit of the sunniest city in Germany during your last couple of weeks there. Won't that be nice?"

Only years of experience in keeping a poker face during business negotiations kept Susanne from grimacing. *Yeah. About as nice as the root canal Franzi just mentioned.*

3

"Uncle Norbert has a lot of friends in the Wiehre," her mother continued. "He could help you find an apartment there. You liked that part of the city when we first took you there, remember?"

"Mama, I was a kid. I liked to pretend I was a princess living in one of the Art Nouveau mansions, waiting for a prince to come along and rescue me." She huffed at her younger self. "I haven't needed rescuing or wanted a prince—or any man— since I was six."

Her sister winked at her. "I hear the women in Freiburg are quite beautiful too."

"I'm not moving there for a woman either."

Their mother put down her empty champagne glass, stepped closer, and put both hands on Susanne's shoulders. From only centimeters away, she sent Susanne one of her famous gazes—the one that had gotten them to eat whatever was on their plates when they'd been kids, even if it was spinach. "He's family, Susanne."

No one said her name quite like her mother. Susanne winced. "I know. It's just…"

"If you refuse to help him, he'll lose the store. It would break his heart. That store is his pride and joy, and it was your grandfather's before him."

Oh hell. Susanne rubbed her face. How could she say no now? "Only until the end of March, then I'm gone. Make sure Uncle Norbert knows that."

Beaming, her mother squeezed her shoulders and then let go. "I will. Don't you worry. It'll all work out great, and I'll help cover the moving costs and the rent."

Susanne blew out a breath and tried to stay positive. Yeah, maybe it wouldn't be so bad. After all, it was kind of what she'd done for her old company—travel somewhere, get the job done, and get the hell out of there as soon as the problem was solved.

Easy as pie, right? Or rather easy as Black Forest cake, in this case. It wasn't as if there was anything in that backwoods city that would make her want to stay.

Chapter 2

"Sunniest city in Germany, my ass!" Susanne mumbled as she got off the streetcar and snapped open her umbrella to ward off the lightly falling rain. She hadn't even seen the sun since she'd arrived in Freiburg on Friday afternoon. The cobblestones of the Kaiser-Joseph-Strasse, Freiburg's main shopping street, were slick beneath her favorite suede ankle boots, and a dusting of snow covered the forested hill rising up directly behind the Old Town.

A street performer playing the accordion didn't seem to mind the weather, and neither did the group of tourists being led through the city by a young man in a medieval costume.

Susanne looked around to get her bearings, but a mob of people getting out of another streetcar blocked her view. Someone popping open an umbrella showered her with droplets of water. She gritted her teeth and counted to ten in German, in English, and then in her admittedly rusty French.

Why the hell had she thought taking public transportation was a good idea?

But it wasn't as if she had a choice. Freiburg's city center was a car-free zone, and even around the edges of the pedestrian area, finding a parking spot was about as likely as winning the lottery, so she had left her beloved BMW in her apartment building's parking garage. She would have to ask Uncle Norbert about parking options and getting a special permit so she could take her car to work.

Once the crowd in front of her cleared, she glanced around and checked her phone to see in which direction she was supposed to be heading. A bronze equestrian statue marked the middle of the busy intersection where all the streetcar lines crossed. According to Google Maps, she had to double back a little. She turned and headed toward the tower gate through which her streetcar had just passed on its way into the city center. Its green copper roof and two corner turrets rose high up over the surrounding buildings. The sidewalks and the streetcar tracks ran under its two arches. Her last visit to Freiburg had been more than twenty years ago, but if she remembered correctly, the gate had been left over from the medieval city fortifications. Now, instead of armed guards, a big McDonald's sign had been placed above the right arch.

Shaking her head, Susanne crossed the street so she could pass through the arch.

A streetcar wildly rang its bell to hurry her along.

Susanne clutched her chest and leaped onto the sidewalk. She hadn't seen the damn thing because the umbrella had blocked her view. "Don't you worry. It'll all work out great," she mimicked her mother. "Yeah, but not if I get killed on my first day at work."

A guy pushing a bicycle gave her a curious look, but she ignored him and marched on.

A familiar green-and-white logo greeted her on the other side of the gate.

At least Freiburg had a Starbucks. Mollified, she headed toward it. No way would she survive this day without caffeine.

But the long line in front of the counter convinced her otherwise. Her uncle's store opened at ten, and if she wanted to be taken seriously by his staff, she couldn't be late.

If he even had any staff.

Following the map on her phone, she turned left onto Gerberau, a smaller cobblestone street. It was picturesque, she had to admit. Cute little stores, cafés, a bakery, an Indian restaurant, and a chocolate shop lined the street. She passed a Turkish restaurant that an artist had decorated with a mural of the gate she'd just passed through and a bearded monk tapping beer. To her right flowed a *Bächle*, one of the narrow canals that lined the streets in the Old Town.

Finally, she caught sight of Paper Love, her uncle's store. Two carousels offering greeting cards had been pushed beneath a blue awning to protect them from the rain.

She headed toward the white-framed glass door with its brass handle, but before she had taken even two steps, an irresistible aroma teased her nose.

Susanne looked around.

Ooh! Right across the street was a little coffee shop. Almost without a conscious decision, she detoured, stepped over the gently gurgling *Bächle*, and walked across a mosaic embedded into the cobblestone sidewalk.

Two minutes later, she held the tallest coffee the shop sold in her hand. She took the first sip right then and there. *Ah. Liquid manna.* Now she was ready to face the disaster that was her uncle's store.

With renewed determination, she strode toward Paper Love.

"Watch your step!" the woman from the coffee shop called after her.

Susanne tried to slide to a stop, but it was too late. Instead of the cobblestones, her foot hit only air—and then crashed down into the clear water of the *Bächle*.

The very *cold* water of the *Bächle*.

Coffee splashed over her hand, soaking the sleeve of her wool coat and the right leg of her slacks.

"Ouch! Goddammit!" She withdrew her foot from the shallow canal and blew on her scalded fingers, all the while trying not to drop the coffee or her umbrella.

"Are you okay?" the coffee shop woman asked.

"Yeah. Just peachy." If she gritted her teeth any harder, she would have to call her sister for dental repairs. She stared down at the sodden mess that was her left suede ankle boot.

Her stay in Freiburg was definitely not off to a good start.

Cursing, she crossed the street and shoved open the door to the stationery store with too much force.

The bell above the door jingled frantically.

She closed her umbrella and rammed it into the stand by the door, then used her now-free hand to tug on her coffee-stained slacks. She grimaced. So much for dressing for success to make a good impression on her first day.

She let the door close behind her and paused to take in her temporary place of work.

The left side of the store was dominated by a well-lit glass case that held gleaming fountain pens. A locked display case for pens? Wasn't that a little over the top? She'd only ever seen them in jewelry stores. Not that she'd spent much time in jewelry stores since she didn't wear much jewelry and none of her relationships had ever made it to the point where she would have wanted to buy a ring.

A floor-to-ceiling shelf along the right wall was filled with notebooks, school supplies, and writing pads of all colors and sizes. Large reels of colorful paper and racks of glittery cardstock hung behind the cash register, which was located on a counter at the other end of the room. One corner of the store held pencils, erasers, highlighters, bottles of ink, quills, nibs, and items that Susanne didn't recognize.

Who the hell needed all this stuff in the age of smartphones? No wonder her uncle was close to bankruptcy.

Since they had just opened, no customers had found their way to the store yet, but a short woman looked up from the leather-bound notebooks she'd been arranging on an island display that dominated the middle of the room.

At first, Susanne thought she might be an intern or a university student who worked for her uncle part-time, but as she took a moment to study the woman, she realized that only her slight build and her large eyes, which seemed almost too big for her delicate face, made her look younger than she was. The faint lines around her eyes and her mouth revealed that she was probably closer to Susanne's own age—thirty-eight—than to thirty, and she had made no attempt to cover them with makeup.

She wasn't beautiful in the classic sense of the word. Her hair was too dark to be blonde and too light to be brown; too wavy to be straight but not wavy enough to qualify as curly. Mostly, it looked windblown.

Not Susanne's usual type for sure. But there was something about her that drew her gaze anyway. If Susanne hadn't been so pissed off, she probably would have found her cute.

But cute or not, this wasn't the look she had expected from a saleswoman. Didn't her uncle enforce a more professional dress code? The woman was wearing blue jeans and a white blouse, for Christ's sake! Admittedly, she looked good in them, but that wasn't the point.

"Good morning." The woman's voice had a surprisingly husky depth for someone so small. She directed a friendly smile at Susanne. "How may I help you?"

At least the saleswoman wasn't rude to potential customers. There might be hope for her yet. Susanne walked toward her.

Splash, splash, splash. Her left boot squished with every step and left puddles of water on the tiled floor. She tried her best to ignore it and appear professional. "My name is Susanne Wolff. I'm looking for Norbert. Is he in?"

"Of course. Um, Nobby?" the woman called toward the back of the room, where an open door led to what might be the office or a supply room. "There's someone here for you. And, um, could you bring the mop while you're back there?"

Nobby? Her uncle was not only on a first-name basis with his employee but also allowed her to call him by his nickname? Such familiarities with employees were often a bad idea. It was high time someone with a clue about managing a business took over.

Things around here would change; she'd make sure of that—as soon as she'd gotten out of this wet boot.

Her uncle entered the sales area through the door in the back. He was a little balder and grayer than she remembered, but he immediately put down the mop and came toward her with open arms. "Susi! There you are!"

"I go by Susanne now." Only her twin sister was still allowed to call her by her childhood nickname.

"Oh. Of course." He squeezed her tightly, then let go and took a step back to look her over. "You look great. You're the spitting image of your father. But, um, what happened to your boot?"

Being compared to her father didn't exactly improve Susanne's mood. With a grunt, she shook her left foot. Her cold, wet toes felt as if they were about to fall off. "I stepped into a gutter." She jerked her thumb over her shoulder, pointing at the death trap.

"It's not a gutter," the employee said softly. "It's a *Bächle*."

"I know what it's called, but frankly, I don't care. Who the hell puts uncovered waterways in the middle of the street? Someone could break a leg!"

The employee didn't back away from Susanne's glare. With her elfin features and her slight build, she might have looked like a pushover, but the tiny cleft in her stubborn chin declared that she wouldn't let herself be intimidated. "Well, look on the bright side."

A snort escaped Susanne. *Oh Christ. She's one of those the-glass-is-half-full Pollyanna types.* Not that she had anything against a positive attitude, but rose-colored glasses wouldn't help them save the store. "There's a bright side to ruining my favorite pair of boots?"

"Oh yes." The woman's smile was irritatingly unshakable. "Legend has it that if you accidentally step into a *Bächle*, you'll marry a local guy and live happily ever after in our beautiful city."

Susanne nearly spat out the sip of coffee she'd just taken. "That's the last thing I want."

Uncle Norbert chuckled and patted her back. "Local girl. Ending up with a guy wouldn't be much of a happy ending for my niece."

The woman's large eyes—they were a warm brown, as Susanne could now see—widened even more. "You…you are…?"

Oh great. Just when she had thought this day couldn't get any worse, it turned out she'd be working with a backwoods person who acted as if she had never met a gay person before. She just hoped the woman wouldn't turn out to be a homophobe. The homophobic attitudes at her former workplace were part of the reason she had quit her last job, and she wouldn't stand for it in her uncle's business either. She squared her shoulders and tried to look as dignified and proud as her coffee-stained clothes and wet boot would allow. "Yes, I'm a lesbian. Do you have a problem with that?"

"W-what? No! That's not what I… I didn't… I just meant…"

Susanne waved away her stammered excuses.

Uncle Norbert wrapped one arm around each of them and beamed as if he hadn't noticed the tension between them. "Susi, um, Susanne, may I introduce you to Anja Lamm, my favorite full-time employee?"

"Only full-time employee," Frau Lamm threw in.

Lamm. Susanne bit back a snort. That was exactly the way Frau Lamm had just stared at her—like a lamb who'd glimpsed a wolf. She gave her a brisk nod, not in the mood for meaningless pleasantries, and then turned toward her uncle. "Is there someplace where I can get cleaned up?"

"Of course. Let me show you." He lightly gripped her elbow and led her toward the door in the back.

Susanne left the room without giving Frau Lamm another glance.

☙∽ৎৄ৵

Anja grabbed the mop that Nobby had left behind, sank against the island display, and stared after them. That was his niece?

It hadn't been hard to guess that the tall woman wasn't a local. In her well-pressed, black slacks, a cream-colored cashmere sweater, and a long, black wool coat, she looked like a lawyer here for a case, a guest lecturer at the university, or an overdressed tourist.

As much as she tried, Anja couldn't see any family resemblance. Even after she had stepped into the *Bächle*, not a single strand of the woman's chestnut hair had been out of place. It was swept up into an elegant twist that accentuated the long line of her neck. In comparison, the ring of gray hair encircling Nobby's otherwise bald head often seemed to defy gravity, lending him an Einstein-ish look. His niece definitely hadn't inherited Nobby's bowlegs either—or his kindness. Her gray eyes had been as cool as the weather outside.

No wonder! She thinks you have a problem with her sexual orientation.

Anja groaned. Nothing could be further from the truth.

When steps approached, she busied herself mopping up the water on the floor, not wanting Susanne to think she'd been staring after her.

But it was just Nobby, who returned alone.

"That's your niece?" Anja whispered, keeping an eye on the door that led to the tiny office and the equally tiny bathroom.

"Isn't it obvious? I have the same arresting cheekbones, don't I?" His blue eyes twinkled as he patted his bearded cheeks.

"Don't forget slender build." She lightly nudged his potbelly.

"That too."

"She didn't look anything like this," Anja gestured toward the back, "in the photo you showed me."

Nobby scratched his beard. "Well, I took that photo the last time she visited with her mother and sister, so it's a few years old already."

"Years? Try decades." In the photo she'd seen, Susanne had been a gangly teenager of maybe sixteen or seventeen.

He tilted his head. "Is that a problem?"

"Yes! I mean, now she thinks I stared at her because I have a problem with her sexual orientation, not because I thought your niece was much younger."

"Oh." He looked helpless for a second before shrugging. "Well, just tell her you're bisexual."

It still amazed her how casually that crossed his lips. Her own father had never had such an easy time with it. "No. I can't do that."

"Why not? Want me to tell her?" He took a step toward the back.

She grabbed his sleeve and held on. "No! She'll think you want to set us up or something."

"And that would be bad…why? As we just established, my niece inherited my good looks. And since she stepped into the *Bächle*, she's destined to marry someone from Freiburg." He winked at her. "You could be the lucky girl."

"No, thanks." Anja bit her tongue before she could tell Nobby she liked her partners less overbearing and abrupt. "Please don't say anything. I'm sure it'll be fine." After all, it wasn't as if she'd have to interact with Susanne again. From what Anja had heard about her from Nobby, she was pretty busy and probably wouldn't stay around for long. Anja would give her a polite nod any time she dropped in to take a break from her sightseeing, and after a few days, she'd be gone.

Susanne swept into the sales area and strode toward the front door like a woman on a mission. "I saw a shoe store on my way here. I'm going to get myself something dry to wear, and then I'll be right back to take a look at the books."

Before Nobby or Anja could answer, the door closed behind her.

Anja stared after her as she marched up the street, giving the *Bächle* to her left a wide berth. "Look at the books? She means the notebooks, right?" She pointed at the rows of Moleskins and Leuchtturms. "Or is she looking for travel guides about Freiburg?"

Nobby ran both hands through his hair in a useless attempt to get it to lie flat against his head. "Uh, no. She's not here for sightseeing. Her mother asked her to, um, help out in the store for a while."

A sinking feeling swept over Anja. "Help out for a while?"

"Just until Easter."

That meant Susanne would be staying not for three days, but for nearly three *months*. "But why? You and I have things well in hand."

"Of course, but…" Nobby looked away to turn one of the leather-bound journals on the island display a little more to the left. "Sometimes it's just nice to have a fresh set of eyes, you know?"

A fresh set of eyes? Why the heck would they need that—especially if it came with an attitude attached? She tugged on his sleeve so he would look at her. "What's going on, Nobby? Why didn't you tell me sooner your niece would be coming?" Keeping secrets from her wasn't like him at all.

He kept his gaze on the journals and touched the leather as if to ground himself. "I didn't want to say anything, but—"

The chime of the bell above the door announced their first customer of the day.

Nobby put on a welcoming smile and bounded toward the woman as if she were another long-lost relative.

The customer took forever to look around. She seemed to leaf through every single notebook in the store and then asked to try out some fountain pens.

Normally, Anja would have proudly presented each of their fine writing instruments, but now she impatiently waited until the woman finally left—after having bought just a cheap notebook and a single pencil.

As soon as she opened her mouth to talk to Nobby, the bell jingled again and Susanne returned, wearing a shiny pair of new black boots. "We'll be in the office," she said to Anja as she walked past and pulled Nobby with her. "Can you keep an eye on the store?"

The door closed behind them before Anja could answer. *Who the heck died and made her queen of the universe?* Nobby had said she was here to help out, not to order people around as if she were the boss. Apparently, his niece hadn't gotten the message. She hoped this kind of attitude wouldn't be going on for the next three months.

No matter what the superstition said, if any local girl ended up marrying this woman, it definitely wouldn't be her.

Chapter 3

By the time Susanne made it back to her temporary apartment south of the city center, darkness had fallen, and she could barely make out the shapes of the beautiful Art Nouveau villas with their ornamental facades in the neighborhood.

She entered the building and unlocked the door of her spacious apartment on the first floor. Her steps echoed through the nearly empty dining room and the kitchen, which was separated from it by two arched doorways.

The fridge was just as bare as the rest of the apartment. *Guess it'll be muesli for dinner.*

At least there were no moving boxes cluttering the space, since she had brought only a couple of suitcases, duffel bags, and one box of stuff for the kitchen. She had figured that the less she took, the less she would need to lug back once her exile was over.

Without any furniture, the dining room was kind of depressing, so she grabbed her bowl of muesli and wandered into the living room, which wasn't quite as bare since she had taken over a recliner and a coffee table from the previous tenant.

The hardwood floor creaked softly beneath her boots. Since she had been gone all day, the air in the room had gone stale, so she opened the French doors that led to the garden she shared with the building's other tenants. The air was cool, but at least it had stopped raining.

She stood in the doorway and inhaled the scent of the wet grass.

An owl hooted from a tree at the edge of the property. No sounds of passing cars interrupted the peaceful atmosphere—only the ravenous growling of her stomach. She hadn't made time for lunch. Instead, she had gobbled down some peanuts while poring over Uncle Norbert's business ledgers and bank statements. What she had seen had ruined her appetite anyway. Her uncle was just as bad of a businessman as his brother. Paper Love was in big trouble. The store hadn't turned a profit in years. It barely made enough to cover payroll and utilities, much less the other monthly bills. Uncle Norbert had used his personal money to help keep the store afloat, but he couldn't keep doing that. If she didn't find a way to turn things around soon, Paper Love would be going under.

Maybe it would be for the best. Why cling to a store that was doomed just for sentimental reasons? Her uncle could sell off the stock and start anew with something else—or enjoy his much-deserved pension. But they weren't at that point yet. Susanne wasn't one for giving up without putting up one hell of a fight. She'd start by taking inventory of the stock and taking a closer look at the products the store sold tomorrow.

A sigh escaped her as she kicked off her boots, stripped off her socks, and sank into the recliner. A blister had formed on her heel where the new leather had rubbed against her foot all day.

Perfect. Just perfect. From the moment she'd arrived in this city, nothing had gone right.

She put her aching feet up on the ottoman and set the bowl on her lap. But when she went to dig into the muesli, she realized she'd forgotten to grab a spoon.

Groaning, she heaved herself up, put the bowl onto the coffee table, and limped into the kitchen.

When she returned with the spoon, a cool gust from the still-open French doors hit her. She shivered and went to close them. As she stepped past the recliner, movement caught her eye.

She whirled around, the spoon raised as if she could chase off the intruder with it.

Instead of the burglar she had expected, a white-and-brown tabby cat stood on her recliner, its front paws on the coffee table, lapping up the milk from her muesli.

"What the hell? Where did you come from?"

At the sound of her voice, the cat turned its head and looked at her. A brown stripe across its nose made it look admittedly cute, but Susanne wouldn't let that sway her. She stabbed her finger in the direction of the open French doors. "Out!"

The cat meowed and went back to enjoying her milk.

"Wow. You've got some nerve, kitty." It was well-nourished and its fur gleamed with health, so Susanne knew it wasn't a starving stray. Since she couldn't eat the muesli anymore, she decided to let the cat finish its stolen meal. "Just this once. Don't think this is going to turn into a bed-and-breakfast for the next three months."

When the cat had lapped up the rest of the milk, it withdrew its front paws from the coffee table, curled up on the recliner, and started to clean its whiskers.

"Oh no, you don't." She reached for the cat to pick it up and carry it outside.

The cat let out a hiss and curled into an even tighter ball so she couldn't get a hold of it.

Not that she would have tried again. With the kind of luck she was having today, she'd probably get the hell scratched out of her.

"This is ridiculous." She was standing in the middle of her nearly empty living room, her bare feet getting cold, and her stomach was still growling because a cat had eaten her dinner. "Okay, I'm giving you an option here. Are you listening?"

The cat's ears flicked in her direction, so she took that as a yes.

"Either you go back outside voluntarily, or I'll, um…" *Yeah, or you'll do what? Call the police to tell them to come arrest this dangerous intruder?* She snorted. "Or I'll have to find a way to get you to leave, and trust me, you won't like it."

The cat didn't move.

"Don't say I didn't warn you." She grabbed the back of the recliner and pushed the piece of furniture with its furry occupant across the hardwood floor toward the French doors.

Her feline visitor let out a startled hiss.

"I told you, you wouldn't like it." When she reached the step leading down to the garden, she tilted the recliner.

The cat slid off the leather seat and landed on the tiled patio. It gave Susanne a disgruntled look.

Quickly, Susanne pushed the recliner out of the way and closed the door before the cat could sneak back inside. Through the glass, she gave the feline a victorious grin. "Mission accomplished!"

She slid the semi-transparent curtain closed and went to get herself a new bowl of muesli.

"Meow!" The plaintive sound drifted after her, followed by the soft thump of a paw against the glass. "Meeoooooow!"

With a groan, she rested her forehead against the fridge. "Be strong." She was here to do a job, not to make friends—not even with a cat.

⚬⚬⚬

"And then she dragged Nobby into the office, and I didn't see much of her for the rest of the day, thank God!" Anja paused in the middle of the footbridge across the lake and waited for Miri's reaction.

Gino, her friend's shaggy mutt, used the opportunity to sniff out the love locks people had placed all over the railing.

Something splashed in the water below them, but in the darkness, Anja couldn't see what it was. Maybe a swan or a turtle?

"Thank God?" Miri repeated. "What would have been so bad about seeing more of her? I thought you said she was hot."

"Hello? Didn't you listen to a word I just said? She's a total snob. Waltzes in there with her ruined five-hundred-euro shoes and thinks she can take over just like that! Besides, I never said she was hot."

"Did too."

"Did not."

A passing jogger with a headlamp chuckled at them.

Now Anja was grateful for the darkness that hid her blush.

Miri didn't seem to mind that he had overheard part of their conversation. When the jogger had disappeared around a bend in the path circling the lake, she asked, "So is she? Hot, I mean."

"I guess she's marginally good-looking."

Miri guffawed. "Marginally good-looking? Now I know I've got to visit the store and check her out!"

Anja grabbed her sleeve. "Don't you dare. I'm in enough trouble as it is. I think she doesn't like me."

"What's not to like?" Miri growled like a mama bear whose cub had been attacked.

Her instant defense warmed Anja despite the cool January wind. She wrapped one arm around her friend and squeezed while they continued to walk. Despite their height difference, their steps matched, probably because they had done this same walk around the lake almost every evening for the past fifteen years.

Anja lowered her gaze to Miri's favorite salmon-colored sneakers that were practically glowing in the dark—probably just like her ears. "She thinks I'm not comfortable around gay people."

"You?" Miri shortened Gino's leash for a second as they reached the end of the bridge and someone on a bicycle whizzed past them. "Why would she think that?"

"Long story." After the day she'd had, Anja didn't have the energy for long explanations. "She misunderstood the way I looked at her when I found out who she was."

"So if she took it personally, I take it she's part of the rainbow family?"

"Yeah, out and proud, according to Nobby. Having a lesbian niece is probably part of why he took it so well when I came out as bisexual to him."

Miri let out a low whistle that made Gino bark once. "So she's hot and gay."

"Forget it," Anja said forcefully.

"What? It was just an observation."

"Sure. Just an observation. Like that time you tried to set me up with the guy from the ice cream parlor who thought being bi meant I'd be eager to have a threesome with him and another woman."

"Hey, how was I supposed to know he'd be such a creep? He seemed nice."

"Well, Susanne Wolff is anything but nice, so forget it."

Miri laughed. "Her name is Wolff?"

"What's so funny about that?"

"Wolff…Lamm…wolf…lamb…" Miri pointed back and forth between Anja and some imaginary person. "Don't you get it?"

"Yeah, well, this lamb is not going to get eaten by the big, bad wolf." Anja kicked a piece of wood out of the way and watched as Gino chased after it until the leash reined him in.

"I want you to know that I'm heroically abstaining from making a suggestive joke about what you just said."

Anja's cheeks heated. She hadn't even realized the double meaning of her words. "Thank you."

"But seriously, you should be more open toward meeting new people." The humor was gone from Miri's voice.

Not this again. "I'm meeting new people in the store every day."

"I'm not talking about customers. You need more than Paper Love. You haven't been on a date, much less had a relationship since the Stone Age. There's this woman I'm friends with on Facebook who—"

Anja groaned. "No Facebook. You know I'm not on any of that social media stuff. If I decide to ask a woman out, I'll do it face-to-face."

"Talk about the Stone Age," Miri muttered.

Anja ignored the comment. "Besides, maybe you've spoiled me for other women."

"Oh, please. We kissed exactly once, and that was enough to nearly convince you that you're not bi after all."

Anja chuckled. "It wasn't that bad."

After a beat of silence, they said at the same time, "Yes, it was."

Their laughter rang through the darkness.

They had met a year after Anja had left the tiny little town where she had grown up and moved to Freiburg. She had been curious to explore that part of her sexuality, but she hadn't worked up the courage to go to one of the few gay bars or parties in the area, and joining the queer sports club hadn't been her thing either. She and Miri had finally met at the Lesbian Film Festival.

They had instantly hit it off. After the third date, Miri had kissed her. Nothing. No fireworks, no butterflies. It had been like kissing her sister, and that had confused Anja for a while. She had needed some time to figure out that just because she was attracted to women didn't mean she was attracted to *all* women.

And she definitely wasn't attracted to Susanne Wolff.

They paused when they reached the fork in the path where Anja had to go right, while Miri and Gino would head left.

"So are you sure you don't want me to come by tomorrow?" Miri asked. "Not to check her out or anything like that. Just for moral support. I could pose as a customer so you can impress her with your amazing sales skills."

Anja laughed but shook her head. "No, thanks. I don't even want to impress her. She's just here to help out for a while, not to take over."

"Are you sure about that? Nobby is what…? Sixty-two? Sixty-three?"

The veggie *Yufka* they had eaten before their walk suddenly sat like a slab of mud in Anja's stomach. "You think…?" She clamped her mouth shut, not wanting to say the words, as if that would make them more likely to happen.

Miri shrugged. "Maybe his niece is sniffing out the store to see if she wants to take over once he retires."

Anja had been dreading the day Nobby would retire for years, but he had repeatedly assured her that she would always have a job at Paper Love, even if that happened. But with his niece at the helm, Anja wasn't so sure about that—and neither was she sure that she'd want to work for Susanne Wolff.

For the first time ever, she was not looking forward to going to work in the morning.

Chapter 4

Susanne was starting to understand how the cat that had visited her last night must have felt—like an unwelcome intruder.

Anja Lamm stood behind the cash register and watched her every move while pretending to flick through a magazine with a red-and-gold fountain pen on its glossy cover.

God, get over yourself. I'm not trying to steal your precious notebooks or pens. I'm here to help! Susanne tried to ignore the gaze following her as she went from product to product, entering data about prices and other details in a note-taking app on her iPhone. So what if Frau Lamm didn't like her? She didn't care. In her old job as a business consultant, she hadn't always been greeted with open arms either. When she had been sent out, it usually meant the company was in trouble, so very few people were warm and fuzzy toward her.

But somehow this seemed different—more personal—and that was why working with family members or someone you were close to was a bad idea. Her mother wouldn't listen, though, and her uncle was obviously just as bad.

Why the hell was he paying someone to stand around and read a magazine? Granted, she was good with customers. Susanne admitted to herself that she wouldn't have been so patient with the people who took forever to check out every item in the store or asked endless questions, only to leave with a couple of cheap ballpoint pens.

The amount of money they made from sales like that didn't even justify having an employee.

Susanne picked up a leather-bound notebook from the center island to look for the price tag. When she found it, she nearly dropped her phone. A hundred euros for a journal? No wonder they hadn't sold any of them all day!

When she carefully put down the expensive notebook, an almost inaudible sigh of relief drifted through the store.

God, the woman really made her feel as if she were out to harm her beloved notebooks. "Is that price tag correct?" Susanne asked, pointing at it.

"If it says ninety-nine euros and ninety-nine cents, it is."

At least she seemed to know the prices of the products they sold by heart, so she wasn't totally useless.

"It's refillable," Frau Lamm added in a defensive tone.

"So is my smartphone," Susanne muttered. With a shake of her head, she moved on to the display case of fountain pens. She leaned forward and peered through the glass to make out the tiny price tags placed near each pen. The tag next to the pen in the middle—a midnight-blue-and-silver pen with engraved letters of alphabets from all over the world—caught her attention.

Two thousand euros? What the hell? She whirled around.

Frau Lamm quickly averted her gaze as if she'd been caught doing something forbidden.

Had she been checking out Susanne's ass? *Nah. She stammered like a scared little girl when she found out I'm a lesbian. No way is she gay.* She had probably just watched her to make sure she wouldn't smudge the glass she'd polished earlier.

"Could you put down your pen porn and explain this to me, please?"

"P-pardon me?" Frau Lamm stuttered.

Susanne bit her lip. Hell, her professionalism really was slipping. Would she have said something like that if this had been any other job? Probably not.

It pissed her off that she'd been sent to Freiburg to rescue another family member who was completely inept as a businessman. Her mother had charged in like the cavalry to save her husband's struggling businesses more than once when Susanne had been growing up, even taking out a loan for him and nearly ruining her own business in the process.

Susanne had been forced to watch helplessly, and she now realized that she'd let that old, pent-up anger color her interaction with Anja Lamm. From now on, she would try to treat her time in Freiburg like any other job.

"That magazine." She pointed. "Could you put it down and come over here… please," she added after a second.

Frau Lamm carefully put down the magazine and walked over with the expression and posture of a prisoner being led to her execution.

"Who sets the prices around here?" Susanne asked.

Frau Lamm folded her arms across her chest, which drew Susanne's attention to the bit of smooth skin revealed by two open top buttons on her blouse.

Annoyed with herself for even noticing, she tore her gaze away.

"Nobby and I decide together, based on what we pay our suppliers and what the competition asks for similar items," Frau Lamm answered.

Okay, that was a reasonable strategy, but still… "Two thousand euros for a single pen seems a bit excessive."

"It's a Montblanc Meisterstück Solitaire LeGrand 146." At Susanne's blank look, Frau Lamm added, "A special edition from one of the best fountain pen makers in the world."

"Still. Who would spend that much when a pen for a couple of euros would get the job done just as well?" Susanne pointed to the cheap pens in the corner.

Frau Lamm sighed. She opened her mouth, then closed it again. When she finally spoke, she asked, "What kind of car do you drive?"

"Excuse me?"

"What kind of car do you drive?" she repeated more slowly, as if Susanne had problems processing the question.

"A BMW." Revealing this tiny bit of semi-personal information made her feel as if she'd said too much, probably because she was used to fiercely guarding her private life against her homophobic boss and his good old boys' club. "What does that have to do with anything?"

"Why spend that much on a car? Why not just get a used Ford Ka or a little Fiat that would take you from A to B just as well?"

"Because I love cars. Driving a car isn't just about getting from A to B. A car is… I don't know… A lifestyle. A personal expression."

"And a status symbol," Frau Lamm added.

"Yeah, maybe that too. People wouldn't be very impressed if their business consultant showed up in a dented, cheap little car."

Frau Lamm waved her hand in a there-you-have-it gesture.

"You want me to believe that fountain pens are like cars?" Susanne eyed her skeptically.

"Maybe not for you. But they are for the customers we target. Personally, I prefer a bicycle to a BMW, but if I made that kind of money," she gestured at the price tag, "I wouldn't hesitate to spend two thousand euros on this beauty." She gave the pen a loving look and trailed her finger along the glass in a sensual caress.

Susanne's mouth went dry. Probably just because she hadn't been drinking enough while working. Maybe she should get herself another coffee. She cleared her throat. "So how many of these BMW-type pens have we sold this year?"

"It's only the middle of January."

"Meaning none."

Frau Lamm wrapped her arms even more tightly around herself, but she refused to avert her gaze, even though she had to raise her head to make eye contact.

"January isn't a good time for pens. We sell more of them around the holidays, and sales will probably pick up again as we get closer to Valentine's Day."

If things continued like this, they'd be out of business by Valentine's Day.

"Is there a specific reason why you're asking all these questions, Susanne?"

The casual use of her first name took her by surprise. No one had ever attempted such a familiarity in her old job. If she didn't deal with it right away, she could have a situation on her hands down the road. "Frau Wolff."

"Pardon me?"

"This is a workplace, Frau Lamm. I don't think calling each other by our first names is appropriate."

Frau Lamm's big eyes widened even more. With her elfin features, she looked so vulnerable that Susanne wondered if she'd been too harsh.

No. Don't doubt yourself. You can't save a business by coddling the employees. You know that.

"B-but your uncle and I have been on a first-name basis for years, and we manage to work together just fine."

The way her uncle managed his business was what had gotten them into trouble in the first place. "My uncle makes his own decisions, but I, for one, would prefer if you called me by my last name."

"Very well, Frau Wolff." She gave Susanne a stiff nod. Her brown eyes, which shone so warmly whenever she interacted with customers or with Uncle Norbert, were now shuttered.

Susanne steeled herself. She had never shied away from doing whatever was necessary to get the job done, and she wouldn't start now. If that meant hurting Frau Lamm's feelings, so be it.

∽⌀∾

Anja went back to her magazine and tried to find new products that could be of interest to their customers, but even reviews of the newest Diamine inks couldn't capture her attention now.

She turned the page with a little too much force, nearly tearing the glossy paper. Her body vibrated with tension. How the heck had her wonderful, fun workplace become this stiff, no-first-names-please situation? The nerve of this woman!

Susanne—Frau Wolff—had been nitpicking all day long, running her critical gaze over every centimeter of the store and documenting any perceived issue. Anja wasn't surprised to see her use some app on her smartphone instead of pen and paper.

Not that she had anything against phones and other digital devices. She owned one too, but for her, it was strictly a tool of communication, or she used it to quickly look things up online. If she needed to capture important thoughts, however, she used her traveler's notebook. At least that never ran out of battery, and the slower writing speed helped her think more clearly. How could Nobby invite a person like his niece, who clearly didn't get the appeal of a fine ream of paper or a leather-bound notebook, to work at Paper Love?

Granted, Susanne's long fingers looked pretty elegant tapping the screen of her smartphone, but that wasn't the point. Just because she was easy on the eyes didn't give her the right to look down on them. Every little thing about the way they ran the store seemed to be wrong in her opinion. Anja hated this new atmosphere and feeling as if she constantly had to justify herself. Did Nobby know what his niece was doing?

Maybe she should let him know. He'd been locked away in his office all morning, so he probably had no clue that his niece was basically trying to take over before he had even decided to retire.

But before she could head into the office to talk to him, Susanne apparently had the same idea. Gripping her cell phone as if it were a box full of incriminating evidence, she strode past Anja's position behind the cash register and stepped into the back rooms. With a cool glance over her shoulder, she pulled the door closed behind her.

Oh, come on! They rarely closed that door. What was she telling Nobby that Anja wasn't allowed to hear?

Curiosity bubbled up inside of her. Should she…? She glanced toward the street. Since people's lunch break had ended a short while ago, foot traffic outside had slowed. No potential customers approached the store or turned the carousels outside to pick a card.

Anja didn't like eavesdropping, but she couldn't help herself. Under the pretense of getting a roll of tissue paper from the stockroom, she opened the door, sneaked into the back rooms, and lingered in front of Nobby's tiny office.

Voices drifted through the door, and she could easily identify Susanne's precise, confident tone. "I haven't finished my review yet, so it's too soon to make any real recommendations, but one thing is clear: you've got to cut your costs."

Nobby said something Anja couldn't understand.

"Well," Susanne answered, "if push comes to shove, it might become…"

Anja didn't catch everything, so she leaned closer.

"…let your employees go."

What? Anja nearly hit her head on the door. Susanne had seriously marched in there to tell Nobby he should fire her and Felix, the student who helped out in the store on Saturdays? *What a bitch!* She should have known Susanne would be the type who got her kicks from firing people. Good thing Nobby would never in a million years go for this…would he?

Nobby answered, but his voice was too soft for her to make out the words. His tone, however, spoke loud and clear: it sounded defeated.

God, no! Her knees became wobbly, so she caught herself with her damp palms against the door. *Please don't let this coldhearted beast tell you how to run your business.*

Susanne spoke again, but now it sounded strangely warped and distorted, like an old cassette tape that had been played one too many times.

Anja sucked in a steadying breath to ward off her rising panic. She didn't know how long she'd been standing there, trying not to hyperventilate, when the door beneath her hands started to move.

She jumped back, but it was too late to pretend she'd been heading toward the stockroom.

Susanne stood in front of her, those cool gray eyes assessing her the same way she'd looked at the Meisterstück Solitaire earlier. "Frau Lamm?"

"I…I, uh…" Past Susanne's shoulder, she caught a glimpse of Nobby, who sat slumped behind his desk. "I wanted to ask if it's okay if I take my lunch break now." She needed to get out of here—now.

"Oh, yes, yes, of course. Go." For the first time ever, Nobby didn't smile or make eye contact. "In fact, why don't you both go to lunch? I'll hold down the fort until you're back."

Anja knew him—he wanted to be alone to think about whatever his niece had told him. She wanted to stay behind and talk him out of following her advice, but she'd already told them she would be heading out for lunch. Under Susanne's watchful eyes, she didn't have a choice. She grabbed her messenger bag from behind the cash register and fled.

❧

Susanne walked along the cobblestone street, glad to escape the little store for a while. Telling a company's owner that it might become necessary to fire people was never easy, but usually, she could hide behind the shield of professionalism. Not this time. The devastation on her uncle's face made her stomach feel as if it were a sheet of paper that someone had crumpled into a little ball.

Oh, now you're using paper analogies? She definitely needed to take a step back and regain a healthy emotional distance—starting with having lunch, even though she'd lost her appetite. She'd just grab a quick bite somewhere and then head back to the store to see if Uncle Norbert was ready to talk about the steps necessary to save his business.

Enticing scents drew her to a food court that had been set up in what appeared to be an old newspaper building. The aromas of dishes from all over the world—Persian, Afghan, Brazilian, Mexican, Chinese, Italian, and German—made her mouth water, but the court was incredibly crowded, and she wasn't in the mood to eat squeezed in between strangers at a tiny bar table, so she walked on.

The bells of the Münster, the cathedral towering over the Old Town, announced that it was one o'clock. Wasn't there a farmers market with food stands at the Münsterplatz? That should be quick.

Susanne headed in that direction. The scent of fresh flowers and frying onions greeted her before she had even reached the square. The crowd of shoppers had thinned, and most of the vendors were already packing up their fruit, vegetables, cheeses, breads, and homemade jams, but the sausage stands along one side of the Gothic red sandstone cathedral were still doing good business.

Maybe Uncle Norbert should invest in a food trailer instead. With a wry smile, she got in line and tried not to feel bad for her uncle or Frau Lamm. There was no place for sentimentality in business.

∽◊◊◊∽

For several minutes, Anja wandered aimlessly without paying the slightest attention to where she was going. If it hadn't been for the finely honed instincts of someone who'd lived here for years, she would have probably stepped into a *Bächle* too. She followed one of the narrow canals through an alley and ended up at the Münsterplatz, with the towering cathedral in its middle.

The vendors were packing up their goods, talking to each other in Alemannic. The soft tones of the dialect she'd grown up with were as soothing as a hug, so she strolled along the edges of the farmers market.

As usual, the trailers of the sausage vendors were soon the only stands remaining. They never seemed to have a problem attracting enough customers, locals and tourists alike, so there was still a bit of a crowd surrounding them. Maybe she'd soon be back to selling sausages too, the way she had right after moving to Freiburg. The supermarket she'd worked for back then had put her behind the meat counter without caring that she was a vegetarian.

Why were some people so cold and uncaring? Anja would never understand people like Susanne. *Frau Wolff,* she corrected herself with a huff.

As if conjured up by the mere thought of her name, Susanne appeared in front of her as the crowd parted. She stood just a few steps away next to one of the food trailers, her mouth wide open, about to bite into one of the popular long, red sausages that were served in a bun. Just as she took a bite, their gazes met.

Susanne froze, and so did Anja.

Someone ran into her from behind, shoving her forward and into Susanne.

Mustard splattered everywhere, and a few fried onions dropped onto the cobblestones. Susanne nearly choked on her bite of sausage and started to cough.

Just when she'd thought the day couldn't get any worse. "Oh God. I'm sorry. Are you all right?"

"Fine," Susanne wheezed. A gob of mustard grazed her elegant scoop-necked top, right where her wool coat stood open.

Anja reached out with a tissue from her pocket.

"Um, thanks. I can do it myself." Susanne took the tissue from her and used it to dab at the stain on her chest.

"Oh." Anja withdrew her hand. Her cheeks burned. *God. You nearly rubbed her breast!* If Susanne hadn't already threatened to fire her, she probably would have done so now. Anja pretended to be busy checking herself for mustard spatter just so she wouldn't have to look her in the eyes.

Susanne crumpled up the tissue and threw it and the rest of the bun into a nearby trash can, as if Anja's appearance had spoiled her appetite. "Are you here for a sausage too, or…?"

"No," Anja said before she could think about it. "I don't eat meat."

"Ah."

Anja hated that judgmental "ah" she encountered all too often, but she held her tongue. Now was not the time to fight that battle. She had enough on her hands fighting for her job already.

"So you're here because you followed me." Susanne made it a statement, not a question.

"What? No! I just…" Anja trailed off since she couldn't very well admit that she'd wandered around upset because she had overheard what she had said to Nobby.

"You what?" Susanne pierced her with those gunmetal gray eyes.

Anja squirmed. God, this woman could push her off her stride much too easily. But enough was enough. She wouldn't be able to bear the strain of waiting for days until someone finally told her what the heck was going on, so she decided on the direct route. After all, Susanne already planned on firing her, so what else could she do to her?

She firmly planted her feet on the cobblestones, bracing herself. "Why do you want to take over Paper Love if you don't even like stationery?"

"What? Who said I want to—?"

"Oh! I get it now!" Anja put her hands on her hips, leaned forward, and glared at her. They were almost nose to nose now—well, nose to chest because of their height difference—and Anja did her best to focus on her anger and not on the distracting closeness of Susanne's admittedly nice breasts. "You want to toss out the pens and paper and sell smartphones or sushi or something."

"I don't even like sushi," Susanne said with an annoying calmness.

God, this woman was maddening. "That's not the point! You—"

"Let's get one thing straight. I don't have any intention of staying here in Freiburg to take over the store, not for sushi and not for anything else."

"Then why do you want Nobby to fire me?"

Susanne slid her hands into the pockets of her slacks and rocked back on her heels to give Anja a disapproving look. "Do you always eavesdrop on your boss's conversations?"

"No! Of course I don't." For some reason, Anja didn't want her to think that. "I just... I couldn't help myself. I needed to know what's going on."

"Oh, come on. Surely you knew it was coming."

"How was I supposed to know? Nobby was always happy with my work, and our customers really seem to like me. It was only when you came in and—"

Susanne cut her off with an impatient wave of her hand. "This isn't about you or me. Don't think I'm having fun doing this."

"Could have fooled me," Anja muttered under her breath.

Susanne fixed her with a sharp glare. "I get that you need to be angry with someone, but that kind of attitude won't help save the store."

"I've worked at Paper Love for fourteen years. Of course I'm angr... Wait a minute! Did you just say...?" Anja couldn't breathe. Tunnel vision set in, and all she saw were the clear gray irises in front of her. "S-save the store? Are...are you saying...?"

"Come on," Susanne said, now much gentler than before. "Let's go find a place to sit and talk." She walked around the cathedral to the three steps that formed the pedestal for a sandstone statue in front of the main portal.

Dazed, Anja followed her like a meek little lamb being lured away by the big, bad wolf, no longer caring if she'd be eaten alive.

૭∾ૡૡ

Since there were no benches or other seating options nearby, Susanne pointed to the sandstone steps at the base of a statue.

Frau Lamm plopped down as if all the strength had drained from her legs.

Susanne sat next to her, close but not touching. Providing comfort to an employee who might have to be let go wasn't part of her job description, but Frau Lamm had gone very pale and she was still her uncle's employee, so for now, Susanne was responsible for her well-being.

She patiently watched Frau Lamm's face and waited until the dazed look had cleared from her eyes.

Finally, Frau Lamm took a shaky breath and half-turned on the step to look at her. "Are you saying Paper Love is in trouble?"

Susanne nodded. "Trouble with a capital T, I'm afraid."

"Can we…I don't know, do a special sale or something?"

"You don't understand. The store isn't just short a few hundred euros, and it isn't just this month. You're nowhere near breaking even, and you haven't been in years."

"Years! But…but…Nobby never indicated that we're in financial trouble. He always paid me on time."

"With his personal money if need be," Susanne threw in.

Frau Lamm gulped audibly. She put both elbows on her thighs and leaned her head onto her palms. Her golden brown hair fell forward, forming a curtain around her face and hiding it from Susanne as if she couldn't bear to be seen at her most vulnerable.

"You didn't know?" Susanne asked quietly.

Without looking up, Frau Lamm shook her head.

"Really? Excuse me for saying so, but I find that a bit hard to believe."

Frau Lamm looked up. Her vulnerable-looking doe eyes narrowed, and she squared her slim shoulders. "Are you calling me a liar? Are you always this suspicious of everyone, or is it just me you don't like?"

Susanne's mouth moved, but it took several seconds before she was capable of answering. It wasn't often that someone confronted her like this, and she certainly hadn't expected it from Anja Lamm. She held up her hands, palms out. "This isn't personal at all."

"Oh yes, it is. This is as personal as it gets for me! Paper Love is a big part of my life. It *is* my life. If we go under…" Her voice became even huskier than normal with every word and then broke.

God, no tears, please! Susanne never knew how to handle those, especially not in situations that were supposed to be unemotional and professional, so she charged ahead. "So you really want me to believe you had no clue? Come on. You're not stupid. You must have noticed that people aren't exactly beating down your door to buy stationery."

"Of course I noticed! But it's not that we don't have enough customers. The store can get busy at certain times of the day. I knew we weren't getting rich, but with Nobby owning the place so we don't have to pay rent, I thought we must at least be getting by."

"It's not the number of customers; it's that you have the wrong customers buying the wrong stuff. You can't survive on the two cents you make off a greeting card and a cheap ballpoint pen. Didn't you ever see the numbers?"

Frau Lamm shook her head. "Nobby doesn't like putting the store's numbers into a computer. He's pretty old-school in that regard."

"Yeah, I noticed. I've seen that thing he calls a cell phone."

A weak smile tugged on Frau Lamm's lips. "I nicknamed it *the brick*."

Susanne laughed and was glad to hear her chuckle a bit too. "Yeah, that's what it looks like. So you never saw his business ledgers either?"

"No. Nobby always told me he wanted me to focus on the customers and the stationery, and he would take care of everything else. He didn't even tell me you'd be coming, probably because he knew I'd start asking questions that he wasn't ready to answer." She sniffed.

Did she see it as a betrayal that he had kept her out of the loop?

Frau Lamm stared up at the saints and apostles decorating the cathedral as if hoping for the patron saint of nearly bankrupt stationery stores to intervene. Finally, she directed her attention back to Susanne. "So that's why you're really here, isn't it? Because we're in trouble."

"Yeah. That's what I do for a living—I help companies in trouble…or advise them to close down, if need be."

Frau Lamm gave a decisive shake of her head. "Not Paper Love. There has to be another solution. What can we do to save the store?"

"Well, there's two sides of the equation," Susanne said, glad that they were back to discussing business strategies instead of dealing with emotions. "Either you have to cut back costs, or you have to increase revenue."

"We."

"Pardon me?"

"We," Frau Lamm repeated. "You keep saying *you*."

Susanne wasn't sure she understood. "Yeah. Something wrong with that?"

"Paper Love isn't just any store. It's your uncle's lifework—and your grandfather's before him. Shouldn't it mean more to you than the other businesses you've worked for?"

Now it was Susanne's turn to stare up at the saints above the cathedral's entrance just so she didn't have to look into those brown eyes. This was exactly the kind of entanglement she'd been trying to avoid. Finally, when the silence went on for too long, she directed her gaze back to Frau Lamm. "It does."

"Good. Then we're in this together." Frau Lamm held out her hand, clearly expecting Susanne to shake it.

Reluctantly, Susanne placed her hand in Frau Lamm's. Her fingers were cool—either from the January temperatures or because she was afraid of losing her job. Engulfed in Susanne's bigger hand, Frau Lamm's felt almost fragile, and Susanne fought the urge to cradle it in both of hers. *No coddling employees, remember?* Frau Lamm's handshake was surprisingly strong for such a slight woman, so maybe she wasn't the type who needed coddling anyway, despite the way she looked.

"Let's go back to the store. We can talk while we walk." Frau Lamm stood and pulled Susanne up with her by their still-linked hands.

When she let go, Susanne curled her fingers against her now-empty palm.

"Come on." Frau Lamm strode across the square like a soldier on a rescue mission.

Hell, when had she lost control of this situation? Susanne shook her head and hurried after her.

With her hand on the brass handle of Paper Love's front door, Anja paused. She had entered the store thousands of times, but now that she knew its very existence was in danger, it felt different somehow. *Oh, come on. This isn't a funeral. Not yet anyway.*

"Everything okay?" Susanne asked behind her.

Anja turned. "Yeah. It's just…" How could she explain?

As if sensing what stopped her, Susanne gently reached past her, pushed the door open, and stepped forward to lead the way into the store.

"Wait!" Anja pulled her back around. "You have a bit of onion on your, um…" *Very nice breasts.* She pointed. "Your shirt."

"Oh. Thanks."

Anja tried not to watch as Susanne picked off the piece of onion and flicked it away. At least this little episode had distracted her from the hopefully premature feeling of sadness that had gripped her. *Yeah, well, I suggest you look for another distraction. Remember that she wanted to get you fired.*

She forced herself to step into the store and pretend she would get to do so multiple times a day for the next thirty years. "Could you keep an eye on the store for a minute? I'd like to check in with Nobby."

For a second, Susanne's normally cool, calm, and collected expression slipped, and she actually looked a bit panicked. "Um, sure. If you give me a minute first to get rid of the mustard stain."

"Oh. Of course."

She disappeared into the bathroom, which gave Anja a chance to fan her overheated cheeks. Why the heck was she blushing just because of some mustard?

When Susanne returned a short while later, Anja resisted the urge to check out her chest to see if the stain was gone. She left her in charge and went to the office.

The door was open so Nobby would hear the bell whenever a customer entered the store, and he looked up as she approached. He greeted her with a smile, but it wasn't quite one of the full-out, warm Nobby smiles she had grown used to. "How was lunch? Did you get a veggie Currywurst, or did you not make it past the cheesecake in the café down the street?"

Why was he still trying to make everything appear normal? He needed his energy to fight against his business going down, not to mislead his employee. Besides, she considered herself much more than an employee. Nobby was more like an uncle than an employer to her, and she had thought he considered her family too.

"Oh, Nobby." She crossed the room and perched on the edge of the desk as she had so many times before. "Why didn't you tell me?"

His weak smile instantly fell. "Susanne told you about…?" He gestured at the business ledgers he'd been brooding over.

She nodded. "Why didn't you? Why let me find out this way?"

"I'm sorry. I thought I'd be able to turn things around and you'd never have to find out. I didn't want you to have to live with that constant, nagging worry."

"I don't need you to protect me. I'm thirty-six. I'm no longer the wet-behind-the-ears girl you first hired. I could have helped. Maybe together, we could have found a way to save Paper Love."

"We still can. At least that's what I'm hoping."

"If your niece doesn't fire me first."

Nobby shook his head so vehemently that his leftover flyaway hair bounced from left to right. "No one is firing you."

Anja looked him in the eyes. Her throat ached, and she had to swallow twice before she could speak. "If that's what you have to do to save Paper Love, then do it."

"No!" He glanced away, and she had a feeling his beard hid a hint of a blush. "I…I always thought… I always imagined you taking over as the new owner once I retire."

It was a wonderful dream, but that's all it was: a dream. "You know I don't have the money to buy the store from you." Even if she worked until she was ninety years old and saved every last cent she made, she would never be able to afford a building in this part of the city—or any building anywhere in Freiburg for that matter.

"Who's talking about buying it? I want to give you the store. You know I don't have any kids, and my nieces… Well, you've met Susanne. I appreciate her coming all the way here to help, but I doubt she wants to stay."

"You can't do that, Nobby. You inherited the store from your father. What would your family say if you gave it to a virtual stranger?"

Nobby shrugged. "I inherited it from my father because, unlike my brother, I shared his passion for stationery. No one else in the family does, so they'll just have to live with my decision."

"That… I…I don't know what to say." She cleared her throat to get rid of the lump that had settled there. "Except you do know that you have to stick around for at least thirty more years, right?"

He chuckled and patted her hand. "Not going anywhere."

"And neither is Paper Love," Anja said.

Nobby sighed. "I don't know. Things don't look good."

She gripped the edges of the old, worn desk. "How long do we have until…?"

"A month or two. If we don't see any improvement by March, I'll have to—"

A knock on the door interrupted the words Anja hadn't wanted to hear anyway.

"Come in," Nobby called so quickly that she knew he hadn't wanted to say them either.

The door opened, and his niece stuck her head into the tiny office. "Um, I have a customer out there, but I don't understand what he wants—and it's not just because of his dialect. He says he's looking for a wet ink. Isn't all ink wet? I mean, it's a liquid."

Anja laughed, leaned over, and gave Nobby's shoulder a quick squeeze before getting up and walking toward Susanne. "All right. I'll come save you, fountain pen novice." She just hoped they could somehow manage to save the entire store too.

"It's *Frau* Fountain Pen Novice, please," Susanne said with a straight face, but a softening around her eyes revealed that she was joking.

So she did have a sense of humor. Good. They would probably need it in the weeks to come.

Chapter 5

Susanne flipped through the pen magazine that Frau Lamm had been reading yesterday, trying to familiarize herself with some of the terms of the fountain pen world. *Dry ink, wet ink, music nib, squeeze converter, breather hole, piston filler…* Dozens of terms buzzed around her brain and made her feel a bit dizzy.

Or maybe her distractedness was responsible for her not grasping any of the terms in the magazine.

After every sentence she read, she peered up from behind the cover of *Pen World* and glanced over at Frau Lamm, who had climbed up on a stepladder to hang a bunch of paper animals so that they dangled over the island display.

The ladder wasn't very high, just a three-step, but she didn't seem comfortable up there. She held on to the grip with one hand while trying to hang a paper flamingo with the other.

It made Susanne a bit nervous too. The last thing her uncle needed was a workplace accident. "Want me to do that?"

For a moment, Frau Lamm looked tempted to let her take over, but then she shook her head. "I can do it."

"Suit yourself." She had offered, so now Frau Lamm was on her own. But she couldn't help keeping an eye on her.

Since Frau Lamm was short, she had to stretch to reach the ceiling. The sweater she wore rode up, revealing a strip of smooth skin and a toned belly.

Admittedly, Anja didn't look bad for a paper geek.

The random thought made Susanne frown. Where the hell had that come from? And since when did she think of her as anything but *Frau Lamm?* She resolved to keep her eyes—and her thoughts—on work. "So care to explain that wet ink/dry ink stuff you were talking about with the customer yesterday?"

Frau Lamm paused in her attempts to hang the paper flamingo. "Basically, it's about the viscosity of the ink. Some inks flow more quickly from the nib, so they're called wet. There are even some companies who add lubricants to their inks. In comparison, a dry ink has a slower flow, so there's a bit more friction when you write."

Wet, lubricants, friction. Susanne hid her grin behind the pen magazine. Who knew that inks could sound so sexy?

At least when Frau Lamm talked about them. She launched into an explanation of various examples for wet and dry inks, gesturing animatedly with both hands. She seemed to have forgotten her earlier discomfort at being on a ladder.

It was kind of cute how enthusiastic the usually quiet woman became when she spoke about inks, but at the same time, on top of a ladder wasn't the best place for that much enthusiasm. It wobbled on the uneven wood floor, making Frau Lamm drop the flamingo as she latched on to the grip.

Susanne put down the magazine and pointed at the paper animals. "Come on. Let me do that."

"I told you I can do it."

"I'm not saying you can't. But I'm taller. If you hand me the animals and I pin them, we'll be done in no time."

After a moment's hesitation, Frau Lamm nodded. "All right. Thanks." She climbed down and picked up the paper flamingo.

Susanne climbed up, ignoring the fact that her thigh brushed against Frau Lamm's shoulder in the process. When Frau Lamm handed her the flamingo, she pinned it to the ceiling by the attached string.

Next, Frau Lamm held out what looked like a fox.

Susanne took it, careful not to let their hands brush. "Who made them?" She nodded down at the zoo of animals waiting to be hung.

"I did. Not during working hours, if that's why you're asking. I enjoy getting creative in my spare time, so I don't want Nobby to pay me for it, and the paper I used is my own."

"No, that's not why I asked." Susanne sighed, but she couldn't blame her for being a little defensive. Even though they seemed to have achieved some kind of truce now, Frau Lamm probably wouldn't forget that she'd told Uncle Norbert he might need to fire her. "I just think they're cute. That's all."

"Oh. Thanks."

Silence descended on them as Susanne pinned the fox. When she looked back down, Frau Lamm stood with her back to her, sorting through the paper animals.

"Listen," Susanne said. "I know you think I'm a heartless bitch, and I really shouldn't care, but when I told my uncle he might need to fire you, I really didn't—"

"No." Frau Lamm turned around.

"No, I should care, or no, you don't think that about me?"

A hint of a smile flitted across Frau Lamm's face. "Either. Both."

Susanne gave her a dubious look.

"You do come across like a bit of a hard-ass, but I don't think you're entirely heartless."

Entirely? Susanne arched her brows. *Thanks a lot.*

"You're here, after all, and I doubt it's because Nobby is paying you handsomely for your services."

Her uncle wasn't paying her at all. He had tried to offer her money, but she had refused to accept it. Susanne said nothing and took the next animal Frau Lamm handed her. It was a dove that carried an olive branch in its beak. Was that supposed to be a peace offering?

The look in Frau Lamm's eyes—a lot friendlier than before—made her think so. Susanne gave her a nod and pinned the dove to the ceiling.

Frau Lamm reached for a frog next, but when Susanne wanted to take it from her, she held on. "What do you think our chances are?"

She spoke so quietly that Susanne had to strain to understand her. "Of saving Paper Love, you mean?"

Frau Lamm bit her lip and nodded.

"I can't give you a specific number. Not yet at least. It's not just this store I'm not familiar with; I also don't know much about the stationery industry in general—and I have a feeling that's part of the problem. The stationery industry, I mean. I bet it's changed a lot since my grandfather first opened the store in 1950."

"It has," Frau Lamm said. "In those early years, he made a living just selling and repairing fountain pens and nothing else, but then ballpoint pens became popular, and he had to branch out."

It was strange that she knew more about that part of Susanne's family history than she did, but, of course, she had heard all the stories from Uncle Norbert since she'd worked with him for years, while Susanne hadn't seen him in ages. "To be honest, I think that all stationery stores will be struggling soon, if they aren't already. They'll probably go the way of the old vinyl record stores. I mean, this is the digital era, so aren't fountain pens and paper notebooks becoming obsolete?"

"Not at all."

Susanne studied her.

As Frau Lamm stood in the middle of the store, clutching a paper frog, she looked a bit like a princess from a fairy tale, not like a real-life modern woman. Maybe it was her slight build or her big, dreamy eyes that made her appear that way, but Susanne couldn't help wondering if she was indulging in wishful thinking when it came to her beloved paper products.

Frau Lamm waved the frog as if it were a defensive weapon. "Like you just said, you don't know the stationery business."

"So enlighten me."

"I know you think any reasonable person would use a smartphone and a note-taking app and that it's just nostalgic, old-fashioned people who resort to pen and paper, but that's not true. Analog products are actually making a comeback as a countermovement to the digital trend—and that includes vinyl records, by the way."

If that was true, it wasn't happening in Susanne's circles. "Really?"

"Oh yeah. Young people want to express their individuality, but you can't do that with digital devices because all the Samsungs and iPhones look the same. That's why they decorate their cell phone covers with pink glitter."

They both shuddered a little and grinned at each other.

"All right," Susanne finally said. "But we're not selling cell phone covers or pink glitter."

"It doesn't stop there. People are taking up hobbies such as hand lettering, bullet journaling, or scrapbooking. Coloring books for adults were a big thing a year or two ago, and even Polaroid-style instant cameras are making a comeback."

"Really?" Susanne's father had owned a camera like that when she'd been a child, and she remembered her parents arguing because he had constantly wasted the expensive photos on snapshots of himself making silly grimaces. As a kid, she had thought it funny, but now she viewed it as a waste of money. "Why would people resort to low-resolution images like those? Nowadays, every smartphone has a better camera."

"Yeah, but the digital photos usually stay on your phone. You can't touch them. People want that instant tactile connection. They are rediscovering the pleasure of doing things with their hands."

If Frau Lamm hadn't been an employee, her words combined with her sexy voice would have made Susanne think of other pleasurable things she could do with her hands, but since they worked together, she wouldn't allow her thoughts to wander in that direction.

Frau Lamm put down the frog and picked up a leather-bound journal from the island display. "I don't know if you have ever tried out a good fountain pen. Not one of those cheap, scratchy things we're forced to use in school, but a really great one. That smooth glide of a nib over creamy paper with just the right amount of pressure." Her gaze went hazy, and a smile played around the corners of her mouth. "That's so much more sensual than punching keys on a keyboard. There's something almost intimate about it."

She smoothed her hands over the leather cover of the journal as she spoke, then opened the book, circled the rounded corners with a sensual stroke of her fingertip, and practically made love to the thick, ivory paper.

Susanne's mouth went dry as her thoughts rushed into territory she tried to stay away from. She grasped the top of the stepladder to keep her balance.

Frau Lamm looked up at her. "Come on. Even you have to admit it. It's nice, isn't it?"

Susanne swallowed and had to tear her gaze away from those delicate yet strong hands before she could answer. "Mm-hmm. Very nice."

"I knew you'd see it my way." Frau Lamm winked and walked away to greet a customer who entered the store.

Susanne's mouth was probably hanging open as she stared at her retreating back. What the hell was that? Had Anja—Frau Lamm, dammit—just flirted with her? Had she practically seduced that lucky journal because she wanted to see what kind of effect it would have on Susanne?

Uncle Norbert stepped up to her, jolting her out of her thoughts. "You're not getting dizzy up there, are you? You look a little…stunned."

Susanne jumped down, folded up the ladder, and dragged it to the side so it wouldn't get in the way of Frau Lamm and the customer. "No. I'm fine," she answered in a voice so low that the customer couldn't hear her. "It's just dawning on me that the stationery business truly is a world of its own. One I don't have a clue about."

And neither did she have a clue about what Frau Lamm was doing. Was she playing with her? Susanne hated straight women who did that. Or even worse, was she using her knowledge of Susanne's sexual orientation to stop her from firing her?

If that was what she was doing, she was wasting her time. No way would Susanne let herself be manipulated like that. She was here to work, not to flirt with an employee. If need be, she would simply stay away from Frau Lamm and keep their interaction to a minimum.

There. Problem solved. She nodded to herself.

"Yes, it is," Uncle Norbert said.

"Huh?" Susanne had nearly forgotten that she'd been talking to him.

"A world of its own. But don't worry. You'll get the hang of it." He patted her arm. "And I've got just the thing to help you." With a triumphant "ta-da," he pulled something from his shirt pocket and dangled it beneath her nose.

"Paperworld," Susanne read the print on one of the two pieces of paper. "Isn't that the name of the pen magazine Anja, um, Frau Lamm likes to read?"

Uncle Norbert chuckled. "That's *Pen World*. This is *Paper*world. It's the world's biggest stationery and office supply trade fair. And I just got two free tickets. I thought you and Anja could go. Maybe you'll come back with some great ideas for how to turn the store around."

Susanne stared at the two tickets in his hand. "It's not in Freiburg, is it?"

"No. It's in Frankfurt at the end of the month."

That meant a two-hour drive each way at the very least. Great. Not even a minute ago, she had resolved to keep her interaction with Frau Lamm to a minimum, and here he was, suggesting that they be joined at the hip for an entire day—or possibly even an overnight stay.

"So?" He held up the tickets again. "What do you think?"

"Stationery road trip. Yay." She hoped he'd put her unenthusiastic tone down to her lack of passion for stationery. At least she had about two weeks before the fair to get her head back into the game.

"If you'd rather have it in another color, I can order whatever we don't have in stock." Anja watched the customer run his hands over the notebook the same way she had just caressed the leather-bound journal.

Okay, maybe not the *exact* same way.

What on earth had she been thinking? It had started out as an attempt to show Susanne the appeal of notebooks but had then snowballed into something much more…sensual. She definitely hadn't planned on doing that. Susanne wasn't a friend and certainly not someone she could joke around and flirt with like that! Even if she hadn't tried to get her fired from her dream job just a few hours ago, she *so* wasn't Anja's type.

She was businesslike and seemed to approach every situation from a purely logical point of view, while Anja viewed life from a more interpersonal, emotional angle. Susanne loved cars; Anja didn't even own one. She had eaten a bratwurst, while Anja had been a vegetarian since she'd been sixteen.

Flirting with her was wrong. But it had also been amazingly fun, especially since she hadn't flirted with anyone in a long time. *No, no, no, no. Stop thinking like that. You're not even the flirty type. Why start now, with her of all people?*

"…open?" the customer asked.

Oh shit. She'd totally missed everything he'd been saying—and Susanne was still in the room and was probably watching her interact with the customer. Anja gritted her teeth. Instead of flirting with her, she should prove to her what a good salesperson she was. She took a wild guess, hoping he had asked her how long the store would be open tonight. "Um, until six thirty."

He gave her a puzzled look. "I asked if the notebook lies open when you use it. The one I'm using right now doesn't lie flat but closes on its own whenever I let go of it."

Anja felt herself blush to the roots of her hair. "Oh. Sorry. I have the perfect notebook for you! We just got a delivery from a little Greek company. They use an entirely new type of binding that allows you to even bend the cover all the way back. It stays open like a dream."

His eyes lit up. "That's exactly what I need."

Phew. "Give me a second. I'll get you one from the stockroom." Glad to escape for a moment, she rushed toward the back. As she passed Nobby and his niece, she caught snippets of their conversation. "Paperworld… Two free tickets…"

Anja gave a joyful hop. They had gotten tickets for Paperworld? She had always wanted to go, but one thing or another had always come up that kept her from making it to the trade fair. Maybe they would find a new trend at the fair, something that would draw more well-paying customers to the store. She barely stopped herself from skipping all the way to the stockroom like a kid who'd just found out she'd be going to Disneyland.

But right as she reached the door to the back, Nobby's voice drifted over. "I thought you and Anja could go."

Oh boy. She had assumed she and Nobby would go, but, of course, they couldn't leave Susanne at the store alone, and Felix, their part-time employee, had never covered an entire day on his own. That left her to spend a day at Paperworld with the resident stationery grump. The resident stationery grump with whom she had just flirted, even though Susanne had no idea she was interested in women.

Anja stepped into the stockroom and pulled the door closed behind her. Leaning her forehead against one of the floor-to-ceiling shelves, she let out a long groan. Why, oh why, was her life suddenly so complicated?

∽∾∾

Susanne steered her car down the steep ramp into her apartment building's parking garage and parked in her spot. Her ankle boots tapped a tired staccato over the concrete as she headed toward the metal door that led to the staircase.

As she reached out to open it, something brushed along her calves. Susanne jumped and glanced down.

In the dim light, a pair of glowing green cat eyes looked up at her.

"God! You scared me half to death! You might have nine lives, but I only have one. How the hell did you even get in here?"

"Mrrreow," the cat answered, whatever that was supposed to mean. It rubbed its head against Susanne's shin.

Dismayed, she stared at the tuft of hair left behind on her black slacks.

Steps sounded behind her, and a woman she recognized as one of her neighbors walked toward her, carrying a car seat with a sleeping baby. "Oh, hello," the woman said, more to the cat than to Susanne. "How did he get in here?"

"I have no idea. It's not mine," Susanne hurried to add. She wasn't sure if pets were allowed in the building, and she didn't want to get in trouble on her first week.

Her neighbor chuckled. "I know. He's mine." She switched the carrier to the other arm so she could shake Susanne's hand. "Katrin Maier."

"Susanne Wolff. I just moved in last weekend." She nodded down at the cat that still rubbed along her legs, ignoring its owner. "He's actually the first neighbor I met. He, um, kinda invited himself to dinner."

"Oh God, I'm sorry. Please don't think we don't feed him or are neglecting him. It's just... He's not a big fan of kids."

Susanne could empathize. It wasn't that she disliked kids, but personally, she had no desire to have one. She gave the cat a sympathetic look.

"Ever since I had Lena," her neighbor cast a loving look at the sleeping baby, "Muesli tends to stay away."

"Muesli?"

"Yeah. Because he—"

"Loves muesli," Susanne finished for her. "Yeah, I found that out the other night."

Her neighbor groaned. "Once again, I'm so sorry. I will gladly pay for any damage he might have caused."

"It's fine. No harm done."

Katrin looked back and forth between Susanne and the cat. "He seems to like you. You wouldn't, by any chance, want to adopt a cat, would you?"

Susanne nearly started to stammer as her answer almost exploded from her. "Oh, no, no. I won't be here for long, just until Easter. That wouldn't be fair to poor Muesli."

Her neighbor laughed. "Relax. I was kidding. Kind of. I really feel bad about him no longer feeling comfortable in his home. But there's not much I can do about it—other than giving him up so he can find a new home, as hard as that would be."

"Sorry. I can't help you there. Maybe the tenant after me would like to adopt a cat." Susanne pushed the heavy door open and held it for her neighbor to squeeze past her with the baby carrier. "Have a nice evening." She tried to make a quick getaway before Katrin could involve her in more small talk about where she was from and why she wasn't staying.

Instead of following its owner, the cat ran after Susanne.

"Muesli, no," Katrin called. "You're coming with me."

The baby started to cry. Her screams echoed through the staircase.

Susanne wanted to cover her ears. After a day like today, this was the last thing she needed. The cat rushed ahead and waited for her in front of her apartment door.

"Come here!" Katrin started after the cat, carrying the screaming baby.

"Uh, you know what?"

Katrin gave her a desperate smile. "You changed your mind about wanting to adopt him? Any chance you might want the baby too?" She held out the carrier with the crying infant.

"No!" Susanne said vehemently, even knowing that the last bit about the baby had been a joke. "I'll just put him into the backyard, and you can let him in once you've taken care of the baby."

"Oh, thank you. That would be great."

"No problem." When Susanne unlocked the door, Muesli strode inside as if he had done so a thousand times before.

Great. Now her neighbor probably thought she'd let the cat in before. She closed the door and breathed a sigh of relief when the baby's screaming faded away.

The cat went straight to the living room, jumped up on the recliner, and sniffed the coffee table, where he had found the muesli the previous evening.

"Sorry, no muesli today."

He looked up as if recognizing his name. "Meow."

"Nope. Forget it. I'm not feeding you, or you'll think this is your new home."

"Mrrrow?" He put his front paws on the armrest to be closer to eye level and looked up at her.

Somehow it reminded her of the way Frau Lamm had looked at her yesterday, when she had confronted Susanne about her use of the word *you* instead of *we* and had told her they were in this together.

"All right, all right. One bowl of milk—no muesli—and then you're out of here, do you hear me?"

The cat followed her to the kitchen.

God, she was getting soft—and at a time when she could least afford it.

Chapter 6

Shortly after nine on Friday morning, Anja zipped east on the bicycle path along the Dreisam River, ducking her head and squinting against the cool wind. God, she was ready for spring and warmer temperatures! She tried not to think of the fact that she might not have a job come spring.

A gray heron that stood stock-still in the middle of the river seemed to be sick of winter too. The bird had fluffed its feathers and tucked its long neck back against its body as it peered into the water, probably looking for breakfast.

She slowed so she wouldn't disturb the heron, then sped up again. Being late to work was not an option today. Since Nobby had given his niece a key to the store a couple of days ago, she had beat them to work every day, so Anja left for work a little earlier too, hoping to get in before Susanne and prove her dedication.

When the beautiful cast-iron railings of Mariensteg, a pedestrian bridge across the river, appeared in front of her, she pedaled harder to make it up the ramp.

Just as she crossed the bridge, a raindrop hit her cheek. Within seconds, others followed, creating a pattern of dark spots on the asphalt. A cold droplet splashed onto her head through the air vents of her bicycle helmet and slowly trickled down her scalp. She cursed under her breath and tried to make it the last five hundred meters to the store without getting completely drenched.

But she couldn't outrun the rain, which was now coming down hard. By the time she chained her bike to a streetlamp, she was soaking wet. She fumbled for her key as she hurried across the street, half-blinded by the rain dripping into her eyes.

At the door, she nearly collided with Susanne, who had arrived at the store at the same time. Unlike Anja, she had an umbrella, so her hair and her immaculate slacks, blouse, and coat were virtually dry.

"Oh wow." Susanne stared at her. "You're wet. Uh, I mean…soaked by the rain."

Her stammering made Anja laugh despite feeling miserable. "Yeah. That's what happens when you trust the weather report. Their cloudy-but-dry just broke loose all over me."

Susanne stretched out her arm to hold the umbrella over her while she unlocked the door with her other hand. Not that it was doing much good at this point, but Anja appreciated the gesture.

Shivering with her wet hair, Anja stepped into the store after her and peeled off her gloves, her bicycle helmet, and her drenched coat, careful not to get any water onto their notebooks and paper products.

Susanne averted her gaze to the puddle of water forming on the floor. "Uh, I'll mop that up. Why don't you go dry yourself off or something?"

"Thanks." Anja carried her wet coat to the back, hung it up to dry, and slipped into the small bathroom. She caught a glimpse of herself in the mirror and had to laugh. No wonder Susanne had stared at her. Her hair was plastered to her scalp, darkened to a brown color, and one soggy strand clung to her forehead. Then her gaze wandered lower. Her jeans clung to her thighs. The rain had soaked through her coat, so even her cotton shirt was damp and stuck to her body, outlining her bra and her nipples, which had hardened in the cold.

Even though she was shivering, her cheeks flushed with heat. *Oh God.* Was that why Susanne had been staring at her? She snorted. *Don't flatter yourself. You look like a drowned rat. Nothing attractive about that. Now get moving and get to work. You wanted to impress her with your dedication to work, not with an impromptu wet-T-shirt contest.*

She dabbed a towel over her face and neck and towel-dried her hair. There wasn't anything she could do about her wet clothes, other than to wait until they dried on their own. She tugged the damp shirt away from her breasts and stepped out of the bathroom.

Susanne had already mopped up the floor and was now behind the cash register, studying an office supply catalog with great intensity, as if her life depended on learning every product by heart. She didn't look up when Anja entered but gestured vaguely at a paper cup she'd placed at the corner of the counter. "Here."

Anja stepped closer and peered into the cup. *Yum.* Coffee with what looked like just the right amount of milk. "For me?"

"Yeah. I thought you could use something to warm up."

Humming, Anja picked up the cup and cradled it in both hands to warm her fingers. "Thank you." Who knew? Nobby's ice-queen niece could actually be nice. She had braved the rain to get her a coffee from the little café across the street. "What do I owe you?"

"Nothing. It's on me."

"Thank you." Anja took her first sip and hummed as the perfect mix of coffee and milk hit her taste buds. "How did you know how I like my coffee?"

Susanne shrugged, apparently not wanting to make a big deal out of it. "I asked the woman behind the counter."

Clever. Anja nodded appreciatively.

"Why don't you go unpack that delivery we got yesterday?" Still not looking up from the catalog, Susanne nodded toward the stockroom. "I'll keep an eye on the store until you're dry or Uncle Norbert gets here."

"Sure." She chuckled. "Wouldn't want to scare the customers, right?"

"Right."

When Frau Lamm's footsteps faded away, Susanne finally lifted her head and stared after her, trying not to take in the way her damp shirt clung to her torso. *Scare the customers. Right.* She doubted anyone would be scared. Fear was definitely not what she was feeling at the moment. She used the catalog she'd hidden behind to fan her face.

God, what are you—twelve? It wasn't as if she'd never seen breasts, even though, admittedly, it had been a while since she'd seen them up close and personal. Frau Lamm wasn't even that well-endowed. Even if she were, it shouldn't matter since she was an employee and probably not interested in women.

When the bell above the door jingled, she looked up, glad for the distraction.

It wasn't her uncle, as she had expected, but a customer—a woman of about forty. She closed her umbrella and slid it in the stand next to Susanne's.

"Good morning." Susanne reminded herself to smile. Working with customers wasn't her strong suit; she preferred the more matter-of-fact style of interacting with behind-the-scenes businesspeople. But if she put her mind to it, she knew she could be good at it. Helping out in her father's many different businesses as a teenager had taught her that.

"Good morning." The woman looked around.

"Can I help you?"

"Yes." The customer stepped closer. "I'm looking for a present for my son. He's starting university next month."

How the hell had she gotten so old that a woman her age had a kid in university? Susanne tried not to grimace. "That's great. Are you thinking of anything in particular? Maybe a leather-bound journal?" She pointed at the ones on display at the center island and tried to remember what Frau Lamm had said about them. "It has wonderful, creamy paper, so pens just glide over the pages like a dream."

The woman took one of the journals and studied it. The price tag didn't make her blink, so maybe Frau Lamm had been right—some people were willing to pay that much for a notebook. "I'll take it."

Yes! Susanne held back a triumphant grin. It looked as if she was getting the hang of selling stationery. "Good choice. How about a fountain pen to go with it? Writing instruments like these are pretty popular with young people at the moment, and we have a nice selection of high-quality ones." She swept her hand toward the glass display along one wall.

They walked over to it, and Susanne used the key her uncle had given her to unlock the case.

The woman picked up the two-thousand-euro fountain pen and studied it from all angles.

Susanne held her breath. If she could sell that one, it might keep Paper Love afloat for another month. What could she tell the customer about it to entice her to buy it? If Frau Lamm had told her any details about it, she couldn't remember, so she said the only thing that had stuck in her mind. "This one is like the BMW of fountain pens."

The customer looked at her with an inscrutable expression, put the pen back down, and picked up another, less expensive one.

Damn. Susanne fisted her hands behind her back.

Finally, the woman seemed to settle on a fountain pen priced at two hundred euros.

Still nothing to sneeze at, Susanne told herself.

"Does this one take standard ink cartridges?" the customer asked.

"I think so," Susanne said, even though she had no idea.

The customer lifted the pen. "May I?"

"Go ahead."

The woman pulled off the cap and tried to unscrew the barrel, probably to see what kind of ink cartridge fit inside. "This doesn't…" She grunted. "It doesn't come off. Is it damaged?"

"Let me try." Susanne took the pen and tried to unscrew it, but nothing moved. Then she noticed that there was another part at the bottom of the pen that looked as if it might unscrew. Maybe that was the way to open the pen. She twisted it with deft movements. It shifted. A triumphant grin curved Susanne's lips. She really was getting good at handling—

Ink seeped from the pen's nib and dripped onto her hand.

Oh shit. Susanne put the pen and her inky fingers behind her back to hide the accident and gave the woman the friendliest smile she could muster. "Let me go ask my colleague. I specialize in paper, but she's the fountain pen expert."

"Yes, of course."

Gritting her teeth, Susanne rushed toward the back. God, she hated looking like an incompetent fool and having to ask for help. Too bad her uncle hadn't come in yet, probably because the rain had delayed him. She would have preferred asking him for help rather than revealing to Frau Lamm—an employee—how clueless she really was.

But her pride wasn't important right now. Making a sale that would help save the store was. She closed the door behind herself and went to the stockroom, where Frau Lamm was busy unpacking yesterday's deliveries.

Susanne opened her mouth to explain the problem, but the sight before her made her close her mouth and pause in the doorway.

Frau Lamm stood in front of a shelf, an open cardboard box next to her and a thick notebook in her hands. She cradled it lovingly, held it up to her face, and sniffed it with a blissful smile that looked almost post-orgasmic.

Susanne leaned in the doorway and watched her with a grin. God, what a stationery junkie. It was weird but in a cute way.

When Frau Lamm looked up and saw her, the journal slipped from her grasp. She caught it before it landed on the floor. Instantly, her cheeks flushed. "Uh, I was just, um…"

"Doing quality control on the way our notebooks smell," Susanne supplied with a straight face. Okay, an *almost* straight face.

"Uh, right. You never know what detail will entice a customer to buy a notebook." Under the obvious pretense of placing the journal on the shelf, she turned away. When she faced Susanne again, her blush had receded. She pointed at the store. "Is there a problem out there?"

Only then did Susanne remember the dripping pen in her hand and the customer waiting next to the display case. "Yes, actually. I wanted to sell a pen, but it exploded all over my fingers." She held up her ink-stained hand.

Frau Lamm frowned like a dog owner who'd been told that her golden retriever had bitten someone. "This one is usually very reliable. I have one at home, and it's never leaked in all the years I've had it. What did you do to it?"

"Nothing. I just tried to unscrew it because the customer wanted to see what kind of ink cartridges it takes. That's all."

Frau Lamm groaned. "It doesn't take cartridges. It's a piston filler."

Susanne tugged on her earlobe as if trying to remove water from her ear. "Translation?"

"It means the body of the pen itself is the ink tank. There's a piston inside the barrel that you move up to fill it with ink. You didn't, by any chance, twist the knob at the end of the pen, did you?"

"Um, yes. I thought that's how you opened it to put in the ink cartridges."

"Nope. When you twist the knob in this direction," Frau Lamm mimicked it with a turn of her wrist, "you push the piston forward, expelling the ink."

Susanne stared down at the ink-smeared writing instrument. "The longer I work here, the more I appreciate a simple ballpoint pen."

Huffing, Frau Lamm took the pen from her and wiped it down with a tissue. "Is the customer still here, or did your little ink explosion chase him or her off?"

Normally, Susanne wouldn't stand for any teasing from an employee, but she knew she deserved it, and Frau Lamm's tone was so good-natured that she couldn't get angry. "Of course she's still here. I even talked her into buying one of those BMW journals."

"BMW journals?"

"Yeah, you know. The expensive leather ones on the island display." Secretly, Susanne referred to all the products that seemed overpriced to her as BMW stationery.

"Ooh. How did you manage that?"

Susanne stared at the pattern of ink on her hand. "I just repeated what you told me about it." *Minus all the sexy touching.*

Frau Lamm chuckled. "See? We'll make a stationery addict out of you before you know it. I'll go take care of the customer." She walked past Susanne to the door, then paused and looked back. "By the way, you've got ink on your ear."

The door clicked shut behind her.

Susanne stayed behind, looking after Anja. *Frau Lamm*, she reminded herself. She reached up to touch her ear but then stopped and glanced at her inky fingers. Now she would have to be the one who stepped into the bathroom to clean up.

Somehow this rescue mission wasn't going the way she had expected at all, and she wasn't sure if that was a good or a bad thing.

Chapter 7

When Frau Lamm turned the sign on the door to *closed* that evening, Susanne did a quick calculation of how much revenue they had made. Not bad. In the week she'd been here, this was the best sales day so far, mostly because of the four-hundred-euro pen Frau Lamm had managed to sell to the customer she had taken over from Susanne.

Uncle Norbert peered over her shoulder. "Ooh! That's promising, isn't it?" Before Susanne could answer, he clapped his hands and added, "How about I take you two to dinner as a thank-you? My treat."

"Yeah, it was a good day, but I hardly think immediately spending any extra money we made will help us." God, it was a wonder the store had survived all these years. Her uncle might have a vast knowledge of stationery and a heart of gold, but a businessman he was not.

Uncle Norbert rubbed his bearded cheeks. "Oh. Right. I just want you to know how much I appreciate your help." He looked at Frau Lamm. "Both of your help."

Frau Lamm gave him a quick hug. "We do feel appreciated, even without a dinner invitation. Right, Frau Wolff?"

"Right."

"Frau Wolff?" Uncle Norbert glanced back and forth between them. "Why so formal?"

Frau Lamm said nothing and walked past them to the back, leaving Susanne to answer.

"We're colleagues, Uncle Norbert." She kept her voice low. "Not friends."

"Why can't you be both?" her uncle asked.

"Because…because I think it's better to keep work and my private life separate." She had made the mistake of mixing both once, and she would never repeat it.

Uncle Norbert fluffed his circle of gray hair with an expression that indicated this concept was completely foreign to him.

Frau Lamm returned from the back, wearing her now-dry coat. She paused in the middle of the store to strap on her bicycle helmet.

Uncle Norbert frowned. "You're not planning on taking your bike home, are you? It's still raining."

Susanne glanced past the paper animals dangling from the ceiling to one of the large windows. It had gotten dark outside, but in the light of a streetlamp, she could make out sheets of rain pouring from the sky, forming puddles on the cobblestoned street.

"No big deal." Frau Lamm zipped her coat and put on her gloves. "I can change into something dry once I'm home."

"But you'll be miserable on your bike. You'll catch a cold."

"He's right," Susanne heard herself say. What the hell? She hadn't planned on getting involved in this discussion. Quickly, she added, "The last thing the store needs right now is a sick employee."

Frau Lamm sighed, opened the buckle beneath her chin, and took off her helmet. "Okay, I'll leave the bike here until Monday and take the streetcar."

"But you don't have an umbrella, do you?" When Frau Lamm shook her head, Uncle Norbert turned toward Susanne. "Could you drive her home?"

"That's not necessary," Frau Lamm said immediately. "I told you I'll be fine on the bike. I'm not made of sugar, so I won't melt just because of a little rain."

Susanne remembered that she had looked pretty miserable in her drenched clothes this morning, and she needed her healthy and at the store to help customers and to answer any questions she might have about stationery products. "No problem. I'm heading home anyway, and I don't mind a little detour." She reached for her car keys and strode to the door. "Come on."

⁓∽∾⁓

Anja threw Nobby a you-shouldn't-have glance, which he answered with an impish grin. She shook her head at him and hurried after Susanne.

With her longer legs, the taller woman had already reached the door, opened it, and unfolded her umbrella. She waited until Anja had reached her side before she set off down the street.

Since the umbrella wasn't meant for two people, they had to press close beneath the cover so their arms were touching. It was slightly awkward but not as uncomfortable as Anja had expected—at least not for her. She had no idea what was going on in Susanne's head since her professional poker face was firmly in place.

"Taking the streetcar really wouldn't be a problem," Anja said.

Susanne led them around a large puddle. "It's okay. You introduced me to your favorite status symbol; now I'll introduce you to mine."

Anja decided to give in. Truth be told, being delivered directly to her doorstep would be nice in this weather. After a long day at work, she couldn't wait to get off her feet. "Where are you parked?"

Susanne slowed and pointed to a still-standing section of the medieval city wall that ran parallel to the sidewalk. The entrance to a small parking garage had been built into the wall just a few steps down the street from the store. "Down there."

"How did you manage to get a parking spot there? It's a private garage, isn't it?"

A quick smile lit up Susanne's gray eyes. "Let's just say I have my ways."

They ducked into the parking garage, and Susanne pressed the fob on her key. The blinkers of a car to their left flashed, revealing a sporty black BMW.

Susanne shook out the umbrella and tossed it into the back of the car before getting in. "Where to?" she asked when Anja climbed into the passenger seat.

Anja settled her messenger bag and the bicycle helmet onto her lap, careful not to get too many raindrops on the gleaming leather seat. This car looked as immaculate as its owner, as if she'd only bought it this morning. Anja had never sat in a BMW, and she had to admit it was kind of nice. "Betzenhausen."

"I have no idea where that is. I haven't had a chance to get to know the city."

Did she even want to? Anja wasn't sure. "It's on the western edge of the city. Just head toward the Schwabentor, and I'll give you directions from there."

Susanne started the engine, and a soft pop ballad drifted through the loudspeakers. *Ooh, the new Jenna Blake album!* Anja gave an appreciative nod. Apparently, they did have one thing in common after all.

Susanne steered them competently through the rain-slick streets, sticking to the speed limit.

Neither said much, other than Anja giving directions. The only sounds in the car were the low music and the fast, monotonous back-and-forth of the windshield wipers across the glass.

Ten minutes later, Susanne maneuvered around the ninety-degree left turn onto the quiet street where Anja lived.

"It's the second gray-and-white building on the left." Anja pointed through the rain-smeared windshield.

Susanne leaned forward and squinted.

The rain pelted down in buckets now. Even though the wipers were set to the highest speed, they couldn't keep up to clear the view.

"Just pull into the parking spot next to the building. It's mine, but I don't use it."

Susanne parked the car and turned off the engine.

For a moment, they sat without moving, the darkness and the heavy rain cutting them off from the rest of the world. Even the three meters to the apartment building seemed like a long distance.

"Thanks so much for driving me. I really appreciate it. Do you know how to get home from here?"

"Not a clue. But I've got GPS." Susanne patted the dashboard.

"Oh. Of course. Until Monday, then."

Susanne cocked her head. "You're not working tomorrow?"

Anja reined in the urge to defend herself. Why would she even need to? She was an employee, not a slave, so of course she had a day off. "I only work Saturdays in December and during the summer, when we're busy. Have a nice weekend, and drive safely." She unbuckled the seat belt, braced herself, and prepared for a mad dash to the front door.

"Wait." Susanne undid her own seat belt and leaned toward Anja. Their shoulders brushed.

What on earth is she...? Anja held her breath.

Susanne angled her arm through the gap between the seats and reached into the back for her umbrella. "I'll walk you to the door, or you'll be drenched within a second."

Anja exhaled. *Jeez, what did you think she would do? Kiss you?* "Thanks."

The patter of rain became louder as Susanne opened the door and then dimmed as she closed it and walked around the car.

Anja grabbed her helmet and her messenger bag, got out too, and ducked beneath the umbrella that Susanne held over both of them. A bike trailer made for transporting toddlers had been left in front of the building, so they had to walk around it to get to the front door.

The light in the staircase was already on, probably because one of Anja's neighbors had arrived home shortly before them. She unlocked the door and stepped inside, while Susanne hovered on the other side, still beneath the umbrella.

"Um…" Anja hesitated. The polite thing would probably be to invite her in, but she felt a little self-conscious at the thought of Susanne seeing her tiny apartment. *Oh, come on. What do you care what she thinks?* Besides, they should talk about Paperworld anyway, since the trade fair was coming up next weekend. She gave herself a mental kick. "Do you want to come up for a minute? Maybe the rain will let up so that you can actually see where you are going."

Susanne hesitated. She glanced over her shoulder at the gray curtain of rain and then back at Anja.

The light in the staircase went out, throwing them into darkness.

Anja reached around the doorframe for the light switch outside since that one was glow-in-the-dark and easier to find. Her shoulder brushed something soft. She bit her lip and tried not to think about what part of Susanne's body it might have been.

The light flared on again, no doubt revealing Anja's blush.

"All right," Susanne said. "Just for a minute."

Their wet shoes squeaked as they climbed up the three flights of stairs to Anja's apartment, which was on the top floor of the building. In front of the door, Anja slipped out of her shoes, and Susanne silently followed her example.

Anja's heart pounded as she unlocked the door, and it wasn't because of the stairs they'd just climbed. Her little apartment was her safe haven, a place that she had created just for herself, and she usually didn't invite near strangers in—especially not ones who might be judgmental. Nobby's niece could be a bit of a snob.

So what? If she didn't like Anja's home, that was her problem. Anja mentally counted to three and then swung open the door.

ᠭᡈᠣᢅᢇᠥ

Susanne normally wasn't the overly curious kind, but now she found herself looking around. In her socks, she stood in a short, gray-tiled hallway. To her left was a closed door with a dozen postcards and humorous quotes taped to it. Another door, this one with a glass insert, stood open, leading to another room.

Frau Lamm went through that door, turned on the light, and waved at her to follow.

Susanne padded across the hardwood floor. The apartment reminded her of how she'd lived as a student years ago. A sleeper couch with a folded duvet and a pillow dominated the wall to her right, while a floor-to-ceiling bookshelf took up the wall to her left. A TV stand on wheels had been rolled up against the foot of the sofa, and directly behind it, a huge, square Ikea shelf had been set up as a room divider that separated the sleeping area from a small desk.

Every last available space on the bookshelf and the divider was filled with books and notebooks, sorted by color, which created a rainbow that spread through the entire room.

Susanne peeked past a row of books to the other side of the divider. The desk was covered in colorful paper, cardboard, and felt. Some of the half-finished craft projects looked as if they would become store decorations for Valentine's Day.

When Susanne stepped farther into the room, she realized that it was L-shaped, curving to the left. A low-hanging white lamp threw shadows onto a tiled mini kitchen with a fridge, a sink, a two-plate stove, a round table, and two chairs.

Compared to her own spacious apartment in the Wiehre, Frau Lamm's home was tiny, but Susanne guessed that with a pair of French doors leading onto a balcony and another window that let in sunlight, it would look bigger than it really was when the sun was shining, reflecting off the caramel-colored hardwood floor. It was cozy, and it fit Frau Lamm perfectly.

"Um, I know it's pretty small, but I don't need much." Frau Lamm's defensive tone made Susanne look over to her.

She stood next to the tiny kitchen, her arms folded across her chest as if to erect a barrier between them.

"I like it," Susanne said, partly to put her at ease and partly because it was true. Plus she knew that rents in Freiburg were expensive and that Frau Lamm didn't make much money working at Paper Love. For a moment, she wondered why Frau Lamm hadn't been more ambitious. She certainly had the intelligence to be much more than a salesperson in a small stationery store. But then Susanne reprimanded herself. If Frau Lamm was happy with the life she had, it wasn't Susanne's place to judge.

Frau Lamm, who had already opened her mouth, probably to defend her apartment, snapped it shut.

Susanne walked up to the balcony doors and peered outside through a gap in the semi-transparent burgundy curtains. A streetlamp cast a yellow circle of light onto the street below. Somewhere behind it, a church tower with a huge bird's nest on top was silhouetted against the near-dark sky.

Frau Lamm unfolded her arms, stepped next to her, and looked outside as if trying to see her neighborhood through Susanne's eyes.

"Hard to believe that we're in Freiburg," Susanne said after a while. "This looks like a little village, not a city."

"That's what it was about a hundred years ago, and it's part of what I like about living here. I can take the streetcar and be in the city with all its restaurants and shops within ten minutes, but if I go the other way," she waved her arm, "I have the river, lakes, and meadows right outside my doorstep. So I kind of have the best of both worlds."

Susanne suppressed a smile. Apparently, that enthusiastic gesturing wasn't limited to stationery but extended to all the other things she loved.

"What?" Frau Lamm asked.

"Nothing."

The doorbell made them both jump.

"Oh shit, I forgot." Frau Lamm slapped her forehead.

Hot date with the boyfriend? Susanne bit back the words before she could ask. Frau Lamm was an employee, she reminded herself, so her private life was none of her business.

"Be right back." Frau Lamm hurried past her before Susanne could offer to leave. "Yes?" she said into an intercom in the hallway.

"It's me," came the slightly distorted answer. The person didn't add a name, but the voice was definitely female.

Not a boyfriend, then. Susanne turned and craned her neck, but, of course, there was nothing to see.

"Come on up." Frau Lamm pressed a buzzer and opened the door.

Seconds later, a knee-high dog rushed into the apartment. The cream-colored mutt looked like a mix of standard poodle and terrier, perhaps with some other breed thrown in somewhere along the line. It greeted Frau Lamm with excited yips, its soaking wet tail going back and forth faster than the windshield wipers had, then bolted across the hardwood floor toward Susanne.

"Gino, no!"

Before Frau Lamm or the woman stepping into the apartment could stop him, Gino jumped.

Susanne stumbled back and protectively threw up her arm. But instead of teeth piercing her skin, a wet tongue licked her hands, and two equally wet paws were planted on her thigh.

"Gino!" A sharp whistle pierced the air.

The dog dropped down and trotted back to its owner with a whine.

Susanne gazed down at the muddy paw prints on her slacks. What was it with the pets in this city? First, a cat decided to move in with her, and now a dog greeted her as if they were long-lost buddies.

"I'm so sorry." His owner rushed over to her. "He doesn't get that from me. I usually introduce myself to a woman before I jump her."

Susanne stared at the stranger. The woman was tall, so Susanne could look into her twinkling hazel eyes without having to tilt her head up or down. The stranger ran a hand through her very short, dark hair and gave Susanne an impish grin.

Frau Lamm groaned. "This is my impossible best friend, Miriam Blattmann. Miri, this is Susanne Wolff, whom I *work* with." She stressed the word *work* and glared at her friend.

"Oh." Miriam's grin fell. "Oops. Sorry. I didn't mean to… I thought you had finally taken my little nudges to heart and had decided to ask someone out on a date."

Date? Did that mean…? Susanne's gaze flicked back and forth between them. Anja…Frau Lamm was gay?

At the moment, she seemed to be mostly embarrassed. Her cheeks were as red as a fire hydrant. She disappeared into the other room and returned with two towels. One she wet at the sink and pressed into Susanne's hands while she started to dry the dog with the other, bending over him in a way that hid her flushed face.

Susanne watched her for a second, then dabbed at the mud stains on her slacks.

"Sorry," Miriam said again. "But hey, I brought Indian food for our Netflix night—which you apparently forgot, Anja. It should be enough for three." She held up two white plastic bags with a logo that said *Kashmir* and sent Susanne an inviting look. "Can I tempt you?"

"Miri!" Frau Lamm groaned from her kneeling position.

"What? I didn't mean it that way. Get your mind out of the gutter, woman!"

Susanne couldn't help it—she burst out laughing. She hadn't expected Frau Lamm to have such an irreverent friend…a friend who very obviously was a lesbian or bi. No matter what her own sexual orientation might be, Frau Lamm apparently didn't have a problem with women who were attracted to women. Why then that weird reaction when they had first met? If it hadn't been Susanne's sexual orientation, what had thrown her for a loop?

"Um, I'm sure Frau Wolff has plans for the evening." Frau Lamm spoke without looking up from the dog that had stretched out on the floor, letting her towel-dry his belly.

Susanne's plans consisted of reading up on the stationery business and trying to keep the cat from getting into her apartment any time she opened a door or window.

"Do you?" Miriam asked. "Because if you don't, you're welcome to stay and have dinner with us. Right, Anja?"

"Uh, yeah. Right." Then, as if realizing how half-hearted her answer had come across, Frau Lamm got up from the floor and looked Susanne in the eyes. "Seriously, if you're not in a hurry, stay. Miriam always gets enough to feed an army."

"Never heard you complain about getting leftovers," Miriam said.

"And you never will. I don't know how it's possible, but their food tastes even better the next day. So?"

They both looked at Susanne expectantly.

Susanne hesitated. Normally, she avoided socializing with co-workers. She had her own circle of friends, independent of work. But they were all in Berlin and London, while she didn't know a soul except for Frau Lamm and Uncle Norbert in this little city. Suddenly, she found herself reluctant to return to her large, half-empty apartment. Must be all that rain, she told herself. It was messing with her mood, making her sentimental. "Is there space for me?" She gestured at the small, round table, which had only two chairs.

"Oh yeah." Frau Lamm left the room. She rummaged around in the hallway and returned with a folding chair, which she unfolded and pushed up to the table. "Is this okay?"

"Sure." Had she come across as so spoiled that Frau Lamm thought she needed a throne or something?

Miriam rubbed her hands together. "Come on. Let's eat. I'm starving." She took plates from the cupboard over the stove, apparently very familiar with where things were kept in Frau Lamm's apartment. She opened the food containers and glanced over her shoulder at Susanne. "Do you like it ho—?"

Frau Lamm clamped her hand over her friend's mouth and nudged her aside. "What she's trying to ask is if you like spicy food."

Their antics made Susanne bite back a grin. Their dynamic reminded her a little of herself and her twin sister. She really should call Franzi this weekend. "I love it. Whenever I was in London for work, I ate nothing but Indian food. They had a chicken jalfrezi that was to die for."

"Sorry, no chicken jalfrezi tonight," Miriam said. "We usually get just veggie options so we can share. I hope you don't mind."

"Not at all."

They took their seats around the small table, while Gino sniffed the floor in the tiny kitchen as if looking for dropped morsels.

"Gino, go lie down." Miriam pointed to the space behind the dividing wall.

He let out a sigh that sounded almost human, trudged to the indicated spot, and plopped down.

Susanne cut the samosa on her plate in half. "So you are the vegetarian, right?" She glanced at Frau Lamm, who nodded.

"She and half of Freiburg." Miriam grinned. "If you're ever looking for a place to get a juicy steak or a schnitzel, I'm the person to ask."

Was this Miriam's way to get her to call her? Susanne couldn't tell. She glanced over at Frau Lamm, who dug into her paneer salad with enthusiasm but didn't say anything. Susanne gave Miriam a noncommittal nod. "I'll keep that in mind. But I won't be here that long. Just until we somehow manage to get my uncle's store out of trouble."

"About that..." Frau Lamm looked up from her salad. "Now that you've been here for a while and know the store a little, what do you think would be the best way to—?"

"Nuh-uh!" Miriam waved her fork. "Remember the rule? No work talk on Netflix night!"

Frau Lamm snapped her mouth shut and started to hunt down the pomegranate seeds in her salad, as if she didn't know what else to talk about with Susanne.

Her friend didn't seem to have the same problem. "So tell me a little about yourself."

Susanne chewed her piece of naan bread extra thoroughly to give herself a moment to think about what she wanted to tell them. Normally, she didn't talk about her private life with co-workers. "I'm thirty-eight, was born and raised in Berlin, have an MBA, and I'm in between jobs at the moment."

Miriam chuckled. "That was the resume version. Now something that wouldn't make it onto your resume."

"Miriam." A warning growl resonated in Frau Lamm's voice. "Frau Wolff said yes to having dinner with us, not to being interrogated."

"That's okay," Susanne said. While she wasn't completely comfortable talking about herself in this context, it wasn't as if she had anything to hide. "What do you want to know?"

"Let's start with the basics. Hobbies?"

"I don't have much time for hobbies, but I love snowboarding and just about any kind of water sports. I'm also a bit of an amateur photographer."

"Water sports, hmm?" Miriam popped half a pekora into her mouth, chewed, and swallowed. "Anja likes getting wet too."

The small table wobbled, and Miriam jumped. "Ouch!"

Frau Lamm flicked a piece of naan bread at her. "She means I like swimming and water volleyball."

"That's what I said, isn't it?" Miriam innocently batted her lashes before turning back to Susanne. "Pets, house plants, siblings, boyfriend…girlfriend?" She drawled out the last word as if it had five syllables.

"Okay, let's see." Susanne put her fork down and ticked each item off on her fingers. "No pets, one plant—species unknown—one twin sister, no girlfriend, and definitely no boyfriend."

"You have a twin sister?" This time it was Frau Lamm who asked the question. "Wow, that must be so cool."

Susanne shrugged. "My sister is great, but I'll have to disappoint you if you're imagining all kinds of shenanigans that we got into as kids, pretending we're the other. We're not identical, so we don't look any more alike than other siblings."

"Still," Frau Lamm said, "growing up together, having someone who's always on your side, who understands you without many words... That must be kind of special."

Susanne had never thought about it much. Since she had never known anything else, maybe she had taken that kind of relationship with her sister for granted. "Yeah, I suppose it is. We're still pretty close."

"What does your sister do for a living?" Frau Lamm asked. "Is she a businesswoman too?"

"No. She lives from hand to mouth," Susanne repeated what her sister always said when asked about her job.

"So she's a starving artist?" Miriam asked.

Susanne chuckled. "No. She's a dentist."

"Ouch." Frau Lamm touched her very white teeth that didn't look as if they had much need for a dentist. "Is she your dentist too?"

"Hell, no! She put a Lego piece up my nose when we were playing doctor as kids. I'm not letting her anywhere near me with a drill."

Miriam burst out laughing so hard that she made the dog wake up. Frau Lamm's laughter was quieter, but it was warm and genuine, making Susanne chuckle along with them.

Finally, when the laughter had died down, Susanne looked back and forth between them. "How about you?" Her gaze settled on Miriam first. She found it easier to address her, maybe because she didn't want to appear too nosy about a co-worker's private life. "Any siblings, Frau Blattmann?"

"Frau Blattmann." Miriam groaned. "God, you make me feel like a school teacher. Why don't we just call each other by our first names?" She lifted her water glass to drink to it.

"Um..."

Susanne and Frau Lamm glanced at each other.

"Miri, Frau Wolff doesn't—"

"It's fine." Susanne suppressed a sigh. They could be professionals and work together efficiently even without the formal barrier of using last names, right? Just because they called each other by their first names wouldn't make them friends.

"Great...Susanne." Miriam enthusiastically clinked her glass to Susanne's, and after a moment's hesitation, Anja lifted her glass too and joined it to the others. "And to answer your question about siblings... I'm the youngest of six."

"Six?" Susanne echoed.

"Yeah. And I'm the only one who doesn't have kids, so Christmas at my parents' is an adventure."

Anja opened her eyes comically wide. "It is. I was invited for Christmas dinner one year, and it took me until the middle of January to recover."

Miriam reached across the table and patted her arm. "Don't say I didn't warn you."

"You did." Anja squeezed Miriam's hand. "My imagination just didn't live up to the real thing."

Susanne observed their interaction. Had these two ever been a couple? But asking something like that crossed a line that she didn't want to cross with someone she worked with. "What about you? Do you have any siblings?"

"No, I don't. My family tree is more like a bonsai." Anja indicated the size of a miniature tree with her hands. "No siblings, no cousins, and not many kids my age in the tiny town where I grew up. By the time I was six, I sounded like an adult."

"And if she says tiny, she means tiny," Miriam threw in. "I think there are more cows in that town than there are people."

Anja rolled her eyes. "There are no cows. Most families there used to grow grapes, not cattle." She glanced at Susanne. "I grew up in a wine-producing region about thirty kilometers from here."

Since she had lived in Berlin for most of her life, Susanne couldn't imagine what it must have been like to grow up in such a tiny village. "Weren't you bored to death as a teenager?"

"No, not really." Anja's tone softened and a bit of dialect came through when she talked about her hometown. Susanne found it charming. "I was used to keeping myself entertained, and I was never one for wild parties."

"No parties?" Miriam huffed and nudged her. "Excuse me, but that's not how I remember the stories about your childhood. What about the time you snuck out at night and rode your bike to a party several kilometers away?"

"It wasn't a party," Anja protested, but her cheeks flushed scarlet. "A couple of friends from school went to see a movie, and I didn't want to miss it."

"The movie. Suuuure, that's why you risked being grounded until graduation."

Anja covered her face with both hands. "Why on earth did I ever tell you that?"

Miriam pulled her hands down and grinned. "Because you can't resist this beautiful face. Just like you couldn't resist kissing M—"

"Enough," Anja said. "Frau Wolff doesn't want to hear that."

"Susanne," Miriam corrected. "First names, remember? And maybe she does want to hear about your adventures in the movie theater."

Truth be told, Susanne did want to hear it. Had Miriam been about to mention a boy's or a girl's name? *What do you care? Even if she kissed all of the people in that movie theater, it wouldn't be any of your business.* She kept her gaze on the karahi paneer on her plate. "Uh, that's okay."

For a minute or two, they ate in silence, which was only interrupted by Gino's snoring from his spot next to the couch.

"So did your parents catch you?" Susanne asked after a while.

"Oh yeah. They were waiting in my room when I snuck back in. And boy, were they mad. I was grounded for three months." With an almost inaudible mumble, Anja added, "That kiss was so not worth it."

They talked about wine, movies, and Miriam's childhood while they finished their dinner. Soon every last bite of food, except for a couple of onion pakoras, was gone.

Susanne stood, stacked the empty plates, and carried them the two steps to the kitchen, where she looked around for the dishwasher. "Where do I...?"

"I don't have a dishwasher," Anja said. "Just put them in the sink. I'll do them later."

Wow. No dishwasher. Susanne couldn't imagine it. But even though the apartment felt almost too small for three people and a dog, she had to admit that she'd had an unexpectedly nice evening in this cozy, little space. "All right, ladies. I'll leave you to your Netflix, then."

"You're welcome to stay," Miriam said. "You could even help us decide between *Lost Girl*, *The 100*, and *Orange Is the New Black*."

Until now, Susanne had thought of Anja as pretty old-fashioned, but she wholeheartedly approved of her taste in TV shows. All the choices sounded great, but she didn't even want to imagine where the three of them would sit to watch Netflix...all cuddled together on the sofa bed?

Definitely not an option. "No, thanks. I think I should go. Looks like it has stopped raining for the moment, so this is my chance to get home. It was nice meeting you." She nodded at Miriam from several steps away, keeping the table between them so she wouldn't invite a hug.

Anja walked her to the door.

"Thanks again for dinner," Susanne said. "That was really good. I had no idea there was such a great Indian restaurant in Freiburg."

"There are a lot of great things in Freiburg if you give it a chance," Anja said softly.

Susanne stiffened. "It's not that I don't like the city. It's just… I'm here to work, not to enjoy a vacation."

Anja gave a short nod. "I understand."

Did she really? But there was no point in asking. "Enjoy Netflix. See you on Monday."

"Yes. See you. Drive carefully." Anja squeezed past her through the door and turned on the light in the staircase for her.

Their bodies brushed, making Susanne glad that she could escape to the cooler air in the staircase. She picked up her umbrella by the door and walked down the stairs. As she rounded the bend after the first set of stairs, she glanced back up.

There were four small apartments on Anja's floor, and since Anja's was the one straight ahead from the stairs, Susanne could still see her. She stood in the doorway, gripping Gino's collar with one hand so he wouldn't run after her.

Their gazes met, and they nodded at each other.

Susanne raised her hand for one last wave before she reached the landing and was out of sight.

∽∾◠∾

"That was the big, bad wolf?" Miri asked as soon as Anja closed the door. She used the flyer that the Indian restaurant had stuck into one of the bags to fan herself. "Damn, girl! How can you work with her without being constantly distracted?"

Anja took the flyer from her and used it to give her friend a playful slap to the shoulder. "I manage just fine. You're the one who can't resist a beautiful woman, even if she's a total ass."

"But that's the thing—she's not. An ass, I mean. She seems nice to me. A little reserved maybe, but she thawed out pretty fast."

Yeah, Anja had to admit that Susanne hadn't been so bad, at least not with Miri there to draw her out. She had even agreed to finally switch to a first-name basis. But would it be like this at Paperworld next weekend—or at work on Monday, for that matter? She doubted it.

"Thanks a lot for embarrassing me with that movie theater story, by the way," she grumbled as she went in search of snacks for their Netflix night.

"Oh, come on. It wasn't that bad. We all have a first-kiss story like that."

"Yeah, but neither of you shared yours. Plus she's my boss. Kind of."

Miri plopped down onto the sofa bed. "Hey, you were the one who insisted that she's not there to take over, so she isn't really your boss."

"Still." Anja tossed a bag of sweet chili chips onto Miri's lap, settled down next to her, and grabbed the remote control before her friend could. "Just for that embarrassing story, I get to pick what we're watching."

Still thinking about her unplanned dinner with Anja and her friend, Susanne entered her apartment and kicked off her shoes. Even in socks, her steps echoed through the hall. God, her bare apartment had all the charm of an impersonal hotel room. Maybe she should get some more furniture, even if it was just for a few months.

She plopped down into the recliner, opened the browser on her laptop, and typed in *stationery business trends* to start doing some research.

Her finger hovered over the enter key, but she couldn't bring herself to press it. *Oh, come on.* Working on weekends was the norm for her, so why this sudden reluctance? Maybe it was all the Indian food she'd devoured or the thought of Anja and Miriam watching a TV show at this very moment. She eyed the Netflix icon in her favorites bar. Should she…?

A soft tap on the glass of the French door interrupted her before she could decide.

When she looked up, she wasn't surprised to see the cat on the other side of the glass door. This tap-and-meow game had been a nightly occurrence since she had moved in a week ago, even though Susanne hadn't done anything to encourage it.

Okay, *hardly* anything. Putting a bowl of milk outside every now and then wasn't an invitation, was it?

"Meeeeeooooowwww!"

This time the nightly concert sounded especially desperate.

Tap-tap-tap-tap.

Susanne took a closer look. "Oh boy."

Apparently, the cat had been caught in the downpour. His white-and-brown fur was plastered flat against his slender body, making him appear thinner. Water dribbled from his drooping whiskers.

Could cats catch a cold?

Susanne had no idea, but he looked miserable.

Another plaintive cry and a tap-tap-tap came from outside.

Well, she had already rescued one unfortunate creature from the rain today, so rescuing another wasn't a big deal, right? She put the laptop aside, stood, and crossed the room.

Muesli's wet tail raised up high in the air when he saw her stride toward him.

She opened the door, and he shot inside as soon as the gap was wide enough for him to squeeze through. "Just this once." She pointed a warning finger at him. "And just until you're dry, understood?"

"Meow."

"Good."

The phone rang, and Susanne stepped into the hall to answer. She expected it to be her mother, who called almost every day to see how things were going with the store, but instead, Franzi's name flashed across the screen. "Hey, Sis. How's the drilling business?"

Franzi chuckled. "Can't complain. How's it going down there in the deep south? Mama says Uncle Nobby is pretty down. Do things really look that bad?"

"Not very promising, to tell you the truth."

"If he needs money, I can—"

"No." Her sister's generosity was touching, but she didn't want her to risk her money when it might not help their uncle anyway. "If that were the solution, I would have given him some money and been back in Berlin by now. But any money you give him would only be a temporary fix. What he needs is some serious restructuring. Otherwise, we're just sticking a Band-Aid on a gushing wound."

"So how do we stop the bleeding?" Franzi asked.

"I have a few ideas, but I need to do more research before I recommend anything. The stationery business is more complex than I thought." Susanne strolled back into the living room, the phone pressed to her ear. "But we're going to Paperworld next—" She paused in the doorway at the sight that greeted her.

The cat had gotten comfortable in her recliner and was now grooming himself.

"Oh, no, no, no. Shoo! That was not part of the agreement! Get your furry little ass off my recliner!"

Muesli glanced her way and then continued to lick his paw.

"Pardon me?"

Susanne burst out laughing. "Not you. I'm talking to the cat."

"You got a cat? You? Are you working up to getting a girlfriend?"

"Hahahaha." Susanne lifted the cat off the recliner, ignoring his protest, dried off the wet leather with a tissue from the coffee table, and sat before he could jump back up. "I don't have a cat, and I don't want a girlfriend right now."

"So it's an imaginary cat you're talking to?"

"No. It's real. It's just not mine. It belongs to a neighbor, but it's always trying to hang out here."

Franzi chuckled. "You've got a feline stalker! And you thought your life in Freiburg would be boring. I was thinking of coming down next weekend to entertain you, but apparently, that's not necessary."

"I'd love that! Wait… Next weekend? Damn, that's not going to work."

"Hot date?" Franzi asked.

"I just told you. I'm not looking for a girlfriend or a date, especially not while I'm here. We're going to be in Frankfurt on Saturday. There's a trade show that'll give me a better idea of where the stationery industry is going."

"We?"

Her sister never missed much. "Anja and me."

"Ah, the famous Anja," Franzi said before Susanne could explain who she was.

"You've met her, of course." Susanne kept forgetting that her sister had spent more time in Freiburg than she had.

"Not yet. I visit Uncle Nobby mostly on the weekends, when Anja isn't there, and the one time I was in Freiburg for a week, she was out sick. But Uncle Nobby talks about her all the time. Don't you ever call him?"

"Of course I do. On his birthday."

While her sister lectured her on not keeping in touch with the family often enough, Susanne's mind drifted. Should she ask Franzi what Uncle Norbert had told her about Anja?

And that would be important why? You're here to keep an eye on the store, not its employees.

The cat chose that moment to jump up on her lap, probably adding more muddy paw prints to her already stained slacks.

"Hey, I'm not your cuddle buddy! Get off my lap!"

Muesli started purring and ran his raspy tongue over her hand.

"Cut it out. No licking!"

Franzi laughed. "Clearly, the cat is not a practice run for a girlfriend, or you wouldn't have said that."

"You'd better keep drilling holes into teeth, Sis. You'd never make it as a comedian."

Once Franzi had stopped laughing, they made tentative plans for her sister to visit sometime in February, then said goodbye and hung up.

Susanne put the phone on the coffee table and stared at the cat on her lap. "Don't think I'll let you stay the night just because you're getting all touchy-feely. I'll have you know I'm not that kind of woman."

Jae

A few raindrops were still falling from the dark sky, but she hardened her resolve. She'd watch one episode of *Orange Is the New Black*, then she'd kick the cat out. It wasn't as if he had nowhere to go, and if she let him stay, she would only make him think he'd found a new home…and then snatch it away when she left.

The cat cuddled up against her belly, settled his chin on her arm, and closed his eyes with a contented sigh.

Okay, maybe two episodes.

Chapter 8

At nine o'clock on Monday morning, Susanne slowed the BMW to a near crawl as it bumped over the cobblestoned street toward the parking garage near Paper Love.

A woman on a bicycle leaned forward over the handlebars as she pedaled in the same direction.

Hey, isn't that Anja? She knew that bike helmet. Okay, and maybe that nice ass was familiar by now too. Susanne shook her head at herself. Since that disastrous relationship with a colleague as a consulting newbie, she had made it a point to ignore the physical attributes of the people she worked with, and now wasn't the time to change that.

When she stepped out of the parking garage a minute later, the woman was bending over a nearby bike rack, chaining her bicycle to it. It was indeed Anja.

"Good morning, Frau L—um, Anja," Susanne called from several steps away so she wouldn't startle her.

Anja straightened and took her messenger bag from the basket on the back of her bike. "Oh. Good morning."

They walked the few steps to the store together.

Susanne found herself unusually tongue-tied. Normally, she never had a problem making small talk or talking business with co-workers, but their dinner on Friday hadn't been a business meeting. Should she just ignore it and pretend they hadn't shared Indian food? Or try for a more friendly tone, ask what Netflix show they had decided on, or maybe thank her again for dinner?

But she didn't want to invite too much familiarity.

Anja seemed to be equally unsure of what to say, so neither of them spoke until they reached Paper Love.

Susanne was glad to see her uncle already inside, going over some order lists behind the counter.

"Morning, Nobby." Anja walked past her to give him a hug.

Watching them greet each other so warmly was a little weird. No way would she have ever greeted her former boss this way. Susanne couldn't put her finger on what exactly she was feeling. Part of it might have been envy because she didn't have that kind of close relationship with her uncle. She remembered what Anja had told her on Friday evening about having a family tree the size of a bonsai. Maybe she didn't have any uncles, and that was why she and Uncle Norbert were so close.

She walked past them to the back to hang her coat. When she turned, she came face-to-face with Anja, who had her own coat in hand but made no move to hang it.

"Listen," Anja said quietly, as if not wanting Uncle Norbert to hear. "I know Miriam kind of steamrolled you into agreeing for us to be on a first-name basis. If you'd rather we go back to addressing each other by our last names, that would be fine."

Did she want to do that? Susanne took the coat from Anja and hung it for her so she'd have a moment to think about it. Her first impulse was to jump at the chance to get back some professional distance, but she had a feeling it was too late for that. She had already seen Anja's home, had met her best friend, and had found out bits and pieces about how she'd grown up—including that story about kissing a person of unknown gender in the movie theater.

"Hey, you two," Uncle Norbert called when they didn't immediately return from the back. "Get a room."

What the hell? Had he really just said what she thought he'd said? Susanne squeezed past Anja and strode toward the counter. "What did you just say?"

"You two should get a room," he repeated. "A hotel room. For the fair in Frankfurt."

"Oh."

"What did you think I was talking about?" His baby blue eyes looked at her with the most innocent expression, and Susanne couldn't tell whether it was real or fake.

It occurred to her that she barely knew her uncle. *You preferred it that way, remember?* She cleared her throat. "Oh, nothing. I was just… Forget it."

Anja joined them. Was it just Susanne's imagination, or were her cheeks a little flushed? "I don't think we'll find a hotel room this late. At least not one that won't cost us an arm and a leg. The hotels in Frankfurt are always upping their prices during the big fairs. We can just go there for the day and travel back in the evening."

"Yes," Susanne said. "I think that's more reasonable. I looked it up on Google Maps. We can be home in about two and a half hours if there's no traffic jam on the A5."

"Or we could take the train," Anja said. "That would actually be faster."

The train? Susanne hadn't even considered it, but maybe it wasn't such a bad idea. She could imagine that finding a parking spot at a trade fair with more than thirty thousand visitors would be a nightmare.

"She's right." Her uncle nodded decisively. "You should take the train. That way, you can just relax and spend the time talking and getting to know each other."

Uh... That wasn't on her agenda for Saturday. They would talk about the trade fair and Paper Love, not about their families or teenage kisses in the movie theater. Determined, she pulled out her phone and started looking for the best train connection.

∽◦◦◦∾

"Aah!" Anja fisted her hair with both hands and stared back and forth between her open closet and her sofa bed, which was covered with slacks, skirts, and tops. How on earth was it possible that her entire closet was full of stuff, yet she had nothing to wear for Paperworld?

She couldn't very well show up in jeans. What did you wear to a stationery fair, especially if going with your extremely well-dressed temporary-kind-of-boss? She glanced at her wristwatch. Almost eleven. Was it too late to call Miri?

She reached for her phone and tapped on the first name in her contact list. "Please tell me what to wear," she burst out as soon as Miri picked up.

"Ooh! You've got a date?" Her friend sounded delighted. "Finally!"

"No! I'm going to Paperworld tomorrow, remember?"

"Oh, that. Yeah." Miri's tone sobered.

Anja pulled a wool sweater from the top compartment of the closet, then discarded it. The halls of the fair apparently became pretty hot with all the people milling about, so if she wore a sweater, she'd feel like a lobster being cooked alive. "So what do I wear?"

"Why are you obsessing over this?" Miri asked. "That's not like you at all. Usually, you just throw something on and are done with it."

"I'm not obsessing. I just… My job might depend on this."

"Your job might depend on what you wear to a stationery fair?"

Okay, that sounded ridiculous. "No, that's not what I meant. But the fair could give us ideas that could save the store, and I want to dress in a way that says that I'm taking this seriously."

"All right. What are Nobby and Felix wearing?" Miri asked.

Anja pushed a pair of corduroy pants off the corner of the sofa and plopped down. "They're not going. Someone has to cover the store. I'm going with Susanne."

"Aha!"

"What's that supposed to mean?"

"That's why you're obsessing over what to wear! You want to impress your hot boss!"

"She's not my boss, and she's not—" Anja snapped her mouth shut as an image of Susanne's high cheekbones, glossy chestnut hair, and tall, slim body popped into her mind. Okay, Susanne was pretty hot…objectively speaking, of course. "I'm not trying to impress her." She eyed the piles of clothes to her right. Was she?

Miri chuckled. "Right. So what will she be wearing?"

"I have no idea. Probably something—"

"Hot," Miri said.

"Yes. I mean, no." She roughly shook her head, even though Miri couldn't see it. "I meant to say something that costs more than my entire wardrobe put together." She stood and rummaged through her closet again. "Do you think the gray pin-striped slacks would work?"

"You still have them?"

Anja frowned. "Why not? It's not like they're going out of style, are they?"

"No, but they are kind of boring." Miri was silent for a few seconds. "I've got it! Wear a skirt. Show off those sexy legs of yours. I bet Susanne would like that."

Anja let out a growl. "I told you I'm not trying to impress her." She pulled out the gray pants and started to shove the other stuff back into the closet. "That's it. I'm wearing the slacks."

"Fine. Be boring."

The closet doors clicked shut. "Thanks for that brilliant piece of advice."

Silence filtered through the line.

"Anja? You're not really upset with me, are you? I didn't mean to—"

"No." Anja sighed. "I'm not upset, just… I don't know. Nervous, I guess."

"I know Paper Love means the world to you. I can't even imagine you in any other job."

Anja flopped down onto the couch. "Me neither."

"You'll find a way to keep the store open," Miri said firmly. "I just know it."

"Thanks. I hope so." She extended her legs and pushed the TV stand back with her toes, as if that would help with that closing-in feeling. "I'll let you go now. Sorry for calling you so late."

"Any time. You know that. Sleep well and good luck tomorrow. Oh, and Anja?"

"Hmm?"

"You know those boots that you bought last fall? They would go really well with a skirt." Miri ended the call before Anja could answer.

"I'm not wearing a skirt," Anja said into the quiet room. "Absolutely not."

Chapter 9

When Susanne arrived at the main station at half past six on Saturday morning, she had only one thought: coffee. Preferably the biggest they had, the stronger, the better. Luckily for her, there was a small coffee stand shaped like a giant paper cup directly on platform one, where her train would be leaving from.

Other tired travelers crowded around it, and Susanne quickly got in line.

Someone tugged on her coat from behind.

With a low growl, she whirled around. She so wasn't in the mood for small talk with some stranger.

Instead, Anja stood in front of her, looking much too bright-eyed for this early hour on a weekend. "Good morning. Here, I already got you one." She held out a huge paper cup with a lid.

Susanne's grumpiness instantly faded. She practically lunged for the cup, making Anja laugh. "Thank you." She lifted the lid and peeked inside.

"Black, no sugar, right?" Anja said.

"Mm-hmm." Susanne took a big gulp, not caring that the coffee was almost too hot to drink. "How did you know?"

"Same way you did. I asked the lady from the coffee shop across from Paper Love."

They walked farther down the platform and sipped their respective coffees while they waited for their train.

Anja bounced on the balls of her feet a few times, and Susanne sensed that it wasn't because she was cold. An excited anticipation emanated from Anja. She seemed like a kid about to embark on a school excursion. Under different circumstances, it might have gotten on Susanne's nerves, but now she had to smile. Maybe the coffee offering had gentled her mood.

It wasn't long before the ICE to Frankfurt arrived. They boarded the high-speed train and took their reserved seats next to each other.

Anja put down her backpack, took off her coat, and leaned past Susanne, who had taken the window seat, to hang up her coat on a hook.

Susanne pressed back into her seat to make more room for her—and froze. Suddenly, she felt wide-awake, even though she knew the effect of the caffeine couldn't have set in yet. She had gotten used to seeing Anja in jeans and simple cotton blouses at work, but today, Anja's coat had covered an entirely different outfit. A formfitting, cream-colored blouse was tucked into a beige corduroy skirt. Susanne's gaze trailed over a short, chocolate-colored blazer that emphasized Anja's slim waist and matched the color of her eyes. As Anja sank into her seat, the skirt rode up a little, revealing a bit of pantyhose between the hem and the top of her knee-high, brown boots.

Oh God, those boots. Okay, it wasn't really the boots she was looking at; it was Anja's legs, toned from riding her bicycle to work every day. Susanne's mouth went dry, so she took another sip of coffee. If she had ever thought of Anja as the conservative type, that opinion flew right out of the window. It wasn't that her outfit was daring or overly revealing, but something about it was just…wow. This was going to be a long day.

She must not have done as good a job of not staring at Anja's legs as she had thought, because Anja asked, "What is it? Am I overdressed…underdressed… what?" She eyed Susanne's black pantsuit and her light-blue blouse.

"Oh, no, no. Not at all. It's fine. Perfect, really." *Careful, or she'll think you like her outfit a little too much.* She focused on folding down the tray table in front of her and putting her paper cup down on it. When Anja followed her example, she breathed a sigh of relief since the tray now covered part of Anja's legs.

"Oh. Good. It took me half an hour and a phone call to decide on an outfit." Almost under her breath, Anja added, "Not that my phone joker was much help."

"Who did you call?" Susanne asked before she could censor herself. "Miriam?"

Anja nodded but didn't offer any information about what kind of fashion advice her friend had given. If Miriam had told her to wear this outfit, Susanne wasn't sure if she should hug her or kick her should she ever see her again.

As the train started to move and quickly gained speed on its way north, Anja leaned sideways to reach past the tray table and rummaged through her backpack, obscuring her face.

Was she blushing?

Finally, Anja straightened and placed an apple, a banana, several muesli bars, and a plastic container on her tray table.

Susanne glanced into the still-open backpack, which held more containers, brown paper bags, and a bottle of water. "Don't they sell food at the stationery fair? I haven't packed anything."

Anja unwrapped a muesli bar. "Don't worry. They do, but it's probably overpriced, and I bet there won't be many vegetarian options. I know you can survive on air and lo—uh, on air alone, but I can't." She offered half of the muesli bar to Susanne, who declined with a shake of her head.

"What's that supposed to mean?" Susanne asked.

"Nothing. Just that except for that one time when you had half a sausage on a bun, I've never seen you eat at work." Anja took a hearty bite of the muesli bar.

When Susanne thought about it, she had to admit that it was true. "Hmm. I guess I sometimes forget to eat when I'm stressed or busy."

"I'm the complete opposite." Anja finished off the muesli bar. "When I'm stressed, I can't stop eating."

She paused, and they both looked at the empty wrapper.

"Is this," Susanne pointed back and forth between them and then pointed in the direction they were traveling, "stressing you out? I could have gone with Uncle Norbert, you know? You didn't have to give up your day off to go with me if you—"

"Oh, no, no," Anja said quickly. "I've always wanted to go to Paperworld."

Just not with me? Susanne wondered.

Anja removed the lid from a container and held it out to her. "Cookie?"

With a wry smile, Susanne reached for one. "Thanks."

⁊◌◖◌⁊

As the train compartment around them fell quiet, most passengers dozing, reading, or working on their laptops, their conversation ended too. Maybe it was better that way since Anja didn't know what to talk about with Susanne.

When the train reached Offenburg, the first of a handful of stops along their route, Susanne's cell phone rang. She pulled it from the pocket of her blazer. With a quick "sorry" to Anja, she lifted it to her ear. "Are you checking up on me?" she asked instead of a greeting. It sounded affectionate, not scolding, though.

Was it her girlfriend?

But she had told them she didn't have a girlfriend when Miri had asked.

"Friday? No, that sounds great. Can't wait."

A female voice came through the phone, but Anja couldn't make out what she was saying. Not that she was eavesdropping or anything.

"Don't be stupid," Susanne said. "You don't need to book a hotel. Of course you can stay with me."

So a woman would visit Susanne next weekend—and she would be sleeping over. Anja didn't care, of course.

When Susanne ended the call, Anja quickly busied herself with unwrapping a second muesli bar.

Susanne put the phone away with a smile on her lips but didn't offer an explanation.

"If you've got a friend from Berlin visiting, I can give you a few pointers about must-see spots in Freiburg." *What are you doing?* She definitely hadn't meant to say that.

"I don't think that'll be necessary," Susanne answered. "Unlike me, my womb mate has been in Freiburg several times in the last few years. I assume Uncle Norbert has shown her around already."

"Womb mate?" Her brain felt as if it were operating in slow motion—not a good thing considering this day could make or break the survival of the store.

Susanne chuckled. "Yes. That's what a friend once called my twin sister. Somehow the name stuck."

"Aww. That's kind of cute."

"I think so too, but should you ever meet her, don't tell her that. She's an incorrigible flirt, so you wouldn't want to encourage her."

The wrapper slid from Anja's hand, and she quickly picked it up and stuffed it into the tiny garbage compartment between the seats in front of them. "Does that mean your sister is gay too?" She peeked over at Susanne to judge her reaction. "Um, please feel free to tell me it's none of my business."

"No, that's fine. It's not like it's a big secret. Actually, Franziska is bi."

"Oh, cool." For some reason, Anja met few people who, like she, were in the middle of the spectrum, so even the mention of another bisexual person felt reassuring. "I'm actually bi too." She blurted it out before she'd had time to think about it.

It was probably just her imagination, but it seemed as if the entire train car went completely silent.

The two businessmen across the aisle looked up from their laptops to sneak a glance at her, and Susanne stared at her.

Great. Her face burned, and she fought the urge to hide beneath the tray table.

The conductor saved the day as he stepped into their compartment, interrupting the awkward silence. "Tickets, please!"

Anja scrambled for the printout of her ticket in her backpack, while Susanne pulled her smartphone from the inside pocket of her blazer.

"Good morning." The conductor scanned their tickets, nodded at them, and continued to the next passenger.

Anja took her time returning the ticket to her backpack.

"So tell me," Susanne said, making Anja hold her breath in expectation of what she would ask, "what should we make sure to see at the fair?"

Now it was Anja's turn to stare. Her unplanned coming-out to Susanne didn't even rate a comment? She wasn't sure if she should be relieved or disappointed. *Oh, come on. Why should it matter? This is a business trip.* She pulled her notebook from her backpack and opened it to the page of notes she had taken at home. "For one thing, there's this manufacturer of really cool notebooks from Croatia…"

⤮

Susanne dashed after Anja, weaving around passengers and their baggage on the crowded platform. Their train had been late, so now they had to hurry to make the connecting regional train that would take them from Frankfurt main station to the trade fair.

This wouldn't have happened if they had taken the car, as she had suggested. But then again, if they had taken the car, she might have caused an accident when Anja had casually revealed that she was bi.

Oh, come on. It's hardly that big of a surprise, is it? But somehow suspecting it and hearing the words from Anja were two very different things.

"Slow down," Susanne called. "There's no need to run. Even if we miss our train, there'll be another one in about ten minutes."

"That's ten minutes we won't be spending at Paperworld." Anja glanced over her shoulder. Her eyes glittered with anticipation.

Susanne held up her hands. "Far be it from me to stand between a stationery addict and her drug of choice."

Anja led her down a set of stairs to the underground platforms. The screeching of metal on metal announced an incoming train.

"Damn! I think that's ours. Come on! We can make it!" Anja grabbed her hand and pulled her down an escalator.

They jumped the last meter onto the platform, and Susanne was glad she had chosen to wear flats, not high heels.

The train was still there, waiting with its doors open, and they rushed through them.

Anja quickly let go of her hand, as if only now becoming aware that she had grabbed it.

Susanne curled her fingers around one of the metal poles instead. Breathing hard, she looked around for free seats, but they were all taken. Apparently, a lot of people had the same genius idea of taking the train to the fair. Other passengers squeezed in after them until Susanne started to feel as if she were using the subway in Tokyo, where professional pushers were employed to stuff humans into subway cars. She muttered a curse as people jostled her from all sides, forcing her to take a step back. Now she had to stretch out her arm almost painfully so she could reach the pole, and the fingers of a stranger brushed hers in search of a spot to hold on to.

Anja wasn't faring any better. A guy was pressed against her backpack so tightly that she squirmed uncomfortably.

"Hey, why don't you back off a little?" Susanne snarled at him. "You're so far into my friend's personal space that you really should buy her dinner first."

Anja gave her a startled look, either because she wasn't used to being defended or because Susanne had called her a friend without meaning to.

"And where do you suggest I go?" The guy gestured behind him, where other people were squeezed in just as close.

She sent him a glare but had to admit that he really had nowhere to go.

Finally, the doors closed, and the train jerked forward.

Susanne clutched the pole more tightly, but Anja didn't have anything to hold on to, so she was tossed forward, against Susanne. She grasped Anja with her free hand, keeping her on her feet.

A startled gasp escaped Anja. Her warm breath brushed Susanne's collarbone where she had opened her coat, sending shivers through her body.

"Uh, sorry." Anja tried to move back, but the people surrounding them had immediately taken advantage of the freed-up space and had crowded closer, so now Anja couldn't back up. "Um…"

"It's okay." Susanne forced a smile and tried to ignore how much more than just okay her body found this unexpected situation. "Better me than that guy. At least this way, you have a chance of me buying you dinner afterward."

Anja let out a nervous chuckle and managed to move back a little so that their bodies were no longer touching all along their lengths. But each time the train changed its speed or another passenger jostled one of them, their fronts brushed, and the temperature in the train seemed to skyrocket.

The train slid to a stop at the next station, jolting Anja backward. She grabbed the lapel of Susanne's coat.

Susanne spread her fingers over Anja's back to steady her.

They stood frozen in this semi-embrace for several seconds, just staring at each other.

God, if she bent her head, she could—

Are you fucking crazy? You're on a business trip. On a train surrounded by dozens of stressed-out, potentially homophobic strangers. With an employee! She cursed the fact that Anja had told her she was bi. Maybe if she hadn't, keeping a professional distance—even if it was just a figurative distance—wouldn't have been so difficult.

Susanne struggled not to sound breathless. "I don't think this is what Uncle Norbert had in mind when he said we should use the train ride to get to know each other better."

Anja burst out laughing, making Susanne smile, and the tension between them receded a little.

The doors banged shut without anyone having gotten on or off, and the train accelerated away from the platform.

Slowly, Anja loosened her death grip on Susanne's lapel and then let go completely. "Next stop is ours." She sounded a bit hoarse.

Susanne bit back a *thank God* and just nodded. By the time they made it out of here, the pole she gripped would probably have permanent indentations from her fingers.

⌒⌒∞⌒⌒

The doors hissed open, and passengers popped out of the train like corks from champagne bottles, clearing space so Anja could finally move. While she was glad to be able to breathe more easily, her body protested as it lost contact with Susanne's.

The four-minute ride from the main station to the trade fair premises had seemed to last an eternity, but her libido insisted that it hadn't been nearly long enough.

They followed the stream of people to the entrance of the massive exhibition complex, dropped off their coats at the coat check, and then made it through the bag check to have their tickets scanned.

She fell into step next to Susanne as they headed down a seemingly endless hallway. It appeared as if they were entering another world. Her body buzzed with excitement, and Anja had a hard time telling if it was because she was about to enter a hall full of stationery or because she was still overly aware of Susanne's proximity.

She snuck glances at her from the corner of her eye, trying to figure out if she felt it too, but Susanne had put on her fully focused business mask and glanced at the fair navigator app she had downloaded to her smartphone. "Where do you want to go first?"

Anja consulted the paper floor plan she had grabbed at the entrance. The trade fair was spread out over several floors of four exhibition halls. "How about hall 6.1? That's where most of the stationery is."

"All right." Susanne pointed to a sign above. "It's this way. Let's just hope it's not as crowded as the train."

Yeah, let's hope so. Her poor body wouldn't be able to take being pressed close to Susanne and breathing in her amber-and-a-ghost-of-vanilla scent for hours.

∽∾∾

Oh my God! They had been in hall 6.1 for less than half an hour, and Susanne's head already felt close to exploding from all the things it had to take in.

Illuminated desktop globes rotated to her right, display cases to her left showed off fountain pens that looked as if they cost more than her BMW, and notebook decorations dangled from the ceiling above her. Never in her life had she seen so many stationery and office products in one place and certainly not the kinds that were displayed here. There were pencils smelling of lavender, pens made from recycled Nespresso pods, and scissors shaped like the Eiffel Tower.

Bright colors and the background noise of conversations surrounded them, taxing her senses.

Anja flitted from booth to booth like a bee discovering the first blooming flowers after a long winter. She touched a notebook here and a writing utensil there, as if she needed to connect with it all. Her cheeks were flushed, either from excitement or from the warm, stuffy air in the hall.

Susanne followed a step behind her so she could watch her take it all in. For her, that was much more fun than looking at stationery.

One vendor had set up walls around their booth, leaving just a narrow entrance. It looked like a tiny castle, but instead of keeping people away, it drew them in since the walls were one huge coloring picture depicting a city scene.

Anja grabbed a red crayon and colored in one of the roofs. She glanced up as if feeling Susanne's gaze on her, and her cheeks flushed even more. "Sorry. I couldn't resist. I know we're here to work."

If Susanne had been here with anyone else, she might have given them a stern nod, but she didn't have the heart to spoil Anja's enjoyment. She pointed at the crayon in Anja's hand. "This *is* work. After all, you can't very well recommend a certain brand of crayons to our customers if you haven't tried them out yourself."

"Right. So try it."

"Uh, I don't know. I've never been good at—"

"Try it." Anja pressed a green crayon into her hand.

Susanne glanced left and right. No one paid them any attention. To her left, a guy in a business suit and a tie colored in a train. If he could do it, so could she. She grabbed a handful of crayons and painted the sail of a boat bobbing on a still-white river in rainbow colors.

Anja paused in her own roof-coloring endeavor and grinned at her.

Okay, this was kind of fun, Susanne had to admit.

Finally, they put the crayons down and continued exploring the booths along the broad aisle. Anja took the lead as they talked to vendors from all over the world and watched product demonstrations and presentations on the latest developments in the stationery business.

Susanne was used to taking control of work situations, so hanging back and letting Anja do the talking took some getting used to. After a while, she found that she didn't mind at all. She knew she could trust Anja to do a much better job than she could.

As quiet and unassuming as Anja was most of the time, she now talked animatedly and asked clever questions. Plus her accent when she spoke English with people from all over the world was kind of cute. She charmed the exhibitors without even trying, so the two extra bags Anja had brought became heavier as the day progressed and they collected free samples, business cards, and product catalogs. They also took turns carrying Anja's backpack, which seemed to be getting heavier by the minute too.

Susanne's feet and shoulders ached. She had no doubt that if she glanced at the fitness app on her phone, she'd find that they had walked at least five kilometers— and the day wasn't even half over yet. She shifted her weight from one foot to the other as she watched Anja take in yet another booth.

This one displayed notebooks that had a computer keyboard embossed on their covers. When she took a closer look, she realized that the letters on the keys spelled out *handwriting beats keyboard.*

Susanne suppressed a chuckle. This was definitely the right notebook for Anja.

Anja lovingly ran her fingers over the cover, tracing the keys, and then opened one of the journals to study the paper.

"They come in hardbound and softbound, and we offer them in three different colors and three sizes," the exhibitor said in heavily accented English. "Customers can choose between ruled and blank paper."

"They are beautiful," Anja said in a tone that most people reserved for little babies—or their lovers.

A shiver went through Susanne despite the overly warm temperature in the hall.

"You should really think about offering them with dot-grid paper too," Anja said. "It's really popular with many customers at the moment."

That started a lively discussion about ways to make the product even better, and when they parted ten minutes later, Anja slid yet another catalog and a free notebook into her bag.

The vendor warmly shook her hand.

Anja glanced at the business card he had handed her and smiled at him. "Dovidenja. Zelim vam ugodan dan."

That got her an excited response, and it took two more minutes before Susanne could finally pull her away from the booth.

"You speak…whatever language that was?" Susanne asked as they headed for the hall's exit.

"Croatian. No, I don't really speak it. Just a few phrases that I remember from when I was a child. My parents and I used to spend every summer in Croatia, but I was just eight or nine when the war broke out and we stopped going, so all I remember are things like *goodbye* and *have a nice day*."

"It's a beautiful country," Susanne said.

Anja's eyes lit up. She got that dreamy look on her face—the same one she got when she talked about pens and notebooks. "You've been there?"

Susanne nodded. "Just once. I spent a week on Krk last year. Not long enough to pick up more than *pivo molim*."

They both chuckled at Susanne's beer-ordering skills.

"So you didn't go back as an adult?" Susanne asked.

Anja shook her head. "September is really the best time to go. It's still warm enough to swim, and most tourists are gone by then. But that's also the time when we're pretty busy at the store with back-to-school sales." After a moment, she added, "Plus vacations like that aren't in my budget."

"Did you never consider getting a better-paying job so you can go on vacations, maybe get a car…"

Anja stopped abruptly, ignoring the fact that they were right in front of the escalators.

Other visitors had to veer around them. Some cursed loudly.

"It might be hard to imagine for you, but not everyone needs a BMW and tailor-made clothes to be happy."

For a second, Susanne didn't know what to say. It was rare that anyone talked to her like that. She opened her mouth to protest but then snapped it shut, lightly gripped Anja's elbow, and pulled her onto the escalator going up to the next level.

There were no exhibitors on this floor, just meeting rooms, so fewer people milled around. Susanne spied a quiet corner with a padded bench across from several computer terminals with a handwritten sign that said *out of order*. She led Anja over and put down her heavy bag.

Anja dropped onto the bench next to her and ran a hand through her hair. "Sorry." She glanced at Susanne, then away. "I don't know what… I'm usually not… I guess all the stress of the store possibly closing is getting to me. Of course, that's not an excuse for being a bitch."

A hint of a smile tugged at the corners of Susanne's mouth. "You think that was bitchy? Compared to some of my former colleagues, that was tame."

Anja shook her head. "Then I definitely wouldn't want to work for that company."

"No, you wouldn't." She couldn't imagine Anja surviving for even a day in that pool of sharks.

"That's what I like so much about working at Paper Love. There's no mobbing, no backstabbing, and the day-to-day work doesn't revolve around who's bringing in more customers or making more money. Yeah, being able to afford expensive vacations and a bigger apartment would be nice, and when I'm caught in a downpour, having a car doesn't sound so bad, but at the end of the day, it's not really important to me. I like my life the way it is, and everything else would just be…glitter. Nice to look at, but not really necessary." Anja looked up from where she'd studied her hands and gazed into Susanne's eyes. "Can you understand that?"

Their eye contact made Susanne swallow. "Yes." She had always thought people who were content with what they had were just passive fools, but the more she got to know Anja, the harder it became to judge her. Maybe there was something to be said for not always being on the lookout for something different, something more, something better. She cleared her throat. "I think I need to apologize too. I didn't mean to attack your, um, lifestyle."

Anja grinned. "Lifestyle?"

"Yeah, you know."

"Let's just forget it and put it down to—"

A loud growl coming from Susanne's stomach interrupted her.

"Hunger pangs," Anja finished her sentence with a laugh. "Come on. Let's take a break." She opened her backpack, pulled out muffins, apples, sandwiches, and small containers of juice, and arranged a little picnic on the padded bench between them. There was two of everything, so clearly, Anja had packed food for her too.

"Oh wow. No wonder the backpack was so heavy."

"Are you complaining?"

Susanne lifted her hands. "Wouldn't dream of it." They could have eaten in one of the restaurants or cafés downstairs, but being away from the hordes of people for a while was nice.

"Good." Anja handed her one of the cheese sandwiches but held hers without eating and looked at Susanne with a serious expression. "Do you think any of this," she waved her hand at the floors below them, "will save Paper Love?"

Susanne put down her sandwich and sighed. "No."

"No."

Susanne's one-word answer seemed to echo through the hall and bounce back from the high ceiling.

Anja had feared this would be the answer. Perhaps that was why she had avoided asking the question so clearly until now. Still, hearing it aloud was like a kick to the gut.

"At least not by themselves," Susanne added. "Carrying a few more items, no matter how nice they are, won't save us."

Anja smiled sadly. "Just glitter, hmm?"

"Exactly. We need to change everything from the ground up."

She had said *we* this time, Anja realized. It made her feel better but only a little bit. Her tongue seemed to stick to the roof of her dry mouth, so she pierced the seal of her juice container with the straw and took a big sip of orange juice. *Change everything.* She hated that word: change. "W-what does that mean?"

"No more school supplies. No more staplers and printer paper and stuff like that."

"But we sell a lot of them, especially in summer."

"Yeah. But we hardly make any profit from cheap items like that because the competition forces us to sell them barely above cost. We can't compete with department stores and big chains like Staples and McPaper."

She was right. They could sell pencils and paper clips all day and still never earn enough to make a living. But it was still hard to let go of products they had sold for so long.

Deep in thought, Anja rubbed an apple clean on her skirt. "You want us to specialize in BMWs." She glanced at Susanne, who stared at the apple…or maybe at her legs. Tingles spread through her body, reminding her of the way she had felt pressed against Susanne this morning. *Are you out of your mind? This isn't the time for thoughts like that.*

Hastily, Susanne looked back up into her eyes. "Basically, yes. We should focus on high-end stuff and specialty items that no one else has. Maybe tie our products to our location by working with little local companies."

Anja's mind went in a hundred different directions at once and finally came up with a few ideas that might be useful. "Greeting cards made by artists from the region, vegan notebook covers, and eco-friendly items like pens made out of recycled plastic bottles."

"Yes. Something like that."

Anja pulled out her notebook and started to scribble down more ideas but then paused. "Is there a big enough market for that?"

Susanne shook her head. "Not in Freiburg alone. If we want to reach enough people to make a living, we need to do business online as well."

Online. Oh shit. She'd been afraid Susanne would say that. "But that goes against everything we've been trying to do with the store."

"Plunging it into ruin?" Susanne squeezed her eyes shut and rubbed her lips as if trying to wipe out those words.

"Ouch." Stung, Anja leaned back against the wall, away from Susanne, who now peeked over at her.

"Sorry. That was harsh. I'm just frustrated." She slid closer on the bench until Anja felt the warmth of her knee against her leg. "Listen. Nowadays no company can survive without a strong online presence. I don't get why you didn't at least set up a website with a webstore years ago."

"Because it lacks the kind of personal touch that our customers prefer."

"Then find a way to provide that personal touch online."

Anja's stomach churned. Susanne made it sound so easy, but for her, it was anything but. While she could use the Internet and get done whatever she needed to do online, it felt like a foreign language in which she had never quite become fluent. "How?"

Susanne shrugged. "I don't have all the answers, but our first steps need to be setting up a website with an integrated webstore, a blog, an Instagram presence, and a YouTube channel. And then we need to spend some serious time finding out where the scrapbookers, journalers, and pen-and-paper geeks hang out online. That's where we need to be too. We need to create content they want to read and that establishes us as trendsetters."

Anja squeezed the apple so tightly that she felt the fruit give under her fingers. Her nails left half-moon-shaped indentations in the apple. "Blogging, social media marketing, making YouTube videos… Nobby can't do any of that."

"I know." Susanne studied her with a serious expression. "The question is: Can you?"

The weight of every notebook and every piece of paper in their entire store seemed to settle on Anja's shoulders. She wanted to argue, wanted to tell Susanne that she was wrong, that this couldn't be the solution, but she knew she had closed her eyes from the truth for too long already. Now she had to face it or live with the consequences. "Yes," she croaked out and then added with a slightly steadier voice, "I can do it."

Susanne reached over and gently squeezed her hand. "I know you can. I will help, okay?"

Her fingers were warm and strong and chased away part of the fear. "Okay. Where do we start?"

"First, we save this poor apple," she gently loosened Anja's fingers, which had held the piece of fruit in a death grip, "and then we save Paper Love, starting with a short video about our top five finds at Paperworld."

"Sounds good." Anja put her other hand on top of Susanne's and looked into her eyes. "Thank you."

Susanne grinned. "Don't thank me yet. I'm not just talking about product videos. If we want to achieve that personal touch, Paper Love needs a face—your face." She pulled her iPhone from her blazer pocket and held it up. "Ready to be a film star?"

Anja groaned. "I hate being on video. My hair's probably a mess; my blouse is wrinkled from the backpack straps, and—"

"Nonsense. You look beautiful. Um, I mean, I bet our customers will appreciate your well-put-together but natural look."

The compliment filled Anja with warmth. "Okay. Let's do this. But first…"

"Yeah?"

"Muffins."

Anja dropped into the seat next to Susanne and stretched out her aching feet as far as the space in the high-speed train allowed. At least the regional train from the exhibition grounds to the main station hadn't been as crowded as this morning. *Too bad,* a little voice commented. She ignored it.

Susanne rotated her shoulders, which probably hurt as much as Anja's since they had taken turns carrying the backpack and had each lugged around a heavy bag too. "I can't believe this was just one day. It feels like we were there all week."

"Yeah." Anja's brain was on overload with all the stimulation from the fair and the things they would have to do in the coming days and weeks, and her feet ached as if she had walked all the way from Freiburg. She closed her tired eyes. "But it was worth it, right?"

"Mm-hmm. Definitely. I mean, I still don't get why an adult woman would squeal over a notebook like a teenager who just met her favorite band, but it was fun and it helped me see the direction we need to take the store in more clearly."

"I did *not* squeal."

"No, of course not. You were just talking excitedly, in a higher than usual voice." Susanne imitated a cartoon character who had inhaled helium.

Anja opened her eyes and reached out to give her a playful slap to the shoulder, then paused and let her hand drop back into her lap. *Oh wow.* When had she become so relaxed around Susanne? Somehow the tone of their interaction had shifted during the course of the day. Hard to imagine that this was the same woman who had insisted on being addressed by her last name less than two weeks ago. Was that a good thing? She hoped so. Having Susanne behind the camera had certainly put her more at ease when they had filmed several short video clips.

"Do you think the videos are good enough to use on YouTube?" Anja asked.

When no reply came from Susanne, she turned her head and looked over.

Susanne had pulled her silver clip from her hair so she could rest her head more comfortably against the seat. Now her hair tumbled loosely about her shoulders. Her eyes were closed and her lips slightly parted. Her usually controlled features had relaxed in sleep, making her look younger and more vulnerable. What a difference from the ice queen who had stormed into the store on the first day, cursing the *Bächle*!

Anja's gaze followed the soft lines of her mouth. God, she was beautiful. Why on earth hadn't they put Susanne in the video instead of her? Her fingers itched to comb back a strand of hair that had fallen onto Susanne's face. *Stop it. This is crazy.* She shoved her hand beneath her thigh to resist temptation.

She sat there watching her until her eyelids became too heavy and she closed her eyes.

Some unknown time later, a touch to her shoulder startled her from her light slumber.

She opened her eyes and looked around, expecting the conductor. But the aisle next to her seat was empty, so she peered to the other side.

Susanne had slid sideways in her seat, and her head rested on Anja's shoulder.

Aww. Anja grinned. If only she could take a photo. She had a feeling not too many people got to see Susanne like this.

She gazed past her out the window to the darkness beyond, trying to figure out where they were, but couldn't make out any prominent landmarks. A glance at her wristwatch revealed that they were about halfway to Freiburg. Oh wow. That meant that she'd slept for an hour.

The automatic doors to their compartment opened with a whoosh, and the conductor entered. "Tickets, please."

Damn. Couldn't he have waited another half hour so Susanne could get a little more sleep? Careful not to move her shoulder, Anja reached into the inside pocket of her blazer and pulled out her ticket.

Susanne didn't stir. A slight frown pulled at her brows but then smoothed out.

Anja handed her ticket to the conductor. Susanne's phone lay on the tray table, but she didn't know the code that would unlock it, so she couldn't show him Susanne's ticket.

With a sigh of regret, she reached out to softly shake her awake.

"Don't," the conductor whispered. "It's okay. She's obviously with you." Grinning, he nodded at the way Susanne trustingly rested her head on Anja's shoulder, using her as a pillow.

With me, Anja mentally repeated. "Yes, she is. Thank you."

He handed her ticket back and went down the aisle to the next passenger.

She watched him until he disappeared into the adjoining compartment. Had he assumed they were a couple? *Doesn't matter. You're not.*

Susanne made a kitten-like noise that had Anja press her hand to her mouth to hold back a giggle. Her long eyelashes fluttered, then lifted. She looked around, clearly dazed and needing a minute to remember where she was. "Oh. Uh, sorry." She sat up and wiped her mouth as if to check whether she'd been drooling. Even the low light in their compartment couldn't hide her blush.

"It's okay." Anja decided not to tease her, but she couldn't keep the corners of her mouth from curling up into an amused grin.

"Where are we?" Susanne asked.

"About halfway to Freiburg. Go back to sleep."

"I wasn't sleeping." Her voice was husky, belying her words. "Just resting my eyes for a moment."

"Mm-hmm. Same way I wasn't squealing over that notebook earlier."

Susanne glared at her in a way that would have made the blood freeze in Anja's veins two weeks ago. But now it just made her grin more broadly.

A yawn interrupted Susanne's glaring. She stretched, and her slightly wrinkled blouse pulled taut over her breasts.

Anja tore her gaze away. Maybe she should rest her eyes for a while too. It would definitely be safer.

∽oඋ∽

Neither had the energy to trudge up the stairs to the streetcar, so they stepped onto the escalator as if by unspoken agreement. The wind tugged on Susanne's blouse, making her shiver, and she quickly buttoned her coat.

God, she was tired. She had forced herself to keep her eyes open the rest of the way to Freiburg because she'd been afraid that she'd use Anja as a pillow again. Somehow that felt even more intimate than being pressed against each other from head to toe this morning. That thought warmed her shivering body.

When they reached the streetcar stops, they had to go their separate ways because Anja had to take the streetcar on this side of the street, while Susanne had to wait for the one leaving from across the street.

They stood next to the tracks and turned toward each other.

Anja bobbed up and down on the balls of her feet. She had slid one hand under a strap of her backpack while holding on to a heavy bag with the other.

"Want me to take that?" Susanne pointed. "I could bring it to work on Monday along with the bag I have and then drive you home so you don't have to take it on the bicycle."

"No, that's okay. Thanks."

Susanne smiled. "Don't want to be separated from all those free notebooks over the weekend, hmm?"

"Well, as you said this morning, how can I recommend products to our customers if I don't inspect them carefully?"

"Right."

In the distance, a streetcar approached from the direction of the city center. A red sign at the top of the windshield indicated which line it was, but Susanne couldn't yet tell them apart, and it was still too far away for her to be able to read the number.

"That's mine," Anja said.

"Oh, then, um, good night and have a nice rest of the weekend."

"You too."

They stood without moving and looked at each other.

As exhausted as she was and as glad as she would be to get home and put up her feet, Susanne realized she didn't want to say goodbye. *What the hell?* She'd never had a problem spending her evenings alone.

The streetcar whooshed past them, slid to a stop several meters away, and opened its doors, but Anja made no move to get in. "You know what? I'm pretty hungry, and I'm not up for cooking. Want to go grab that dinner you owe me?"

"I owe you dinner?"

"Yes. Remember this morning? You said I had a chance of you buying me dinner after our little, um, snuggle session on the train."

Susanne chuckled. Snuggle session, hmm? So was Anja still thinking about it too? "Right. I did say that, and I'm a woman of my word, so let's go. Any good restaurants around here?"

"Oh yes. Plenty of them. What are you in the mood for?"

Susanne honestly didn't care. She wasn't picky about food, and if the Indian dishes they had shared last week were any indication, they had similar tastes. "You're the local. Why don't you surprise me?"

"All right. Come on." Anja took her arm, pulled her away from the windy bridge where the streetcars stopped, and led her down the street.

⟳∽∾⟲

"Careful." Anja reached for Susanne's elbow as they stepped across a *Bächle*. She hesitated in front of the restaurant's heavy-studded oak door, not sure if Susanne would enjoy this type of place. It might be a bit too rustic for her, with tasty but simple regional dishes.

But Susanne was already reading the menu that was posted on small blackboards attached to the shutters. "Ooh, that sounds good."

"Are you sure? It's pretty simple. No frills. Don't expect fine dining."

Susanne shook her head at her. "You've really got the wrong impression about me. I'm not the glitter type either. No frills is fine."

Before Anja could think of a reply, Susanne opened the door and held it for her. "Thanks."

Lively conversations drifted over as they entered the large dining room. The dark hardwood floor and the wood ceiling gave the restaurant a cozy feel. It was pretty busy, and they were lucky to find a free table for two in the corner.

The vegetarian options were limited, but Anja already knew what she wanted, so she watched Susanne study the menu. She didn't look out of place here at all.

She had taken off her blazer and had opened the top button on her blouse. Her hair tumbled to her shoulders and was still a little mussed from her nap on the train. Anja found that she liked this more down-to-earth look.

"Do you mind if I order meat?" Susanne had to lean across the table to make herself heard above the noise.

The question caught Anja off guard. She hadn't expected Susanne to be so considerate. "No, not at all. I don't like people trying to talk me into eating meat, so I try not to be a missionary and convert people to vegetarianism either."

"I don't eat a lot of meat, but Franzi—my sister—says I have to try the *Rindfleisch*." Susanne tapped the item on the menu.

Anja took a closer look. It was the beef with horseradish sauce, boiled potatoes, and cranberries. "Good choice. It was my grandmother's favorite."

"What did she think about having a vegetarian granddaughter?"

Anja chuckled. "She was always worried about me starving to death. For her, a meal without meat wasn't a real meal."

"My mother was the same when Franzi went through her short-lived vegan phase."

The waitress stepped up to their table, and Anja ordered the cheese spaetzle and a small salad.

"Do you want it with the caramelized onions or without?" the waitress asked.

Anja hesitated for only a second. "With onions, please." This wasn't a date, after all, so she didn't need to keep her breath fresh for the good-night kiss. An image flashed through her mind's eye—Susanne and she standing at the streetcar stop where they had to go their separate ways, leaning closer and closer until… She roughly shook her head to chase away the image.

It didn't take long for their food to be served, and they both dug in with gusto.

The spaetzle was sprinkled with butter-fried bread crumbs and tasted delicious.

The loud group at the large table next to theirs got up and left, and the noise level in the restaurant instantly dropped so they could talk without raising their voices.

"This is good." Susanne sounded almost surprised. She swiped a piece of beef through the horseradish sauce on her plate.

"What, you thought our little backwoods region couldn't produce anything worth eating?" Anja tried for a teasing tone, but, truth be told, it rankled her a little that Susanne didn't seem to like Freiburg.

Susanne put down her knife and fork. "I didn't say that—or think it," she added before Anja could say anything. "In fact, no matter where I have traveled, I have often found that the best food is served away from the big cities in little, rustic restaurants like this."

"So you travel a lot?"

Susanne picked up her cutlery. "Yeah, I do. I did. I worked for a big international consulting firm."

"Worked," Anja repeated. "Right. You said you're in between jobs."

Susanne nodded.

"Can I ask what…?"

"What happened at my old job?" Susanne hesitated, and for a moment, Anja thought she wouldn't answer, but then she said, "I finally had enough, so I quit."

Anja paused with her fork hovering in mid-air. "Enough of what? The bitchy colleagues you mentioned earlier today?"

"Them too. The whole company climate was pretty toxic…at least for women. My boss always picked the shittiest, most difficult jobs for me just because he wanted to see me fail, while his boys got the easy jobs and all the praise." Susanne's voice was tight with frustration.

And now Susanne was here in Freiburg, trying to save Paper Love. Did she consider it a shitty job too?

"I thought I could prove myself and make him respect me, but I finally realized that my career wouldn't go anywhere as long as I stayed," Susanne continued. "So I quit."

"Good for you." They clinked their wineglasses on that final statement, then Anja asked, "What's next for you?"

"A company where people are judged by their skills, not by their gender, hopefully. It shouldn't be too hard to find one, especially since I'm not tied to a specific location. Maybe I'll even work out of the country for a while."

Wow. They couldn't be more different if they tried. Susanne would move to a foreign country in a heartbeat, while Anja couldn't imagine living anywhere but Freiburg.

Susanne chewed and swallowed a bite of potato. "What about you?"

"Me?"

"Yeah. At the risk of sounding as if I were conducting a job interview, where do you see yourself in five years?"

"Behind the counter of Paper Love," Anja said firmly.

Susanne regarded her with a serious expression. "But what if that's not possible? What would you do if—?"

"Are you trying to find out if I have a plan B?" Anja shoved back her half-eaten salad. "I don't have one. I don't *want* one."

"Maybe you should. Even if we can turn things around for now, my uncle won't run the store forever, and who knows what will happen once he retires."

"I know what Nobby wants to happen." Anja raked her fork through her spaetzle and peered up at Susanne from under half-lowered lids, watching her reaction. "He wants, um…" She hesitated, not sure how Susanne would take it, then forged ahead. "He wants me to take over as the new owner."

To her surprise, Susanne nodded her approval. "I'd be all for that. Selling you the store might be a good solution."

"No. That's not what I…what he…" Anja took a deep breath. "I don't have the money to buy the store from him. He wants to *give* me Paper Love."

Susanne took her time cutting a slice of beef in half. Finally, she raised her gaze to Anja and studied her thoroughly.

Anja squirmed under the intense scrutiny of those gray eyes. God, she suddenly felt like a crook trying to cheat Susanne out of her inheritance. She forced herself not to duck her head in shame.

Finally, Susanne shrugged. "If that's what Uncle Norbert wants."

"You…you would be okay with it? With Paper Love going to someone who isn't family?"

Susanne took a large sip of wine. "My sister has her own practice, and I have no intention of staying around past Easter."

"What about…well, your father? The store belonged to his father after all."

Susanne barked out a bitter laugh. "Oh God, no. I'd rather you have Paper Love than my father. At least with you, the store might have a fighting chance."

Anja didn't know what to say. They ate in silence for a while. Once the last bites of her spaetzle and Susanne's beef were gone and they had asked for the bill, Anja said, "If it ever comes to that…to Nobby giving me the store, I'll try to set aside some money every month to pay your family back in some way."

"Let's worry about that once we've managed to save the store, okay?"

"Okay."

They nodded at each other, and the mood lightened.

The waitress brought the bill. "Are you paying together or separately?"

"Separately," Anja said, while Susanne answered, "Together."

Anja looked at her.

"This is on me. I said I'd invite you for, um, the train situation," Susanne said with a glance at the waitress.

"I was just kidding about you having to buy me dinner for that."

Susanne handed the waitress a fifty-euro bill. "I wasn't."

Anja finally decided to accept the invitation. "Thank you, then."

"You're welcome."

Once Susanne had received some change from the waitress, they headed out.

The temperature had dropped, and Anja buttoned her coat while they walked toward the streetcar stop.

A group of students, apparently a little buzzed, passed them, forcing them to move closer, and neither of them increased the distance between them once the young people had passed. In the cool night air, the warmth of Susanne's arm against her own felt good.

Anja's streetcar stop was the first they came to, and Susanne lingered next to her instead of continuing on to her own. "The stop you need is over there." Anja gestured.

"I know. I'll wait here with you, then catch mine."

Anja had to smile at Susanne's good manners. For a second, she could imagine what it would be like to go on a date with her. Susanne would probably insist on walking her to her door.

The streetcar sliding to a stop next to them interrupted her thoughts.

Passengers veered around them to get in, but Anja and Susanne stood without moving, facing each other.

"Thanks for going with me," Anja finally said. "To Paperworld and to the restaurant."

"My pleasure. I think it was really, um, productive." Susanne shuffled her feet. "Kind of fun too. I learned a lot, so now we should be ready to—"

"Are you getting in?" the streetcar driver asked.

"Yes. Sorry." Anja climbed onto the streetcar and then turned back toward Susanne. "See you on Monday," she called through the closing doors.

As the streetcar accelerated down the street, Anja dropped into an empty seat and looked through the window at the lone figure on the sidewalk until she could no longer see her.

Chapter 10

On Monday afternoon, Anja was scribbling furiously, filling page after page in her notebook. Every now and then, she paused to brush a strand of hair out of her face with the end of her pen, and somehow she had managed to get a smudge of black ink right where the dimple on her chin was.

It repeatedly drew Susanne's gaze, and each time she had to force her attention back to what they were doing. The temperature in her uncle's office didn't help her focus either.

The room was tiny, and with two people sitting close together so they could peer at the screen of her laptop, it was starting to feel a bit like a sauna. Or maybe it was just her.

Anja didn't seem to be affected. She was focused entirely on the different social media channels Susanne showed her. A wrinkle of concentration had formed on her brow, deepening with every site they visited. Finally, she leaned back and rubbed her eyes. "This is kind of a lot."

In the past, Susanne had always ruthlessly enforced whatever was necessary for a business to prosper, with no regard to how the employees might feel about it. But now, after spending the previous Saturday at Paperworld and having dinner with Anja, she couldn't quite muster a cool, businesslike response. "I know. But it's the only way."

"It's really not that I'm too lazy to learn all of this new stuff. I just can't help thinking what if it's all wrong for us? It feels as if we're killing what we're trying to save."

"Killing? Definitely not. Studies show that companies that employ online—"

"Forget the studies." Anja dropped her fountain pen on the desk without her usual gentleness when handling her beloved writing instruments. "Our store is more than just numbers."

Oh man. Not that argument, please. Susanne couldn't help groaning. If she never again had to hear that same old the-spirit-of-the-company-is-more-important-than-making-money discussion, she'd die a happy woman. "Maybe, but without the numbers, there is no store. I thought we agreed on that."

"We did. But what if by making the numbers, we suffocate what Paper Love is all about—the love for stationery?" Anja gestured at the laptop. "We've been in here all day. I haven't seen a customer—a real-life customer, not just anonymous people on some stationery forum—or touched a notebook besides my own for even a second. What I love about this job is working with stationery, not just posting pictures about it."

The sadness in Anja's tone tugged on her heartstrings, but Susanne suppressed the feeling. Personal sensitivities had no place in business, and just because she kind of liked Anja didn't change that fact. "Listen, I don't mean to come across like a bitch, but—"

"If someone needs to preface a sentence like that, they usually are about to do just that," Anja muttered.

Susanne gritted her teeth so tightly that her jaw started to ache. "Listen," she repeated, pronouncing the two syllables carefully in an attempt not to shout. "Loving stationery is nice. But it's a hobby. And this," she pounded the desk, "is a business. It can't survive on love alone."

Anja stared at her and opened her mouth as if to argue back but then closed it and lowered her gaze to her notebook.

Damn. She had been a bitch, hadn't she? *Yeah well, so what if you were?* Knocking some heads was the only way to wake up people who didn't want to see reality. As much as she had enjoyed spending the day with Anja on Saturday, she wasn't here to make friends. But the internal monologue that usually guided her well didn't feel right this time, so she added more softly, "Not if we don't find a way to share that love with potential customers—and have them back up that love with their wallets."

Anja slumped against the back of her chair. The fight went out of her eyes, and that was worse than when she'd practically accused Susanne of being a bitch.

Susanne fought the urge to take her hand. "Don't worry." She allowed herself a quick pat to Anja's shoulder. "All the social media stuff only takes up a lot of time in the beginning. Once we have everything set up and you get the hang of things, it should only take you about an hour a day. We'll prepare plenty of blog posts and a few newsletters ahead of time so we can send them out once the website goes live. Those are the two most important things."

Anja nodded, but the overwhelmed expression on her face didn't fade. She picked up her fountain pen and clutched it as if it were a lifeline keeping her afloat.

Genius. You shouldn't have mentioned the blog and the newsletter. For Anja, they were probably just two more things that she didn't know how to handle yet. This was getting them nowhere. Susanne closed the laptop, pulled the fountain pen from Anja's grasp, and screwed on the cap. She slid the laptop, Anja's pen, and her notebook into her laptop bag. "Come on. I think we need a change of scenery."

"Working on the sales floor isn't going to help us focus," Anja said. "We'll have to take a break each time a customer comes in."

"Then it's a good thing we're going somewhere else."

Uncle Norbert looked up when they left the back rooms. "Are you calling it a day?"

"No, we'll be back in an hour." Susanne dragged Anja out the door, not giving her time to stop and commiserate with Uncle Norbert about the new direction she was steering the store in. She crossed to the other side of the street and carefully stepped over the *Bächle* with an extra long stride.

Anja laughed. "Still afraid you'll end up married to a local?"

"No. Afraid I'll end up with wet feet again." For once, Susanne didn't mind being laughed at since it seemed to shake Anja from the mood she'd been in. Hopefully, where she was about to take her would help even more. After all, Anja had said that food was her favorite coping strategy when she was stressed.

When Susanne stopped in front of the café down the street and held open the door for her, Anja paused next to her instead of entering.

"Thank you," she said quietly.

"Don't thank me yet. We're going to continue working in there."

Anja's eyes twinkled. "Well, we're women so we can multitask. We'll be able to work and eat cake at the same time, right?"

"Right." With just a few centimeters of space between them, Susanne couldn't help taking in every detail of Anja's face—her slightly upturned nose, the curve of her lips, the dimple in her chin.

"What?" Anja asked.

"Uh, you've got a bit of ink there." Susanne gestured.

"Where?" Anja ran her hand over her face as if she could find the ink stain that way.

"There." Susanne reached out but stopped herself before she could touch her. Instead, she tapped her own chin.

Anja pulled a little bottle of hand sanitizer from the messenger bag she'd grabbed on the way out and scrubbed at her chin with a tissue. "Gone?"

"Yes."

"Thanks for telling me. I know you said we need to do more promotion, but wearing our inks on my face doesn't seem like the right way to show them off."

Susanne chuckled, glad to see that Anja hadn't lost her sense of humor. She followed her into the café, past a glass counter with half a dozen different cakes and pies, to a small, square table at the back of the room.

Two glass doors to either side of their table led to a patio overlooking the Gewerbekanal—a canal that was a much bigger version of the *Bächle*. It gave this part of the city a bit of a Venetian flair, and Susanne could imagine how nice it would be to sit outside, right over the water, in the summer.

But, of course, she would no longer be here in summer, and that was a good thing, right? For a moment, she wasn't so sure.

"If you'd rather go somewhere else…" Anja said, as if sensing her conflicting feelings.

Susanne forced a smile. "No, this is fine." She took a seat at the small table and reached for the menu to discourage further questions.

Anja followed suit.

They ordered, and within a few minutes, the waitress brought their hot beverages—black coffee for Susanne and a chococcino for Anja—and two pieces of cake to the table.

Susanne's eyes widened as the waitress slid the plate with the Black Forest cake in front of her. "Oh my God. That thing is huge."

"Mm-hmm." Anja was already digging into her cheesecake, making little sounds that were a bit too erotic for Susanne's comfort.

"No Black Forest cake for you?" Susanne asked to distract herself.

Anja shook her head, looked left and right, and leaned across the table as if about to reveal a national secret. "Don't tell anyone, or I'll be sent into exile, but I don't like Black Forest cake."

Susanne clutched her chest in a dramatic gesture. "That's like being from Berlin and not liking *Currywurst*!"

"What can I say? It's too rich for me. I'm a woman of simple taste."

"No glitter, hmm?"

"Not in my cake."

Susanne slid a forkful of Black Forest cake into her mouth. The combination of whipped cream, dark chocolate, and liqueur-soaked cherries exploded on her taste buds. It was delicious but maybe not the best choice for a cake to be eaten during work hours. "Oh wow. I think they used about a liter of cherry liqueur. You might have to carry me back."

They finished their cake, then pushed their cups to the side so Susanne could place the laptop on the table.

Instantly, the glow that had settled on Anja's face while she had devoured her cheesecake faded. "You mentioned that a blog and a newsletter would be the most important things. But honestly, if I get things like that in my in-box, I just delete them. All this promo stuff just feels like…like being on a date with a really sleazy person."

The comparison made Susanne smile. "Then we'll have to make sure we're not that sleazy date."

"How?" Anja gathered some cheesecake crumbs on her fingertip and then licked them off.

The sight of it derailed Susanne's answer for a moment. She took a long sip of coffee to clear her head. "How do you make sure the person you're going out with wants a second date?"

Anja gave a wry smile. "I think that analogy is not going to help us. I haven't dated much in the past few years."

Susanne wanted to ask why. Was it because relationships were like glitter for Anja—nice to have but not really necessary? That was kind of how Susanne viewed relationships. Work had always been her number one priority. Was it the same for Anja? She shouldn't ask; she really shouldn't.

"We should use your dating life as an example," Anja said.

"God, no. It's about as disastrous as Paper Love's finances, so that's not going to help us either." Susanne decided to change the subject. "How about this? Imagine Uncle Norbert gives you a raise."

"He can't. He can barely afford to—"

"Just imagine it. Imagine you have a couple hundred euros to blow on pens and stationery stuff each month. What would be the first thing you'd buy?"

Anja stared off into space with a dreamy look. "Hmm, tough choice. Maybe a Pilot Capless, a Lamy 2000, or a Platinum 3776 Century."

"How would you decide on one?"

"I would go into a store with a decent selection of fountain pens and try out each one. See which one fits me best."

Okay, that wasn't helping. "But let's say there's no store in Freiburg that carries all these pens."

"There isn't," Anja said. "Some will probably have the Lamy, but not the others."

"So how do you decide, then?"

"Read some reviews and look at writing samples online, maybe see if there's a video comparing them on YouTube."

Susanne pointed her finger at her in a you've-got-it gesture. "So that's the kind of thing we need to put on our blog. Give potential customers what they are looking for, let your passion for geeky stuff shine through…and then discreetly point them to our webstore."

Anja brightened. "No sleazy sales copy?"

"No. You can put up lists of your favorite inks, review notebooks, and do Q&As for people just getting into fountain pens."

Anja gave her a teasing grin. "You mean things like how to avoid having a piston-filling pen seep ink all over your fingers?"

Susanne returned the grin and looked down at her hands, but of course the ink stains were long gone. "Yeah, stuff like that."

"I can do that." Anja clapped her hands, then paused. "But probably not all during normal opening hours."

"Can't Felix help out more?" Susanne asked. "I know he's only a part-timer, but I've barely seen him at the store since I got here."

"He's preparing for his exit exams, so since the beginning of the year he's only been working a few hours a month, mostly on Saturdays. Once he's done in March, he'll probably move away. Hiring someone else is probably out too, huh?"

"Oh yeah. At least for the moment."

"That's why Nobby needs me in the store during business hours."

Susanne rubbed her chin. That was a problem. She wanted to have at least a dozen blog articles ready to be posted by the time the website would go live next month. While she could edit them to make sure they had good search-engine-optimized keywords, she couldn't write them. She needed Anja for that. "What about…?" She hesitated. "After hours? Or maybe an hour or two on the weekend? I know it's a lot to ask, and you're under no obligation to—"

"I'll do whatever I can to save Paper Love. If that means giving up a few hours in the evening or on the weekend, then so be it," Anja said without a hint of hesitation. "We can start right now."

Wow. The passionate fire burning in Anja's brown eyes made Susanne speechless for a moment. "Right now won't be possible."

"Oh." Anja glanced away. "Of course not. It was stupid of me to assume you don't have any plans either."

Susanne shook her head. "I don't. Have plans, I mean. But I need to walk off some of that cake before we get started on the first blog post."

The smile returned to Anja's face. "We could take a walk around Fischerau," she swept her hand toward the area along the broad canal, "stop by the store and tell Nobby not to wait for us, and then come back here."

Susanne emptied her cup. "Sounds like a plan."

∽০৵৹

"Let me guess," Miri said when Anja called her on Thursday during her lunch break. "You're not going to be home in time to join me and Gino for a walk tonight either."

Anja paused next to the *do not feed* sign someone had put up in front of the stone crocodile that lifted its head out of the rushing water of the broad canal. She felt a bit like a beast too. "Yeah. I'm sorry, Miri."

Miriam sighed.

When silence stretched between them, Anja tried to cheer her friend up with a joke. "Aren't you glad we decided to be friends instead of girlfriends? I'd make a horrible partner at the moment."

"Well, if you put as much energy and passion into lovemaking as you put into these overtime projects you've been doing…"

"No offense, but ew."

When Miri laughed, Anja smiled but then sobered. "I really am sorry. It's not that spending time with you is no longer important to me. We're just under a lot of pressure to get everything up and running by the first of March, when we're hoping to have the webstore go live. I swear I'll make it up to you."

"Oh yeah, you will—and a lot sooner than March. All you've been doing lately is working, and that can't be healthy. I'll be dragging you up to the Schlossberg this weekend, and lunch afterward will be on you."

Anja knew resistance was futile, so she didn't even try. "All right. I guess Susanne and I could both use a break. I think she has plans this weekend, so we won't be working anyway."

"How's that going? Working with Paper Love's resident hottie, I mean."

"I thought I was the store's resident hottie."

"Compared to that tall sip of water? I love you to death, and you're really cute, but she's…" Miri made a sizzling sound.

Anja couldn't deny it. In fact, she had thought the same more than once this week, whenever she had looked up from the laptop to read Susanne a passage she had just written.

"So?" Miri prompted. "Is she a total slave driver or what?"

Two weeks ago, Anja would have assumed the same. "No, she's not. She's actually kind of fun to work with." She leaned against the railing and watched a duck settle down on top of the stone crocodile and start cleaning its feathers. "Most of the time, it doesn't even feel like work. We brainstorm ideas, then I write the posts while she takes the photos and proofreads."

"And you think that's not work? Are you at least taking breaks to eat?"

"Oh yes, don't worry. Susanne picked up Indian food twice this week."

"You're having Indian food without me?" Miri sounded as indignant as if she'd just found out her girlfriend was cheating on her. "Oh, you're so going to pay for lunch on Saturday! And I might just have the venison ragout instead of the *Flammkuchen*."

Anja laughed, knowing it was an idle threat. Miri never ate anything but *Flammkuchen* whenever they hiked up the Schlossberg, the hill rising to the east of the Old Town. "I need to get back. Thanks for understanding."

"You're welcome. I'll call you tomorrow."

Anja pressed the end-call icon and slid the phone back into her coat pocket. "See?" she said to the crocodile. "That's why I'm glad I'm not in a relationship. I doubt a girlfriend or boyfriend would have been so understanding."

Of course, the crocodile didn't answer, but the duck sitting on its head quacked once.

A second duck swam closer and climbed up onto the crocodile's head too.

As Anja watched them huddle close, she admitted to herself that not being in a relationship wasn't as great as she pretended most of the time.

∽◦◦◦∾

On Friday evening, an hour before closing time, Anja felt as if she finally had a good enough grasp on at least one of the social media channels the store now had.

The same couldn't be said of Nobby. His forehead wrinkled as he watched her scroll through the photos Susanne had posted so far, making him look like a pug—a pug whose favorite toy had been taken away. "Are the Instantgram and all those other things really necessary?"

"It's Instagram, Nobby." Anja gave him a sympathetic smile. "And yes, they're necessary. Once you get used to them, it's not so bad. You'll see."

It was the truth, even though she still occasionally struggled. Susanne was a patient teacher, never making Anja feel like a fool for asking questions or for taking a while to understand the many things she now had to learn.

"You just tap here and here, select a photo, write a description, click here and here…and voila, you posted a fun stationery picture." She demonstrated her newly acquired skills by posting the photo of the pastel-colored highlighters she'd taken earlier.

Susanne, who had just stepped out of the back room, peered over her shoulder. Since Anja was sitting on a stool, she had to bend down to see the phone, and a few strands of her hair tickled Anja's neck. "Um, not to take away from your great explanation or all the things you learned, but you forgot to add hashtags."

"Oh shit." Anja slapped her head. And here she had been so proud of her Instagram skills. "God, can't we just go back to printing flyers?"

Nobby nodded eagerly.

Susanne gave them both a stern but not completely unsympathetic look. "You know we can't. It's not so bad. You can just edit the post and add the hashtags." She reached around her and tapped the screen of Anja's phone.

Her arm brushed Anja's shoulder in the process, making her tingle all over.

"You tap here, press *edit*, and type in whatever hashtags you want." Susanne did it. "See?"

Anja could only hope that she would remember all of the steps. Susanne's closeness as they both gazed at the small screen was seriously distracting.

When the bell above the door announced the arrival of a customer, Anja hopped up from her stool behind the counter, glad to escape Susanne's proximity and the social media stuff that, at times, still threatened to put her brain on overload.

A woman in her late thirties entered the store and unbuttoned her long leather coat while she looked around, revealing jeans and a formfitting sweater.

"Good evening." Anja walked over and gave her a welcoming smile. "Can I help you?"

The woman's gaze took her in from head to toe. "Oh yes, you certainly can." Her tone and the smile she directed at Anja appeared almost a little flirty. "I'm looking for an old woman who's supposed to work here."

Old woman? Anja was the only woman on payroll, and while she had felt like an eighty-year-old after the trade fair last Saturday, she certainly didn't consider herself old. "Um…"

She felt more than heard Susanne walk up behind her. "I'm just seven minutes older, so if I'm old, what does that say about you?" She stepped past Anja and hugged the stranger.

Anja stared at them. That was Susanne's twin sister?

They were roughly the same height, and they both had the same slender build, but her sister's eyes were more blue than gray and her brown hair didn't have the subtle red highlights that shimmered in Susanne's hair.

Anja had, of course, known that they weren't identical twins, but somehow she had expected that she would recognize Susanne's sister immediately should she ever meet her. So much for that theory.

Susanne's sister greeted her uncle with a hug and then turned toward Anja. "You must be Anja. I'm Franziska, Susi's younger, better-looking sister. I'm glad I finally get to meet you. Uncle Nobby has told me so much about you."

Anja threw him a glance. "I hope only good things."

"Oh yeah. He always sounds as if he's ready to adopt you." Franziska took her hand in a strong but gentle grip and winked at her. "But I'm glad he didn't because that would make us cousins."

"Behave!" Susanne gave her sister a playful slap to the back of her head. The glare she sent her wasn't so playful, though.

"Hey!" Franziska rubbed her head. "I come all the way from Berlin, and that's how you greet me? To make up for it, you should have to pay for dinner. And lunch tomorrow. Who's on board?" She looked from her uncle to Anja.

Anja didn't want to intrude on Susanne's time with her sister, and she certainly didn't want to encourage her flirting. "Sorry. We're open for another hour, and I promised my best friend a hike up to the Schlossberg tomorrow."

"Ooh, that sounds great," Franziska said. "That's the one thing I haven't done on any of my visits. Uncle Nobby always claims he's too old to make it up there."

Nobby put on his most pained expression and pressed a hand to his back. "You young people go ahead and enjoy yourselves."

Anja bit back a smile. She knew Nobby was quite capable of making it up the Schlossberg, at least if she lured him with a beer and a *Flammkuchen* in the beer garden halfway up the four-hundred-and-fifty-meter-high hill. She squinted at him. Was he sending them off alone to play matchmaker and set her up with one of his nieces…and if yes, which one?

"Don't worry. We will." Franziska looked at Anja. "As long as you think your friend is okay with us tagging along."

Anja stared at her. How could twin sisters be so different from each other? While Susanne tended to be more reserved, Franziska had apparently never met a stranger.

"Are you crazy?" Susanne slapped the back of her sister's head again. "You can't just invite yourself along like that!"

"It's okay. I don't mind." Anja realized she hadn't just said it to be polite. She really didn't mind.

"Are you sure?" Susanne asked. "I don't want to hijack your plans for the weekend. After we've worked together so much this week, I bet you're sick of spending time with me."

Usually, Anja did relish having time to herself, but now she found that she wasn't sick of Susanne's company at all. Quite the opposite. While they had spent every evening together for the past week, their interactions were mainly about stationery and online promotions, and now she was curious to see how Susanne would be away from work with her sister. "I'm sure. The more, the merrier. As long as you don't mind getting slobbered on."

"Slobbered?" Franziska repeated. "Oh, you mean because you and your friend will drool over—ouch!" She glared at her sister, who had pinched her.

Susanne glared right back.

Anja had to laugh at their antics. "No. My friend has a dog."

"Oh, cool. I love dogs." Franziska's grin faded. "Seriously, though, are you sure your friend is fine with having us join you?"

"Yes," Anja said. Miri was always up for meeting new people and probably wouldn't mind spending part of the day with two beautiful women. "Don't worry about it. I'm sure you'll hit it off."

They arranged to meet in front of Paper Love at ten, then Susanne and her sister were out the door, with Susanne sending one last apologetic glance over her shoulder.

Anja sank back onto her stool. "Are you sure one of them isn't adopted?"

Nobby laughed. "I'm sure. They've always been very different. Franzi reminds me of my brother, while Susi…Susanne takes after her mother's side, at least when it comes to her personality."

"Is that the reason her sister kept visiting you, while Susanne didn't? Just different interests?"

Nobby's laughter abruptly stopped. "I really don't know what made her stop visiting."

"She's been here for three weeks, and you still haven't asked her?"

He glanced down and traced a faded ink stain on the counter with his fingertips. "Now that she's here, I don't want to chase her off by bringing it up. I don't want her to think I'm trying to make her feel guilty. I'd rather just enjoy her company while it lasts, you know?"

"Then why not come with us tomorrow? We wouldn't have to go all the way up. We could just have lunch at the beer garden if it's open and then walk back down."

He softly squeezed her shoulder. "I appreciate it. But I'll be meeting Ulrike to go to the farmers market tomorrow morning."

Ulrike had been his neighbor and close friend for as long as Anja had known him, but lately, there had been a twinkle in his eyes whenever he mentioned her, so Anja couldn't resist teasing him. "Ooh! You've got a date! Why didn't you just say so?"

Even his beard couldn't quite hide his blush. "It's not a date. We're just buying vegetables."

"Oh, is that what people over sixty call it?" Then she stopped teasing and gave him a sincere look. "I'm really happy for you."

"Hey, I said it's *not* a date. It hasn't even been a year since Ulrike lost her husband, and at my age, you're not ready to jump into something new that fast." But he smiled every time he mentioned her name.

"Well, then I'll just be happy that you're buying vegetables and getting your vitamins."

"Thanks." He nudged her. "Come on. Let's crunch the numbers for today and try to get out of here on time. We've both got big plans tomorrow."

Chapter 11

Anja and Miriam were already waiting when Susanne and Franzi arrived in front of the store at ten o'clock. While the dog excitedly jumped around them, Anja made the introductions.

She looked good this morning in a pair of faded jeans, scuffed hiking boots, and a red-and-black, fleece-lined jacket that she'd left open because the sun was shining. For once, Freiburg lived up to its reputation as the sunniest city in Germany, and the temperature was almost springlike, even though February had just started.

Susanne unbuttoned her own coat too.

Two people on bikes whizzed past them on the cobblestoned street, so Anja led them across the street to the sidewalk and then continued on in the direction of the Swabian Gate.

Susanne couldn't help noticing how effortlessly Anja and Miriam stepped over the *Bächle* without even giving it a glance, as if they just sensed that the narrow canal was there. In contrast, Susanne had to consciously pay attention not to step into one of them again. "What purpose do they serve?"

Uncle Norbert or one of her other relatives who lived in the area had probably explained it to her when she'd been a child, but back then, she hadn't really paid attention.

"I think in the Middle Ages, they were used as a water supply for animals and for preventing fires," Anja said. "Nowadays, they're just—"

"Glitter," Susanne finished the sentence, remembering what Anja had said about things that were nice to look at but not really necessary.

Anja laughed. "I guess you could see it that way."

Franzi and Miriam traded confused gazes, but neither Susanne nor Anja explained the *glitter* comment.

"But I like them," Anja added. "They're just so…so Freiburg."

Susanne admitted to herself that she was coming to like them too. They were a remnant of a time long gone and no longer served a real purpose, but being around Anja and her notebooks and fountain pens was starting to give her an appreciation for the more old-fashioned things in life.

"Sounds like you haven't had much time to play tourist," Miriam said. "What parts of our beautiful city have you seen already? Have you seen the Schwabentor?" She gestured toward the medieval tower guarding one of the city gates.

Susanne glanced up at the knight standing over a slayed dragon depicted on this side of the tower. "I've driven by this guy a few times."

"This guy is St. George, patron saint of Freiburg," her sister said. "And what do you mean…driven by? You've been in Freiburg for nearly a month now, and you still haven't really seen anything?"

"Like Miriam said, I haven't had much time to play tourist. But I've seen the Gerberau and the Fischerau," Susanne said, naming the two streets closest to Paper Love. "And, of course, the famous *Bächle*."

"You didn't see it," Anja corrected with a smile. "That's why you stepped into it."

Franzi roared with laughter. "You stepped into a *Bächle*? You know what that means, don't you?"

Susanne huffed. "I'm not superstitious."

Anja led them up a couple of steps to a bridge crossing a busy street. Once they made it to the other side, they followed a path that circled up the Schlossberg, which despite its name—Castle Hill—looked more like a forested mountain to Susanne. She fell into step next to Anja, while Franzi and Miriam followed behind them, deep in conversation, and the dog trotted ahead with his tail wagging the entire way.

After a few minutes, they passed a beer garden. Long, orange tables and wooden benches had been set up beneath old chestnut trees. People were sitting outside, eating pretzels and *Flammkuchen*. The scent of bacon, onions, and melted cheese from the pizza-like dish drifted over.

Susanne shook her head at the people.

"What?" Anja asked. "You don't like *Flammkuchen*?"

"I love it. It's just… In Berlin, beer gardens aren't even open in February."

Anja shrugged. "Well, that's Freiburg for you. At the first rays of sun, the street cafés and beer gardens open, even if they have to provide blankets to their customers."

"It's the same in Berlin—but a month later."

Soon, the paved footpath turned into a hiking trail through sun-dappled woods. Birds were singing all around them, and a woodpecker hammered away in a tree above them. Susanne admired the way the fresh air brought color to Anja's cheeks. She breathed in deeply. God, how long had it been since she'd taken the time to go hiking or just enjoy a day outside?

For a while, only birdsong, low chatter from a group walking ahead of them, and the crunching of their shoes over the path interrupted the silence.

"How come your sister knows Freiburg so well and you don't?" Anja finally asked.

Susanne took several more steps while she thought about how much she wanted to tell her. Usually, she would just claim that her career and her busy life had left her no time to visit relatives, but it seemed wrong to fob off Anja with that excuse. Because that was what it was, she realized now: not much more than a feeble excuse.

"I stopped coming here after…" She threw a glance back over her shoulder to make sure Franzi was still talking to Miriam. It wasn't that she wanted to keep secrets from her twin; she just didn't want to bring up painful memories for her. Or maybe she didn't want to make herself even more vulnerable by having her and Miriam listen in.

"You don't have to tell me." Anja touched her hand. "I didn't mean to be nosy."

Susanne looked down at her hand. "It's okay. It's not like having your parents go through a divorce is such a unique experience."

"Guess not. But it can still be painful."

Something in Anja's tone made Susanne look up to study her face. "Your parents divorced too?"

"No. But maybe they should have. They don't have the best marriage. It's not like they hate each other, but there's not much love there either. Basically, they are just roommates who hardly talk." She sighed. "Was it that way between your parents too?"

"Oh no. They talked plenty. Well, argued, really. My father was not fit to be a husband…or a father." Susanne kicked a branch out of the way. "I mean, he was a fun playmate, and he always bought the latest gadgets, so we loved spending time with him as kids, but when it came to taking responsibility and setting rules to raise us right, he left it all to our mother. She always says it was like having a third kid. I guess he never really grew up."

"Wow. I had no idea," Anja said. "I met him once, when he visited Nobby. He seemed…nice."

Susanne nodded. "He is nice. But he lives in his own world with high-flying dreams that never work out. He'd start a business, then grow bored with the everyday details and jump onto the next brilliant idea. By the time my parents divorced, they were up to their necks in debt—which he stuck my mother with. She had to work like a maniac to save her own company. Nearly ruined her health over it."

Anja paused for a second before continuing on, leading them around a bend in the winding path. "I'm sorry. Is she okay now?"

The question and the compassion in Anja's tone touched her. "Yes. She's fine. But she had to cut off contact with my father to not be dragged back into his mess."

"Is that what you did too?" Anja asked quietly. "Cut off contact with him and his side of the family?"

"No. I…" Susanne bit her lip. That wasn't what she had done…was it? "I'm still in touch with him." Well, she called him on his birthday and on Christmas, just as she talked to Uncle Norbert and the rest of that part of the family a couple of times a year. She had always put it down to work and the physical distance, but she had to admit that she kept in touch with her mother's side of the family much more.

Anja let her chew on that in silence for a while, as if sensing that Susanne needed some time to think.

"Nobby isn't like that, you know?" she said when the path became steeper. "I mean, he might be a bit of a dreamer, and he's not a great businessman by any means, but he's the most constant, loyal person I know. He's worked at Paper Love for nearly fifty years. He's not chasing after new dreams every other week."

"I know." Susanne struggled to breathe evenly, and it wasn't just because of the hike up the hill. She was stunned at how much she had told Anja. She couldn't remember ever telling anyone this much about her family history.

Before she could decide if she should say anything else, the path took one last turn, and they reached a square. Benches were set around several massive, old trees and close to the edge of the square, which offered a breathtaking view over the city and the surrounding area.

Susanne walked up to the waist-high railing. The cathedral and the Old Town lay below them, and behind them, a mountain range stretched out in the distance. "Wow."

Anja stepped next to her. "That's the Vosges."

"So that's France already?" Susanne pointed at the horizon.

Anja nodded. "We're just thirty or forty kilometers from the border and not much farther from Switzerland. There's an observation tower a bit higher up. You'll probably have an even better view from there. Want to go?"

"Sure." She turned toward her sister. "Are you up for a bit more hiking?"

Normally, Franzi was up for pretty much anything and never admitted defeat before Susanne did, but this time she hesitated. She exchanged a glance with Miriam. "Miri has promised to introduce me to the *Flammkuchen* in the beer garden."

What the hell…Miri? Half an hour ago, her sister hadn't even known Miriam existed, and now she was already calling her by her nickname? Well, at least she was no longer flirting with Anja. "If you wait a little, we could all have *Flammkuchen* together."

"We can't take Gino up to the observation tower." Miriam pointed at her dog and threaded her arm through Franzi's. "We'll wait for you down there. Just join us whenever you're ready."

Before Susanne could think of something to say, the two strolled back to the path leading to the beer garden.

Anja stared after them. "I was pretty sure they'd hit it off, but I didn't expect this." She gestured at the disappearing act they were pulling. "Your sister isn't going to break Miri's heart, is she?"

"Hey, why do you think my sister's going to be the heartbreaker? It might be the other way around." Truth be told, she wasn't too worried about her sister. Franzi usually was quick to jump into flings but slow to lose her heart to anyone.

"True." Anja shook her head at them, then turned toward Susanne. "Well, they're both adults."

"At least according to their passports," Susanne threw in.

Anja chuckled and set them off toward an even steeper, winding path.

For a moment, Susanne half expected Anja to thread her arm through her own the way Miriam had done with Franzi, but she didn't. Susanne shoved her hands into the pockets of her coat and pushed away the weird feeling of disappointment coursing through her.

It took a bit of searching for them to find the tower because there were no signs pointing out which path they needed to take. "Sorry," Anja said, sounding a little breathless from the hike. "It's been a while since I was here."

"I don't mind," Susanne said and found that it was true. It was nice to be so far removed from her everyday life and the problems they dealt with at work. She looked around the slopes of the hill. "Why is it called Schlossberg?" They were nearly at the peak now, and still there wasn't a castle in sight.

"There was one…or rather several throughout the centuries, but they were all destroyed in one war or another. You can still see the ruins in some places, though."

Finally, a thirty-meter-high lookout tower rose up in front of them. With its long steel supports it looked like a huge bundle of Mikado sticks. A narrow spiral staircase with hundreds of metal-grate steps circled up to a round platform halfway up and then continued to two other platforms at the very top and slightly below it.

Susanne paused to catch her breath for a second, then headed toward the tower. Several steps up, she stopped again.

Anja hadn't followed her. She stood rooted to the spot at the base of the tower, clutching the metal railing.

"Aren't you coming?" Susanne called down to her. "I know this is probably old hat to you, but…"

"No, that's not it." Anja scraped the bottom of her hiking boot along the ground. "I've never been up there. I'm, um, not too fond of heights."

Susanne jumped down the few steps she had already taken. "We don't have to go up there if you don't want to. We can join Franzi and Miriam for some *Flammkuchen*."

"No, no. You go up. I'll wait here."

Susanne hesitated. "But don't you want to see the view from up there?" She pointed at the top of the tower.

"Yes, of course I do, but—"

"Then come on. We'll do it together." She offered Anja her hand.

Anja's gaze darted back and forth between her hand, her face, and the tower. She swallowed audibly.

Susanne waited patiently, not pressuring her or trying to grab her hand to pull her up the stairs. Anja had to decide this for herself.

Finally, Anja loosened her white-knuckled grip on the railing and accepted Susanne's hand.

Her fingers were cool and clammy. Susanne entwined them with her own in a secure grip. "You can do this. But if it gets to be too much, just tell me, and we'll go back down, okay?"

Anja pressed her lips together and nodded.

Hand in hand, they took the first step, then another. The staircase was winding and narrow, so they had to walk with their shoulders brushing. Susanne let Anja walk on the outside, where the stairs were broader.

"Couldn't they at least have built concrete steps, not these see-through metal grates?" Anja grabbed the railing with her free hand.

"Don't look down. Keep your eyes on the horizon."

The higher they climbed, the paler Anja became, but she followed Susanne's advice and kept her gaze on the horizon…or on Susanne.

When they neared the circular platform halfway up the tower, Susanne paused. "Want to keep going or stay at this level?"

Anja's grip on her hand tightened. "Keep going…I think. As long as I focus on the physical activity of climbing, it's not so bad."

"Okay." Susanne led her higher up on the winding staircase.

Steps pounded on the metal stairs above them, and a family with two kids climbed down toward them, forcing them to let go of each other's hand and continue single file so the family could pass.

As they lost contact with each other, Anja latched on to the back of Susanne's coat.

Susanne turned her head to look at her. "You okay?"

Anja nodded. "Let's keep going before I lose my courage." Once the family had passed them, she took up her spot next to Susanne again and they continued.

They hadn't even taken two steps before Anja shyly reached over and took her hand again.

Smiling, Susanne squeezed her fingers. She couldn't help admiring Anja's courage.

It didn't take long for them to reach the next platform, almost all the way at the top of the tower. There was another, slightly bigger one right above them.

The muscles in Anja's jaw tightened, but she marched on without Susanne having to ask if she wanted to go higher up.

Seconds later, they emerged onto a circular platform. From there, another, much shorter winding set of metal stairs led up to the crow's nest at the very top of the tower.

Susanne looked back and forth between it and Anja. "We don't need to go all the way up…unless you want to."

Anja hunched her shoulders against the cold wind and stared up at the crow's nest. "I made it this far, so what's a few more steps? No big deal, right?" Her wide-eyed gaze belied her words, though.

"You don't have to prove anything to me."

"I'm not. I just…" Anja raked her teeth across her bottom lip.

God, did she have to look so sexy doing that?

"I feel like I've been avoiding things I was too afraid to take a closer look at, and I don't want to do that anymore."

"You mean Paper Love?" Susanne asked.

Anja nodded. "Yeah. That and maybe a couple of other things. It's time to face my fears."

Susanne's admiration for her grew. She wondered what other things Anja had been afraid of but decided not to ask. They had already told each other too much for two people who had only just met three weeks ago. But that didn't mean she would let Anja go through this scary experience alone. "Is there space for two up there?"

"I think so."

"Then let's go up together. Just like saving Paper Love, you don't have to do it alone."

Anja exhaled shakily. "Thank you."

Susanne chuckled. "Don't thank me yet. I was the one who practically dragged you up here."

As they walked to the stairs leading up to the crow's nest, Anja's grip on her hand tightened until it was almost painful, but Susanne didn't complain. She put one foot onto the first step and looked at Anja. "Ready?"

Instead of an answer, Anja climbed the first step too and then kept going. She mumbled something with every step they took.

"Are you counting the steps?" Susanne asked.

Anja stared straight ahead. "No, just telling myself how crazy I am." A tremor ran through her voice.

"You're not crazy. You're brave."

"Debatable." Anja's steps slowed, and she stared down at the ground thirty-five meters below. She became even paler, if that was possible. "Oh God, that's really high."

Susanne wanted to take her into her arms and wrap her in a bubble of safety. But since that was not a bright idea, she searched for something to say that would distract her. She asked the first thing that popped into her mind. "That person you kissed in the movie theater…was it a boy or a girl?" As soon as she'd said it, she wanted to take it back.

At least it got Anja to look up, away from the ground, to stare at her. "Uh, what?"

"Forget it, okay? I was just trying to distract you. And it worked. Look where we are."

Anja looked around as if only now realizing they had reached the crow's nest. The tiny platform was shaped like a half-circle and was just big enough for two people if they didn't mind being close—and Susanne didn't mind at all.

They huddled together, with the wind tugging on their coats and hair. Up here, she could sense the slight swaying of the steel tower beneath her feet.

Susanne told herself that it was the incredible three-hundred-and-sixty-degree view, not Anja's proximity, that took her breath away.

Below her, the spire of the cathedral soared above the gables of surrounding buildings. She could make out the Rhine Valley and the Vosges in the distance, while the hills and mountains of the Black Forest framed them from the other side.

"Wow," Anja murmured next to her. "My knees feel like overcooked spaghetti, and my stomach has relocated to my throat, but this might actually be worth it."

"Yeah." Susanne chuckled. "I feel like spreading my arms wide and shouting, 'I'm the king of the world.'"

"Queen. And it was a boy."

"What?"

They faced each other. The wind had put some color back into Anja's cheeks.

"The person I kissed in the movie theater. It was a boy."

"Oh. And you didn't like it?" Susanne couldn't keep herself from asking. Her feeble attempts at staying professional had been doomed the moment she had agreed to spend part of the weekend with Anja.

"He was cute and all, but it was so awkward." Anja let out a laugh that sounded nervous. "Neither of us had any idea how to kiss. One of my best friends volunteered to teach me, and kissing her was…oh wow. It was pretty confusing because I knew I liked boys too."

"And you never suspected you might be bisexual before that?"

"No. I mean, I had crushes on a girl or two, but I thought they were just straight girl crushes. I thought everyone felt that way. Until Nicole kissed me."

Despite the cold wind, Susanne felt warm all over. Maybe the height was getting to her too, or maybe it was the mention of a kiss, but Susanne couldn't look away from Anja's lips.

They trembled just the tiniest bit.

"Are you still scared?" Susanne asked, her voice low.

"No. Yes."

"Which one?"

"I…I'm scared…and a little cold," Anja said.

Susanne moved even closer to provide some warmth and comfort.

Anja gripped her coat again, this time bunching her fingers into the fabric at Susanne's hips.

They stared into each other's eyes. Susanne's gaze darted down to Anja's mouth, which seemed to be coming closer and closer until Susanne could feel her warm breath on her lips.

This is wrong. So wrong. Oh God. Her eyes fluttered shut.

A pounding noise made Anja jerk away at the last moment.

Susanne's eyes flew open. She needed a second to realize it wasn't her thumping heartbeat but another person tramping up the stairs.

He paused halfway up and shaded his eyes with his hand. "Are you coming down?"

That was exactly how Susanne felt—like a drug addict coming down from a high, crashing back into reality. She wasn't sure her vocal cords would work, so she just nodded.

Without saying anything, they squeezed past him, went back down to the platform, and then kept going as if by a silent agreement.

"Are you okay?" Susanne asked after a few steps. Then she realized that Anja might interpret it as an invitation to talk about that near kiss, and she wasn't sure she was ready for that. "I mean, with your fear of heights, going down is probably not any easier. If you need to hold on to me…" She held out her hand.

Anja visibly hesitated. "Not a good idea."

"Holding my hand? Or…?" Susanne pointed toward the crow's nest.

"The latter…both… I don't know."

They paused on the second platform, which was thankfully empty except for them.

Susanne ran her hand through her wind-ruffled hair. "You're right. I mean, we both know I'm not staying, and we're starting to work really well together. It would be madness to risk that for a fling that can't go anywhere…right?"

"Uh, right."

Had there been a flash of regret in Anja's eyes?

Don't flatter yourself. Move on. "So we're fine? I, um, I like working with you, and I don't want there to be any awkwardness between us."

"We're fine," Anja said. "No awkwardness."

Susanne should have been relieved, but somehow she felt less than satisfied as they continued down the stairs.

Anja tentatively went from one step to the next, clinging to the railing. Going down was probably even harder for her because now she couldn't keep her gaze on the horizon; she had to look down so she wouldn't miss a step.

Maybe she should have kept her mouth shut, but Susanne couldn't watch her suffer like this. "Anja? Since we established that we like working together…how about we treat this as a team-building experience?"

"Meaning?" Anja asked, her voice tense. She continued to stare down at the metal grates and the ground beneath.

"Rely on your team members to get you down safely." She extended her hand.

Anja hesitated. "I never said I like working with you." A twinkle chased away the scared look in her big eyes.

"Oh, so you're suffering through your workdays, and all that laughter I heard from you when we played around with the Instagram filters yesterday was just... what?"

"Tension," Anja said with a straight face.

"So then why don't I hear the same sounds now? I'd think being up here would make you very tense."

"Um, because... Okay, okay, maybe I like working with you too. Not at the beginning, but now you seem...bearable."

"Bearable?" Susanne tried her famous ice-queen glare but couldn't quite manage it. "All right. That's good enough. Come on." She stretched out her hand a little farther, and this time Anja reached for it.

They held on to each other more tentatively than before. The gesture seemed to have lost its innocence.

Don't overthink it. It was okay to like working with Anja. Trying to be an effective, emotionless robot at work might have proven successful in her previous job, but it wouldn't get her far in her uncle's store. Even liking Anja as a person was okay. As long as she didn't start liking her too much or giving in to this damn attraction, they would be fine.

∽ი௦ℓᔕ

Miri waved until Susanne and Franziska, still standing at the streetcar stop, were out of sight. She dropped into the free seat next to Anja and pulled Gino closer so he wouldn't get in the way of other passengers. "I never thought I'd ever say this about a dentist, but, God, she's cute!"

"Yes, she is." Anja buried her hand in Gino's fluffy fur—the same hand that had held on to Susanne's earlier today. She could still feel the warmth of her skin and the reassuring pressure of her fingers as Susanne had led her up the observation tower. Before she could think too deeply about what had happened—or almost happened—up on the crow's nest, she shook herself out of her daze. Only then did she realize what she'd just said. "I mean, she seems like a very nice woman, but she lives in Berlin, and if she's anything like her sister, she has no intention of moving to Freiburg. Plus Susanne said she's a big flirt. Heck, she even flirted with me when she came to the store yesterday."

"Hold your horses. I never said I want to marry her. You know me. I'm the queen of casual dating and hot sex. I'll leave that whole happily-ever-after commitment thing to you. But you have to admit that she's cute…and hot." Miri fanned herself with both hands. "And one hell of a kisser."

Anja's head jerked around. "You…" She lowered her voice so the other passengers wouldn't be able to listen in. "You kissed her?"

"Well, technically, she kissed me, but I wasn't exactly an unwilling participant." Miri flashed her a grin.

"Christ, Miri! You've known her for all of…what?" She glanced at her wristwatch. "Five hours?"

"So?" Miri turned in her seat to face her. "Anja, you know I love you to death, but you and I…we're very different people. If I see something I want, be it a promotion at work or a kiss, I go after it, while you…"

"While I…what?" Anja prompted when Miri fell silent.

"While you hesitate and double-check and think about it for so long that by the time you finally make up your mind, your chance is gone."

Was that what had happened up there on the crow's nest? "Well, thinking about it first before jumping in with both feet is a good thing, isn't it? Otherwise, you could make a mistake that you'll end up regretting."

"So what if you make a mistake or two?" As they approached Betzenhausen, Miri pressed the button for the streetcar to stop and nudged her to get up. "That's life. Without taking a few risks, you miss out on so many good things."

Anja followed her out of the streetcar. "Who says I'm not taking risks?"

"When was the last time you kissed someone? And I'm talking about an I-want-to-tear-your-clothes-off kind of kiss, not just a friendly peck on the cheek."

Anja's mind flashed back to that moment on the crow's nest, with her hands on Susanne's hips and Susanne's breath on her lips. *That was not a kiss. It was just…a momentary confusion.*

When Anja didn't answer, Miri did it for her. "Two years ago!"

Two years, three months, and a couple of days. Not that she was counting or anything.

"And I know it's not because you're still hung up on your ex. You're just too chickenshit to get involved with someone new and potentially get hurt."

"Hey!" As they paused at the intersection where they had to go separate ways, Anja nudged her. "I'm not chickenshit. I'm…risk-averse. But I'm working on it, okay? I'll have you know that I went all the way up the observation tower earlier."

Miri dropped Gino's leash and then bent to pick it up. "What? Last time I wanted to drag you up there, you said even wild horses couldn't get you on that thing!"

Heat crept up Anja's neck. "There were no horses involved."

Miri gave her a knowing look. "Just one business consultant who's just as hot as her sister."

"It wasn't like that. She just encouraged me, and she was with me every step of the way, so climbing the tower wasn't as scary."

"So I take it you don't think she's an ass anymore?"

It was hard to believe that she'd ever thought that, but Susanne hadn't exactly been on her best behavior at first. "No. She's not an ass." She held up her hand. "But that doesn't mean I want to get involved with her."

"If she's even half the kisser her sister is, you don't know what you're missing."

"Miriam." Anja growled.

"Okay, okay. Suit yourself. But you'll join us tomorrow morning, right? Franzi invited us to have brunch with her and Susanne."

Anja loved brunch, but she needed to use Sunday to get her equilibrium back before the workweek started and she would once again spend her days and most of her evenings huddled close in front of a laptop with Susanne. "No. I'm not going. I promised myself I'd start going swimming on Sunday mornings again."

"Come on. You can start up swimming next week."

"You were the one who said I have to get out more, meet new people, so I signed up for water volleyball after I swim my laps."

Miri sighed. "Are you sure you don't want to postpone that and have brunch with us instead? Poor Susanne will sit there like an idiot while Franzi and I stare into each other's eyes."

The thought of Susanne feeling ignored and neglected almost made her give in, but then she strengthened her resolve. "No, thanks. You go have brunch; I'll go swimming." At least while she was swimming laps, she'd stop thinking about that moment up on the observation tower and imagining what might have happened if they hadn't been interrupted.

❦

Later that day, Franzi put down her cutlery, dabbed her lips with the red napkin the restaurant had provided, and leaned across the table. "What's up with you, Sis? You haven't said more than three words since we got here."

Susanne looked up from where she had cut her salmon-spinach-and-potato gratin into little squares. "Nothing. Just focusing on my food."

"Uh-huh. Are you angry because I kind of ignored you most of today?" Franzi covered her face with both hands and peeked through her fingers. "God, I'm the worst sister ever. I come here to spend time with you, and then I abandon you for

Miri. It's just that she's fun and really great to talk to. I feel as if we've known each other for ages. But, of course, that's no reason to just—"

"I'm not mad at you." If anything, she was mad at herself for nearly kissing Anja.

Franzi lowered her hands to the table. "You're not?"

"You know me. Is this," Susanne pointed at herself, "my angry face?"

Her sister studied her carefully. "No." She squinted and leaned even closer until Susanne squirmed. "This is your I'm-pining-over-a-woman face."

"Nonsense!"

"The lady doth protest too much, me thinks. Wait!" Franzi shoved her half-eaten plate of Swiss raclette cheese away as if she'd lost her appetite. "Now I get it! That's why you're not mad at me for abandoning you today. Because you got to spend time alone with Anja. You *like* her."

Susanne shrugged as casually as possible. "Not at first, but…yeah, she's all right, I guess."

Franzi shook her head. "No, I meant you like *like* her. As more than just a colleague."

"You're imagining things. You're the one who gets crushes on people at the drop of a hat, not me." But the conviction she'd aimed for wasn't there.

"Oh, cut the bullshit, Susi. Remember, you're talking to me—your womb mate. What's going on between the two of you?"

Susanne sighed and pierced one of the gratin squares on her plate with her fork. "Nothing. She's an employee."

"Uncle Nobby's employee, not yours."

"Which still makes us colleagues, and you know I don't mix business with pleasure. It always gets messy."

"But you are interested in her?" Franzi asked.

"I'll be gone in less than eight weeks."

"So that's a yes. I knew it."

Susanne put her fork down with a clank. "That's a big, fat no. Besides, I wasn't even thinking about her right now." It was the truth…if you left out the fact that she now wanted to save Paper Love for Anja as much as she wanted to save it for her uncle.

"What were you brooding about, then?"

Susanne sighed. "Money."

Franzi sent her a worried gaze. "You're not in financial trouble, are you? I know you're not getting any money for helping out Uncle Nobby, and the rent in Freiburg is not exactly cheap. If you need help, I can—"

"No," Susanne said firmly. "I've got enough money saved to keep me afloat even if I didn't work for the rest of the year, if that's what I wanted."

"Why are you thinking about money, then?"

"Because Paper Love needs a website with an integrated webstore, plus a newsletter and plenty of online ads to survive."

Franzi nodded and started eating again. "That makes sense."

"Yeah, but a professionally designed and developed webstore will cost about ten thousand euros."

Franzi nearly choked on a bite of potato. "Ten thousand?" she gasped out and took a large gulp of wine. "Wow. And people think dental work is overpriced."

"There are cheaper options, but we'd have to upgrade eventually, so in the long run, we would just be wasting even more money." Susanne forced herself to continue eating as she remembered Anja pointing out that she ate too little whenever she was stressed.

"Yeah. It's the same in my job. If you go for cheap fillings, you'll only end up paying more later."

"The problem is that Uncle Norbert doesn't have that kind of money. His savings are just about depleted." Susanne took her time chewing a forkful of salmon. "I'm thinking about lending him the money."

Franzi froze with her wineglass in hand. "You…you want to lend him ten thousand euros?" Her voice came out in a squeak.

"I don't know if *want* is the right word, but I don't see any other way to save Paper Love."

"It's not that I want to talk you out of it. I'm all for helping him. It's just that you always said you'd never, ever make the same mistake that Mama made with Papa when she gave him all her money and cosigned his loans."

"I know what I said. But this is different." She wasn't sure that it really was. She had promised herself to keep work and her private life separate, to never go into business with family or friends, and to never lend large amounts of money to anyone. Now it felt as if she was doing all three of these things.

"I agree. And you know what makes it different?" Franzi asked and then continued without waiting for a reply. "Mama was alone back then. You aren't. I want to give you half of the money you need for the webstore."

Susanne vehemently shook her head. "No. I'm not taking a cent from you."

"Why not? I'm his niece too. Why should you carry all the risk alone?"

"Because you just had to replace a…" The correct word failed her, so she made a drilling sound.

"Actually, it was an automatic autoclave. Not that it matters. I still want to help out. So fifty-fifty?"

Susanne groaned. "Why do I have to have such a stubborn sister?"

"Genetics, dear womb mate." Franzi winked at her. "Come on. Just say yes. You'll have a much easier time selling this idea to Uncle Nobby if we're sharing the costs."

That much was true. "All right, you little pest."

They finished the rest of their meal in companionable silence. Susanne was too deep in thought to say much. Somehow the unshakable rules and convictions she had lived her life by had been turned upside down within just three weeks. Less than a month ago, she had assumed her uncle was a sentimental fool for wanting to hold on to his little store, and now she was pumping her own personal money—and that of her sister—into it, with no guarantee that they'd get even one cent of it back.

This city was really messing with her head.

๛๛

An unfamiliar noise ripped Susanne from the middle of a dream. She mumbled a protest. "Mmpf, Anja?"

Then the cobwebs of sleep receded. Of course it couldn't be Anja, even though faint impressions of the dream she'd had still lingered. She and Anja had climbed a giant fountain pen, walking hand in hand as they had today, and when they had reached the golden nib at the top, she had pulled Anja close, threaded her fingers through her windblown hair, and—

And then nothing. Just as they had been about to kiss, something had woken her. She curled her empty hand into a fist. God, it had felt so real. She could still feel Anja's hand in hers and her breath on her lips.

Yawning, she mentally cursed whatever had woken her. She couldn't get involved with Anja in the waking world, so at least getting to kiss her while asleep would have been nice.

But her sister's bad timing had ruined that. Had Franzi gone to the bathroom, and the unfamiliar noises of another person in the apartment had woken her up?

Susanne opened her eyes, now fully awake.

The room was dark except for the faint glow of her alarm clock, which revealed that it was three o'clock. She had left her door ajar in case her sister needed something, but in the hall leading to the living room, where Franzi slept on the new couch, everything was quiet.

The same couldn't be said about her bedroom.

A rhythmic rrrrr-rrr-rrrrr sounded right next to her.

"What the…?" Susanne flicked on the lamp on the bedside table. Light flared on, blinding her for a moment.

Once her eyes had adjusted to the sudden brightness, she could make out the cat that was perched in a sphinxlike position on the mattress right next to her.

"Muesli! What the hell are you doing here?"

The cat continued to purr.

Her bedroom window was closed, as were all the other windows in the apartment—at least they had been when she had gone to bed—so he couldn't have sneaked in that way.

Susanne gritted her teeth. Franzi must have let him in. Earlier, when they had returned from the restaurant and Muesli had given his usual tap-and-meow concert on the other side of the French door, Franzi had voted for letting him in, but Susanne had refused. So much for her sister respecting her decision. Franzi had probably intended for him to sleep on the couch with her, but instead, Muesli had gone looking for Susanne.

It was strangely touching. *Yeah, well, he probably thinks the bed is more comfy than the couch.*

Should she pick him up and put him outside? It would be the right thing to do, or he would get attached to her and then end up being hurt when she left.

Muesli stretched out more comfortably on his side and kneaded the covers at her hip with his front paws.

The rhythmic touch and the soft purring were soothing and chased away the loneliness that had settled over her at the abrupt ending of the dream.

Loneliness. Bah. She scoffed. *Since when do you get lonely? You've got work, and Franzi is in the next room.*

But despite that pep talk, she couldn't bring herself to climb out of her warm bed and put the cat outside. Besides, if she kicked him out now, he would probably keep her and Franzi awake with his tapping and yowling.

"Don't get used to it," she mumbled as she closed her eyes and curled around the small, warm body. She fell back asleep within seconds.

A wet tongue licked a path up her neck.

Susanne moaned. "Mmm, a little softer, honey."

The rough licking stopped, then something pulled her hair.

"Ouch! What the fuck?" Susanne pulled her head away and opened her eyes.

The cat sat next to her pillow. When he saw that he had successfully woken her, he jumped off the bed and strutted to the half-open door, where he paused and looked back at her with a demanding "meow."

Susanne sat up and wiped her neck. "You honestly think I'm gonna feed you as a reward for waking me up—again?"

"You talking to me?" Franzi asked from the kitchen. The hardwood floor in the hall creaked, then she stuck her head into the bedroom. "Ah. This is where he ended up. I thought so. I'm making coffee. You want a cup?"

"Yeah, in a second." Before she could take her sister to task about letting the cat in, Franzi disappeared.

Muesli followed.

"Don't feed him," Susanne called after her.

"Why not? No wonder you don't have a girlfriend if this is how you treat your overnight guests!"

"Haha." With a grunt, Susanne tossed off the covers and padded to the kitchen.

Franzi rummaged through the cabinets, probably in search of something she could feed the cat.

"And if this is how you listen to the person you share living space with, it's no wonder you don't have a girlfriend...or a boyfriend either. I told you not to let him in or to feed him."

Muesli circled them both, purring and meowing.

"Come on, Susi. Give him some tuna or something."

Susanne shook her head. "You know I'm not staying. It would be mean to lead her on."

Franzi leaned against the counter and studied her. "Her? Muesli is a male, isn't he?"

Oh shit. Had she really said that? "Him. It would be mean to lead him on."

A grin curled Franzi's lips. "Why do I get the feeling it's not the cat that's on your mind?"

"Because you have an overactive imagination." Susanne threw up her hands. "Fine. Give him the tuna. I need a shower." She fled to the bathroom before her sister could start another discussion about Anja.

Chapter 12

"What do you think?" Anja peered across her kitchen table at Susanne. The article about gift ideas for stationery addicts was the tenth blog post Anja had written, but she still held her breath while she waited for Susanne's judgment.

Or maybe it was the way Susanne looked that made her breathless.

Since it was Saturday, they had met at Anja's apartment to prepare more blog posts for the website launch. Susanne had traded her power suit for faded jeans that clung to her in all the right places and a sweater with its sleeves pushed up, revealing her toned forearms. Her hair tumbled loosely onto her shoulders.

Susanne held up one finger in a give-me-a-minute gesture while her eyes flicked left and right over the laptop screen. A wrinkle of concentration formed between her brows. Finally, she looked up, and the wrinkle smoothed out when she smiled. "It's great."

"Really?" Anja couldn't help beaming. Susanne's praise warmed her more than the mug of hot chocolate she had made for them.

"Really," Susanne said with a decisive nod. "It almost makes me want to buy a fountain pen."

"Ooh. That's high praise coming from a pen-clueless, digital-only snob like you."

"I'm not pen-clueless. I'll have you know that I can now tell a Lamy 600 from a Pelikan 2000."

A giggle rose up in Anja's chest. "It's Lamy 2000 and Pelikan M600."

"I knew that. I just wanted to make you laugh."

Anja studied her. Had she really done it on purpose, just to hear her laugh?

Susanne tapped the edge of the laptop screen as if to direct Anja's attention back to the blog post. "So I would keep the second half exactly as it is. But maybe you could revise the beginning a little."

Anja slid her chair around the round table in her mini kitchen, closer to Susanne, so she could glance at the opening of the blog post. "It's not working?"

"It is, but I think it would work even better if you could add a more personal touch. You keep saying that it's what your…our customers want, right?"

"Right." Anja rubbed her chin and tried to think of something but came up empty. "Any suggestions?"

"Maybe you could weave in a personal experience. Have you ever gotten stationery or writing instruments as a gift?"

Anja grimaced. "Yes. I once got a fountain pen from my first girlfriend, but I sold it a year later because it wasn't working."

"The pen?" Susanne asked. "Or the relationship?"

"Neither. It was stiff and about as bendable as a nail—and that's true for both the nib and my ex." Anja surprised herself by answering honestly. She had been the one to do all the compromising in the relationship, even contemplating moving halfway across the country to Hamburg, while her girlfriend hadn't been willing to meet her halfway to make their life together work.

"That sucks." Susanne gave her a compassionate look. "I hope it got better after that."

"Are we talking about gifts or relationships?" Somehow she got the feeling Susanne was more interested in hearing about her relationships than about any stationery presents she might have received.

Susanne hesitated.

"It's okay to be curious and ask questions, you know?" And it really was okay, she realized. In the past four weeks, she had gotten more comfortable with Susanne. She didn't even feel self-conscious about the size of her apartment anymore, maybe because Susanne really seemed to like it. "That's what people do when they make new friends, right?"

Susanne's gaze flicked over to her. "Are we? Friends, I mean?"

The memory of their almost kiss up on the tower flashed through Anja's mind, as it had more often than she cared to admit in the week that had passed since then. It had been a decidedly more-than-friendly moment, but she ignored it. "We could be. I don't think I've ever spent so much time with anyone, and we haven't killed each other yet, so…"

"We've been too busy working to hatch murder schemes." After a moment, Susanne cracked a smile. "But let's assume I was asking about relationships. I mean, I could report them to the LGBT police if the lesbians and bi women down here in Freiburg are not treating you the way they should."

Anja chuckled. "I didn't have another girlfriend after her, so the lesbian and bi women in Freiburg are safe for now."

Susanne's eyes widened. She put down the mug she had just picked up without taking a sip of her hot chocolate. "Wait. You mean bendable-as-a-nail woman was your first and *only* girlfriend?"

Anja's defenses went up so fast that she could almost hear the metallic clank as the parts of her steel armor snapped into place. "Yes, but that doesn't mean I was just experimenting or confused or taking the easy way out because my two other relationships were with men."

"Whoa!" Susanne held up both hands, palms out. "I never said—or thought—any of that. Do you really think my sister would let me get away with such a stupid biphobic attitude?"

Anja's cheeks flamed hot. "Sorry." She averted her gaze and stared into her almost empty mug instead. "I've been faced with some pretty ridiculous assumptions when I told people about my relationship history. The last woman I was interested in didn't want to date me after finding out I'm bi because she was convinced it wouldn't be long until I'd cheat on her with a man."

"Christ. She definitely deserves being reported to the LGBT police for that." Susanne's voice sounded rough, as if she'd love to help dole out any kind of punishment they would decide on. "I haven't known you very long, but I'm pretty sure you'd never cheat on anyone."

The invisible armor Anja had surrounded herself with shattered into a million little pieces. Susanne's instinctive trust in her felt incredibly good. "Never."

Susanne nodded. "So you've only ever had three relationships?"

"Yes, unless you count Miri. Is that so out of the ordinary?"

"No, but—wait! You and Miriam were a couple?"

Anja laughed at her wide-eyed look. She always found it satisfying to see the controlled woman lose her cool. "No. We tried, but there just wasn't any…" She gestured, searching for the right word.

"Spark," Susanne finished for her.

Their gazes met and held until Anja forced herself to look away. "Yes." *Unlike the two of us.* She pushed the thought away, as deeply into the recesses of her mind as it would go. "How about you?"

"No spark between Miriam and me either," Susanne answered with a straight face. "I think my sister would kill me if there was. Did you know Miriam is in Berlin, visiting her, this weekend?"

"Yes, Miri told me."

Susanne shook her head. "They've known each other for all of a week. I'll never understand how some women get involved so fast!"

"Don't worry. Miri isn't the U-Haul type, and Franzi seems to be more into fun than commitment too. But don't think I didn't notice that you're trying to distract me from my question." Anja poked Susanne's shoulder, then let her hand linger there as she sensed the warm skin beneath her sweater. *God, get a grip.* She snatched her hand away. "If you want to be friends, I can't be the only one confessing embarrassing relationship stories."

Susanne shrugged. "That's the thing. I don't really have any relationship stories, embarrassing or otherwise. Compared to the long-term relationships you must have had, mine really don't deserve that name."

"So you've just had one-night stands or short flings?" A hollow feeling settled in the pit of her stomach at the thought, even though she told herself it didn't matter whether Susanne was the relationship type or not.

"I'm not a womanizer by any means. I've had flings, but I've also had just as many long-term relationships."

"Then why do you say they don't deserve that name?"

Again that one-shouldered shrug from Susanne. It was kind of cute how awkward or maybe embarrassed the confident woman suddenly appeared.

"I don't know," Susanne said. "Even those relationships that lasted longer stayed kind of superficial. More like casual dating than let's-bare-our-souls-and-move-in-together relationships."

Anja tried to imagine what that must be like. Probably dinner and sex but very little talking about things that really mattered. But she drew the line at asking her that. It was bad enough that she kept having flashbacks to that near kiss; she didn't need to start fantasizing about what Susanne would be like in bed.

"I guess I was…am too caught up with work to invest much time or energy into a relationship," Susanne added.

Anja studied her, trying to figure out if Susanne was happy with that kind of love life. But before she could make sense of the complex emotions darting across her face, Susanne tapped the laptop. "You know what? Let's just leave the gift ideas blog post the way it is. It's one of many, so it's not worth wasting that much time on it. Want to do the next one?" She held out the list of blog topics they had brainstormed.

For a moment, Anja considered tackling the *Beginner's Guide to Traveler's Notebooks* or *Eco-Friendly Pens and Paper*. But at the thought of having to write yet another blog post, her brain threatened to go on strike. "No. I need a break from all the blog prep." She took the list from Susanne and closed the laptop. "Let's do something fun instead."

"Fun?" Susanne repeated with a dubious expression, as if she'd forgotten the meaning of the word.

Anja smiled. "Yeah. Something fun…with our hands," she couldn't resist adding. She told herself she wasn't flirting, just teasing a new friend a little.

Susanne's gaze went to Anja's hands, and a sensual smile played around the corners of her mouth. "Were you thinking of anything in particular?" Her voice was a seductive purr.

Anja shivered as goose bumps spread over every centimeter of her skin. That would teach her not to tease Susanne. Apparently, she could out-flirt her without making half an effort. "You don't want to know what I was thinking of," she mumbled under her breath. More loudly, she added, "Paper boats."

The look on Susanne's face made Anja burst out laughing.

"Paper boats?" Susanne repeated.

"Yes. Were you expecting something else?" Anja asked in her most innocent tone.

"No. I was thinking of origami all along, of course."

Anja grinned at her. "Mm-hmm. Sure. I've been thinking about what you said at Paperworld. About tying our products to our location. One of the things that make Freiburg special is the *Bächle*. They even sell *Bächle* boats at the farmers market."

"Yeah, I saw them. What about them?"

"I thought we could make our own. Not for sale, just as a decoration to point passersby toward the store. We could make paper boats, place them on a sheet of Plexiglas, and put it on the *Bächle* right across from Paper Love. That way, the paper boats would look like they are bobbing on the water."

Susanne leaned back on her chair, stretching her long legs out beneath the table. When she put one hand behind her head and directed her gaze to the ceiling while she seemed to think about it, Anja's gaze was drawn to the delicious line of her body.

God, she really needed to get a hold of herself.

"I like it," Susanne finally said. "We would need to get a permit from the city, but I think it's worth the trouble. If we had an entire armada of paper boats, they could form an arrow pointing at the store."

"Ooh, great idea!" Anja jumped up and rummaged through her desk drawer for colorful paper and other craft supplies. When she returned to the table, she slid her chair back to its old position, away from Susanne's distracting closeness, before she sat down. "Okay, let's get started."

"Uh, I think you should be our designated boatbuilder. I'm the digital expert, remember? I'm not very good at that creative stuff." Susanne held up her hands and wiggled her fingers as if to prove a point.

Anja studied her long, slender fingers. She seriously doubted that those fingers would fumble awkwardly, no matter what they were doing. Her mouth went dry, and she emptied her hot chocolate, which had long since gone cold. "Nonsense. We said we're in this together. Anyone can build a paper boat, even a five-year-old kid. It'll all come back to you once we start."

Susanne shook her head. "I don't think I ever made one, even as a child."

"Seriously?" Anja had never heard of anyone not knowing how to build a paper boat. "No one ever showed you?"

"Not that I remember."

Determined, Anja slid a turquoise sheet of paper in front of her. "Then I'll teach you how to do it." She ignored Susanne's grumbling and took the pink sheet for herself. "First, you fold your sheet in half. Then you fold the top corners to meet in the middle."

She hadn't made a paper boat in a very long time, but muscle memory kicked in. Apparently, her fingers remembered the steps. After each one, she waited until Susanne had copied what she was doing. "Now fold up the flaps at the bottom and tuck in the corners."

Susanne did as instructed. "I thought we were making a boat, not a party hat."

"Patience, young Padawan." Anja playfully poked her with one corner of her own party hat before taking it and opening it up. "Pull the two sides of the hat apart in the middle and push the corners together so that it forms a square."

"Jeez, I've put together Ikea furniture that was easier to assemble," Susanne mumbled.

"You have Ikea furniture? You?"

"What, you think I have only artisan solid wood furniture, where a single bedside table costs a thousand euros?"

"Um…" Truth be told, Anja had assumed something like that.

"I splurged on a really nice couch and a massive desk for my apartment in Berlin, but other than that, my furniture is mix and match. A friend of mine loves finding furniture at flea markets and then restoring the various pieces. She even had me help with my dresser and a bookcase."

Anja imagined Susanne lovingly running a sanding block or a paintbrush along a piece of wood but quickly banished the image from her mind. "And yet you're complaining about a simple paper boat? Keep going, woman!"

"Yeah, yeah. What's next?"

"You fold up the bottom points on each side." She held up her piece of paper, which now was a triangle again. "And then you repeat what you did earlier, pulling the sides apart in the middle to make it a square again."

Susanne struggled a little. The cute line between her brows made a reappearance. Finally, she held up her own square. "Got it."

"Now comes the tricky step. You pull the top parts outward."

"Which parts?"

"This and this." When Anja reached over to show her, their fingers brushed. Both froze.

Warmth spread from Anja's fingers to the rest of her body. God, how could an innocent little touch like this affect her so much? It took all her self-control not to caress Susanne's fingers, trail her hand up her wrist to the soft skin on the inside of her forearm, and then…

She swallowed heavily. *Stop torturing yourself.* With a trembling finger, she tapped the two points at the top of the square, this time careful not to brush Susanne's hand again. "These two." Her voice was husky.

Was it just wishful thinking, or were Susanne's hands a little unsteady too as she pulled the two parts outward? "Oh. What do you know? It's a boat. Well, kind of."

The sail in the middle was coming apart where she hadn't folded it quite right.

Susanne chuckled and ran her thumb along the sail to fix it. "I think we should name this one the *Titanic*."

Anja put a yellow sheet of paper in front of her. "Try another."

This time Susanne did it without help, and Anja wasn't sure if she should be proud of her student or disappointed that there would be no more accidental brushes of their fingers.

Once Susanne had all the steps memorized, they raced each other to see who could make a boat faster or who could make the smallest paper vessel.

"Hey, you're cheating!" Anja threw the *Titanic* at her. "Don't think I didn't see you using two sheets of paper for the first two steps so you can finish the next one faster."

Susanne continued folding unrepentantly. "All is fair in love and paper boat making."

"God, you're so competitive!" But Anja's complaint wasn't for real. Secretly, she liked that Susanne challenged her to do things differently and to push herself.

Finally, they had used up Anja's entire package of craft paper. They finished their last boats and looked up at the exact same moment.

The table was covered in a fleet of colorful paper boats in various sizes.

"Wow. I think we went a little overboard." Susanne laughed. "That's way more than we need." She picked up one that Anja had made before they had started racing each other and traced the skull-and-crossbones toothpick flag Anja had inserted at the top. She looked over at Anja. "Beautiful."

Her gray eyes held such a soft expression that Anja couldn't believe she had ever thought them cold. She wanted to thank her for the compliment, but looking into Susanne's eyes, she couldn't get the words out.

Susanne cleared her throat and redirected her gaze back to the boat in her hands. "You should do this in the store, you know?"

"Fold paper boats?"

"Offer a seminar on origami or that calligraphy thing you do with the brush pens. Once people see what works of art you can create, they'll want to do it too, and they'll buy the craft supplies they need in the store."

"I'd love that! When can we start?"

Susanne laughed. "Let's wait until we've built up our newsletter a bit. Otherwise, you might sit there with me as your only student."

Anja wouldn't mind at all. She bit her lip so the words wouldn't slip out. "Pick one." She gestured at the pile of boats and chose a purple one with a smiley face on the sail for herself.

"Why?"

"Because as you keep saying: how can we recommend our products to our customers if we haven't tested them out? We're going to float them on the lake."

"Lake?" Susanne repeated slowly.

"Yes. It's not even a ten-minute walk from here, and it'll be nice to get some fresh air after being stuck inside all day."

"You want us—two mature adults—to float paper boats in public on a Saturday afternoon, when there'll be plenty of people at the lake?"

Anja smiled. "Too chicken to do it?"

Susanne huffed, stood, and grabbed the boat she had dubbed the *Titanic*. "Come on. The one whose boat sinks first buys dinner."

∽∾∾

It was after nine and the sun had long since gone down by the time Susanne finally got up from Anja's sofa. When Susanne's paper boat had been kidnapped by a curious swan, Anja had laughed and declared herself the winner of their bet, so Susanne had paid for takeout from Kashmir. They had taken the food back to Anja's apartment, and the time had flown by while they ate, decorated their boats, and talked.

Anja followed her into the hall and stood watching while Susanne put on her coat.

Susanne opened the door but made no move to step through it. They had spent most of the day working, so why did this feel like saying goodbye after a date? An amazing date even. She couldn't remember when she had last had so much fun and talked so openly.

"Thanks for coming over." Anja shuffled her slippered feet. "I had a great time."

"Yeah, me too."

Anja grinned. "Even when your boat got swan-napped?"

The term made Susanne laugh. "Maybe I shouldn't have named it *Titanic*. With a name like that, it was doomed from the start. But at least now we can say even swans love our paper products, right?"

"Right."

They smiled at each other. Seconds ticked by, then Susanne gave herself a mental kick before she could get sucked in by the warm glow in Anja's brown eyes. "Well then, I'd better go."

"Yeah."

Susanne hesitated. Should she hug her? They had decided to be friends, and that's how friends said goodbye, right? But was it really a good idea to—?

Before she could finish her internal discussion, Anja stepped forward, right into her personal space, and wrapped her arms around her in a quick hug.

Anja was several centimeters shorter, her forehead coming up to Susanne's mouth, and she hugged with the same mix of carefulness and abandon that she'd put into making the paper boats.

Susanne enfolded her into her arms. When she felt Anja's warmth, her body pressed a little closer without her conscious decision. Her eyes fell closed of their own accord. How could a simple hug feel so amazing?

Then, before Susanne was ready, Anja let go and stepped back.

Susanne quickly opened her eyes.

"Want to get together to prepare two more blog posts tomorrow?" Anja asked.

A part of her wanted to nod enthusiastically. *Yeah, the part called libido.* But she knew it was more than that. She genuinely enjoyed Anja's company, and somehow that was even worse.

"Hey, if you want to have a real day off, that's no problem," Anja said when Susanne took a while to answer. "We can do it on Monday or—"

"No, that's fine. We can do it tomorrow." She was an adult, after all, not a teenager who couldn't control her hormones.

"All right. Just call whenever you want. Other than water volleyball in the morning, I don't have any plans."

That conjured up visions of Anja in a bathing suit or, God help her, a bikini. She tried to swat the thought away, but like an annoying fly, it returned immediately. "Will do. Good night."

"Good night. Drive safely."

Before Susanne could do something stupid, like try for another hug, she turned on her heel and jogged down the stairs.

Just as she reached the front door, someone on the other side prepared to unlock it.

Susanne opened the door and held it open for the couple in their sixties. She had seen them before and knew they lived on the same floor as Anja. She gave them a polite nod.

Instead of returning the nod and walking past her, the woman paused and stuck out her hand. "I'm Regina, and this is my husband, Volker. I thought now that you moved in with Anja, we'll be seeing more of each other, so we should introduce ourselves."

Susanne had already extended her hand when she realized what Anja's neighbor had just said. Her fingers went limp in the woman's enthusiastic grip. "Oh, no, no, I haven't moved in. I'm not... We're not a couple."

"Oh. I'm so sorry." Regina hastily let go. "I thought..." She gestured upstairs. "Since you spend so much time at Anja's..."

"We're working. We..." Susanne snapped her mouth shut. She didn't owe them an explanation, and why did she care what they thought? She just hoped Anja had closed her apartment door already and wasn't still standing in the doorway, where she might be able to hear their conversation.

Volker patted his wife's shoulder. "Well, it's nice to meet you anyway."

"Uh, likewise. Have a nice evening."

"You too." They squeezed past her and climbed the stairs.

Susanne stepped outside and let the door close behind her. God, that had been awkward. But then again, there were worse things than being mistaken for Anja's girlfriend. If things were different, she could see herself... She cut herself off before she could finish the thought and marched to her car without looking back.

Chapter 13

Drumbeats and the sounds of trumpets and trombones drifted into the store when Susanne opened the door to drag in the carousels of greeting cards.

Anja looked up from the ink bottles she was restocking.

"Did you see that?" Susanne pointed outside. "A coven of witches is checking out our paper boats."

Anja stepped next to her and peered through the glass door.

Half a dozen witches in costumes and carved wooden masks had paused in front of the paper boats they had set up on the *Bächle* across the street that morning. One of them pulled out a handful of confetti and sprinkled it over the boats before the group moved on toward the Schwabentor. The medieval gate was the meeting place for the marching bands and carnival groups gathering for the Rosenmontag parade. The huge carnival parade was held every year on the Monday before Ash Wednesday, but it had been a couple of years since Anja had attended—mostly because watching alone wasn't much fun.

Anja and Susanne grinned at each other.

"I guess now we can say that both swans and witches like our boats," Susanne said.

Nobby shook his head. "There is no carnival group dressing up as swans."

"We know." Anja patted his shoulder. The swan incident was hard to explain, and the recounting probably wouldn't be as funny as watching Susanne's face when the swan had escaped with her boat. "It's an inside joke."

Never in a million years would she have thought that she and Susanne would one day have inside jokes that only they understood. She had never had that with anyone but Miri.

"Guess I'm too old to understand it," Nobby muttered. "You two should get out of here if you don't want to miss the start of the parade. I'll finish up."

Susanne wheeled the carousels farther into the store. "I'm not going to the parade."

"Oh, yes, you are," Nobby said. "All the other stores in the city center are closing for the rest of the day too, so there's no way I'll let you keep working. That stuff you do on the computer can wait until tomorrow. Anja, get her out of here and take her to see the parade."

Well, an afternoon off would be a nice change of pace, especially if she got to spend a part of it with Susanne. Anja got their coats and pressed Susanne's into her hands. "Come on. I've got to do what my boss says. You don't want to get me fired, do you?"

Susanne snorted but put on her coat and followed her to the door.

"Thanks, Nobby," Anja called over her shoulder.

"You don't need to show me the parade," Susanne said when they got outside. "It's not like we don't have carnival parades in Berlin. Well, they aren't as big or as popular, and there won't be one this year, but that doesn't mean we have to go see the parade here. You can just go home, if you want."

"Actually, I can't. I left my bike at home this morning because last year at carnival someone decorated it with paper streamers, and it took me half an hour to get it all off."

"What about the streetcar?"

"They aren't running until after the parade, so I'm stuck here for the next three hours."

Susanne sighed. "Guess that means I'm stuck too, hmm?"

Anja glanced up at her. Would it really be so bad for Susanne to spend some time with her away from work? The thought stabbed her chest like a sharp needle. "No. Not if you don't want to. I'm perfectly fine watching the parade on my own."

A twinkle entered Susanne's eyes. "Nah. Someone has to protect you from all those witches."

"Oh, so you're going to take on the role of my protector?"

Susanne shrugged. "I wouldn't want to have to face Nobby and tell him I let his best employee be witch-napped."

"And that's the only reason you'll go to the parade with me?" Anja had meant to make it a teasing joke, but her tone was much more serious than she had intended.

They looked at each other, then both glanced away.

"No," Susanne said so quietly that Anja almost didn't hear her over the sound of the trombones. "I also really like spending time with you."

A slow smile curled Anja's lips, then grew into an ear-to-ear grin. "I enjoy your company too. Very much so. I…"

Two people in cat costumes rushed past, probably late for the parade. The jingling of the bells around their wrists interrupted Anja before she could say more—and maybe that was a good thing. Susanne had made it clear from day one that she wouldn't be staying, so getting too attached to her was guaranteed to end in heartache.

Susanne placed a hand on the small of her back and urged her forward. "Come on, or we'll miss the best candy."

"I think they hand out candy mainly to the kids."

"To kids and to people with an irresistible smile," Susanne shot back.

Anja nudged her. "God, you sure aren't suffering from an inferiority complex." Of course, she secretly had to agree. Susanne did have an irresistible smile.

"Who said I was talking about me?"

Anja's stride faltered. Heat rose up her chest and fanned out over her cheeks. "Oh."

Laughing, Susanne led her down the street, with her hand still on Anja's back.

Anja peeked over at her. Did Susanne really think her smile was irresistible?

Nonsense, she told herself. *So far, she has managed to resist it just fine, hasn't she?*

By the time they made it to the Schwabentor, the parade had already started, and they ended up squeezing in among the crowd lined up at the side of the street, watching the costumed groups, marching bands, and the occasional carnival float pass by.

Since Anja was shorter than most of the people around them, she chose a spot in the front, where she could see all the costumes. It didn't take long to dawn on her that it probably hadn't been the best idea. The kids in front of her grabbed all the candy, and as the first adult in the crowd behind them, she was the target of all the practical jokes.

A sailor marching alongside a horse-drawn boat on wheels painted a lipstick heart on her cheek, a bunny rubbed its giant stuffed carrot over her head until her hair was a mess, and a devil in a fiery-red costume tickled her nose with a horse tail on a stick.

Anja whirled around to her self-appointed protector, who was bent over with laughter. "You're a complete failure as a bodyguard." She had to lean close and shout to be heard over the loud music from the marching bands. "Everyone is picking on me. Why am I the only one who's getting singled out?"

Grinning, Susanne plucked a bit of confetti from Anja's hair. "It's because you look cute and approachable. I'm more intimidating."

"Oh, if you're so intimidating, then come here and do what you promised—protect me." She pushed Susanne in front of her as a human shield, and Susanne let herself be dragged around with a laugh.

But now she blocked Anja's view, so she peeked around her. Her cheek rested on Susanne's shoulder, and when the crowd behind her surged forward to catch some candy being thrown, she had to grab hold of Susanne's hips not to lose her balance.

It instantly reminded her of being pressed against her in the overly full train to the stationery fair, but at the same time, it felt different. In the two and a half weeks since Paperworld, she had really gotten to know Susanne. She wasn't pressed up against an attractive woman she barely knew—this was Susanne, the person who had helped her climb a thirty-meter tower and who had gone to the lake with her to float paper boats.

Susanne glanced back at her. "You okay?" The mirth dancing in her eyes had been replaced by a look of concern.

Anja nodded, even though she wasn't sure how okay she really was.

A squeak from the little girl in front of them directed her attention back to the parade.

Another group of witches marched past. The eyes carved into their wooden masks glowed an eerie green. One of them approached, swishing a broom over the feet of the people in the first row, while his—or her—other hand slowly reached into one of the two canvas bags strapped to the costume.

Anja ducked behind Susanne's back and grinned triumphantly. Finally, Susanne, who so far hadn't been hit by a single bit of confetti, would get her share of it.

But when the witch's hand reappeared, it held a piece of candy instead. "For you," a female voice came from behind the mask. She knelt and offered it to the little girl, who took it and then ducked behind her mother.

Susanne laughed. The sound vibrated through Anja since she was still holding on to her hips.

The witch rose and stood toe-to-toe with Susanne.

Anja held her breath. She knew there was nothing to fear; the practical jokes were all in good fun. But suddenly, a wave of protectiveness swept over her and she regretted putting Susanne in the line of fire.

Susanne stood without squirming, staring into the glowing green eyes.

The witch reached into the other bag and pulled out a handful of pink confetti.

Anja tried to drag Susanne back, but with the crowd surrounding them, there was nowhere to go.

The sorceress took a step forward. Instead of tossing the confetti at Susanne, the gloved hand reached around her and deposited it on Anja's head.

"Hey!" A bit of confetti trickled into her collar, making her hunch her shoulders.

The witch tapped her long, wooden nose as if to mock Anja and continued on her merry way.

Anja shook herself like a dog trying to get rid of fleas, but that only dislodged more confetti from her head and made it slide down her back. "Why me again?"

Susanne's laughter, loud and unrestrained, drowned out the drums and trumpets for a moment. "Well, you love paper, so…"

Anja pulled a bit of confetti from her hair and flicked it at her. "I love it on my desk, not in my hair."

Another witch approached, but this one sidestepped Susanne too and tossed confetti at the person next to her.

"See?" Susanne grinned. "They're scared of me."

"Oh yeah? Well, I'm not." Two quick steps, then Anja reached into the witch's bag, pulled out a handful of confetti, and dragged Susanne down by her unbuttoned coat. Without pausing to think about what she was doing, she stuffed it into Susanne's collar.

Her knuckles brushed the warm skin on Susanne's upper chest.

Anja froze. *Oh my God. I've got my hand down her shirt.*

Susanne stood without moving, not backing away. Her pupils were wide as she stared at Anja.

"Uh, sorry. I didn't mean to, um…" Anja withdrew her hand and let go of Susanne's coat.

Still, Susanne made no move to step back or to get rid of the confetti that was now probably trickling down her chest, down her flat belly, and maybe even finding its way—

A tap on her shoulder stopped Anja's mind from imagining exactly where that confetti might end up.

When she turned, she came face to face—or rather face to mask—with the witch whose confetti she had just stolen. The sorceress or sorcerer towered over her and reached into one of the bags.

Uh-oh. Anja prepared for yet another confetti shower. Well, she deserved it.

But instead, the witch pulled out a piece of candy and held it out to her.

Dazed, Anja took it and stared after the witch, who ran off to catch up with the rest of the group. For a second, she wanted to run too, but she knew she had to face Susanne. Slowly, she turned back toward her. "Sorry. That went a little far."

"It's okay. I was asking for it."

"Were you?" Anja murmured, more to herself than to Susanne.

When Susanne shrugged, a bit of confetti trickled out of her pant leg.

Anja tried hard not to imagine all the places it had touched in between. *Lucky confetti.*

Grimacing, Susanne pulled her blouse from her slacks and shook out as much of the confetti as she could. "Come on. I think we both got as much carnival as we can take."

"The streetcars still aren't running," Anja said.

"Then come home with me."

The words and a bit of huskiness in Susanne's voice made shivers run up and down Anja's body.

Susanne laughed and nudged her, easing the tension between them a little. "To *work*. Get your mind out of the gutter! I was talking about us writing another blog post, and since I live within walking distance, we might as well do it at my apartment. I can drive you home once we're done."

"I knew what you meant," Anja said, even though her head was spinning and she didn't know much of anything anymore. *Work, work, work,* she told herself every step they took toward Susanne's apartment. They were just going to work.

Right?

⸻

Susanne was very aware of Anja's presence behind her as she unlocked the door to her apartment. Her body was still buzzing from the brush of Anja's fingers along her chest.

When she took Anja's coat from her to hang it on a hook next to her own, the fleeting touch of their fingers sent heat coiling through her. *Get yourself together. She's not some woman you're taking home to have sex with.*

It didn't feel like it either—she had never cared much what the women she had occasionally taken home thought about her apartment, but Anja's opinion mattered.

As she led her through the hall and into the dining room, she tried to see her temporary home through Anja's eyes. She hadn't hung any pictures or added other little touches that would have made the place feel more homey. The only piece of furniture she had bought since moving in had been a couch so Franzi would have a place to sleep. The dining room, however, was still as bare as ever, and the kitchen hadn't gotten much use either.

Compared to Anja's small but cozy home, her apartment was seriously depressing.

"Um, I didn't see the point of buying a lot of furniture since I…" Her voice echoed through the nearly empty dining room, making her return to Berlin sound like something threatening instead of something to look forward to. She forced herself to say it anyway. "Since I'm not staying much longer."

Anja said nothing. She followed Susanne into the living room, which thankfully looked a little homier. Since there were only three pieces of furniture—the recliner, the coffee table, and the couch—it wasn't as if Anja needed long to take it all in, but to Susanne the seconds seemed to tick by slowly.

She shoved her hands into the pockets of her slacks and watched while awaiting Anja's final judgment.

"Is that why we always meet in the café or go to my apartment when we work on promotional stuff?" Anja asked. "Because you don't have much furniture?"

Susanne nodded, even though deep down, she knew it wasn't the only reason. Inviting Anja into her apartment felt like giving her even more insight into her life and personality, adding one more layer of intimacy, and that was probably not a good idea.

Yeah? So then why bring her here now? They could have gone to a café in the city center and passed the time until the streetcars were running again.

Anja bent over the coffee table and studied the framed photo that Franzi had brought as a housewarming gift. "Oh my God, that's so cute! Is that you and your sister?"

Susanne groaned. This was exactly why she had never let colleagues visit her apartment. But then again, Anja was more than just someone she worked with, wasn't she? "Yes. Please ignore the hair."

"What happened? Don't tell me you cut each other's hair!"

"That's what it looks like, right?" In the photo, their bangs almost reached their hairline, and one side was shorter than the other. "But, no. That was the year my father thought he could make money selling Atari consoles, even though the video game industry was crashing for a couple of years in the eighties, and my mother tried to make up for it and save money by giving us haircuts instead of sending us to the hairdresser. She couldn't get the bangs right and kept trying to even them out, so they became shorter and shorter."

Anja giggled. "How old were you?"

"About four or so. Too young to defend myself against this accidental mullet."

Still grinning, Anja traced the crooked line of four-year-old Susanne's bangs with her index finger, a gesture that looked so tender that adult Susanne shivered.

Cut it out, idiot!

Anja directed her attention to Susanne's parents, who stood behind them in the picture.

Both of them were smiling, even though Susanne remembered the fight they'd had over the haircuts gone wrong.

"You really look a lot like your father," Anja commented.

Susanne heard that a lot, but she could never see it. Or maybe she didn't want to see it. "I guess."

Anja turned away from the photo and studied her instead. "That's not a bad thing, is it? He's a good-looking guy."

"So you think I'm good-looking too, hmm?" That almost made up for being compared to her father.

Anja's cheeks flamed a bright pink, but she held Susanne's gaze. "You don't like being compared to him, do you?"

A sigh worked its way up Susanne's throat. "I don't hate him or anything, but whenever my mother points out that I'm like him in some way, she doesn't mean it as a compliment."

"If he's anything like Nobby, he can't be all bad, can he? I mean, your parents went through a divorce. Has it ever occurred to you that your mother isn't totally objective when it comes to your father?"

"Yes, of course," Susanne said, but it was more of an automatic response. Then, when Anja kept looking at her with that patient, understanding gaze, she paused and took a moment to think about it. "I know that. But maybe you're right. He's got a great sense of humor, he's not afraid to venture off the beaten track, and he probably has other positive traits too. Maybe I should remind myself of that more often."

Anja nodded. "Maybe you should."

Their gazes connected and held.

In the past, Susanne had never liked giving people such insights into her psyche, making herself vulnerable, but now she found to her surprise that it wasn't a bad feeling at all—maybe because she sensed that Anja liked what she saw.

Finally, Anja glanced away. Her gaze went to the French doors, and her eyes lit up.

Susanne turned to see what had caught her attention.

Muesli was on the other side of the glass, crouching down like a sprinter in the starting block, waiting for the signal to launch himself forward. "Meow!"

"Ooh! You have a cat? Didn't you say you don't have any pets?"

Susanne groaned. "I don't. He's the neighbor's cat."

Tap-tap-tap-tap. Muesli did his best drummer imitation and let out another piercing meow.

A wrinkle formed between Anja's brows. "Is he okay?"

"He's fine. That's just the usual dramatics he pulls when he wants me to let him in."

"Can we? Let him in, I mean. I'd love to meet him. He looks so cute with that stripe across his nose." Anja tilted her head and looked up at Susanne, her big, brown eyes hopeful.

Faced with that kind of look, Susanne didn't have it in her to say no. When the hell had she become such a pushover? "Just for a minute. You can say hi while I go get changed and get rid of that confetti." And maybe use the couple of minutes alone to find her backbone where Anja was concerned.

At the door, she glanced back.

Anja hadn't wasted any time. She had already opened the French door and knelt on the hardwood floor, letting the cat sniff her fingers.

When Susanne returned a few minutes later, now dressed in jeans and a sweatshirt, the French door was closed. For a second, she breathed a sigh of relief, glad that Anja had put the cat back out without her having to be the bad guy.

But then she walked farther into the living room and found her in the recliner.

Muesli was snuggled up to her, lying more on her chest than her lap. His purring was so loud that Susanne wondered how she could have missed it, and it became even louder as he rubbed his head all over Anja's chest.

Lucky cat.

Maybe it was just her imagination, but as she plopped down on the couch, she thought the cat gave her an I-win-you-lose grin.

Susanne glared at him but didn't have the heart to pluck the cat off Anja's lap and kick him out. She would give them a few minutes before she did that.

Anja looked over at her with a blissful smile. She scratched Muesli beneath his chin, making him stretch his neck so she could get to every spot. "God, I really miss this, and I didn't even know how much until he hopped up on my lap. When I was growing up, we always had at least one cat, but now I haven't had one in years."

"He's up for adoption." Those two were kind of cute together, and Susanne would rather Anja cuddle with a cat than with some other woman...or man. She didn't want to examine that thought too closely. "His owner just had a baby, and he's not a fan. So if you want him..."

Anja leaned forward and rubbed her cheek over Muesli's head. "I wish I could. But my apartment is too small for a cat. It wouldn't be fair to the poor animal."

Just like it wouldn't be fair to Anja to start something between them, Susanne reminded herself.

"What's his name?" Anja asked.

Susanne watched the cat rub his nose along Anja's in a feline version of a kiss. "Lucky." God, had she really just said that? "Um, Muesli. That's his name. Yeah. Muesli."

"Muesli?" Anja laughed.

Susanne held out her hands. "Hey, don't look at me. I didn't name him. But he really seems to love muesli, so the name fits."

"Cats." Anja shook her head and continued to pet him. "I could do this forever, but I've got confetti stuck in my shirt, and it's starting to itch like crazy." She rubbed one shoulder against the back of the recliner and then stood, lifting the cat up with her.

"Come on. I'll put him out and point you to the bathroom." Susanne took the cat from her, and Muesli immediately snuggled up and brushed his head beneath her chin. Anja's scent clung to his fur, making her want to bury her face in it. She gave herself a mental kick and showed Anja to the bathroom, still holding the cat.

At the door, Anja turned back around and reached out to pet Muesli, who seemed completely relaxed about being carried around, his front paws hanging over Susanne's arm. "Oh damn! I got lipstick from the heart on my cheek all over his fur."

"Really?"

They both bent over him to look for traces of red in his fur. There were indeed a few red streaks on the back of his head, where Anja had rubbed her cheek over his fur.

"Ah, it's not too bad," Susanne said. "I'll clean him up before I put him out."

When Anja straightened and looked up, their faces were only centimeters from each other.

Susanne's breathing picked up. Her gaze darted back and forth between Anja's eyes and the soft curve of her mouth. She knew she should step back. They needed to work together. She would leave in six weeks. But she stayed where she was, staring into Anja's eyes that seemed to draw her in.

The world around them receded as they gravitated toward each other, Anja rising up on her toes and Susanne dipping her head, both watching each other for any signs of hesitation until the very last moment.

Their lips met in a tentative brush, then paused for a beat of Susanne's thudding heart.

Anja lifted one hand; Susanne wasn't sure whether it was to push her away or pull her closer.

She held her breath.

Anja's fingers curled around the back of her neck, warm against Susanne's skin, igniting something deep inside. Her eyes fluttered closed. She lost her grip on the cat, along with the last shreds of her common sense. Muesli landed on the floor with a meow of protest.

Their mouths met in a careful caress that quickly grew more heated when Anja made a soft sound of pleasure in her throat. She pressed closer, her body fitting perfectly against Susanne's, despite the difference in their heights.

Anja's lips were even softer than they looked. Susanne traced their outline with the tip of her tongue.

Immediately, Anja parted her lips on a soft gasp, allowing Susanne to slip inside.

Mmm, raspberries. Anja tasted of the candy she had eaten and something Susanne couldn't name. Something that made her head spin. Susanne's knees wobbled, and Anja looped her arms around her neck and held on tighter as if she was afraid of falling too.

Anja gave Susanne's tongue a tentative flick.

Heat spiked through her, jolting her senses, and her rational mind shut down completely. She forgot that they were co-workers, forgot that she wasn't staying, forgot everything but the taste and the scent and the feel of Anja.

Soon, Anja lost her tentativeness and matched her caress for caress. Their tongues slid along each other, retreated, then met again.

God, she never wanted this to end. *You have to.* She knew she should stop this madness, but she couldn't. Instead, her hands started to move of their own accord, sliding under Anja's shirt to caress the indentation of her lower back.

Her skin was silky and warm, instantly making Susanne want to feel more, to explore every single part of her.

Anja tangled her fingers in Susanne's hair and pulled her even closer.

Crazy. This was crazy. *Crazy good.*

A loud "meow" and the brush of a warm, small body along her calves finally jolted Susanne out of her erotic trance. Somehow she summoned the willpower to break the kiss and drew back with one last nibble on Anja's full bottom lip.

Anja leaned her forehead on Susanne's shoulder, her breathing as ragged as Susanne's own.

Holy shit. Her heart thudded against her ribs.

When Anja lifted her head, her eyes were dazed. She touched her fingertips to her lips, which were as red as the raspberries she tasted like.

The sight made Susanne long to kiss her again. She took a step back to resist temptation until the wall stopped her. "I'm sorry. I shouldn't have… I didn't mean to… I had no business kissing you, and I promise it won't happen again." She rushed out the words in one breath, then paused and stared at Anja, who stood in the middle of the hall, nibbling her lip.

God, what would it feel like if she bit Susanne's lip like that?

Stop it, dammit! Usually, she had no problems keeping her libido in check, but at the moment, all she could think about was kissing Anja again. She peered over at her, half hoping, half fearing that Anja would say it was no big deal; it had been just a kiss after all.

Anja regarded her with a frown. "Why are you taking all the blame? I can't even remember who started it. Maybe I was the one who kissed you first."

"Then I shouldn't have kissed you back."

"Do you…" Anja swallowed audibly. "…regret it?"

She should have said yes and left it at that, but she couldn't get the words out. "Getting involved makes no sense, Anja." She tried to inject certainty into her voice, but she mostly sounded resigned. "Our lives don't mesh—yours is here, and mine is in Berlin. You should focus on Paper Love and I on finding a new job and getting my career back on track. Neither of us needs the complication of a relationship right now, especially a long-distance one."

Anja sank against the wall next to her, and Susanne could only hope that she wouldn't touch her because she knew that would make her resolve melt like ice cream in August.

"But maybe we could…" Anja trailed off as if realizing that there really weren't any good options.

Susanne turned toward her and leaned one shoulder against the wall. "I wish it were different, but I can barely make a relationship work when I live in the same city as my girlfriend, and you are not the one-night-stand type." She searched Anja's face. "Or are you?"

In the silence between them, Susanne's heartbeat pounded in her ears. What would she do if Anja said she was? But, of course, that was wishful thinking. She knew Anja well enough to have a good idea of the answer before she even opened her mouth.

"No, I'm not." Anja lowered her gaze to the floor as if not having one-night stands was something to be ashamed of. Then she glanced up. "I think I'd better go wash off that lipstick before I can no longer remove it."

"Lipstick?" Susanne had trouble following, her brain still focused on things other than processing words.

Anja gestured at the smeared mess on her cheek.

"Oh. Right." She opened the bathroom door for her and watched as Anja stepped inside and closed the door between them. "Goddammit."

"Meow?" Muesli answered.

With a sigh, Susanne pushed away from the wall to finally put him outside. If only she could lock out the memory of their kiss as easily.

❧

Anja turned on the faucet, bent over the sink, and scrubbed her face with cold water, as much to remove the lipstick as to cool her overheated cheeks and to clear her head. She watched the water swirl down the drain. It looked like the mini tornado wreaking havoc inside of her.

When she straightened and reached for the towel, her gaze went to her reflection in the mirror above the sink.

Her cheeks were flushed and her lips red and a little puffy. They still tingled from Susanne's kisses. If she had ever been kissed like that, she couldn't remember. She could barely remember her own name when Susanne had kissed her. God, the things that woman could do with her lips and her tongue.

Enough. She wrenched her shirt over her head and shook it. Confetti drifted to the floor, and when she put the shirt back on, the itching was gone. What stayed, though, was the feeling of Susanne's lips on her own that seemed to be imprinted on her body and mind.

But no matter how overwhelming, how good that kiss had felt, she had to put it out of her mind. Susanne was right. She should focus on Paper Love. At least that kind of love was safe and wouldn't end up breaking her heart.

The buzz of the cell phone in her back pocket made her jump.

Grateful for the distraction, she pulled it out, expecting it to be Miri, back from her weekend in Berlin. But instead, the name of Nobby's not-quite girlfriend flashed across the screen.

She accepted the call and leaned against the sink. "Hi, Ulrike."

"Sorry to…" Static crackled, obscuring Ulrike's voice. "…didn't have the number for his niece, so I…"

"The connection is pretty bad. I can barely hear you." Anja stuck her finger in her other ear, but, of course, that didn't help. "Where are you?"

"…the hospital."

That word came through loud and clear, as did the worry in Ulrike's voice.

A bolt of panic ripped through her body, hot and cold at the same time. "Hospital? Who's in the hospital? What happened?"

"Nobby fell when he came over after work. He…" An overhead announcement drowned out even more of Ulrike's explanation. "Lot of pain… In the ER. Anja? Can…hear me?"

"Yes. Yes, I heard you. We're on our way! We'll be there as soon as we can. Hang in there!"

Ulrike didn't answer. The connection had cut out for good.

Cursing, Anja shoved the phone into her pocket, ran to the door, and tore it open.

Susanne was just stepping out of the living room and looked at her with wide eyes as Anja came charging toward her.

"We have to go," Anja blurted out.

"Calm down. I can drive you home if you need a little distance right now, but I really hope we haven't ruined our friendship because of—"

"It's not about that. Nobby's in the ER!"

"What?" Susanne crossed the hall with long strides, and they gripped each other's forearms in silent support. "What happened?"

"I don't know. The connection was shitty, probably because they're in the ER. All I understood was that he took a fall, and now he's in a lot of pain and… Oh God! What if he…?"

Susanne squeezed her arm, wrenching her from the panicked visions of a fractured spine or a gushing head wound. "Hey, let's not assume the worst. Maybe it's just a few scrapes. He's going to be fine, okay?"

Anja nodded and clung to those words and to Susanne's arm.

"Come on." Susanne wrapped one arm around her waist. "Let's go see him."

∽◯◯◯∽

Susanne's dazed brain still hadn't quite grasped the situation as they hurried toward the sliding glass doors of the ER. This day was giving her emotional whiplash—one minute she had shared this incredible kiss with Anja and the next she was rushing off to the ER.

She kept one arm around Anja as they burst into the reception area. Anja trembled against her, making Susanne want to hold her closer.

Someone else was talking to the receptionist behind the glass window, so they had to wait a few steps away.

"God, I'm so glad you're here," Anja whispered. "I'm not family. If I were alone, they probably wouldn't tell me anything."

Susanne soothingly trailed her hand along Anja's back. "I'm here. He'll be fine."

"I know. I know." Anja rocked back and forth for a moment, then gave Susanne a grim smile. "Just look at me. He's *your* uncle, and yet I'm the one who's a complete mess."

"You're not a mess." Susanne's fingers itched to reach out and cradle her face. "You're just worried. You've spent way more time with him than I ever did." And, unlike her, Anja hadn't kept an emotional distance. That was one of the reasons why getting involved with her would not be a good idea. She would only end up hurting her, and that was the last thing Susanne wanted.

"Anja?" someone called from the waiting area.

They whirled around.

A woman in her sixties waved at them. Her chin-length silver-blonde hair was in disarray, as if she'd run her fingers through it several times.

"Ulrike!" Anja grasped Susanne's hand and pulled her over to the woman. "How is he?"

"I don't know. He's still in there." Ulrike pointed at the door separating them from the treatment area.

They sank onto a padded bench in the waiting area, with Anja in the middle. "What happened?"

"He slipped and fell going up the stairs to my house," Ulrike said. "I'm pretty sure he broke something. Maybe his hip or his tailbone. I think they're doing X-rays right now."

Anja slumped against Susanne's side, and Susanne again wrapped one arm around her without much thought. It felt like the natural thing to do. Just providing some comfort, right?

They waited in silence for a minute, then Susanne realized that she hadn't even introduced herself in the commotion. She extended her hand and reached around Anja. "I'm Susanne...Norbert's niece."

"Oh. You're his niece? I thought you were..." Ulrike's gaze went to Anja. "Her girlfriend."

"Oh, no, no. I... No." Of course Ulrike would think that. They sat much too close to be just co-workers, her arm was around Anja, and Anja's head rested on her shoulder.

As if only now realizing what she'd been doing, Anja tried to slide back and put some distance between them, but Susanne squeezed softly, indicating that it was okay.

"Nice to meet you, even under the circumstances." Ulrike shook her hand. "Nobby has promised to introduce us for years, but..." She trailed off with a vague gesture.

Susanne lowered her gaze to the grayish floor. "Well, I, um... My job kept me busy, so I didn't visit very often." *Try never.*

"You're here now; that's what counts," Anja said.

Susanne gave her another squeeze and a grateful look.

Ulrike nodded. "I know Nobby will be very glad about that. That man!" She shook her head. "He didn't want to go to the ER, even though he could hardly move."

Anja and Ulrike talked about this and that to pass the time, while Susanne preferred to wait in silence, focused partially on the comforting pressure of Anja's body against her side and partially on the sliding door to the treatment area.

Every time those doors swished open, they looked up, but each time, the nurse or doctor either called out another name or bustled through the waiting area on their way to someplace else.

The ER was busy, probably with cuts, intoxications, and other little injuries from the carnival parade.

Susanne glanced around for something to distract her, barely resisting the urge to tap her foot. Her gaze repeatedly went to Anja to see how she was holding up. A single piece of pink confetti still clung to Anja's hair, and Susanne reached out to remove it. Then she felt Ulrike's gaze on her and quickly let her hand drop back to her lap.

It seemed to take forever until a nurse stepped out and called, "Is somebody here for Norbert Wolff?"

"Yes!" Susanne and Anja jumped up, while Ulrike got up more slowly.

The nurse nodded. "The patient will be right out."

"How is he?" Anja asked.

When the nurse hesitated, Susanne added, "I'm his niece."

"We X-rayed his pelvic region, and it seems he was really lucky. He's got a coccyx contusion—a bruised tailbone—but nothing is broken or dislocated."

Anja exhaled sharply and leaned against Susanne's shoulder. "Thank God!"

"He's still in quite a bit of pain, so we'll be giving him a prescription for painkillers," the nurse said. "He'll have trouble sitting and maybe even walking for a week or two."

"Anything else we can do?" Ulrike asked.

"Get him a donut cushion and apply ice for the first few days." The nurse shrugged. "Other than that, there's not much we can do."

"What about work?" Susanne asked. "We're in the middle of restructuring his store."

"Well, he doesn't need to be on bed rest, but if his work requires a lot of sitting or bending and lifting, he should sit it out."

Susanne grimaced at the poor choice of words and traded glances with Anja, who was finally getting some color back in her cheeks.

The nurse said goodbye, and it wasn't long before Uncle Norbert came out of the treatment area. He walked gingerly, as if every step hurt, but he grinned when he saw them. "The X-ray tech said I have a great-looking ass!"

"She...or he did not say that!" Ulrike slapped his arm, but her fondness for him was obvious from the way she looked at him.

Susanne smiled, glad that her uncle had someone in his life and that he was already feeling well enough to make jokes.

"Okay, maybe he said the X-rays look good, but it was an X-ray of my ass, so..."

Anja gave him a careful hug.

Susanne instantly missed her warmth against her side. *Stop being stupid. You've never been the touchy-feely type.* She crossed her arms in front of her chest.

Anja stepped back. "God, Nobby, never scare us like this again!"

"Wasn't my intention. Ulrike was the one who insisted on calling you." He gave his friend a little glare before addressing Anja and Susanne again. "Sorry you didn't get to see the rest of the carnival parade."

"We had already left the parade," Anja said.

Oh shit. Did she have to tell him that?

He looked back and forth between them. "Please don't tell me you went to the café to work!"

"No, we..." Anja studied the floor as if she had found something very fascinating down there. Her face had taken on the color of the paper flamingo she'd made for the store.

Under different circumstances, Susanne would have found it cute.

"I promise we didn't work for even a minute," Susanne said. For once, work had been the last thing on her mind.

Uncle Norbert continued to look at them.

His scrutiny made Susanne nervous. Didn't he believe her, or could he sense that something had happened between them?

"I think we should fill that prescription and get you home so you can ice that great-looking ass of yours." Ulrike gently took his elbow and led him to the exit.

"I could drive him home," Susanne offered.

Ulrike shook her head. "That's not necessary. Nobby and I are neighbors, so I'm going there anyway."

"But who'll make him dinner?"

"Hey, I'm not an invalid," Uncle Norbert protested. "I hurt my tailbone, not my hands. I can take care of dinner myself."

Ulrike patted his arm. "You eat dinner over at my place almost every night anyway." She looked at Susanne. "Don't worry. I'll keep an eye on him and make sure he takes it easy at home."

"At home?" Uncle Norbert echoed. "I'm not staying at home. The doctor said I could work."

"He or she probably said you could work as long as you're not sitting for any length of time or bending down and lifting stuff," Anja said. "And that's ninety percent of what you do at Paper Love. You won't be able to restock the shelves or work in the office, and even if you stand behind the counter, you'll be uncomfortable and grouchy. That's hardly the way to make our customers happy. So why not finally take some time off, like you promised me you would back in December?"

Oh wow. Susanne struggled to hide her grin. Anja was a force to be reckoned with when she was protecting the people she cared about.

Uncle Nobby looked completely steamrollered. "But—"

"Don't worry." Anja rubbed his arm. "We've got it covered. Right, Susanne?"

"Right." Then Susanne's amusement faded as they left the ER and she remembered that she'd be in the car with Anja in a minute and that she didn't have a clue what to say to her.

♋

Now that the emergency was over, awkwardness settled between them. Anja missed Susanne's arm around her. Not even the soothing notes of Jenna Blake's latest song drifting through the car's speakers could drown out the silence between them—quite the opposite. The romantic ballad made her all the more aware that there would be no romance for her and Susanne.

"I'm so glad he's not seriously hurt," Anja said when she couldn't stand it any longer.

"Me too." Susanne took a right onto Lehener Strasse, then stopped at a red light at the next intersection. She peeked over at Anja. "But I guess it changes things, doesn't it?"

"Between us?" Anja said before she could stop herself.

"No!" The light turned green, and Susanne accelerated across the intersection a little too fast. "No. I mean..." She eased up on the gas pedal. "The fact that he'll be out for a week or two and Felix isn't working either. I'll have to step up my stationery game and help out more at Paper Love."

Great. Anja squeezed her eyes shut for a second. That meant they'd spend even more time together than before, just when they could use a little distance.

"What?" Susanne sent another quick glance over at her. "You don't think I can do it?"

"No, no, that's not…" Anja bit her lip. "I'm sure you'll do just fine." The question was, how well would she be doing, having to work with Susanne more closely than ever, while all she could think about was that kiss and what Susanne had said afterward?

Chapter 14

"Hey, slow down!" Miri called as Anja marched along the lake's shore. "This is supposed to be a relaxing walk, not a race."

Anja slowed so Miri and Gino could catch up. "Sorry. I guess with everything that happened today, I've got a lot of nervous energy to burn."

"But you said Nobby will be fine, right?"

"That's what they said at the ER. We just need to keep him from returning to work too soon."

"Then what else has got you so…twitchy?" Miri asked.

Anja opened her mouth to tell her she wasn't twitchy, but what slipped out instead was, "I kissed her." She gripped Miri's arm the way she had gripped Susanne's earlier that day. "I kissed Susanne."

She expected Miri to stumble to a halt and stare at her, but her friend waved her hand dismissively. "Oh, that's nothing. I slept with her sister."

Now Anja was the one stumbling to a halt and staring. "You…what?"

Miri dragged her over to a bench beneath a streetlamp and pulled her down next to her. The dog flopped down at their feet. "I slept with Franzi." A big grin spread over her face, and her eyes shone. "Well, there wasn't actually much sleeping going on last weekend."

"Oh wow," was all Anja could think of to say.

Miri's grin became even broader, if that was possible. "You can say that again," she said in a dreamy, faraway voice. "God, it was fantastic. Best sex I ever had."

Anja covered her ears with both hands. "No details, please. She's Susanne's sister."

Miri laughed. "Okay, okay. I'll just daydream about the mind-blowing details in silence."

"So now what?"

"More great sex." Miri's eyes twinkled. "Franzi will try to come down here next weekend."

"She knows that's all it is, right? Great sex?" Anja knew Miri was usually very up-front about the fact that she wasn't into commitment, but since they were talking about Susanne's sister, she wanted to make sure. The situation was complicated enough as it was.

"Actually…" Miri's grin transformed into a soft smile. "This time that's not all it is. I thought it was, but she keeps surprising me. *I* keep surprising me when I'm with her."

"Oh wow." Anja hadn't expected that. She had rarely seen her friend like this. Miri jumped into relationships much faster than she did, but she didn't often become serious about it so quickly.

"We don't know each other very well yet, except in the Biblical sense, of course," Miri added with a wink, "but I could easily fall in love with her. Being with her is just so easy. So right."

Anja nodded to herself. That's what being with Susanne felt like too, and the flutter in her belly told her that she, too, could easily fall in love. *If you aren't already,* a voice in her head helpfully pointed out. She silenced it immediately.

"God, listen to me." Miri laughed and scrubbed her hands over her face. "Gooey like a marshmallow."

"What about Franzi? Is she open to more than a weekend fling?"

"She feels the same." Miri beamed. "We decided to try to make this work."

"How? She lives eight hundred kilometers away."

Miri shrugged. "That's what planes and trains are for." At the skeptical look Anja gave her, she added, "Look, we're not sending out wedding invitations quite yet. Maybe it'll work out; maybe it won't. But I really enjoy her company, in and out of bed, and I want to see where this can go, so why not give it a try?"

It sounded so easy. Could it be as simple for her and Susanne?

Miri slid closer and nudged her. "Now let's stop talking about me and start telling me about you and Susanne! You really kissed her?"

"Well, we never established who kissed whom first, but…" She exhaled. "Yeah."

Miri did a little dance on the bench, wiggling her shoulders. "Woo-hoo! How was it? Is she as good a kisser as her sister?"

Anja glared at her but then gave in. "Let's just say that if Franzi was a better kisser than her sister, you would still be in Berlin."

"Oh, it was a close call, believe me. So you and Susanne decided to give it a go too? That's so cool!" Miri clapped her hands, making Gino jump up and bark once. She shushed him. "We can go out on a double date next Saturday before I drag Franzi back to bed."

Anja studied her shoelaces. "Um, no. We decided to just be friends. The store needs my full attention, especially now that Nobby is out sick for a week or two."

"So you just…shut off your feelings?" Miri made a cutting-off motion with her hand. "How's that working out for you?"

A sigh escaped Anja. "Not very well. It'll probably take some time to get over it, but it's for the best." Maybe if she told herself that often enough, she'd start to believe it.

"Oh, come on, you don't believe this pile of bullshit, do you?"

"We've got to work together for the store to survive, Miri. If we mess this up…"

"For six more weeks! You'll be working together for just six more weeks. It's not like you would be stuck with her until you retire if it doesn't work out."

Anja folded her hands behind her neck and massaged her stiff muscles while swaying back and forth twice. "That's just it. Six weeks. Then she'll be gone."

"To Berlin, not on a mission to colonize Mars!" Miri pulled one of Anja's arms down so she could study her face. "Come on, Anja. She's hot, she's intelligent, and she spent an entire afternoon building paper boats with you, indulging your stationery geekiness. Why not give it a try? If I can do it, so can you! What have you got to lose?"

Anja swished her feet through the grass beneath the bench. "My heart."

Miri softened her grasp on Anja's arm. "So that's what this is really about. You're scared."

Was that it? Anja slumped against the back of the bench. "Of course I am. I'm not like you, Miri. I don't take risks. I like to keep my feet firmly on the ground instead of jumping into the unknown."

"I know. I'm not asking you to go skydiving or to give up your life here and move to Berlin with her. But, sweetie, you can't lock your heart away and wait for a guarantee that you won't get hurt." Miri slid her hand down Anja's arm and squeezed her fingers. "There are no guarantees. When you climbed that observation tower, you didn't have any guarantee that you wouldn't have a panic attack halfway up, and yet you did it anyway."

Yes, she had braved the observation tower. With Susanne's help. Hope fluttered in her belly. Maybe if she and Susanne were in it together, she could do this too. "But she hasn't given me any indication that she wants something beyond those six weeks with me. She wants to go back to Berlin, find a new job, get back to her old life. After we kissed, she immediately apologized and said that getting involved makes no sense."

"Sense? Since when do feelings have to make sense?" Miri shook her head. "Maybe she said that because she's just as scared."

Anja wanted to object. Susanne was the epitome of confidence, never afraid to take risks and make the hard decisions. But then she thought about it. Maybe that was just business Susanne. Maybe private Susanne was different. She remembered the discouraged slump of Susanne's shoulders when she had told her she could barely make a relationship work even if she lived in the same city as her girlfriend.

She jumped up from the bench, nearly stumbling over Gino in her haste.

Miri stared up at her. "Did I say something wrong?"

"No. I think you said something very right. Do you mind if we cut this walk short?"

"Uh, no."

"You're the best." Anja bent and kissed her cheek. "Thanks for kicking my butt."

Miri clapped her shoulder. "You're my best friend. Ass-kicking is included in the package. Now go get your woman, tiger!"

Anja rolled her eyes but couldn't help smiling. She tousled Gino's shaggy fur, waved at Miri, and fell into a jog as she headed for the nearby streetcar stop.

∽◦◦◦◦∽

Susanne trudged through her apartment, which felt even emptier than before. She had tried to settle down with her laptop and work on a blog template for Paper Love yet couldn't focus on it. She called her uncle to see if he needed anything, but Ulrike assured her that she was taking good care of him.

Grunting, she stalked to the kitchen and filled the electronic water kettle to make some tea. Maybe that would help with her restlessness.

Once the kettle clicked off, she grabbed it and dumped some water into a mug, promptly spilling half of it all over the counter.

"Dammit." Disgusted with herself, she grabbed a dish towel and mopped up the water. God, she felt as if she had a hangover—just without the fun of getting drunk first.

Well, she had felt drunk on Anja's kiss.

Oh great. There we go again. Her brain started the mental slideshow of that kiss in the hallway. Anja had barely touched her, yet she could still feel her everywhere. How was that possible?

Tap-tap-tap. "Meeeooow?"

This time Muesli's let-me-in concert was a welcome distraction. She left her attempts at making tea behind and went to the living room.

The sight of Muesli staring at her from the other side of the glass was starting to become familiar. The red streak on top of his head was new, though.

Oh, right. She had forgotten all about getting the lipstick off his fur as soon as Anja's lips had touched hers. And afterward, they had rushed off to the ER.

Sighing, she opened the French door so she could clean him up.

He shot into the apartment as if trying to not give her time to change her mind and close the door in his face. Once inside, he trotted to the kitchen at a more leisurely pace, stood in front of the fridge, and meowed up at it.

Susanne followed. "I don't think you're supposed to have human food." Not that there was much in her fridge. She opened it and found a package of sliced turkey breast behind two cups of yogurt. "This should be safe, right?"

"Meow."

"Yeah, of course you'd say that." She sliced up a bit of turkey breast, put it on a plate, and slid it in front of him. As an afterthought, she added a bowl of water. "Don't get used to it. It's just this once, as an apology for the lipstick thing."

As she watched him gobble up the meat, the doorbell rang.

Maybe her neighbor, Muesli's owner, was looking for her cat.

She went to the door and peered through the peephole, but the hallway beyond was empty, so she pressed the button for the intercom. "Yes?"

Only silence answered.

Just as Susanne was about to storm back into the kitchen, thinking it was some stupid practical joke, a female someone cleared her throat.

"It's…it's me. Anja."

She didn't need to add that. Susanne would recognize her voice anytime, anywhere. Adrenaline spiked through her. "What's wrong? I just talked to Uncle Nobert. He's not doing worse, is he?"

"I talked to him too. He's fine. Can I come in? I think we need to talk."

The panic Susanne felt at that was only slightly less than when she'd thought something might be wrong with her uncle. She hesitated.

"What, you don't think we're capable of talking without tearing each other's clothes off?" Anja's chuckle sounded a little forced.

Susanne groaned. "Don't give me any ideas," she muttered under her breath. "Of course we are. Come on in." She pressed the buzzer and opened her apartment door, clinging to it with one hand.

Anja's steps approached slowly. She paused and looked at Susanne from the other side of the doorway. Her face was pale, and her eyes held that same look she had sported when she had taken that first step up on the observation tower—scared and not sure she would ever make it to the top.

Susanne's throat tightened. Suddenly, the last thing on her mind was ripping her clothes off, but God, she wanted to hold her. She opened the door wider. "Come in." She led the way into the living room.

They sat on opposite ends of the couch.

Anja stared at her hands. For someone who had come to talk, she was now very silent.

"Are you okay?" Susanne asked and then instantly felt stupid. *Does she look like she's okay?*

"Yes. No. Yes." Anja's chest rose and fell under a deep breath. Finally, she looked at Susanne. "I am okay. I'm always okay. But I'm never great. Because I always play it safe."

Susanne watched her. Where was she going with this? But she didn't ask because she sensed that if she interrupted her now, Anja might never again work up the courage to say what she obviously needed to say.

"I've never been one to take chances, especially not with my heart."

"That's not a bad thing," Susanne said softly. "Probably saves you from a lot of hurt."

Anja tilted her head in a vague nod. "Sure, but by trying to protect myself, I sometimes lose out on good things too. If I had given in to my fear and avoided climbing that observation tower, like I always have before, I never would have gotten to share that breathtaking view with you."

And that equally breathtaking almost kiss. Susanne reined in her impatience and waited for Anja to go on.

"I know there are plenty of reasons why we should keep things between us on a strictly friendly basis, but…" Anja's gaze darted to her face, then away. "Do you think…? Could we just…try?"

Everything in Susanne screamed at her to say yes, but she forced herself to hold back. "God, Anja, believe me, if things were different, I'd date you in a heartbeat, but I can't make you any promises."

Anja shook her head and now fully looked at her. "I'm not asking for promises. Can't we just take it one day at a time and enjoy each other's company without worrying about the future for now?"

It was exactly what Susanne had done in many, maybe even most of her past relationships. But did she want to do that with Anja? Could she do that *to* her?

Muesli chose that moment to jump up on the couch between them.

"Hi, boy." Anja immediately buried her fingers in his fur, and Susanne's heart clenched when she saw that they were trembling. "Hey, you've still got that lipstick on your head."

"Yeah." Susanne laughed shakily. "He can't seem to get rid of it." Just as she couldn't get rid of the memory of their kiss. She slid closer to her on the couch.

Muesli took it as an invitation to climb on her lap.

Susanne absentmindedly ran her hand over his fur once but then ignored him to focus solely on Anja. "Are you sure you want to do this? Can you really enjoy our time together, knowing it might not last?"

"I think so. Using those six weeks to find out if it could work is better than wondering forever if…"

"If?" Susanne prompted when Anja fell silent.

"If that kiss earlier today was a fluke, or if you can make my toes curl every single time you kiss me." Anja peered over at her from under half-lowered lids. How could she look so shy and yet so damn sexy at the same time?

"You know I can never resist a challenge, don't you?" Susanne murmured, her voice husky.

"Then don't."

With a groan, Susanne tossed the remainder of her reservations overboard and decided to do exactly what Anja wanted her to do: live in the moment—and kiss her senseless.

She slid even closer on the couch and turned until her knee touched Anja's thigh. Gently, she put one hand on her hip, just resting it there, even though her fingers wanted to explore immediately. "Are you really—?"

Anja surged forward, and then Susanne was the one being kissed senseless.

Their mouths connected with urgency, as if both of them wanted to make the most of every minute together.

Anja clasped the back of Susanne's neck with one hand while cradling her jaw with the other, holding her against her.

Not that Susanne had any intention of pulling back. She returned the kiss with equal heat.

The cat gave a meow of protest as he was squished between them and then jumped to the floor.

Susanne slid her other hand onto Anja's waist and pulled her even closer. The heat of Anja's body seeped through their clothes, making Susanne's temperature skyrocket too. She nipped at Anja's bottom lip and then slipped inside her mouth, teasing her with lips and teeth and tongue until the small noises Anja made were nearly constant. Or maybe some of them were hers. She could no longer tell.

Finally, she broke their kiss with reluctance.

Anja straightened and took her hand away from Susanne's neck but left the other where it was, softly brushing her thumb along Susanne's jaw.

Susanne tilted her face into the caress and stared into her eyes. So much emotion—passion but also something gentler—swirled in those brown depths that Susanne had to look away. She bent, untied the laces of Anja's sneakers, and pulled off one shoe and sock.

A giggle burst from Anja, and she pulled back her foot as if she was ticklish. "What are you doing? If this is your attempt to undress me, I've got to tell you, it's not very sexy."

Susanne suppressed a moan as visions of undressing Anja and exploring each centimeter of her warm, soft skin danced before her mind's eye. "Believe me, when I undress you, it'll be very sexy." She lowered her voice to a seductive burr. Then she paused as she realized what she'd said: when. Not if.

The flush on Anja's cheeks deepened. She licked her lips. "Then what's this?" She wiggled her toes.

Susanne grinned. "Just looking to see if I could make your toes curl."

Anja fell against her, laughing, and it only took that contact to have them tumble into another kiss.

When it ended several minutes later, Susanne was breathless. For her, kissing hadn't been this intense in a very long time. She glanced down at Anja's cute toes. "Yep. Definitely curled."

"What about yours?" Anja's husky voice sent shivers through Susanne's body.

"You could take off my socks and kiss me again." Susanne invitingly lifted one foot. "And I wouldn't mind if you don't want to stop at my socks."

One hand already on Susanne's ankle, Anja stopped and glanced up at her with wide eyes.

"Hey." Susanne put her hand over Anja's, pulled it away from her sock, and held it in both of hers. "I was just kidding. Well, mostly." She gave a wry smile. "I admit I wouldn't put up much of a struggle if you wanted to drag me to bed right now. But I know you're not the kind of woman who jumps into things like that, and that's perfectly fine."

Anja searched her eyes. Whatever she read there seemed to reassure her because a smile eased across her face.

Muesli jumped onto the coffee table as if to check whether they were done kissing.

Susanne pointed at the floor. "Get down!"

The cat sat and looked at her without blinking.

Anja laughed. "You've never had a cat before, have you?"

"No. And I don't have one now either." Susanne picked him up and carried him toward the bathroom. "Come on. Let's clean him up."

She sat on the edge of the tub, holding him, while Anja took a cloth, wet a corner of it at the sink, and gently ran it over his fur to remove the traces of lipstick.

The cat nestled into Susanne, trying to escape the wet cloth, and Anja had to step closer to reach him. She stood between Susanne's spread legs, her knee resting against the inside of her thigh. A tingle rippled through Susanne, and she couldn't decide if this was heaven or hell.

She distracted herself with one of the questions they still needed to talk about. "How are we going to handle this?"

"Oh, I think it's working the way we're doing it. Look, the lipstick is all gone." Anja took away the cloth and nodded down at the cat.

"No, I meant…" Susanne waved her hand between them. "This. Do you want to tell people? Tell…Uncle Norbert?"

"I don't know. Do you want to tell him?"

Hell, no. She was fairly sure her uncle wouldn't like their day-by-day arrangement. "I'm not saying I want us to sneak around and make each other feel like this is our dirty little secret. But maybe we could be…discreet."

"Discreet, hmm?" A teasing smile tugged at the corners of Anja's lips. "So no making out in the middle of the store?"

A vivid image of her pressing Anja against the island display while she captured her mouth in a demanding kiss flashed through Susanne's mind. "Uh…"

"All right. We can do discreet."

Susanne suddenly wasn't so sure she could.

Anja ran her fingers over Muesli's damp fur. "All done. Good boy." She bent and kissed his head, then straightened.

"Hey, what about me?" Susanne tapped her chest. "I helped get him clean. Don't I get a kiss for that?"

"You're not the one who got her fur all wet."

"Oh, I'm plenty—"

Anja pressed her mouth to Susanne's. "Don't say it," she playfully whispered against her lips.

"If you don't want me to talk, maybe you should find a way to shut me up."

So Anja did.

By the time they finally managed to pry themselves away from each other, it was already nine o'clock. Susanne reluctantly walked Anja to the door. She didn't want her to go, but she knew they both needed some time to process what had happened, so a sleepover wasn't an option tonight.

"Are you sure you don't want me to drive you?" Susanne asked for the third time.

Anja nodded. "If you drive me, I have a feeling we'll still be sitting in your car at midnight, exchanging one last kiss goodbye."

Susanne couldn't argue with that. "At least send me a text so I know you made it home safely."

"It's just two quick streetcar rides, not a trip halfway across the country."

"Still. I'm allowed to worry about my…" Susanne cut herself off, not knowing what to call Anja. Did she have the right to call Anja her girlfriend when she wasn't sure what would happen once the six weeks were up? "To worry about you."

Anja smiled and softly touched her palm to Susanne's cheek. "I thought you were a total ice queen when we first met, but you're actually pretty sweet."

Heat flared up her neck. "Am not."

Grinning, Anja rose up on her tiptoes and kissed her, just a light caress of her lips this time.

It was sweeter than the most delicious chocolate.

"I like it," Anja whispered against Susanne's lips. Then she dropped down onto her heels, took her hand away from Susanne's face, and opened the door. "I'll see you bright and early tomorrow morning."

"See you," Susanne said with a nod, already wondering what it would be like to see Anja again, away from the safe haven of her apartment. Would things between them feel weird? "Good night."

"Sleep well." Anja stepped outside, but instead of walking away, she faced Susanne and lifted her hand in a silent goodbye.

Susanne mirrored the gesture. She watched as Anja reluctantly turned and walked toward the building's front door. The hallway veered to the right, so Susanne couldn't track her all the way to the door. Suddenly, she understood how Muesli probably felt every time she put him outside and closed the French door between them.

Stop being so melodramatic. This so isn't you. Get back inside, put the cat out, and get some work done.

But she stood rooted to the spot until she heard the front door open.

In a second, it would fall closed behind Anja, and she would be gone.

"Anja!" she called, then immediately wanted to slap herself. She barely recognized herself. She had never acted like this with any other woman. In the past, she'd always been in control of herself and her actions.

Anja's footsteps paused before hurrying back toward her, as if she'd been waiting for Susanne to call her back. It took only two seconds for Anja to reappear, a question in her eyes.

Damn. What was she supposed to say now? "Uh, I...I just thought you probably need another kiss to tide you over."

A twinkle lit Anja's eyes. "Oh, do I?"

Susanne nodded. "You do."

"Well, then you'd better come here and kiss me."

Susanne took off one slipper and used it to block the door so it wouldn't fall closed since she didn't have her keys with her. On one sock and one slipper, she padded through the hallway. God, if any of her friends or former colleagues could see her now! Cool, calm, and collected Susanne Wolff was making a fool of herself over a woman. That was definitely a first.

Any embarrassment she might have felt quickly vanished when she bent and kissed Anja. She loved the way Anja curled her fingers around her neck to tug her down and hold her against her. She could spend hours exploring Anja's warm mouth and nibbling her soft lips.

But they were standing in the middle of the hallway for all her neighbors to see, so she reluctantly broke the kiss and traced Anja's reddened bottom lip with the pad of her thumb. "Good night."

"Sweet dreams," Anja whispered.

Oh yeah, she would definitely have those. Although they might be more hot than sweet after that last kiss.

Still looking dazed, Anja walked backward to the door. Their gazes held until the very last moment. Then, with one final wave, Anja turned and was gone.

Susanne trudged back into her apartment.

Muesli sniffed her abandoned slipper, but when she approached, he stopped and greeted her by rubbing against her legs as if he hadn't seen her all day.

She really should put him outside, but she couldn't bring herself to do it. Not today. "Come on. You can share my bed—just this once, okay?" She'd rather curl around Anja than around a cat, but for now, his company would do.

Chapter 15

Anja didn't sleep much, too keyed up from their make-out session and thoughts about their uncertain future. She tried to tell herself to just enjoy each day and that a lot could happen in six weeks, but that didn't help calm her racing thoughts.

At five o'clock, she gave up on sleep and crawled out of bed. She showered and dressed and then slipped her laptop and a travel mug of coffee into her backpack.

At least she'd be able to get some work done on the blog before the first customers started coming in, and she could take a look at the stock and what she needed to order now that Nobby was out for a couple of weeks.

Maybe Susanne would come in to work early too. She admitted to herself that was part of the reason why she was getting her bicycle out and heading to the store before dawn. This eagerness to see her was exciting and scary at the same time.

All was still quiet on the cobblestoned street as she chained her bicycle to the stand next to the parking garage. She had half expected—or maybe hoped—to be greeted by a light already on in the store, but Paper Love lay in darkness.

With a sigh, she unlocked the door and went inside.

She busied herself with her usual morning routine and additional tasks Nobby normally took care of. She even managed to finish writing a blog post on her laptop. As opening time approached, she wheeled the carousels with the greeting cards outside and carried the Plexiglas sheet with the paper boats to the Bächle across the street. The sheet was as long as the distance between her fingertips and her elbow, but thankfully, it wasn't heavy.

Under the pretense of looking around for potential customers, she glanced toward the parking garage where Susanne usually left her BMW.

Still no sign of her.

In the five weeks since she'd been in Freiburg, Susanne had never been late. What if something had happened to her?

Anja shook her head. More likely, Susanne had second thoughts about them and didn't know how to tell her that she didn't want to get involved with her after all, and that was why she was staying away.

The thought made her stomach clench into a tight knot. *Come on. Have some trust. Since when are you such a pessimist?* But the knot in her belly didn't loosen as she went back into the store.

The first customer came and went. Still no Susanne.

Anja fingered the cell phone in her pocket. Should she call her to make sure she was okay?

Just as she pulled the phone out, the bell above the door jingled wildly and Susanne rushed in.

Anja's mouth went dry, not just from relief but probably also because most of her bodily fluids had gone south. Anyone looking so sexy in public should come with a warning label. The top two buttons on her blouse were open as if she had dressed hastily, revealing a glimpse of her cleavage. Her chestnut hair wasn't tied back or put up into a twist today; it tumbled onto her shoulders in wild strands that looked finger-combed.

"Sorry." Susanne leaned against the counter and put down her laptop bag. "I overslept."

"Really?" Anja couldn't help asking, even though she knew her insecurities were stupid. Susanne wasn't the type to change her mind once she'd made a decision.

"Yeah. I only fell asleep around four and must have shut off my alarm clock. If not for Muesli, who woke me up because I don't have a litter box and he needed to go outside, I'd probably still be asleep."

The tension that had gripped Anja all morning vanished. "Aww. How cute."

"I'm not sure how cute it is to have a cat pulling on my hair because he needs to pee."

"Not the cat. You." It was good to hear that she hadn't been the only one who hadn't slept a lot last night. Maybe Susanne needed to hear it too, so Anja gave herself a mental kick. "I didn't sleep much either."

Susanne's gaze softened. She pushed away from the counter and slowly walked up to Anja. "You didn't?"

Anja shook her head. Now that Susanne was so close, she drank in her face, her eyes, her soft lips… As if pulled in by gravity, she leaned toward her.

The bell above the door jingled again, tearing them apart before they could touch.

No! Not now! Anja forced a pleasant smile onto her face and turned toward the customer, a well-dressed woman in her thirties. "Good morning. May I help you?"

"Good morning." The customer glanced around. "I'm looking for a Valentine's Day gift for my boyfriend. I hear fountain pens are like jewelry for men, so…"

Oh shit. Valentine's Day! Despite the paper heart decorations in the store's window, Anja had temporarily forgotten that Valentine's Day was tomorrow. For the past three years, the day had held little meaning for her beyond increased sales of fountain pens and gift cards. But now... Her gaze darted to Susanne. Should she get her a gift or do something special for Valentine's Day too?

The customer looked back and forth between Anja and Susanne. "Did I hear wrong?"

"Oh, no, no. You heard exactly right," Anja said. "Getting him a fountain pen for Valentine's Day is a great idea."

The woman beamed. "So do you have one you can recommend?"

Anja opened her mouth to give her several options when the store's phone rang. She glanced toward the counter. That was probably Herr Schneider calling to check if his order had come in.

"Go take the call," Susanne said. "I've got this."

Anja gave her an are-you-sure look, which Susanne answered with a smile and a nod. It hadn't been that long ago that Anja wouldn't have trusted her with a customer, but she felt bad about doubting Susanne when she'd been late, so she didn't want to do it a second time. After a quick pat to Susanne's arm, she hurried to the counter, picked up the phone, and carried it to the back room so Susanne and the customer could talk without being bothered.

It was indeed Herr Schneider, and she only needed a minute to assure him that his order had arrived and could be picked up any time. When she returned to the sales area, Susanne and the customer stood next to the unlocked display case. The woman held a Pelikan Classic M205 and admired its pretty marble swirls from all sides.

Oh no. That pen wouldn't work for her boyfriend at all. It was too small and too light for most men.

But before she could cross the room and say so, Susanne shook her head. "I don't think that one is going to work. Men usually prefer a more substantial pen with a longer barrel and a thicker grip section. They have bigger hands, so a dainty pen is going to make them cramp up if they write for a longer period of time."

Wow. Anja paused in the doorway and watched with a stunned smile as Susanne handed the woman a Pelikan Souverän M805. Apparently, Susanne had listened attentively whenever Anja had explained their pens to customers.

The woman laughed. "So size does matter after all."

Susanne chuckled, and the sound warmed Anja all over. "It does when it comes to pens."

"I like it." The woman studied the pen. "How much is it?"

Again, Anja resisted the urge to step in and supply the information.

Susanne glanced at the tag inside of the glass case. "This one is four hundred and thirty euros."

The woman let out a little gasp. "I'm not sure I want to spend that much. The relationship is still pretty new, and I don't want him to think that I'm trying for too much, too soon."

Maybe that answered Anja's earlier question about whether to get Susanne a gift for Valentine's Day. They had agreed on no promises and no expectations beyond the right now, and a Valentine's Day gift, especially traditional presents such as jewelry, implied a certain level of commitment. Putting that kind of pressure on Susanne wouldn't be fair.

"Totally understandable," Susanne said, as if agreeing with Anja's unspoken decision. "I'm sure we can find something more affordable." She turned her head and didn't seem surprised to see Anja in the doorway, watching her. Maybe she had sensed her presence. "What would you recommend?"

Anja loved that Susanne had deferred to her, even though she had done well with the customer so far. "How about the Diplomat Excellence? It's about the same size as the M805, and it looks really classy for only one hundred euros." She crossed the room and bent over the glass case to find the pen. Her shoulder brushed Susanne's, making a shiver trail across her skin.

The woman inspected the pen Anja handed her. "Perfect. Thank you so much."

Within a few minutes, their happy customer was out the door with a gift-wrapped pen in her purse.

Susanne pretended to dust off her hands. "Not too bad for a digital snob, right?"

Anja rounded the counter and wrapped her arms around Susanne's neck in an exuberant hug. "You were great! We're gonna make a pen geek out of you after all."

Susanne slid her arms around Anja's waist and spread her fingers wide as if to cover as much of her as possible. "Is that a threat?" she purred.

"That's a promise," Anja answered, trying for the same tone.

Apparently, it worked, because Susanne shuddered.

Anja ran her fingers through Susanne's hair the way she had longed to since the moment Susanne had stepped into the store earlier. She wanted to tell her how much she liked this just-out-of-bed look, but before she could, Susanne kissed her, and the words faded away.

Susanne's lips moved over hers in a tender caress. Anja sensed that the kiss was more about reconnecting than about passion. Maybe Susanne had felt a bit insecure too when she had entered the store, not knowing what to expect.

Anja returned the kiss with the same gentleness and lost herself in the warmth and softness of Susanne's mouth.

Just as Susanne fitted her body against hers and deepened the kiss, the bell above the door announced another customer.

God, their customers' timing sucked. They jumped apart, and Anja wiped her mouth as inconspicuously as possible, trying not to look as if she had just shared one of the best kisses of her life.

Instead of a customer, Miri entered the store. She let the door close behind her, put her hands on her hips, and regarded them with a broad grin. "Now, that gives a whole new meaning to the name Paper Love!"

So much for being discreet. Anja hoped she wasn't blushing as she hugged her friend. "What are you doing here?"

"I had to pick up a new showerhead for the women's shelter. I'm a social worker," Miri added, turning toward Susanne. "From the looks of it, you two could do with a shower too—a cold one anyway."

Anja ignored her teasing. "So your search for a showerhead brings you to Paper Love...how?"

"The department store isn't far from here, and after the way you left the lake yesterday, I thought I would drop by and check on you. See if I needed to dry any tears. But I can see that you actually need a dental dam more urgently than tissues."

"Miriam Blattmann!" Now Anja couldn't fight the flush that swept up her neck. Her cheeks burned fiercely. "Don't mind her, Susanne. She grew up among wolves."

Susanne looked more amused than scandalized. "Oh, don't worry. I'm used to comments like that from Franzi, and she doesn't even have the wolf-pack excuse."

Miri's teasing grin turned into an imploring gaze. "I take it you two are fine?" She searched Anja's face. "*You* are fine?"

"I'm fine. More than fine, actually." Anja gripped Susanne's hand.

Susanne grinned. "She's very, very fine."

New heat shot into Anja's cheeks. "What's this? A competition to see who can embarrass me the most?"

Miri shook her head and winked at Susanne. "Why compete if we can both do it, right?"

"Right." Susanne rubbed her thumb along the back of Anja's hand.

Miri glanced at her wristwatch. "I have to go. How about that double date on Saturday?"

"Double date?" Susanne stiffened and eyed Miri cautiously. "The three of us and...?"

"Your sister, of course!" Miri rolled her eyes. "I might be pretty irresistible, but contrary to popular belief, I don't have women lined up at my door. One woman at a time is enough for me, thank you very much."

"Sorry," Susanne mumbled. "I didn't mean to imply... I guess I get a little protective when it's about my sister, and I didn't know Franzi was coming back to Freiburg so soon."

"Like I said, I'm pretty irresistible." Miri swiped at her very short hair, pretending to flick it back over her shoulder.

"You're pretty impossible." Anja threw one of the paper hearts from the center island at her.

Miri caught it. "See? Even your girlfriend is throwing her heart at me."

Girlfriend? Anja's cheeks warmed again. She sneaked a glance at Susanne to see how she would react.

But Susanne showed no reaction at all. Either she had put on her impenetrable I'm-at-work mask, or someone calling Anja her girlfriend was the most normal thing in the world for her.

Anja hoped it was the latter but had a feeling it might be the former.

With a wave and a "see you Saturday," Miri slipped out of the store.

Susanne stared after her. "Hey, she didn't give your heart back."

She never had it, Anja wanted to say. *Not the way—* She cut herself off before she could finish the thought. *One day at a time, remember?*

She tugged on Susanne's hand. "I wrote a blog post about scented inks earlier. Want to see it?"

"Sure, but do I have time to get myself a cup of coffee first?"

Aww. Apparently, Susanne had jumped out of bed and rushed to work without making coffee, either eager to see her or not wanting to leave her alone with the work at the store. Both options were pretty touching.

Anja flashed a teasing grin. "There's coffee-scented ink."

"Is it drinkable?"

"I wouldn't recommend it."

"Then I need coffee first. And this." Susanne pulled her close by their joined hands and kissed her quickly but firmly. Then she went to get coffee for them both, leaving Anja with a kiss-induced smile on her lips.

"Finally!" Susanne leaned back in her recliner and pressed the phone to her ear. "Reaching you is harder than getting an audience with the pope! I've been trying to call you since yesterday, but it kept going to voice mail."

"Sorry about that," Franzi answered. "But you'd better get used to it. I talk to Miri a lot right now, and that's not going to change anytime soon."

Was that what she and Anja would be doing in the future too? Seeing each other only two or three weekends a month and talking on the phone every evening?

Would that be so bad?

"So this isn't just some fun weekend fling, is it?" Susanne asked.

"That first weekend when I met her, I thought that was all it was gonna be, but now… I admit I'm pretty smitten with her."

"That's great. I like her. I mean, she's a little crazy, but that makes her a good fit for you."

"Hey! It's not my fault that I got all the fun genes and you ended up with the dependable, boring ones."

Susanne let out a snort. "You wish."

"By the way, I'm coming down to Freiburg this weekend. I want to check on Uncle Nobby."

"Uncle Norbert. That's who you'll come to see. Sure."

"Well, maybe not just him," Franzi admitted. "No need to make up the couch for me this time. I'm staying with Miri."

Susanne hadn't expected anything else. "God, you really are smitten."

"Oh, and you aren't?"

The line went silent while Susanne took several deep breaths. Was she?

"Come on, admit it. Miri told me she caught the two of you in the middle of a hot make-out session, during business hours no less!"

"It wasn't a make-out session. I was just kissing her hello."

"Hey, no need to get defensive. I'm happy for you." Franzi chuckled. "Wouldn't it be crazy if both of us ended up moving to Freiburg? And I didn't even have to step into a *Bächle*!"

"Whoa!" Susanne held up her free hand even though Franzi couldn't see it. "I didn't say anything about moving to Freiburg! Right now, we're just seeing where it might go. Are you really at that point already? Franzi, this is crazy! You've known her for all of two weeks!"

"What, you think you lesbians have a monopoly on the U-Haul phenomenon? I'll have you know that some of us bisexuals aren't immune to premature-moving-van syndrome either."

"Franzi…"

Her sister laughed. "Just kidding. God, lighten up. We're not moving in with each other anytime soon, although I wouldn't rule it out for the future. But for now, we're taking it one day at a time."

Jae

Susanne exhaled and rubbed the back of her neck. The muscles there were tense. Maybe Franzi was right—she really should lighten up and not worry so much or she wouldn't survive the next six weeks. But she wasn't as good as her sister at living in the here and now; she always thought five steps ahead and never went into any situation without a solid business plan.

"Sorry. I didn't mean to go all big sister on you." Susanne paused. "So are you giving her anything for Valentine's Day?"

"What? Are you afraid I'm going to send her a ring?" From Franzi's tone, it was obvious that she was grinning.

"I'm serious. Are you getting her a gift?"

"I thought about taking her to a tree-top ropes course on Saturday afternoon. Is that non-U-Hauly enough for you?"

Susanne laughed. "Yes, that has my sisterly approval." But it didn't help her decide what to do about Valentine's Day herself. With her fear of heights, Anja probably wouldn't enjoy an afternoon up in the trees.

"You're not just asking because you're worried about me and Miri moving too fast, are you?"

Her sister knew her too well. Susanne sighed. "It's been a day, an hour, and twenty minutes since Anja and I...since we agreed to give it a chance. We said no promises. So do I give her something for Valentine's Day? What if I don't and she's got something for me? I don't want her to think I don't care, but I also don't want to make any promises I might not be able to—"

"Susanne," her sister said, instantly getting her full attention. Franzi never called her anything but Susi. "You're overthinking things."

Susanne let her head drop back against the recliner. "I know you're right, but..."

"Just do whatever feels right. Anja doesn't seem like the type of woman who would expect grand gestures anyway."

Susanne remembered the no-glitter conversation. "She's not."

"If all else fails, why not give her a pen? She's crazy about that kind of stuff, isn't she?"

"God, yes, she is." Susanne chuckled a little as she thought about what a geek Anja could be. "But a pen is out of the question. Fountain pens are the new jewelry."

"They are?"

Susanne shrugged. "Apparently. I think I'll just try to play it by ear tomorrow." After all, that was what Anja and she had decided to do—enjoy the moment without worrying about where it would lead.

"Yeah. That's what you always do when it comes to relationships," Franzi said. "You never agonize over stuff like this. Why should it be different now?"

Because everything feels different with Anja. But she wasn't ready to voice that thought, not even to her twin sister. "Thanks. Guess I'll see you on Saturday, then. Don't break your neck on the ropes course, okay?"

Franzi chuckled. "Not planning on it."

They said goodbye and ended the call.

"No agonizing. Just play it by ear," Susanne told herself. Determined to stop thinking about it, she reached for her laptop to check in with the company setting up Paper Love's webstore.

Chapter 16

The store didn't have a lot of customers the next afternoon, maybe because everyone else was preparing to spend the evening with their partner. Would Anja get to do the same? She wasn't sure Susanne would want to. Maybe she would think doing something on Valentine's Day would imply too much of a commitment, and they were trying to avoid that for now.

Just ask her and find out instead of brooding over it! She peeked over at Susanne, who sat behind the counter and adjusted her camera lens to take photos of fountain pens and ink bottles for the blog.

But before Anja could open her mouth, Susanne put down the camera and looked over at her. Her gray eyes twinkled. "Want to get inky with me?"

Anja forgot the questions plaguing her and walked over. She couldn't help smiling. "Get inky, hmm? What did you have in mind?"

"Remember the pen that dripped ink all over my fingers? I still have no clue how to fill up one of those. Can you show me?"

Anja beamed. Susanne showing an interest in her beloved pens was the best Valentine's Day gift she could imagine. "Sure." She grabbed a bottle of her favorite ink—a rich, dark-bluish purple—slid a second stool behind the counter, and took a seat next to her.

Susanne handed her the pen she had just photographed.

"That one is not a piston filler. Let's try it with this one." Anja reached for another pen.

Susanne directed an expectant gaze at Anja's hands, watching every motion.

A tingle went through Anja at having Susanne's intense focus on her. Somehow it felt incredibly intimate to have her look at her hands. She cleared her throat. "Here." She gave Susanne the pen. "You try it. I'll talk you through it."

Susanne grinned. "Want to see how well I take instructions when it comes to… manual tasks?"

Anja nudged her with her elbow. "Focus." When Susanne opened her mouth, she added, "On the pen."

Smiling, Susanne closed her mouth and unscrewed the bottle of ink. "So what do I do?"

"First…" Anja reached out and slid the long sleeves of Susanne's shirt up over her elbows to avoid getting ink on it. Her hand slid over Susanne's bare skin in the process, giving her a glimpse of what it might feel like to undress her.

Now it was Susanne's turn to nudge her. "Focus—on the pen."

Heat rose up Anja's neck at being caught daydreaming. God, she hadn't blushed this much in years. "First, you turn the piston knob at the end of the barrel counterclockwise. That extends the piston inside of the pen toward the nib."

Susanne did it.

"Mmm, you follow instructions well," Anja murmured.

Susanne looked up, and their gazes met.

Was it just her, or was it getting really warm inside the store?

Anja had to clear her throat before she could continue. "Then you dip the nib into the ink."

Susanne carefully slid the nib into the ink bottle.

"Deeper." Anja gently guided her hand.

"Jesus," Susanne breathed. "You can't say things like that to me. Not in that sexy voice of yours."

"What…oh! I…I didn't…" Anja yanked her hand away from Susanne's fingers. "All I meant was that the entire nib needs to be submerged, or it won't work."

Susanne fanned herself with one hand while guiding the nib more deeply into the ink with the other.

"Just like that." Anja bit her lip. Why did everything coming from her mouth suddenly sound like something she might say during sex?

Susanne groaned. "Are we filling up a fountain pen or engaging in verbal foreplay?"

"The latter. Uh, the former! I meant the former!" God, this entire conversation while sitting so close to Susanne made Anja's head spin. She hid her face behind her hands. Her cheeks probably looked like a ripe tomato.

Laughing, Susanne pulled her hands away from her face, leaned over, and kissed one of her overheated cheeks. "You know," she said, her voice hoarse, "I'm starting to see why you love fountain pens so much."

"I have a feeling you appreciate them for very different reasons than I do. But you just wait until you try this one out. The nib is amazingly smooth. It glides over paper like…"

"Naked skin over satin sheets?" Susanne's eyes twinkled.

The words created images in Anja's mind that made her feel even warmer. "Now who's engaging in verbal foreplay?"

"Okay, okay. Let's focus on the pen. What's next?"

"You turn the knob in the other direction to draw the ink into the pen." Anja watched Susanne's long, slender fingers as she twisted the knob clockwise. "Now turn the knob just a tiny bit in the other direction to release a few drops. That gets the air out."

"And you have to do this every time your pen runs out of ink?" Susanne asked. "Wouldn't it be easier to just use cartridges? Open pen, old cartridge out, new one in, screw back together, done."

"On the danger of sounding like verbal foreplay again, a fast in and out isn't always best. A true pen aficionado wants to savor the process."

Susanne hummed. "Savoring… Mmm, yeah, I'm all for that."

Wow. This really had to be the sexiest ink refilling of all time. Anja had trouble focusing on the task at hand. "All right. Now wipe it clean, and you're done."

Susanne took a tissue from a box on the counter and wiped down the ink-smeared section and the nib of the pen. When she crumpled up the tissue and threw it into the wastebasket, her fingers came away a bit inky.

"Oops." Anja handed her another tissue.

Susanne wiped at the stains and grinned. "Don't worry. I don't mind getting my fingers wet."

Anja gulped in air. "Getting inky with you is dangerous."

"Nah. I'm totally tame."

"Uh-huh." If there was one word Anja didn't associate with Susanne, it was tame. She had a feeling she could be dangerous for more than her libido. "So want to try it?"

Susanne stared at her for a few seconds. "Oh, you mean the pen."

"What else would I mean?" Anja tried for her most innocent expression. She slid a sheet of paper in front of her and watched the way Susanne's long, strong fingers seemed to cradle the pen rather than gripping it.

"Ooh, nice." Susanne studied whatever she had written for a moment and seemed to hesitate before holding the paper out to Anja.

She expected to find Susanne's name or *hello, hello, hello*. That was what most people wrote while testing out a pen. Instead, Susanne had written a short message to her.

Want to have dinner with me tonight?

Oh wow. Susanne had to be aware of what day it was. The store was covered in paper heart decorations, and half of the customers coming in yesterday and this morning had been looking for last-minute Valentine's Day gifts.

Anja swallowed. She didn't trust her voice, so she took the pen from Susanne and wrote *yes* with three exclamation marks beneath Susanne's message. Then she held the sheet of paper out for her to read.

"Great." Susanne beamed. "Where do you want to go?"

The bell above the door jingled, announcing another customer.

"Surprise me," Anja whispered to Susanne.

***

"Surprise me, she says," Susanne growled as she shoved her cell phone back into her pocket. "Yeah, she will be very surprised when I take her to some fast-food place."

She had called a dozen restaurants, but none of them had any free tables for tonight, no matter how much money she offered. Maybe it shouldn't have come as a surprise; it was Valentine's Day after all.

Well, there was always option B: she could cook for Anja. Usually, she didn't like wasting her time cooking, but she was a more than decent cook if she put her mind to it. Plus dinner at her place would be more intimate than a restaurant—no other diners and no waitress to interrupt them at just the wrong moment.

Susanne nodded as she warmed up to the idea.

Then she remembered that she didn't even have a table or chairs in her dining room. No way could she invite Anja to a romantic Valentine's Day dinner and then expect her to eat bent over the coffee table.

Dammit.

Anja stuck her head out of the store. "Everything okay?"

Susanne paused her pacing along the cobblestone street. "Oh yeah. Everything's fine."

"Did you find us a place to have dinner?"

"Um, yes." Susanne glanced at her watch. If she hurried like crazy, maybe she could buy a table and two chairs and cook a not too extravagant but delicious dinner. "But I'll have to take off now. Is that okay?"

Anja sent her a startled gaze. Then a smile curled her lips. "Don't tell me you're one of those women who need three hours to get ready for a date."

"No, I… You'll just have to wait and see what I have in store for you. I'll pick you up at seven. Um, better make it seven thirty."

"I'm looking forward to it," Anja said, her voice soft as a touch.

Susanne knew she needed to get going, but she couldn't resist giving her a gentle kiss. "Me too," she whispered against her lips.

After lingering for a moment longer, she forced herself to step back and hurried down the street toward her car. She had three and a half hours to get furniture, assemble it, buy groceries, and cook dinner. It was crazy, but as she skidded down the ramp and into the parking garage, she decided that Anja was worth it.

∽༄∾

The irony wasn't lost on Anja: a few hours ago, she had teased Susanne about taking three hours to get ready for a date, and now she was the one who was taking forever. She had put on three different outfits before finally settling on the beige corduroy skirt and the knee-high, brown boots she had worn to the stationery fair last month. If she wasn't mistaken, Susanne had checked out her legs several times when they'd been on the train. Instead of the conservative blouse she had worn to the trade fair, she had paired the skirt with a long-sleeved, deep-red top with a sweetheart neckline that dipped low, revealing the swell of her breasts if she moved a certain way.

She studied herself in the mirrored sliding closet doors. Was she overdressed? Underdressed? Too sexy? Not sexy enough? It was impossible to say since she had no idea where Susanne would be taking her.

Not that it really mattered. All she wanted was to spend time with her because that was the one thing they didn't have a lot of: time.

She brushed the thought aside and went to dab some perfume on her neck and wrists.

Seven thirty—the time Susanne had said she'd pick her up—came and went, but the doorbell didn't ring. Had she been unable to decide what to wear too?

By seven forty, Anja was pacing her small apartment. She would have called Susanne to make sure everything was okay, but she didn't want to come across like the overbearing girlfriend.

When the doorbell rang, it startled her, even though she'd been waiting for it.

Finally! Not bothering with the intercom, she locked the door behind her and rushed down the stairs.

Susanne's BMW was parked in front of the building, and Susanne waited next to it. She wore jeans that were so faded they appeared almost white and a black, long-sleeved shirt with big, white letters saying, *I like coffee and maybe three people.*

Anja hoped she was among the lucky three. *Okay, I'm definitely overdressed. Where on earth is she taking me?*

"I'm so sorry." Susanne kissed Anja hello. "I'm running behind my admittedly ambitious schedule. I didn't have time to change."

"So I'm not overdressed?"

Susanne's gaze roved over the formfitting top, the knee-length skirt, and the boots that Miri always said emphasized her slender legs. The open admiration in her eyes made Anja stand a little taller. "No, you're perfect. Very beautiful." She kissed Anja again and then opened the passenger side door for her.

Susanne got in on the other side and started the car.

"Do we have time to go to your place so you can change?" Anja asked. "What time is the dinner reservation?"

"Oh, the chef said they're pretty flexible, so yes, we've got time."

Anja stared at her. "You talked to the chef?"

"Guess you could say that." A tiny grin played around the corners of Susanne's mouth.

Anja regarded her through narrowed eyes. "You're planning something."

"Me? Nah. Not a thing."

"Uh-huh." By now, Anja knew her well enough that Susanne's poker face couldn't fool her. She resisted the urge to reach over and nudge her only because Susanne was driving.

Soon, they pulled into the parking garage beneath Susanne's apartment building.

"Want me to wait here while you go get changed?" Anja asked.

"No. Come on in." Susanne walked around the car and opened the door for her.

Anja smiled. She liked this feeling of being courted. Next time, she would do the same for Susanne.

When they entered the apartment, the first thing Anja noticed was the heavenly scent drifting through the hall from the kitchen. Then, as she walked closer, she discovered a table and two chairs that hadn't been here at her last visit.

She whirled around to Susanne, who stood with her hands in her pockets, almost as if she were uncertain or embarrassed. "You…you did all of this? Today?"

"Yeah. All the restaurants I called didn't have any free tables, so it was either this or taking you to a fast-food place for a *Yufka*."

"I would have been fine with *Yufka*, but…wow." Anja walked into the dining room and slid her palms over the backrest of one chair. "How did you get the table and the chairs so fast?"

"Good old bribery." Susanne grinned. "That and some elbow grease. I assembled them myself."

"Wow," Anja said again because her brain failed to find the words to express her feelings. No one had ever done something like this for her. "Thank you for going to all this trouble."

"My pleasure. Can you keep an eye on the lasagna while I go take a quick shower and change?"

"Ooh, lasagna! Sure. But you'd better hurry, or I can't guarantee that there'll be any left over for you."

Susanne smiled. "So I picked the right thing to cook?"

"Absolutely. It's one of my top five dishes—as long as it's a veggie one."

"Of course it is," Susanne said, sounding almost insulted. "I'll hurry." She disappeared into the bathroom, and Anja tried not to imagine her stripping out of her clothes and stepping beneath the warm spray of the shower, soapy suds running down the planes of her belly.

Admittedly, her attempt to not picture it was a complete failure, so to distract herself, she peeked into the oven.

The lasagna sizzling away in a large pan looked ready to be served, so she turned down the temperature on the oven. She opened the cabinets until she found plates and glasses. Susanne had already done all of the work, so the least she could do was set the table.

"There's white wine in the fridge and a bottle of red on the counter," Susanne called from the bathroom. "Feel free to open whatever you prefer."

Since the lasagna was a veggie one, Anja opened the bottle of pinot blanc chilling in the fridge. Just as she looked around for napkins, a meow and a tap-tap-tap drifted over from the living room.

Anja hesitated, then shook her head. Susanne seemed insistent on not letting the cat think this might be his new home, and she had to respect that. Besides, she wanted this evening to be just for the two of them. "Sorry, Muesli. Not tonight."

When she heard the bathroom door open, she took the lasagna out of the oven. A cloud of steam wafted up. Her mouth watered at the scent of tomato, ricotta, and melted mozzarella cheese. Carefully, she put two huge pieces on their plates.

She felt more than heard Susanne come up behind her. "How does it look?" she asked right next to Anja's ear.

Anja shivered and inhaled deeply. Susanne smelled of cocoa butter, maybe from a shower gel, and a subtle but sexy perfume.

"Yummy," Anja answered, not sure if she meant Susanne or the lasagna. Probably both. She turned and found herself nearly body to body with Susanne, who had changed out of her jeans and the long-sleeved shirt. Black slacks hugged her hips, and a silver-gray top emphasized the color of her eyes. Its cowl neck dipped low, giving Anja a tantalizing glimpse of her cleavage, while the capped sleeves showed off her toned arms.

Anja's mouth watered again, and this time the lasagna had nothing to do with it. Susanne looked good enough to eat. "You look…nice." Gosh, she really was out of practice at complimenting women. "Very, very nice."

Okay, that wasn't much better, but the warm glow in Susanne's eyes revealed that she knew how much Anja appreciated her outfit.

"Thanks. Come on. Let's eat before the lasagna gets cold."

Anja carried the plates to the table, while Susanne followed with their glasses of wine.

"Sorry I don't have any napkins," Susanne said as they sat.

"Doesn't matter. This is perfect just the way it is. Much better than a restaurant."

"Really?"

Anja nodded.

Susanne lifted her glass. "To a perfect evening."

To us, Anja wanted to say, but since they were taking it one day at a time, that might have been too much, so she nodded and looked into Susanne's eyes. "To a perfect evening."

They clinked glasses and then dug into the steaming lasagna.

The taste of tomato, fresh mushrooms, zucchini, bell pepper, and cheese burst on her taste buds. "I know I keep repeating myself, but…wow! You can cook, and you can ink up a fountain pen. You might be—" She stopped herself before she could say, *The perfect woman for me.*

Again, that implied too much of a long-term commitment, didn't it? Anja suppressed a sigh. This taking-it-one-day-at-a-time thing was tougher than she had expected.

"Might be what?" Susanne prompted when Anja fell silent.

"A much better date than your sister. Did you know she's taking Miri to a tree-top ropes course on Saturday?" She shivered at the thought of flying from tree to tree on a zip line.

Susanne laughed. "Yeah, I know. Not your idea of romance?"

"No! If I sink into your arms, I want it to be because your kisses make me weak in the knees, not because I'm toppling over in sheer panic."

"Well, I didn't have time to make a dessert, so we can test out if I can actually make you topple over after dinner."

Even though she wanted to savor every bite of the delicious lasagna, Anja found herself eating a little faster.

After dinner, they worked together to clear the table, rinse the dirty dishes, and put them in the dishwasher. It felt very domestic, and Anja found that she loved those quiet moments when their hands brushed as she handed plates to Susanne.

Once the kitchen was clean, Susanne led her over to the couch.

Muesli was still sitting on the other side of the French doors, and he started tapping on the glass when he saw them.

Susanne gave a weary sigh. "Want to let him in?"

"Well, that depends."

"On?"

Anja smiled. "If he stays outside, is there an alternative source for some cuddles?"

Susanne tapped her chin as if having to think about it. "I guess since I'm the hostess, I could provide some."

"Poor you." Anja put on a faux sympathetic expression. "That sounds like a horrible sacrifice."

Susanne nodded gravely. "Yeah, but someone's gotta do it."

Anja rose and pretended to head to the French doors. "If it's such a hardship to you, I'm sure we could get Muesli to—"

With a firm grasp on her corduroy-covered hips, Susanne pulled her back and turned her around. Her lips found Anja's, gentle at first, then, when Anja wrapped her arms around her and drew her closer, nipping and teasing with more heat.

Anja's legs went to jelly, and she sank back onto the couch. Susanne tasted like tomatoes and wine, and Anja instantly felt drunk on her.

When Susanne's mouth left hers, Anja let out a groan of protest, which turned into a low moan as Susanne kissed her throat and slid one hand between them to trace the bare skin just above the neckline of her top.

Oh God.

Almost drowsy with pleasure, Anja couldn't keep her eyes open any longer. Not that she needed to see. Her other senses took over as she tugged the shirt from the back of Susanne's slacks and slipped her hands beneath to caress the warm, soft skin.

In return, Susanne slid her hand down and gently palmed one breast through the fabric of Anja's top.

Anja pulled back with a gasp. Dazed, she realized that she was no longer sitting on the couch. She had slid down on the sofa, and Susanne lay half on top of her, her body warm and pleasantly heavy against her own. Anja's skirt had slid up, and one of Susanne's thighs had slipped between Anja's legs, making her head spin. All she wanted was to pull her closer or, even better yet, take her to bed, but something held her back. "Susanne…"

"God, the way you say my name…" Susanne trailed her thumb along Anja's lips.

A shiver went through Anja, and she nearly forgot what she had wanted to say. "Susanne."

Susanne paused and studied her, her gray eyes questioning. "Are we moving too fast for you?"

"No. Yes." Her body and her mind gave her conflicting signals. Her heart thumped wildly, as much from arousal as from apprehension of how Susanne would react to what she would say next. "I want you, but…" Her cheeks heating, she looked away. "I'm on the last day of my period, so…"

"Ah."

"Sorry. I know that's not romantic or sexy or—"

Susanne framed her face with both hands, leaned down, and kissed her softly. "It's okay," she whispered against Anja's lips. "We're not in a hurry."

Aren't we? Susanne would be gone in six weeks. Shouldn't she be eager to make good use of the time they had, period be damned?

Before she could decide, Susanne navigated them around so they were both lying on their sides, facing each other, and opened her arms. "I believe I promised you cuddles."

Anja sank into her arms with a sigh. "Thank you. For dinner and, you know, understanding."

Susanne kissed her forehead. "No need to thank me. Just because it's Valentine's Day doesn't mean we need to have sex. We get to make up our own rules as we go along. And to tell you the truth, the first time we make love, I could do without this blister on my hand too."

Had she just said *make love*? Anja stared at her, but Susanne's expression didn't change. *She didn't mean it like that. It's just a figure of speech.* Belatedly, Anja's brain processed what Susanne had just said. "Wait. Did you just say…you've got a blister?" She examined one hand, then the other. The skin in the middle of one palm was reddened, and a small blister had formed. She caressed the fingers of the affected hand. "How did that happen?"

"It's from the screwdriver when I assembled the chairs and the table."

Anja shook her head. "What kind of lesbian are you? Aren't you supposed to own power tools like a rechargeable screwdriver?"

"I have one—in my apartment in Berlin, so I borrowed an old-fashioned one from one of my neighbors."

Anja ignored the reminder that Susanne's home wasn't here in Freiburg and instead pressed a kiss to the base of her thumb. "So we're both out of order, in a manner of speaking."

"Just my hand, not my mouth," Susanne answered.

A flush swept through Anja from head to toe as erotic images of what Susanne's mouth could do danced through her mind.

"What?" Susanne tickled her lightly. "I was talking about another kiss."

"Sure."

"No, really." As if to prove it, Susanne slid down on the couch a little and kissed her, and Anja forgot about the conversation and about everything else.

∽∾∾∿

"If I don't leave now, I'm going to fall asleep like this," Anja murmured, sounding already half asleep. Her head was tucked beneath Susanne's chin and her cheek pressed to her chest. Her warm breath teased Susanne's skin where the front of her top dipped low.

Susanne opened one eye. She'd been pretty close to drifting off too. After her libido had finally settled down, she was content to just hold Anja. "What would be wrong with that?"

"This couch isn't meant for two."

"Then come to bed with me," Susanne said.

Anja lifted her head off her chest to look at her.

Susanne chuckled. "To sleep."

The eager glow in Anja's eyes was just too cute. "I'd love that. The thought of traveling all the way across town and crawling into my cold and lonely bed isn't very appealing right now."

Driving her home and then returning to her empty—well, now slightly less empty—apartment didn't sound great to Susanne either. "So then stay."

"If you're really okay with it…"

"Why wouldn't I be? It's been a long day with all the rushing around to get everything ready in time for our date, so I'll probably fall asleep as soon as my head hits the pillow. You don't have to worry about me not being able to keep my hands to myself."

"Who said I was worried?" Anja's tone was low and husky. "At least not about you."

Susanne grinned. It was good to know that Anja was affected by their physical closeness too. Not that her reaction to their kisses had left much doubt about it. She kissed her softly. "I've got faith in you."

Susanne gave her a T-shirt to sleep in and a spare toothbrush, and they took turns in the bathroom. She settled into bed with her back against the headboard and pulled the duvet up to her hips while she waited for Anja. Her hands curled around the blanket. God, why was she so nervous? Nothing would happen tonight.

But if she was honest with herself, she knew that wasn't true. Even if they didn't have sex, something significant was about to happen. Susanne was used to having her own space, and sharing it with someone had never come easy for her, maybe because it left her with a strange feeling of vulnerability. The first time a new girlfriend had slept over had always been a natural progression of sex, never this very conscious decision of inviting her to stay because she didn't want their time together to end.

The door opened, and Anja stepped into the bedroom.

The T-shirt Susanne had given her was a perfect fit on her own taller body, but on Anja's short, slim frame, it appeared more like a mini-dress, almost reaching her knees.

A grin curled up the corners of Susanne's mouth. *God. I think that's the cutest thing I've ever seen.* There was also something very intimate about seeing Anja wear her clothes.

Anja tugged on the hem of the shirt with a self-conscious smile. She crossed the room, and Susanne lifted up the covers for her to climb in.

The mattress dipped, and Susanne suddenly became aware of the fact that her bed was just a queen, which forced them to lie pretty close to each other.

Anja's arm brushed hers as they both settled down on their backs.

A tingle ran through Susanne's body, which was obviously expecting an activity other than sleeping to follow. *Settle down,* she firmly told her libido.

Anja turned on her side, slid her arm beneath her pillow, and regarded Susanne intently.

"What?" Susanne asked.

"I like this." Anja waved the hand that wasn't beneath her pillow back and forth. "Sleeping with you. In the same bed, I mean."

"What can I say? I'm good in bed, even if all I'm doing is breathing." Then Susanne sobered, knowing that Anja's confession deserved more than a joking answer. God, for a relationship that was supposed to be the let's-take-it-easy-and-see-where-this-is-going type, this was getting pretty intense, intimacy-wise. "I really like it too. It takes a bit of getting used to, but it's nice. Really nice."

Anja nodded. "Although…"

Tension seeped into Susanne's muscles. "Although?"

"I'd like it even better if we could…" Anja fell silent and nibbled her lip.

Ah. Susanne's tension was replaced by a warm feeling spreading through her like sunshine on a Sunday morning. She slid to the middle of the bed and pulled Anja into her arms. "This?"

Anja exhaled. "Yes." She placed her head on Susanne's upper chest and wrapped one arm around her hips above the covers. "Is this okay?"

Susanne took her arm, pulled it beneath the duvet, and put it back where it had been. She wrapped her own arm around Anja and spread her fingers across her back, holding Anja safely against her. "Now it's okay."

After a minute or two, her libido got the message that nothing would be happening tonight and finally settled down.

Mmm. This is nice. She deeply inhaled Anja's fresh scent.

"Good night," Anja said. "Sweet dreams."

Susanne trailed her fingers through Anja's hair, evoking a sound that resembled a purr. "You too."

She could tell the exact moment Anja fell asleep. Her body relaxed more fully against her own, her even breathing warmed the cotton at the swell of Susanne's right breast, and her arm seemed to become heavier, holding Susanne in place. Normally, she couldn't fall asleep on her back, but now she felt a pleasant exhaustion settle over her. It didn't take very long for her to follow Anja into the realm of dreams.

Chapter 17

If this was a dream, Anja didn't want to wake up. She lay cuddled up to Susanne from behind, spooning her. Despite her being considerably shorter, their bodies fit against each other amazingly well. Anja's cheek rested against Susanne's back, and she snuggled her face deeper into the soft cotton. Her arm was wrapped around Susanne, who clutched it even in her sleep, pressing Anja's hand against the warm spot at the top of her breasts.

Anja held very still so she wouldn't wake her. She wanted to enjoy this as long as she could. It had been too long since she had woken up next to someone—and not just any someone. Someone she cared for.

After a while, Susanne stirred and stretched against her. The brush of her body along Anja's front made her bite back a moan.

Susanne rolled over and smiled as their gazes connected. "Good morning."

"Good morning."

"Are you always such a bed hog?" Susanne asked, still smiling.

Anja groaned. "Oh no. What did I do?"

"I had to get up to use the bathroom once, and when I got back, you were on my side of the bed."

Only now did Anja realize that she wasn't where she had fallen asleep. Apparently, Susanne had solved the problem by crawling in on the other side. She covered her face with her hand. "Sorry."

"No need to apologize. It's cute as hell." Susanne gently pulled Anja's hand away and caressed the length of her back, making Anja arch against her like a big cat.

She slid closer to feel more of Susanne's warm body pressed against her own, but when Susanne leaned forward to kiss her, Anja placed a hand on her chest and stopped her.

Susanne paused and gave her a questioning look.

"Sorry, I…" Anja hid her face against Susanne's shoulder, then peeked up. "God, first I can't have sex, and now I refuse to even kiss you. Please don't think I don't want you. I do. I really, really do, but…"

"Hey, it's okay if you're not the morning-sex type. Or the morning-kisses type."

"Oh, I'm all for morning sex and for morning kisses," Anja said, not bothering to hide her enthusiasm, "after I've used the bathroom and had time to brush my teeth."

Susanne laughed. "You might be the most down-to-earth woman I've ever dated. You know what you want and what you don't want. I like that."

Anja had a feeling she was grinning like a fool. She loved Susanne for taking everything in stride without making her feel bad about it. It proved that even though they hadn't made any commitment to each other beyond the six weeks, this wasn't just a physical fling for Susanne either.

"So," Anja slid her arm beneath the covers to return the soft caresses to Susanne's back, "I take it you're a morning-sex person?"

"Most of the time, I'm the rushing-off-to-work type, but I have a feeling with the right woman, I could be an any-time-of-the-day-sex person."

Am I the right woman? Anja hoped they would get a chance to find out sometime soon. For now, she would settle for a kiss or two. Determined, she tossed the covers back and swung her legs out of bed.

"Hey, where are you going? We've still got," Susanne glanced at the alarm clock, "fifteen minutes before we have to get up."

"To the bathroom." Anja gave her a meaningful look. "To brush my teeth."

"Ooh! Wait, I'm coming with you."

They chased each other to the bathroom, and Anja was amazed at Susanne's unexpectedly playful side. Since they spent most of their time together working, that part of her didn't often make an appearance, and she had a feeling she was one of the lucky few who ever got to see it.

Side by side, they brushed their teeth, sharing the sink.

Finally, Susanne showed off her shiny white teeth in a broad grin. "So now that we both have fresh, minty breath, how about—?"

Anja didn't wait for her to finish the sentence. She pressed her against the sink and kissed her.

The alarm clock going off in the bedroom finally tore them apart.

Susanne groaned and broke the kiss. "We'd better get dressed. We have to open the store on time."

"Yes, and we should check on Nobby on the way to work." Anja kissed her one last time before she slipped out of the bathroom so Susanne could take a quick shower. Sometimes, being a responsible adult sucked.

"You did it, didn't you?" was the first thing out of Miri's mouth as she entered Anja's apartment for their Friday Netflix night. She took Anja by both shoulders and studied her from head to toe, then let out a little squeal that made Gino woof. "You slept with her!"

"Jesus, Miri, keep your voice down!" Anja peeked past her to the staircase, which was thankfully empty. She grabbed Miri's arm, dragged her farther into the apartment, and closed the door.

Miri unleashed the dog and then immediately went back to scrutinizing Anja. "You slept with her."

"No. I mean, yes, but not—"

"Oh, don't bother denying it. I can tell. You've got this glow about you."

Anja glanced at the mirror in the hallway. She was blushing, but otherwise, she didn't look any different. "Nonsense. I'm not glowing."

"Yes, you are. You're sporting the infamous after-sex glow."

More warmth flooded Anja's face. "That's not even a thing."

"Oh yes, it is. Trust me. I should know." Miri smirked. She pulled her to the sofa bed and pressed her down on it before getting comfortable next to her. "So how was it? Come on, details! I need details!"

"You want all the graphic details? Are you sure you're ready to hear them?"

That gave Miri pause. "Um, well, there are some things no one needs to know about their best friend, but otherwise…hell yes, I'm ready!"

"All right. Here are the details of my very exciting first night with Susanne."

Miri slid closer as if not wanting to miss a thing.

Anja struggled to keep a straight face. "She prepared a very romantic dinner and basically courted me all night, and then we had a little make-out session on the couch that got pretty heated, so she asked me to go to bed with her."

"And? Come on!" Miri waved her hand. "Get to the interesting part!"

"We got into bed, and she took me into her arms. God, her body felt so good against mine." Anja's eyes fluttered shut, and for a moment, she could almost pretend to be back in Susanne's arms. "She caressed my back and trailed her fingers through my hair and then…"

"And then?"

Anja opened her eyes. "We fell asleep."

"You did not!" Miri slapped Anja's thigh. "Come on. Tell me what happened in between the back caresses and the falling asleep."

"Nothing, I swear." Anja held up three fingers. "We didn't make love; we just slept together. In a nonsexual way."

Jae

"But…but…why? Why wouldn't you sleep with her—*really* sleep with her? When I caught you kissing in the store, you both looked ready to tear each other's clothes off."

"I…" Anja tugged on a tiny hole at the knee of her jeans. "I wanted to, but I had my period, so I stopped her before it could go too far."

"Ah. Got it." Miri wrapped one arm around her and squeezed. "That sucks." She paused as if considering what she'd just said, then grinned. "Or doesn't suck, in this case."

Anja groaned at the bad pun.

Miri turned on the sofa, curled one leg under her, and studied Anja intently. "There's something else, isn't there?"

Her friend knew her too well. Anja avoided her gaze. "I think it would have happened if it wasn't for my period, but I can't help thinking maybe taking it slow is for the best."

"Is it?" Miri asked. "I thought the whole point of dating her was to see if there could be something worth pursuing after she leaves. Why wouldn't sex be part of testing it out?"

Anja cringed at the reminder that Susanne would only be staying a handful of more weeks. She lowered her gaze to the hole in her jeans again. "Because I don't think it would be just sex."

Miri pulled her around by the shoulder so Anja would look at her. "What do you mean?"

Anja peeked up at her. "I think if I made love to her and she to me, it would shove me over the edge."

A smile curved Miri's lips. "Isn't that the point of having sex? For your partner to take you over the edge?"

"Not that edge. I'm talking about my feelings for her. I think if we made love, it would make me fall for her all the way."

"Ah." Miri gave her a knowing look. "So that's why you stopped her. You were afraid of falling."

Anja wanted to deny it. When she and Susanne had kissed on the couch and she had ended up deliciously trapped beneath Susanne's body, she hadn't consciously thought about it. But deep down, she knew it had probably influenced her decision to stop.

"You know what I think?" Miri said. "That look on your face when I got here? That wasn't the after-sex glow."

188

"Of course it wasn't. Didn't we just establish that Susanne and I didn't have sex?"

Miri waved her away. "Now that I think about it, maybe it was more the goofy I'm-so-in-love glow."

"No, I'm not... I..."

"I think it doesn't really matter whether you have sex with her or not, Anja. You'll fall for her even without mind-blowing orgasms. If you haven't already."

Anja sank against the back of the couch and stared at the wall, which blurred before her eyes. Something quivered deep inside of her. God, Miri was right. Her feelings for Susanne had grown with every day they spent together, and even abstaining from sex wouldn't change the fact that she was falling in love with her. "Shit."

Miri laughed and patted her knee. "Hey, look on the bright side. After Easter, you and I can keep each other company on the long drives or the flights to Berlin and back, and Franzi and Susanne can travel together too."

"Assuming Susanne wants a long-distance relationship with me."

"Why wouldn't she? You're great."

The genuine compliment and the unshakable conviction in Miri's voice sent a faint smile to Anja's face. "Thanks."

"So Indian food and Netflix now?" Miri rustled the bag of food she'd put down on the end of the couch. "Maybe the sex scenes in *Orange Is the New Black* will give you some pointers for your sadly nonexistent sex life."

Anja took the bag from her. "For that remark, you're not getting any samosas."

Chapter 18

"Hey, you bought more furniture, Sis." Franzi stepped into the dining room, hand in hand with Miriam. "I thought you didn't want to do that because you'd only have to sell it again. Does that mean—?"

"It means I didn't want my guests to have to eat from the floor or crouched over the coffee table," Susanne said before her sister could finish the sentence. She didn't want to get Anja's hopes up, making her think she'd be staying.

"And this guest for one is certainly grateful." With a groan, Miriam eased herself down on one of the two folding chairs Susanne had borrowed from Anja. "God, I'm so sore."

Susanne covered her ears with her hands. "No details, please," she and Anja said in unison.

Miriam snorted. "I wish. Get your minds out of the gutter, you two. I'm sore from spending all afternoon on the ropes course."

While she and Franzi rested their sore limbs, Susanne and Anja worked together to get the food on the table. They sidestepped each other in the small kitchen area as if it were a choreography they had rehearsed all day, never getting in each other's way. It had been the same when they had prepared the meal together, Susanne taking care of the potato salad while Anja made zucchini balls.

Susanne stole a quick kiss as she handed Anja the glasses and then another one after dinner, when they put the dishes in the dishwasher.

When they walked into the living room after cleaning up the kitchen, Miriam was leaning sideways on the couch so she could whisper into Franzi's ear. Whatever she said made both of them blush, and they exchanged a kiss before Miriam let herself sink against the back of the couch.

Susanne placed tortilla chips and guacamole on the coffee table. "You're moving a lot better now. Looks like you found a miracle cure for your sore muscles."

"What can I say? Your sister is one talented doctor." Miriam winked. She took a chip, dipped it into the guacamole, and then fed it to Franzi.

Susanne huffed. "She's a dentist."

"Must be why she can do amazing things with her mouth and her teeth."

"TMI, TMI." Susanne lowered herself into the two-person inflatable lounger next to Anja. Buying it didn't count as furniture shopping, so she wasn't sending out mixed signals, right?

Warmth suffused Susanne's side as Anja immediately leaned in to her shoulder. She slung one arm around Anja. Buying the lounger had definitely been a good idea since it forced them to cuddle up.

Anja looked at Franzi. "I forgot to ask earlier because I got distracted by your crazy story about the kid with the braces. How was the ropes course?"

Franzi hastily swallowed a mouthful of tortilla chip. "Amazing! They had rope swings, suspension bridges, zip lines, and an obstacle that had you slide from one tree to the next on a surfboard. We had a blast. You should try it sometime."

"Anja is afraid of heights, remember?" Susanne took her hand.

Anja stroked her thumb along the side of Susanne's index finger as if thanking her for protecting her.

A tingle swept up Susanne's arm and through the rest of her body. She stared down at her hand in disbelief. Wow. If this innocent little touch had that effect on her, she would probably spontaneously combust the first time Anja touched her more intimately.

"There was a guy ahead of us who said he was afraid of heights too, but he did great," Franzi said.

Anja hesitated. "If they have a kiddie course or something like that, I would consider trying it."

"You would?" Susanne searched her face. She didn't want Anja to feel pressured into it just because Miriam and Franzi had done it.

"Mm-hmm. If you go with me."

Susanne nearly suggested doing it in the summer, when being in the cool, shadowy forest would be a nice change of pace from the heat, but she bit her tongue before the suggestion could slip out. By the time summer came, she would be long gone from Freiburg. "Sure. We could do that sometime if you really want to."

"Why not? I mean, there's no shame in climbing back down if I really can't do it, as long as I try first, right?"

Susanne knew she was talking about the ropes course, but the words fit their relationship too. "Right. No shame in it at all."

Franzi launched into an enthusiastic recap of every obstacle on the tree-top ropes course, but Susanne missed half of the descriptions because she was too distracted by the slow caress of Anja's thumb across her finger.

Not too much later, Miriam let out an exaggerated yawn. "Oh gosh, sorry. I'm really beat."

Franzi got up immediately. "Yeah, me too. Must be all that fresh air. I think we should drag our tired asses home."

"Now?" Susanne glanced at her watch. It was a quarter to nine. They had barely touched the tortilla chips and the guacamole Anja had made.

"Sorry," her sister said, already on the way to the door. "I'll see you for brunch tomorrow before I drive back."

Quick hugs and they were out the door.

Anja and Susanne stayed behind and traded gazes.

"I think we've just been ditched for sex," Anja said with a grin.

"No doubt. But I have to admit they are kind of cute together." She studied Anja. "Are you tired too? I mean, tired for real. I know we've been working our asses off all week to get things ready for the website launch. I could drive you home if you want to make it an early night."

Anja's gaze darted away, then back to Susanne's eyes. "Could I...stay over?"

Susanne smiled. Truth be told, she had secretly hoped Anja would consider another sleepover. "Sure. That would be great, actually. And we already proved that we can keep our hands off each other...for the most part." She chuckled.

Anja didn't laugh. The look on her face was intense. "Who said I want us to keep our hands off each other?"

"You, um..." Susanne had to swallow against her suddenly dry mouth before she could continue. "You want to...?"

"Make love to you."

There was not even a hint of doubt in her tone, so Susanne didn't ask if she was sure.

"Unless you're too tired."

"Are you kidding me? I'll never be too tired to make love to you, even when I'm ninety." She bit her lip. *Damn.* That sounded like the promise of forever that she'd been trying to avoid.

But luckily, Anja didn't seem to notice. She took Susanne's hand and led her to the bedroom as if it were her apartment, not Susanne's.

God, this newfound confidence was kind of hot, especially when Anja gently pressed her down on the bed. She put her knee on the bed between Susanne's legs, and a groan escaped Susanne, as she could already imagine what that slender thigh would feel like pressed against her more intimately.

About to follow her down on the bed, Anja paused. "Oh, I forgot. What about your blister?"

"It's nearly healed. Besides, it's on my left hand."

"So you only said you were out of commission so I wouldn't feel bad on Wednesday?"

Susanne shrugged. "Yeah, well…mostly."

"You are so sweet. Sweet and hot." Anja's gaze raked over her. "Have I told you how much I love seeing you in jeans?"

"How about seeing me out of them?"

"Let's find out." Anja knelt between Susanne's spread legs and reached for the button on her jeans. Despite her confident tone and actions, her fingers trembled.

Susanne gently covered them with her own. "You okay?"

Anja dug her teeth into her bottom lip and nodded. "It's just… It's been a while."

Susanne smiled softly. "Want me to remind you?" She dipped one finger beneath the waistband of Anja's jeans and caressed the smooth skin of her lower belly.

Anja sucked in a breath, and the muscles of her belly quivered beneath Susanne's hand. "God, yes."

Susanne wasn't sure if it was an answer to her question or a reaction to her touch. It probably didn't matter. She wanted to feel more of Anja. Now. She withdrew her hand, sat up, and maneuvered both of them back so that she sat on the edge of the bed and Anja stood between her spread legs. After glancing up at Anja's face, she opened the button on Anja's pants and slid down the zipper. To her surprise, she fumbled a little. Her hands were clumsy from nervousness and excitement. That hadn't happened to her in…forever.

Anja seemed to sense it; she helped push her jeans down over her hips and kicked them off, then reached for the hem of her sweater and pulled it over her head. It wasn't a well-practiced striptease, but there was still something so inherently sexy about the movements that it made Susanne's breath catch.

Susanne was barely aware of the top dropping to the floor since her gaze was focused on Anja, who stood before her in just a burgundy bra and matching panties. "Oh wow." Susanne drank in her creamy skin, the delicate arc of her ribs, and the swell of her breasts peeking out from the lace edge of the bra. Eager to feel that soft-looking skin against her own, she all but ripped her own sweater and tank top over her head and wrestled out of her jeans.

The cool air in the bedroom brushed over her skin and made her nipples tighten.

Her gaze was on Anja again, and Susanne couldn't understand how she'd ever thought she wasn't classically beautiful. She was stunning.

"You are the stunning one." Anja stared at Susanne as if she'd just been shown an especially beautiful fountain pen.

Only then did Susanne realize that she'd spoken out loud.

"Nuh-uh. *You* are." Before Anja could open her mouth to argue, Susanne drew her down on top of her and then rolled them until they were both on their sides, facing each other. She cupped Anja's face in her hands and kissed her long and deep and slow. God, she had never before felt anything so good as Anja's body against her own.

At the skin-on-skin contact, Anja moaned into her mouth and clutched her back with both hands.

Susanne kissed her until her senses were reeling. She slid down the straps of that sexy bra and placed a kiss on each smooth shoulder before slipping her hands around her to unhook it. The cups fell away, baring Anja to Susanne's heated gaze.

"Stunning," she repeated as she took in every centimeter of Anja's body until she reached her panties. "I think you should take these off too."

"You too," Anja answered breathlessly. "I want to see you."

They stripped off their remaining clothes almost in sync with each other, then sank back onto the bed, with Susanne on top this time. God, she didn't know where to begin. She wanted to touch her everywhere all at once. She trailed her hands up her arms, across her collarbones, along the top of her breasts.

Anja's skin felt so wonderful beneath her fingertips that she lost herself in sensual pleasure for a minute or two, until Anja let out a low, thick hum and pulled her down into another kiss.

Susanne eagerly returned the kiss and finally ended it with a tiny nip of Anja's bottom lip. Then she kissed her way down her neck. At the curve where Anja's neck joined her shoulder, she paused and breathed her in.

Her senses were on overload—her intoxicating scent, the silkiness of Anja's skin against her own, and the sound of her elevated breathing.

She nuzzled the spot where Anja's heart beat furiously at the base of her neck, matching the thudding of her own heart, then continued her path down. When she reached the indent of her collarbone, she dipped her tongue into it and tasted Anja's slightly salty skin. "Mmm, you taste good."

Anja slid her hands restlessly up and down Susanne's back, causing shivers to rush through her body. "And you feel good."

"So do you." Susanne moved down in the bed and cradled one of Anja's breasts in her palm. Her breasts were a perfect handful and so incredibly soft that Susanne gave in to the urge to rub her cheek against them.

Anja's hands came up, and she threaded her fingers through her hair. "Susanne, please."

At the pleading note in her voice, Susanne closed her mouth over one nipple. It instantly hardened against her lips, and she teased it, first with her tongue, then, carefully, with her teeth.

Anja's head tilted back, and a low moan rose from deep in her throat.

It resonated through Susanne's body, driving her crazy. She wanted more of those little sounds. More of Anja.

When she sucked on her nipple, Anja bucked beneath her and tightened her grip on Susanne's hair, urging her on.

Not that Susanne needed any encouragement. She trailed a string of kisses from one breast to the other and circled Anja's nipple with her tongue, every now and then playfully flicking it.

"God, this is torture," Anja breathed.

Susanne slid back up a little and caressed Anja's flushed cheek with her thumb. "Want me to stop?" she asked, more teasing than anything.

"No! I want…" Anja raked her bottom lip with her teeth. "You. I want you."

"Where?" Susanne asked, her voice husky. "Where do you want me?" Hearing Anja say it would be so hot.

But instead, Anja flushed and reached out.

Susanne held her breath, expecting her to take her hand and guide it to where she wanted her to touch. That would be even hotter than hearing her say it.

In a move that was strangely shy and bold all at the same time, Anja slid her hand between them and gently cupped Susanne between her thighs, where she was already wet with need.

A jolt of raw desire blazed through her, and her hips instinctively arched to meet Anja's touch. She choked back a curse and struggled for control.

"There," Anja murmured, her eyes hooded. She left her palm where it was, cradling Susanne intimately. "I want you there."

Susanne gritted her teeth. "Then you'd better take your hand away, or I won't be able to move a muscle in about thirty seconds."

"Really?" Anja moved her fingers experimentally.

Susanne sucked in a breath, her mind already hazy with pleasure, nearly unable to think or form words. "Yes, really."

"Thirty seconds?" Anja repeated, her tone half teasing, half full of wonder.

Susanne shifted into her touch without conscious thought. "Twenty-five."

Anja's pupils were so wide her brown eyes nearly looked black. "Let's see if we can make it fifteen when I do this." She stroked the pad of her finger across Susanne's clit.

"Oh God!" Susanne's eyes slammed shut, and bright points of pleasure flared behind her lids. She closed her fingers around Anja's wrist, caught between needing to draw her hand away and wanting to press it more firmly against herself. She forced her heavy eyes open. "Not this time, Anja. I don't want just fifteen seconds. I want—" *Forever.* She pushed the sappy thought away. "I want to savor this. Savor every centimeter of you. Make you feel me everywhere."

Anja groaned. "Yes. I want that too. And we will take our time—later. But first, I want to see you lose control." She swirled her fingers through Susanne's wetness again.

A shudder of need rippled through Susanne, and she let out a long groan, her breathing ragged. "I will if you keep this up. Oh hell. I didn't think you'd be so... so...God!"

Anja stopped moving her fingers and looked into her eyes. "Is it okay?"

"Okay?" Susanne let out a shaky laugh. "It's hot as..." Then Anja moved her fingers again, and she lost her train of thought.

"Good." Anja urged her to roll over, and to her own surprise, Susanne eagerly settled on her back with Anja on top.

"Thank you," Anja breathed against her lips, as if sensing that Susanne normally wasn't so at ease handing over control. She held herself up on one elbow and planted openmouthed kisses on every bit of skin she could reach.

Each touch, each kiss sent tremors of pleasure through Susanne. She clutched Anja's back as Anja lightly sucked on her neck and then paused to nibble on her shoulder. "God, you have amazing shoulders. Did anyone ever tell you that?"

Susanne grunted. "My shoulders aren't the part of me that needs attention."

"No?" Anja smiled down at her. "How about this part?" She dipped her head, and the wet heat of her mouth closed over Susanne's breast.

Lightning-swift desire shot through Susanne. She sucked in a breath, already feeling a tightening deep inside of her. She arched into Anja. "We might beat those...mmm...fifteen...oh God...seconds."

"Yeah?" Anja's pupils flared wide.

Susanne's throat was too dry and her brain too fuzzy to form words, so she nodded shakily.

"That's okay." Anja slid up and pressed a kiss to her lips. "I'll just start all over again." She set a slow, deliberate rhythm with her fingers, keeping her strokes light.

Susanne's pulse thudded through her entire body, and she drew in a ragged breath as Anja kept exploring.

"Susanne…" Anja breathed her name as she moved with her, the expression of intense focus on her face assuring her she wouldn't stop for anything in the world. Their gazes locked.

This was so intimate. Almost too intimate. But Susanne couldn't close her eyes. Didn't want to close her eyes. She gripped Anja's back with both hands to ground herself.

Each stroke drove her deeper into the swirl of sensation. Already the first little tremors shook her body. *No. Not yet. Please not yet.* She wanted this night to last forever. But when Anja circled her fingers faster, with a little more pressure, there was no holding back. Pleasure coiled into a tight ball, then spread outward. She choked out mumbled words that probably made no sense at all. Or maybe she shouted Anja's name.

She must have blacked out for a couple of seconds because the next thing she was aware of was Anja cradling her in her arms, their bodies slick with sweat. Even though Susanne was the taller one, it felt incredibly good to let herself be held.

As her heartbeat and her breathing slowly settled and her limbs started working again, she lifted her hand and traced the faint laugh lines around Anja's mouth, which was smiling at her. "God, that was amazing. You were amazing…and a bit surprising. It was a good surprise," she added quickly. "A very good surprise."

Truth be told, she didn't know what had surprised her more: Anja taking control or her handing it over so willingly. But then again, maybe it shouldn't have surprised her. At work, they had taken turns too. Sometimes she'd been in control, teaching Anja how to handle social media, and sometimes Anja had taken over and introduced her to the world of stationery.

Anja kissed her fingertips. "You take my breath away. You're so beautiful. I loved being the one to, you know, make you come."

Susanne chuckled, charmed by the crimson color that crept into Anja's cheeks. It was hard to believe that the woman who had driven her crazy with desire only a minute ago now blushed at her honest admission. Somehow it fit Anja, though. "I loved it too, in case you couldn't tell."

"Oh, I could tell. Those little sounds you made gave you away. Especially that gasp you made when I did this…" Anja slid her hand down Susanne's body and swirled one finger around her swollen clit.

Susanne's heartbeat tripped, and renewed pleasure surged through her, but she drew Anja's hand away. "Oh no. Now it's my turn." Vibrating with the need to feel her, Susanne kissed her.

Anja surged against her and returned the heated kiss.

When Susanne swiped her thumb over Anja's nipple, Anja tore her mouth away to gasp for air, her breath hot on Susanne's lips.

"So responsive. I love that." Susanne replaced her thumb with her mouth while she slid her hand down Anja's body. Goose bumps rose in the wake of her touch, and she lingered to rub them away but only succeeded in creating more of them. The muscles of Anja's belly tightened as she responded to each small caress. Susanne traced the curve of her hip, then down the outside of her leg before caressing the soft skin of her inner thigh.

When Susanne trailed her fingers upward, Anja went taut with anticipation beneath her and spread her legs farther.

Susanne glanced up and made eye contact.

Anja lay completely open to her, her cheeks flushed and her lips parted.

Susanne couldn't wait any longer—and she didn't need to since Anja's eyes telegraphed the same need.

They both groaned as her fingers dipped into Anja's wetness.

Susanne stroked her, matching her pace to her tongue's motion on Anja's breast.

Anja rocked against her. "Oh. That," she gasped out, her voice strangled. "Do that again."

"This?" Susanne flicked her tongue across her nipple. "Or this?" She stroked her clit more purposefully.

Anja let out a shaky moan. "Yes. Either. Both. God."

Susanne lifted her head from Anja's breast and stared at her. Anja looked so beautiful writhing beneath her, and Susanne felt drunk on the power to make her so desperate but also eager to give her everything she needed.

Tiny moans and gasps rained down on her. God, what those noises did to her. She reveled in the sound and the sight of Anja coming undone in her arms.

When Anja's legs started to shake, Susanne made eye contact as she gently slid two fingers inside.

A throaty sound escaped Anja, somewhere between a sigh and a cry. She arched up against her and rocked her hips faster. "Susanne." She clamped her teeth onto her bottom lip as if trying to hold herself back, to make it last.

Oh no. Susanne didn't want her to hold back. She wanted to see her face and the look in her eyes when she came. "Let go." She curled her fingers, searching for that perfect spot that would send her spiraling.

With a shout, Anja surged up against her. She stiffened and tightened around Susanne's fingers. She clutched at Susanne's shoulders, her hair, trying to anchor herself.

Breathless, Susanne slowed but kept moving, prolonging her pleasure until Anja fell back onto the bed. She followed her down. The sensation of their sweat-glistening skin against each other made her head spin. She drew Anja into her arms and kissed her damp forehead, her flushed cheeks, her mouth.

As life returned to Anja's limp body, she brought her arms up, wrapped them around Susanne, and kissed her back. When she opened her eyes, the dazed pleasure in them made Susanne want to make love to her all over again.

But that could wait. For the moment, she was sated, and all she wanted was to hold her close. She trailed her hand up and down her back in a long, tender caress and luxuriated in the feel of Anja's naked body against her own.

Normally, she would have rolled over, needing a bit of space to fall asleep, but with Anja, she didn't want to move away. Ever.

Careful. That's just post-coital thinking. Pondering life-changing things like that in the afterglow of great sex was dangerous, so Susanne decided to shut off her brain for the rest of the night—and she knew one surefire way of doing that.

On the next swipe down Anja's back, she slid her hand a little lower until she could palm her ass. "So," she whispered into Anja's ear, loving the shudder that went through her, "want to see if you can beat my fifteen seconds?" She seductively rasped her fingernails down the curve of her ass and over her thighs.

"If you keep using your nails like that, I won't have a problem beating your record." Anja moaned. "God, who knew the back of my thighs were such an erogenous zone?"

Susanne held on to her and rolled them both over. "Let's see what other erogenous zones you might have," she murmured against her skin and then started to trail a string of kisses down her belly.

ᔓᗢᘐᗢᔓ

"Wow! I suddenly feel like a queen." Franziska looked around the large room where the restaurant served brunch.

Everything gleamed and sparkled: the crystal chandeliers, the torch-shaped lamps on the very white walls, the large mirrors, the cutlery on the white tablecloths, and the polished hardwood floor. Ornaments that looked like lilies in a medieval coat of arms decorated the high ceiling.

Anja felt like a queen too—not so much because of their location, although it did remind her a little of the Hall of Mirrors in Versailles, but more because of the way Susanne looked at her.

Susanne had spent most of the night making her feel as if she was the most desirable woman on earth, and she had tried to do the same for Susanne. They hadn't let go of each other's hand on the short walk up to the Greiffenegg Schlössle, which was located partway up the Schlossberg. The food from the buffet smelled heavenly, and Anja was starving, but what she really wanted was to drag Susanne back to bed.

The glimmer of heat in Susanne's eyes told her she thought the same.

"Come on," Susanne whispered into her ear. "Let's pretend to be social for a while. My sister will need to hit the road in an hour or two anyway, and then…"

She didn't finish the sentence, but Anja's imagination did it for her. Shivers raced through her body. Her skin hungered for Susanne's touch. God, what was going on with her? She'd never been this way before. It was probably because she was very aware that Susanne would be leaving next month, so she wanted to experience as much as she could with her in whatever time they had.

She forced herself to let go of Susanne's hand so she could get some food from the buffet.

They stayed close together, piling food onto each other's plates and laughing about the way Miri headed straight for the chocolate mousse.

When they sat at their table, which offered a great view over the Old Town, Miri and Franzi were already there.

"Oh wow." Miri eyed their plates and giggled. "Looks like the two of you worked up quite an appetite."

Heat rushed to Anja's face. She lowered her gaze to her plate, which was piled high with cheese, fruit, jams, a roll, and a croissant, and to the bowl of muesli next to it.

"Anything you want to tell your favorite sister?" Franziska grinned and nudged Susanne, who pretended to be busy arranging two rolls, a huge plate of scrambled eggs, and a piece of apple pie on the table.

Slowly, Susanne looked up. "Actually, yes. I do have an announcement to make."

Anja tensed, even though she didn't quite know why. Miri was her best friend, and she talked freely about her own love life. It wasn't as if she was ashamed of having slept with Susanne, but it didn't feel right to talk or joke about it—as if it would diminish their magical night.

"So let's hear it," Franziska said when Susanne paused.

"I…" Susanne flicked her gaze to Anja and gave her a reassuring smile. "…need coffee."

Franziska stared at her sister. "That's it? That's your announcement?"

"Yes." Susanne nodded gravely. "Oh, and…"

"Yes?" Franziska prompted.

"Anja needs some too."

"Forget it, Franzi." Miri put her hand on Franziska's. "If your sister is anything like Anja, we won't get any juicy details out of either one of them. Not that we need to. Their faces say it all."

"It's not like I *want* any juicy details." Franziska shook herself at the thought. "She's my sister after all. I just want to know if she…if you…" She glanced at Susanne. "…are happy."

Without looking away from her sister, Susanne found Anja's hand beneath the table and entwined their fingers. The almost businesslike poker face she had put on wavered, and an ecstatic smile shone through for a moment. "I'm having a great brunch on a gorgeous Sunday morning with my womb mate and her…" She hesitated and flicked her gaze at Miri.

"Girlfriend," Miri quietly provided.

"Wow," Anja mouthed at her and beamed. So Miri and Franzi were really trying for something serious, not just a bit of fun on the weekend.

Susanne nodded with a smile. "With my sister and her girlfriend…and with the most beautiful stationery geek I know. How could I not be happy?"

Anja's cheeks heated again, but this time it was more from pleasure than embarrassment. They weren't quite at the level of commitment that Miri and Franziska had reached, but for now, feeling Susanne's honest admiration was enough. She tightened her grip on Susanne's hand.

Their gazes met and held, and the hall of mirrors around them retreated.

"Anything you want to add, Anja?" Miri asked.

"Yes." Anja didn't look away from Susanne, speaking mostly to her. "I'm also pretty happy…and I need coffee too."

They all burst out laughing.

Chapter 19

Anja had never been one to hate Mondays, but when Susanne's alarm clock went off on Monday morning, she groaned and buried her face against Susanne's shoulder.

Susanne reached out from beneath the duvet to shut off the alarm but made no move to get out of bed either. She slipped her arm back beneath the covers and rubbed both hands along Anja's back in ways that made her even more reluctant to get up. "Still tired?"

"Yes. Guess making love for half of the night, two nights in a row, will do that to you."

Susanne's eyes twinkled. "Are you complaining?"

"No. God, no." But being tired wasn't the only reason she was reluctant to get up. Except for the brunch with Franziska and Miri, they hadn't left Susanne's apartment all weekend. As soon as they went to work, the real world would intrude, and she'd have to face the fact that not all weekends for the rest of her life would be spent like this. Just because they'd had sex—amazing sex—didn't mean Susanne would stay.

"Want me to offer some incentive for getting up?" Susanne asked.

Anja gave her a hopeful look. "Are you offering to make coffee?"

"I could. Or we could grab one on the way to work and use our time to shower together." Susanne's voice dropped to a seductive murmur.

"Shower sex is overrated," Anja answered, but admittedly, the thought of Susanne's soapy hands gliding all over her body sent a tingle through her.

Susanne looked stunned for a moment, then burst out laughing. She rolled out from beneath Anja, leaned over her, and framed her face with her hands. "You're pretty unique. I don't think I've ever met a woman like you."

Anja stared up into her eyes. "Is that a good thing?"

"It is." Susanne trailed her thumbs across Anja's cheekbones, and she had to struggle to keep her eyes open.

"Even if it means no shower sex?"

"Even then." Susanne nodded. "But I might go on a mission to change your mind about that. You know I love a challenge." She placed a soft kiss on the corner of

Anja's mouth, then threw off the covers and climbed out of bed, pulling Anja up with her and to the bathroom.

Maybe this Monday morning wasn't so bad after all.

∽∾⤫∽

They made it to Paper Love fifteen minutes before opening time. Susanne pulled Anja to a stop by their entwined hands and kissed her one last time before she'd have to be a professional. But at least she'd get to sneak long looks at her in between selling notebooks and preparing things for the website launch.

"I'll put the card carousels outside if you go get us two coffees," Susanne said when they finally broke apart, both breathless.

"Sure." Anja let go of her hand with obvious reluctance and turned toward the little coffee store.

"Make mine a tall one, please," Susanne called after her. She watched her gracefully step over the *Bächle* before turning back toward Paper Love.

Only then did she notice that the lights in the store were already on. Something moved inside.

Alarm flared through her, but then she made out her uncle's bearded face.

He was behind the counter, staring at her through the glass.

Oh shit. Had he seen them kiss? The deep furrow between his bushy brows said yes. For a moment, Susanne considered waiting for Anja, who was so much better at dealing with him. But that wouldn't be fair, not to Anja and not to her uncle. She'd put off talking to him—*really* talking to him—for much too long already.

Her throat tightened as she reached for the brass handle and pulled the door open.

The jingling bell sounded like a harbinger of doom.

"Good morning. What are you doing here?" Maybe going on the offense would help. "Shouldn't you be resting at home?"

Uncle Norbert scrunched up his nose like a little boy. "I've done nothing but rest for a week. I'm sick of it, and the doctor said I can go back to work if I feel up to it. At least when I'm at work, I'll be distracted from the pain." He walked around the counter, still moving a bit stiffly, but much better than he had last week. "Speaking of distraction, is that what you're doing with Anja?"

Susanne stiffened and had to fight down a wave of defensiveness.

"Looking for a nice little distraction while you're here? Because if that's what you're after, I suggest you look for it elsewhere." His normally gentle blue eyes drilled into her like laser beams. "Anja is a person who feels things deeply, even if she doesn't always show it. If you—"

"Stop it!" The words finally burst out of Susanne. "Why the hell would you assume I'm just playing with her? Why aren't you out there"—she waved toward the coffee shop, where Anja waited for their coffees to go—"warning Anja not to hurt me? I'm your niece after all, not Anja."

"You never behaved like it," he murmured, his voice so low that Susanne almost didn't catch it.

Susanne swallowed. Her rush of anger faded away. She'd hoped to avoid this conversation, but that was probably the same bullshit strategy that had estranged her from her uncle in the first place. She gathered her courage and stepped up to him. "Listen. I know I shouldn't have stayed away for so long, but—"

"Then why did you?"

Susanne flinched. Straight to the jugular. Apparently, her uncle wasn't always a dreamer who avoided conflict—and she would have known that if she hadn't cut him out of her life. "I...I don't know."

He continued to look at her. "I know it had nothing to do with your mother forbidding you from visiting after the divorce; otherwise, Franzi would have stayed away too."

"No, Mama would never do that."

Uncle Norbert paled beneath his beard. "Then was it something I did?"

"No!" Susanne leaned against the counter and sighed. "It had nothing to do with you, okay? I just... I needed some distance."

"Distance? Susi, we only saw each other once a year—if that—even before the divorce. How can you need distance from that?"

Susanne studied the grains of the wood floor.

The bell above the door jingled, and Anja's warm presence filled the store. "Nobby!" She rushed to him, put down the two paper cups, and gave him a careful hug. "It's so great to see you. How are you? Did the doctor say it's okay for you to come back to work?"

Susanne watched them smile and talk. Uncle Norbert was right. Anja had been much more of a family member for him than she had been. No wonder he was so protective of her.

Anja looked back and forth between them. "Am I interrupting something?"

The familiar twinkle returned to Uncle Norbert's eyes. "I get the feeling *I* was the one interrupting something."

A flush rose up Anja's neck and colored her cheeks, but she didn't try to deny it. She wrapped her arm around Susanne's hips and held on tightly. "Susanne and I...

We've grown close. But please don't get your shotgun out, okay? We agreed to take it day by day and to see where it goes."

Uncle Norbert's forehead wrinkled. "Are you really fine with that?"

"Yes, I am. Don't worry about me." Anja gave a soft squeeze to Susanne's hip, then let go and kissed Uncle Norbert's bearded cheek before wheeling the first carousel outside.

"Sorry," Susanne mouthed because she had promised to take care of the carousels.

Anja smiled and mouthed, "It's okay."

As Susanne watched her wheel the carousel through the door, her uncle's question resounded in her ears. Was Anja really fine with their agreement?

Uncle Norbert cleared his throat, drawing her attention back to him. "Why did you never give me that chance?" He waved his hand toward where Anja had disappeared. "I would have been fine with even the occasional, casual contact."

Susanne reached for her coffee cup to have something to do with her hands and took a sip of the hot beverage. "It wasn't about you. After seeing what my father put Mama through with his immature ways, I wanted to distance myself from him as much as I could."

"I'm the first to admit that my little brother often acts like a carefree kid with no responsibilities, but not everything about him is bad, you know? Not everything about this side of the family is bad."

"I know." Susanne stared into the black depths of her coffee. "I think I threw out the baby with the bathwater, and I shouldn't have done that. I shouldn't have punished you for things he did. I'm sorry, Nobby. Uh, Uncle Norbert."

A smile deepened the lines around his eyes. "Nobby's just fine. I don't want to be stuffy Uncle Norbert who you call only out of obligation once a year. Will you give me a chance to be Uncle Nobby?"

Unexpected tears burned in her eyes. Jesus, what was that? The past two nights with Anja had probably made her much more emotional. Not trusting herself to speak, she just nodded.

Uncle Nobby pulled her into his arms.

His cologne—the same brand that her father had used when she'd been a child— wafted around her, and for the first time in years, she allowed herself to enjoy it.

Anja stepped back into the store, and when Susanne looked at her over her uncle's shoulder, Anja gave her a smile so warm that Susanne felt as if she were the one hugging her, not Uncle Nobby.

When Anja wheeled the second card carousel outside, Uncle Nobby let go and regarded Susanne. "So you and Anja, hmm?"

Susanne shuffled her feet. "Yeah."

"I should have seen it coming. She was fascinated by you from the start."

Susanne couldn't help beaming. "She thought I was a controlling asshole out to fire her."

Uncle Nobby chuckled. "That too." He sobered. "Just don't lead her on, please. I don't want to see her—or you—hurt."

"That's the last thing I want either. I can't make any promises since I have no idea where I'll be in a month, but we're talking openly about that. I…" She glanced through the glass door to make sure Anja was still outside and couldn't hear her. "I really like her."

Uncle Nobby patted her shoulder. "Good. Then you should know that her birthday is coming up."

"Really? When?"

"The first of March."

"That's next Thursday—the day the website and the new store will go live! She never mentioned it's her birthday when we set the date with the web design firm."

Uncle Nobby shrugged. "That's Anja."

"What about me?" Anja asked as she returned to the store.

"You're the person responsible for calling Herr Schneider to tell him his order is in," Uncle Nobby answered smoothly. "You know the old grouch gets grumpy if I'm the one calling. I think the only reason he orders a new notebook every week is so he'll get to talk to you."

Susanne couldn't blame him.

"Well, whatever works to help save the store, right?" Anja grinned and picked up her coffee. "I'll go call him."

When the door to the back rooms clicked shut behind her, Susanne turned back toward Uncle Nobby. "I need a present."

"Maybe a refill for her traveler's notebook." Uncle Nobby gestured at the center island.

"No." Susanne knew what she wanted to give her. She glanced at the locked display case, where a dozen expensive fountain pens gleamed like diamonds. Her gaze zeroed in on the one in the middle. "I want to buy the BMW pen from you."

"BMW doesn't produce pens. You mean the Porsche ones?"

"No." Susanne walked over and tapped the middle of the case. "I mean this one."

"The Meisterstück Solitaire? Are you sure? It's our most expensive pen."

Susanne hesitated but not because of the price tag. Expensive fountain pens were like jewelry, Anja had said to the customer looking for a Valentine's Day gift. If she gave Anja a pen for her birthday, would she be making a promise she might not be able to keep?

It's a pen, idiot, not a wedding ring. Even if Paper Love could be saved, Anja would probably never make enough money so she could afford to blow two thousand euros on a pen. This was something Susanne could give her, and she wanted to buy Anja the pen with an intensity that scared her a little.

"How about this one?" Uncle Nobby tapped the case above the writing instrument to the left of the BMW pen. "It's a Montblanc too, with the same great nib, and I can sell it to you for four hundr—"

"No," Susanne said firmly, decision made. "It has to be this one. And don't you dare sell it to me below cost. I'm paying what's on the price tag."

Uncle Nobby stared at her. "Wow. You weren't kidding, hmm? You *really* like her."

"Yes, I do. So will you sell me the pen?"

"I might not be the best businessman in the world, but I'd never say no to a sale like that. I'll slip it into your laptop bag when Anja is on her lunch break."

"Thanks. I'll transfer you the money tonight."

They nodded at each other.

"When she opens that particular present, she'll either kiss you or kill you," Uncle Nobby predicted.

"Let's hope for the former. I'm pretty fond of my life...and of her kisses." She sent her uncle a grin, but doubt began to take root. Would Anja be able to accept and enjoy the gift when she couldn't promise her anything else?

She took a long gulp of coffee, hoping it would help against the lump in her throat. *Guess I'll find out next week.*

⌖

This morning, Anja had looked forward to the evening, when she could have Susanne all to herself, but as closing time approached, she wasn't so sure she had anything to look forward to.

Susanne had been on the phone or sending emails back and forth with the web design company for most of the day, and Nobby had been around as a chaperone, so they hadn't had much time or opportunity to talk, much less exchange a quick kiss. So far, Susanne hadn't mentioned any plans for this evening, nor had she invited Anja back to her apartment.

Come on. Don't be so clingy. She hadn't been home since Saturday. She knew she should go back to her own place and resume her regular life, including walks around the lake with Miri. At least that was what her brain said. The rest of her didn't share that opinion. She wanted to enjoy every second with Susanne since she was very aware that they were on borrowed time and the clock was ticking.

As Susanne walked past her to drag in the card carousels, she smiled and touched Anja's hand.

The fleeting touch sent a rush of warmth through her body, and she smiled back, forgetting her brooding thoughts.

When the door closed behind Susanne, she reluctantly turned back toward her own task, which was locking up the display case. She inserted her key—and then froze. Since she knew every single pen in that case so well, she immediately noticed that they had been rearranged and one of them was missing.

Anja whirled around. "Nobby! The Meisterstück Solitaire is gone!"

Nobby looked up from behind the counter. "I know. I sold it when you were out for lunch."

"What? Wow. That's, um, great." It was, wasn't it? Selling an expensive fountain pen like that would definitely bolster this month's numbers. But a part of her couldn't help being sad. They'd had that pen for a year, and she had admired it every time she walked past the glass case. Now she felt almost as if she'd lost a friend.

The bell jingled as Susanne stepped back into the store. Her gaze zeroed in on Anja immediately, and a look of alarm shadowed her face. She let go of the carousel, crossed the room with long steps, and clutched Anja's shoulders. "What's wrong?"

Anja forced a smile. "Nothing. Nobby sold *the* pen." She knew she wouldn't have to clarify.

"Hey." Susanne wrapped both arms around her and held her close for a moment. "Don't be sad. I'm sure it went to a very loving home."

"Oh yeah," Nobby threw in. "Couldn't have gone to a more pen-crazy person."

"I know I'm being silly." Anja pressed her face to Susanne's shoulder for a little longer.

Susanne rubbed her back. "No, you're not. How about I take you out to dinner at Kashmir to help distract you? We could run by your apartment on the way back and pick up some clean clothes for you." She lowered her voice. "That is if you want to stay over again."

Anja didn't even try to play it cool. She gave Susanne a warm smile. "I'd really like that. Could we ask Miri if she wants to come? I don't want her to think I've forgotten all about her now that I have you."

"Sure." Susanne squeezed her softly before letting go and turning toward her uncle. "Want to come too? If you don't like Indian, we could go someplace else."

Nobby laughed and raised both hands. "Oh no. I'm sure you will enjoy yourselves much more without me. Besides, sitting for any length of time is still a pain in the ass—literally."

He shooed them out of the store with a promise to be careful on his way home.

Anja threw one last glance back over her shoulder to the place in the glass case where the Meisterstück Solitaire had been, then she forgot all about pens for the rest of the evening.

Chapter 20

Ten days later, Anja unlocked the door to her apartment with the same feeling she sometimes got when returning from a long vacation—a vacation she hadn't wanted to end. In the nearly two weeks since she and Susanne had made love for the first time, they had slept apart only a handful of times.

Why did today of all days have to be the one that Susanne had other plans? She had hurried off right after work, saying she had to take care of something important.

Well, Anja couldn't complain since she hadn't told her it was her birthday. Miri hadn't called either, and even Nobby seemed to have forgotten about her birthday. She couldn't blame him. He was still recovering from his accident, and with the new website and a lot of new products launching today, they had run around like chickens with their heads cut off, too busy to think of anything but work.

Sighing, she closed the door behind her and kicked off her shoes.

When she opened the door to the bedroom/living room, a chorus of "surprise!" greeted her.

Anja clutched her chest. "God, you guys! What are you doing here?"

"Throwing you a surprise party! Isn't it obvious?" Miri blew a pink-dotted party horn.

Her ears ringing, Anja stood in the doorway and stared. Her small apartment was full of balloons—probably Miri's idea—and people. Nobby was there with his not-quite girlfriend; Franzi had come all the way from Berlin, and her favorite neighbors had dropped by.

Anja went from guest to guest, getting hugs and kisses from everyone. Finally, there was only one person left to greet: Susanne stood in the middle of all the chaos and regarded her with a quiet smile. "Happy birthday."

"You...you planned all of this?"

"Yes. Well, Miri and I, since she's the one with a key to your apartment. You didn't really believe we had forgotten your birthday, did you?"

"No, I... Um, yeah. So this was the important thing you had to take care of tonight?"

Susanne nodded. "I wasn't lying. I'd say my girlfriend's birthday is very important."

Girlfriend. Anja liked being called that. She sank into Susanne's embrace and kissed her softly. "Thank you."

"Oh, don't thank me yet. This isn't the real party. Since there's not enough space here, we thought we'd kidnap you and take you to your favorite restaurant."

Anja chuckled. "Good idea, especially since there's probably only a yogurt and a jar of mustard in my fridge."

Twenty minutes later, they were all seated at a table next to a huge painting of the Taj Mahal.

"My sister tells me there's a lot to celebrate today," Franzi said once they had ordered.

Anja's gaze darted to Susanne. "There is? You ran the numbers already?"

"I've been looking at the data until right before you entered your apartment," Susanne said. "I knew neither of us would be able to sleep without having at least some idea of how things are going."

"So?" Anja nudged Susanne's knee with her own. "How does it look so far?"

"Very encouraging. Not only are the February numbers much better than January and even December, but the new website is off to a really great start too. The blog is getting a lot of hits, we have about fifty subscribers to the newsletter already, and the first orders via the webstore are coming in."

Anja barely resisted the urge to bounce up and down on her chair. "Does that mean Paper Love won't have to close?"

Susanne held up her hands. "Too soon to give any definitive answers." When Anja gave her a pleading look, she relented. "But if we keep up the momentum, we should be fine."

Anja threw her arms around her. "That's the best birthday present I could wish for."

"Wait until you open your presents," Nobby said.

Everyone pushed brightly wrapped gifts across the table at her.

Maybe adults weren't supposed to love getting presents, but Anja did—at least when they came from people who knew her well and had put some thought into what to get her. And her friends clearly had. She slid her hands over a year's worth of refills for her traveler's notebook from Nobby. Her neighbors surprised her with a vegetarian cookbook, and Miri had gotten her a box of hard-to-find ink bottles. Finally, she unrolled a sheet of ivory paper and found a gift certificate for a beginner's ropes course from Franzi.

She looked at each of her friends in turn. "Thank you, guys."

"There's one more," Susanne said quietly. "This one's from me." She put a small, rectangular package in front of Anja.

The laughter and chatter at the table stopped. Everyone else seemed to hold their breath along with Anja. Why was her heart pounding all of a sudden? She knew it wasn't a piece of jewelry or something like that. It took some effort to steady her hands as she carefully peeled away the tape.

Susanne had used too much of it, as if she'd wanted to make extra sure the gift wrap would stay put. Had she been nervous too?

Finally, the paper fell away, revealing a slender, black box with a familiar white logo. Anja gasped. "You didn't get me a Montblanc, did you? Susanne…"

Susanne smiled. "Open it."

With trembling fingers, Anja opened the lid.

On a bed of white satin lay a silver-and-dark-blue fountain pen with tiny, engraved letters gracing the barrel.

Anja forgot how to form words. Her mouth moved, but her vocal cords didn't produce sound. "You…you didn't," she finally got out.

"Looks like I did."

"That's…that's crazy." Anja still stared back and forth between the gleaming pen and Susanne's face.

The waiter chose that moment to start serving the food, and they quickly cleared the table of presents to make room for the deliciously smelling dishes. Anja kept hold of the box with the pen.

"Is it okay?" Susanne whispered. "You said you would buy it in a heartbeat if you could, and I wanted you to have something special for your birthday. But if you don't feel comfortable accepting it…"

"It's a lot of money. I won't be able to give you a gift like this." Would they even last until Susanne's birthday, which, according to Nobby, was in November?

"I don't want money to ever matter between us." Susanne's gaze was fierce. "Even a gift with a smaller price tag can be special if it's picked with l—" She bit her lip. "Um, with care."

Anja wrestled with her pride for a while and then finally nodded. She touched the pen, sliding her fingertips over the silver engravings. She had always admired the simple beauty of this pen, but now she knew it would forever hold a special place in her heart—not just because it was an exquisite writing instrument but also because Susanne had given it to her. "It's beautiful, and it means the world to me that you remembered our conversation."

The tension on Susanne's face eased into a broad smile. "So you like your gift?"

"I love it!" *I love you*, Anja mentally added but bit back the words, even though she knew they were true. This wasn't the right time or place. Maybe there would never be a right time for them. "Thank you, Susanne. I...I'm still speechless."

Susanne leaned over and kissed her cheek. "Thank *you* for accepting it."

Anja softly kissed her lips.

"Hey, lovebirds," Miri called from the other end of the table. "Your food is getting cold."

Susanne unhurriedly kissed Anja a second time and then heaped rice onto her plate. "You can test out how bendable the pen is as soon as we get home. Just to make sure this one isn't as stiff as a nail too."

"I would do that, but..." Anja leaned to the side to whisper in her ear, "Once we get home, I'll be too busy testing out how bendable *you* are."

Susanne stared at her, then went for her water glass as if her mouth had gone dry.

Franzi reached over with her fork and tried a bit of her sister's food. "It's not that hot," she said once she'd chewed and swallowed.

"You have no idea just how hot it is," Susanne mumbled.

Anja struggled to not burst out laughing.

"All right, people!" Nobby said. "Let's toast the birthday girl. To Anja!"

Everyone raised their glasses. "To Anja!"

"And to Paper Love." Anja clinked glasses with Susanne first, looking deeply into her eyes. She knew she would remember this moment, this birthday for the rest of her life.

Chapter 21

Anja arched her hips against Susanne's mouth and bit onto her fisted hand to hold back a scream as a surge of pleasure ricocheted through her. She collapsed back on the bed, breathing hard, and tried to focus so she could watch Susanne slide up along her body.

"Hey there." Susanne's eyes held a deep satisfaction as if she, not Anja, had been the one to come twice in a row. "You okay?"

Anja nodded, still a little dazed. "Ecstatic."

Susanne chuckled. "Good. Come here." She spooned against Anja, her front pressed to Anja's back, their legs tangled intimately. Her hot breath fanned over Anja's sensitized skin, prolonging the pleasure still rippling through her.

Anja lay with her eyes open, even after Susanne had switched off the light, throwing the bedroom into darkness. The alarm clock clicked over to 00:01. She sent the damn thing a resentful glare. Another day with Susanne had ended, and only nine more were left.

They both seemed to be very aware that their time together would soon be coming to an end. They made love for hours every night, both insatiable, and even at work they searched each other out for a smile, a soft touch, a quick kiss, as if trying to create enough memories to sustain them for a lifetime.

Anja knew it wasn't working. She would never get enough of her. She didn't want things between them to end; she just didn't know how to move forward. Would they be able to make it work long-distance? Would Susanne even want to try?

Susanne always made it clear that she would be leaving right before Easter, but she never talked about her plans for the time afterward in detail. She hadn't even mentioned any specific job offers, which, now that she thought about it, was a little weird. Anja hadn't asked about her plans either, preferring to enjoy life on cloud nine for a while longer. The thought of Susanne leaving hurt too much, but Anja knew she couldn't postpone it any longer. She needed to face it. Just because they would no longer live in the same city didn't mean they had to break up, right? They had options.

Maybe I should move to Berlin. The thought surprised her. Freiburg was her home, deeply ingrained in her heart. But so was Susanne. They fit in ways that Anja had never expected.

But even if she was willing to move all the way across the country, how could she leave Nobby and the store after they had fought so hard to save it?

Anja suppressed a sigh. They needed to talk. "Susanne?"

"Mmm?" Susanne sounded as if she was close to falling asleep already.

Anja sighed. This wasn't a conversation to have at midnight. If they started to talk about the future now, they'd be up all night, and they had to work tomorrow. She would suggest doing something nice for just the two of them this weekend—maybe a picnic at the lake or in the Japanese garden—and then broach the subject, when they were both more awake and had time to talk for hours.

"Good night," she said.

Susanne mumbled something against her skin that sounded like, "Sweet dreams." Her breathing eased into the quiet rhythm of sleep.

Anja settled Susanne's arm more tightly around herself, covered Susanne's fingers against her breast with her own, and closed her eyes, willing herself to go to sleep too.

❧

The weather in Freiburg had turned springlike, and the farmers market around the cathedral was bustling on Saturday morning. Susanne squeezed through the crowd, trying not to drop the cell phone pressed to her ear or her basket full of vegetables, cheeses, and fresh bread.

"Has Miriam made it to Berlin yet?" Susanne asked as she strolled through one of the narrow alleys back toward the streetcar stop. Most of the time when she headed to the city center, she took the streetcar now, like a true local, instead of taking the car.

"Would I be on the phone with you if she had?" Franzi shot back, and they both chuckled. "She's still en route. But she took the first train this morning, so she should be here in about two hours and twenty-three minutes."

"Not that you're counting or anything." It still amazed Susanne to see her sister like this. Franzi had been much more casual in her relationships so far, never this eager to see her previous lovers. But she could definitely understand. In a week or two, she would be the one to count the seconds until Anja's train arrived.

"What about you?" Franzi asked. "Are you eager to get back to Berlin?"

Was she? Not really, she admitted to herself. "It's going to be strange. I've gotten pretty involved with things at Paper Love."

"Yeah, right. Paper Love. That's what you got involved with." Her sister snorted. "Speaking of work, any idea what you'll do once you're back? Knowing you, you probably have a bunch of job interviews lined up already, right?"

Susanne paused at the end of the alley, not yet ready to join the bustle of people on the main shopping street. "Actually, no. I haven't even been looking."

"What? That's so not like you, Susi."

Susanne gripped the handle of her basket more tightly. "I didn't have the time, okay?"

"Hey, no need to get defensive. This is me—your womb mate. I'm not judging, just trying to understand what's going on."

Susanne still struggled to understand it too. She had always carefully planned out the next step in her career ahead of time. "Don't tell Mama, okay? I don't want her to think I'm like—"

"Oh Christ, Susi! Is that the only reason you're coming back? Because you don't want Mama to think you're changing your mind and your career at the drop of a hat, like Papa did?"

"No! Of course not." But her tone lacked conviction, and even Susanne could hear it.

Susanne pushed through the crowd of shoppers and crossed the street to head to the streetcar stop on the other side. Then she paused and turned back around.

Behind her, a *Bächle* gurgled pleasantly, the sun glinting off its clean water. She had stepped over the narrow stream without giving it any thought, the way Anja did. Like a local.

"Shit," she breathed into the phone.

"What?" Franzi's voice rose in alarm. "What's wrong?"

"You're right. Maybe the reason I haven't started looking for a new job is that I don't want it—any of it. I don't care about a great career with a fat salary or about my nice apartment in Berlin. I like Freiburg. And I…I love Anja. I want to stay."

Franzi laughed. "And you just now figured that out?"

Susanne thought about it. Deep down, she must have known for a while, or she would have looked for a new job, but she had stubbornly clung to the thought of returning to Berlin because she'd been afraid. For the first time in her life, someone meant more to her than her career, and that was scary as hell.

"Yeah, well," she said, her voice thick with emotion, "looks like I'm a little slow when it comes to love."

Saying that word out loud, admitting that she loved Anja—was in love with her—sent a warm thrill through her. "Wow. I can't wait to tell her." She lengthened her steps.

"Tell whom?" Franzi asked. "Mama? Well, you can. She's in the kitchen, making a cake for Miri. Here." A door creaked open, and then the sounds of the phone being handed over filled Susanne's ears.

"What? No, Franzi, wait! I—"

"Susanne?"

"Mama? What are you doing at Franzi's? Um, I mean, I didn't know you were at her place."

"I want to meet that new girlfriend of hers. And if I wait for Franziska to bring her around, I'll be ninety by the time I finally get to meet her, so I just dropped by unannounced."

For once, Susanne was glad she wasn't in Franzi's shoes, but then she remembered that at some point, she would be if things continued to go well between her and Anja. "I met someone too."

"Oh, that's wonderful. What is it about the women in Freiburg?" Her mother chuckled. "I assume that's where you met her?"

"Yes, I did. We—"

"Then make sure you bring her over for coffee when she visits you. I'd love to meet her too."

"She won't be coming for a visit." Susanne cursed her sister for getting her into this mess long before she was prepared for it. She gave herself a mental nudge. "I won't be coming back. I've decided to stay in Freiburg."

For a while, only her mother's harsh breathing filtered through the phone.

"Mama? Did you hear what I just—?"

"I heard you loud and clear. Do you really think that's a good idea? Why rush into things? That's not like you at all."

Susanne braced herself, prepared to defend herself should her mother compare her to her father.

"Franziska isn't moving all the way to Freiburg to be with her new girlfriend," her mother said instead.

"That's different, Mama. All Franzi and Miri had were a few weekends, but I've spent every day of the past two and a half months with Anja, and I can't imagine not seeing her for a week or two or even longer when I travel for work."

"But…but…if you stay in Freiburg, what will you do about a job?"

"I have no idea. I guess I'll figure it out."

Her mother gasped. "I never thought I'd hear something like that from you. That's something your—"

"Don't say it. I'm not Papa, and even if I do something he might have done, that doesn't mean it's wrong. I need to make my own decisions without worrying about whether it might make me like him." She realized that she'd let herself be guided by her need to be different from her father for much too long. She had defined herself by what she didn't want to be instead of thinking about what she wanted.

But that would stop right here, right now. She wanted a life with Anja.

"That's not what I…" Her mother sighed. "I never meant to make you feel that way, Susanne. I just… It's just so unexpected."

"I know. I didn't plan on it either. But I'm not sorry at all. In fact, I'm pretty happy about it."

Her mother took several steadying breaths. "Then I'm happy about it too. But I still want you to bring her by to meet me, do you hear me?"

"Yes, Mama. I will. I have to go now. I'm meeting Anja for a picnic in less than two hours, and I have a lot to do before then. Tell Franzi bye for me." Not giving her mother a chance to say anything else, she ended the call and stared at the black screen.

For a moment, she felt dizzy. Her life had changed so fast. But then again, it had taken almost three months for her to end up where she was now.

As she stepped onto the streetcar and stamped her ticket, an idea occurred to her. In the past, she would have immediately dismissed it as foolish, but now she decided to just go with it—that was, if she could remember how to make a paper boat.

Ten minutes later, she hurried toward her apartment building.

Muesli sat on the low wall encircling the lawn, and when he saw her, he immediately jumped down and greeted her by rubbing against her legs.

"I see he's still enamored with you," Katrin, his owner, called from the mailbox.

Susanne bent to pet him and was about to walk past Katrin with a smile and a "hello," but then she paused. "I admit I'm pretty enamored with him too. Were you serious about giving him up for adoption?"

Katrin clapped her hands, dropping her mail in the process. "Seriously? You want to keep him?"

"I think it's the other way around." Susanne smiled. "He's keeping me. I haven't talked to our landlord yet, but yes, I want to stay…and I'd like to give Muesli a home too."

"I'd love that. At least that way, we could visit him whenever we want…right?"

"Of course. Drop by any time you want to see him."

Katrin beamed. "God, that's such a relief. I love knowing he'll be happy and nearby. I'll bring over his litter box, his cat bed, and the rest of his stuff later."

And just like that, Susanne found herself the new owner of a cat.

She only hoped Anja would be as happy about her staying.

∽◦◦∾

"This is beautiful." Susanne stretched out her long legs in front of the bench.

"Very beautiful," Anja said, but her gaze was on Susanne, not on the Japanese garden.

Spring was in the air today. The rays of the sun shone through the branches of the blooming tree they sat under, and the scent of cherry blossoms trailed on the light breeze. Every now and then, one of the soft pink petals rained down on them. Birds were singing, and an artificial waterfall pattered over large boulders and ran beneath a small wooden bridge.

The Japanese garden was only a few steps away from the popular Seepark—the park surrounding the artificial lake near Anja's apartment—but it was tucked away at the edge and most people didn't seem to know it existed, so they had this part of the garden all to themselves.

This spot was almost ridiculously romantic, and under different circumstances, Anja would have really enjoyed sitting here with Susanne. But right now, she was too nervous to fully relax and appreciate it.

Today was the day. She would finally take the leap, put herself out there, and tell Susanne how she felt.

Susanne opened the picnic basket she had brought and started piling fruit, veggie sticks, olives, cheese, and bread onto the red-and-white-checkered cloth she had spread on the bench between them.

Anja nibbled on a strawberry and a piece of cheese. Both were delicious, but she didn't have much of an appetite.

Either Susanne had snacked while preparing the picnic, or she wasn't hungry either. She didn't touch any of the offerings she had brought. Instead, she peeked into the basket, closed it, opened it again, and stared inside.

Anja decided to forge ahead despite Susanne's strange distraction. If she waited any longer, she'd go insane. "Susanne, can we talk?"

"Of course. In fact, there's something I wanted to tell you too. Or maybe rather show you." Susanne held out the basket.

Anja waved away the offer. "No, thanks. I'm not hungry. There's something I have to—"

"It's not edible."

Anja threw a fleeting glance at the one remaining item in the basket. It was a bottle of some kind. "I'm not thirsty either." She took a deep breath and then just blurted it out. "I know this is really unfair of me since we said no promises and all, but… God, I can't stand the thought of you leaving. Susanne, I…" She swallowed and forced herself to hold Susanne's gaze. "I love you."

For a moment, even the birds seemed to fall silent.

Quickly, Anja added, "I'm not saying that to manipulate you into staying, and it doesn't mean you have to say it back or that I expect you to—"

"Anja." Susanne interrupted her babbling with the biggest grin Anja had ever seen on her. "Take the bottle and open the ship, please."

Bottle? Ship? She was in the middle of putting her heart on the line, and Susanne was talking about some strange nautical stuff? Thoroughly confused, she reached into the basket and pulled out a plastic bottle.

The bottom had been cut out, and inside was a red, slightly crooked paper boat. The name written on the side of the boat was *Anja*. A toothpick stuck out of the sail, and a tiny paper flag attached to it said, *Unfold me.*

"W-what's this?" Anja asked. This wasn't a goodbye present, was it?

No. If it were, Susanne would look much more sober instead of grinning from ear to ear.

"Open it," Susanne said hoarsely.

With trembling fingers, Anja pulled out the boat and carefully unfolded it. As she smoothed out the paper, she realized there was something written on the inside.

I love you.

The paper fell from her fingers, and she stared at Susanne, who gave an embarrassed shrug.

"I'm not usually one for romantic gestures, but I guess you bring it out in—"

Anja threw her arms around her, ignoring the strawberries that rolled off the bench, and interrupted Susanne with a heartfelt kiss.

Unknown minutes later, they drew back a little and gazed into each other's eyes.

"So is that a yes?" Susanne asked.

Dazed from the kiss and the emotions rushing through her, Anja cocked her head. "I think at the moment, I'd say yes to pretty much anything, but…what exactly am I agreeing to?"

"Uh, didn't you read it?"

Anja picked up the unfolded paper boat that had fluttered to the ground. She hadn't read past those all-important three words, but now she realized there was more.

And I kind of grew to love your city too. What would you think of me staying?

Anja traced the words. "You...you want to stay?" It came out in a reverent whisper. "For good?"

"Yes. I realized that as much as I like Berlin, it's just a place. This could be home. *You* could be home."

Anja sank into her arms again and kissed her cheeks, her nose, her lips. "Yes. Yes, yes, yes." They got lost in each other again for a while, then Anja asked, "What about your career? I was afraid to ask, but do you have something lined up?"

"No. Which should have been a pretty good indication that I didn't want another job. I didn't think I would, but I like the one I have now. And since Felix just quit because he graduated, I thought maybe I could..."

Anja couldn't help squealing a little. "You want to take over Paper Love?"

Susanne firmly shook her head. "No. I don't want to force Uncle Nobby into retirement just because I've decided to stay. Even if he decides he wants to retire at some point, the store is yours. I know that's what Uncle Nobby wants, and it feels right. But I thought maybe you'd want to hire me."

"You...as an employee...taking orders from Nobby...or from me?" Anja laughed. "I just can't see it. Besides, I like the thought of us being partners, in business and in life. Now that the online business is picking up, you could take over the webstore, while Nobby and I handle the brick-and-mortar store. What do you think?"

Susanne's gaze went to some spot in the distance, as if she was already picturing it. "I'd love that. And I love you." She cradled Anja's face in both hands and kissed her again. When they came up for air, she laughed giddily. "So the local superstition was right after all."

"What superstition?" Anja's brain, drowning in endorphins, couldn't keep up with everything that was happening.

"I stepped into the *Bächle* on my first day here, remember? And you people from Freiburg believe that whoever steps into a *Bächle*..."

Anja stared at her as the local superstition played through her mind. "Does that mean...you...you want to marry me?"

"Uh, maybe we should take it a bit slower." Susanne's eyes twinkled. "Ask me again next year."

They grinned at each other.

Anja lovingly refolded the paper boat and tucked it away in the inside pocket of her jacket, right over her heart. "Oh, I will," she whispered against Susanne's lips. "I most definitely will."

If you enjoyed this book, you might want to check out another workplace romance by Jae, *Under a Falling Star*.

Other Books from Ylva Publishing

www.ylva-publishing.com

Under a Falling Star

Jae

ISBN: 978-3-95533-238-9
Length: 369 pages (91,000 words)

Falling stars are supposed to be a lucky sign, but not for Austen. The first assignment in her new job—decorating the Christmas tree in the lobby—results in a trip to the ER after Dee, the company's COO, gets hit by the star-shaped tree topper. There's an instant attraction between them, but Dee is determined not to act on it, especially since Austen has no idea that Dee is her boss.

Popcorn Love

KL Hughes

ISBN: 978-3-95533-265-5
Length: 347 pages (113,000 words)

Her love life lacking, wealthy fashion exec Elena Vega agrees to a string of blind dates set up by her best friend Vivian in exchange for Vivian finding a suitable babysitter for her son, Lucas. Free-spirited college student Allison Sawyer fits the bill perfectly.

Worthy of Love

Quinn Ivins

ISBN: 978-3-96324-494-0
Length: 237 pages (77,000 words)

Top lawyer Nadine was ruined by a political scandal. Now she's out of prison, broke, and in a retail job.

College drop-out Bella can't believe her boss hired the hated woman. But Nadine isn't like the crook on TV, and Bella is drawn to her troubled co-worker.

Their chemistry is confusing. How can such different people ever be a match?

Hotel Queens

Lee Winter

ISBN: 978-3-96324-457-5
Length: 319 pages (104,000 words)

An opposites-attract lesbian romance as layered, sassy, and smart as its characters.

At a Vegas bar, two powerful hotel execs meet, flirt, and challenge each other—with no clue they're rivals after the same dream deal. What happens now they've met their match?

About Jae

Jae grew up amidst the vineyards of southern Germany. She spent her childhood with her nose buried in a book, earning her the nickname "professor." The writing bug bit her at the age of eleven. Since 2006, she has been writing mostly in English.

She used to work as a psychologist but gave up her day job in December 2013 to become a full-time writer and a part-time editor. As far as she's concerned, it's the best job in the world. When she's not writing, she likes to spend her time reading, indulging her ice cream and office supply addictions, and watching way too many crime shows.

CONNECT WITH JAE

Website: www.jae-fiction.com
E-Mail: jae@jae-fiction.com

Paper Love
© 2018 by Jae

ISBN: 978-3-96324-066-9

Available in e-book and paperback formats.

Published by Ylva Publishing, legal entity of Ylva Verlag, e.Kfr.

Ylva Verlag, e.Kfr.
Owner: Astrid Ohletz
Am Kirschgarten 2
65830 Kriftel
Germany

www.ylva-publishing.com

First edition: 2018

Credits
Edited by Miranda Miller
Cover Design by Streetlight Graphics

Printed in Great Britain
by Amazon